THE DISAPPEARED

ALSO BY C. J. BOX

THE JOE PICKETT NOVELS

Vicious Circle
Off the Grid
Endangered
Stone Cold
Breaking Point
Force of Nature
Cold Wind
Nowhere to Run
Below Zero
Blood Trail
Free Fire
In Plain Sight
Out of Range
Trophy Hunt
Winterkill
Savage Run
Open Season

THE STAND-ALONE NOVELS

Paradise Valley
Badlands
The Highway
Back of Beyond
Three Weeks to Say Goodbye
Blue Heaven

SHORT FICTION

Shots Fired: Stories from Joe Pickett Country

G. P. PUTNAM'S SONS | NEW YORK

THE DISAPPEARED

A JOE PICKETT NOVEL

C. J. BOX

G. P. PUTNAM'S SONS
Publishers Since 1838
An imprint of Penguin Random House LLC
375 Hudson Street
New York, New York 10014

ISBN 9780399176623

Printed in the United States of America
10 9 8 7 6 5 4 3 2 1

BOOK DESIGN BY MEIGHAN CAVANAUGH

For the people of the Upper North Platte River Valley,

and to Laurie, always

PART ONE

He ain't gettin' nowhere and he's losin' his share,
He must have gone crazy out there.

—Michael Burton, "Night Rider's Lament"

1

WYLIE FRYE WAS USED TO SMELLING OF SMOKE AND THAT WAS LONG before he became a criminal of sorts.

Wood smoke permeated his clothing, his hair, and his full black beard to the point that he didn't notice it anymore. He was only reminded of his particular odor when drinkers on the next barstool or patrons standing in line at the Kum-N-Go convenience store leaned away from him and turned their heads to breathe untainted air.

But he didn't mind. He'd smelled worse at times in his life, and wood smoke wasn't so bad.

On cold nights like this, after he'd used the front-end loader to deliver bucket after bucket of sawdust to the burner from a small mountain of it near the mill, he could relax in the burner shack and let the warmth of the fire and the sweet blanket of smoke engulf him.

Wylie sat at a metal desk under a light fixture mounted in the wall behind him and stared at the dark screen of his cell phone. It was two-forty-five in the morning and his visitor was fifteen minutes late. Wylie was starting to fidget.

He watched the screen because he knew he wouldn't hear the phone chime with an incoming text over the roar from the fire outside. In the rusting shack where Wylie sat, fifty feet from the base of the burner, it sounded like he was inside a jet engine. The west wall—which was made of corrugated steel and faced the burner—radiated enough heat that he couldn't touch it with his hand. In the deep January winter of the Upper North Platte River Valley, Wylie had the warmest blue-collar job of anyone he knew. So there was that.

If he had to stink in order to stay warm on the job, it was a trade-off he was willing to make. He still had nightmares about that winter he'd spent working outside on a fracking rig in North Dakota where he'd lost two toes and the tip of his little finger to frostbite.

Every minute or so, Wylie looked up from the phone on the desk to the small opaque portal window that faced the road outside, expecting to see headlights approaching. He couldn't see clearly because the smoke left a film on the glass that distorted the view, even though he wiped it clear nightly with Windex.

There was nothing to see, though.

It wasn't just the heat from the fire that was making him sweat. He tapped the top of the desk with his fingertips in a manic rhythm. He felt more than heard his belly surge with acid and he tasted the green chili burrito he'd eaten for dinner at the Bear Trap in Riverside. It was going to be a long night.

THE CONICAL STEEL STRUCTURE, known alternatively as a "beehive," "tipi," or "wigwam" burner for its resemblance to each, roared in the dark and belched a solid column of wood smoke into the frigid night sky of Encampment, Wyoming. The burner was fifty feet high and its fuel was sawdust from the mill.

Its biggest fires took place at night by design—when sleeping residents couldn't see the volume of smoke and complain about it. The flames often burned so hot that the walls of the wigwam glowed red like the cherry of a massive cigar and errant sparks drifted out of the steel mesh at the top like shooting stars. When the base was filled with sawdust and fully aflame, the temperature inside exceeded a thousand degrees Fahrenheit.

THERE WAS A WINDOW of time to do what they wanted to do, he'd told the men who would be texting him. Even though it was rare when anybody was up and around in the middle of the night in Encampment, a tiny mountain hamlet of barely four hundred people at the base of the Sierra Madre range, there was a very specific window of time when their plan would work. It lasted from two-fifteen to around three-thirty.

After two, some drunks were still driving around after the trio of bars in the immediate area closed. There was a bar for every one hundred and fifty residents, which Wylie thought was just about right—two bars side by side in the tiny village of Riverside, with its population of fifty residents, and one bar in adjoining Encampment. When two o'clock finally came around and they closed, ranch hands headed back to their bunkhouses, lumberjacks went home for a few hours of sleep, and unemployed drunks drove off to wherever unemployed drunks went.

Wylie could see the last drinkers of the night through the portal either driving recklessly up McCaffrey or motoring home so slowly and cautiously it was almost comical. Large clouds of condensation coughed out of their tailpipes in the cold, and he could sometimes see the drivers themselves if they were inebriated and had forgotten to shut off their interior dome lights. But he couldn't hear the vehicles because of the roar of the fire. He couldn't hear *anything*.

The town cop, known as Jalen Spanks—he'd been given the nickname Jalen Spanks (His Monkey) by the regulars at the Bear Trap—did the same routine every night, arriving at three-thirty. Often, Wylie would emerge from his burn shack and wave hello. In return, Jalen would raise two fingers from the steering wheel in a reciprocal salute. Sometimes, when it wasn't below zero outside, Jalen would roll down his driver's-side window and ask Wylie how he was doing. Wylie kept his responses pleasant and short. He didn't want to become friends with Jalen the cop, because Jalen the cop was kind of a dick who took himself and the authority his uniform bestowed upon him a little bit too seriously, Wylie thought. Too many small-town cops were like that.

WYLIE LOOKED AT HIS PHONE AGAIN. They were twenty minutes late. If they didn't show soon, they might run the risk of being at the mill when Jalen cruised through. That could be a hell of a situation, and one that Wylie would have a tough time explaining away without incriminating himself and getting fired or worse.

So when his phone lit up with the message *Running late*, Wylie said aloud, "No shit."

Five minutes appeared in a text balloon immediately afterward.

"Better fucking hurry," Wylie admonished.

Then: *Hit the bricks*.

"Yeah, yeah," Wylie said as he pulled on his heavy Carhartt coat and jammed a Stormy Kromer rancher hat over his head with the earflaps down. He thrust his hands in the pockets and stepped outside the shack in time to see a pair of headlights turn his way from the road.

The cold instantly tightened the exposed skin of his face and Wylie tucked his chin into his coat and walked away from the burn shack and the burner. He guessed it was twenty below zero based on how quickly the crystals formed inside his nose as he breathed in.

He wasn't supposed to see the vehicle come in, or the faces of the men inside it, or observe what they were doing at the wigwam burner.

That was the deal.

That was the reason Wylie was a criminal of sorts.

IN THE VERSION told by Jeb Pryor, the owner of the mill, the U.S. Forest Service had sat idly by while pine beetles bored into nearly every tree in the Sierra Madre range and, over ten years, killed them where they stood. While millions of board feet of lumber went to waste, hundreds of unemployed timber workers stared at the mountains as they turned from pine green to rust brown. Only after several five-month-long fires had gone out of control were the logging roads reopened.

The federal policy of not logging the dying trees had had something to do with combating global warming, Pryor complained.

Now thousands of dead pine trees were being hauled down from the mountains to the big lumber mill in Saratoga, eighteen miles to the north, as well as to the Encampment mill, the much smaller outfit where Wylie worked as night manager.

Beetle-killed lumber was different from traditional pine, and it surprised nearly everyone when there was high demand for it. Unlike regular pine, beetle-killed wood contained whorls within the lumber that were often tinted blue and green, and these bore holes gave it "character" that furniture makers and designers seemed to prize. The Saratoga mill was struggling to harvest the dead timber in the mountains before it burned or rotted and fell apart.

After he'd lost his job in North Dakota, Wylie had jumped at the opportunity to work at the mill, even though it paid less and the hours were brutal.

But Wylie had child-support payments for two daughters, and a wife who had left him but refused to work. Plus he wanted to insulate and improve his garage into a shop where he could tinker with discarded personal computers and reload his own ammunition. And there were all those gambling debts from his disastrous foray into the world of online poker.

So when he'd received a call a few months before from an unknown number while he sat at the desk in the burner shack, he'd punched it up out of curiosity and stepped outside so he could hear.

The man on the other end had known his name, his occupation, and his hours at the mill. He'd asked about the temperature of the burner at full capacity. His deep, almost guttural voice had sounded like a steel file sawing on a length of metal pipe. It was a strident voice, the kind that usually made Wylie bristle because it meant authority, but Wylie had listened anyway.

The man asked: Would Wylie Frye like to pick up some extra money by doing literally next to nothing?

Wylie was interested. He'd asked the man what he had in mind, and was told that if he needed that answer, the deal was off.

Wylie said he really didn't need to know.

"Just tell me you're not planning to burn hazardous waste," Wylie said. "I've got to breathe the air around here."

"It's not hazardous material," the man assured him.

And now it was an ongoing thing. Every ten days to two weeks, they showed up.

UP AT THE MILL NOW, he circled the sawdust pile on foot, careful not to stare at the burner or the vehicle below. They'd obviously backed their truck to the feeder door, though, because Wylie had seen headlights from the pickup sweep across the front of the mill as it did a three-point turn.

After his second circuit around the pile, Wylie noted that the pickup was driving away. They'd worked quickly. He watched as the red taillights narrowed in the dark and the pickup turned onto the road headed north toward Saratoga.

He was surprised how rapidly his legs had stiffened in the cold despite the flannel-lined jeans he wore, and he beat it back toward the burner shack. He was nearly to the door when he was suddenly bathed in white light.

Wylie turned on his heels, his eyes wide.

"Out for a stroll?" Jalen Spanks asked from his open SUV window. Wylie had not seen the cop enter the yard because the burner had blocked his view of the side road. Had Spanks seen the departing vehicle?

"Just getting some air," Wylie said as he raised his gloved hand to block the beam.

"Kind of a cold night for that, isn't it?"

"It's cold as a witch's tit, all right," Wylie said as he nodded toward the shack. "But it gets pretty smoky in there."

Spanks slid his spotlight to the side so it wouldn't continue to blind Wylie.

"You've really got that thing blasting tonight," Spanks said. Wylie wasn't sure whether it was a statement or a question. It was something a cop would say, though.

"It'll start to burn down," Wylie said. "I put the last bucket of sawdust in it for the night."

"Any more and you'll heat the whole town."

And that's a bad thing? Wylie thought but didn't say. It had been arctic cold in the area for a week.

Spanks leaned toward the open window and sniffed the air.

"What's that smell?"

"Burning wood."

"No, there's something else, it seems to me."

Wylie smelled it, too. The acrid and distinct smell of burning hair and something that smelled a little like roast chicken. Wylie kept his glove up so Spanks couldn't see his face, even though the spotlight wasn't as direct as it had been.

"Oh," Wylie said, "I threw the garbage in the fire. That's probably what it is. Guys throw what's left of their lunches in the garbage barrel."

"Ah."

"Is that a problem?" Wylie asked. "Do we need a permit or something to burn our garbage?"

"I don't think so, but I'll ask the chief," Spanks said.

"Okay."

"Well," Spanks said as his window whirred back up, "have a good night."

"You too," Wylie said.

The police SUV rolled away, gravel crunching under the tires.

Wylie let out a long shivering breath.

Inside, on the desk, was an envelope. In it was twenty-five hundred dollars in cash, as agreed.

Wylie closed his eyes for a moment and he tried not to think about what the men in the pickup had tossed into the burner.

Whatever it was had turned to ash by now, and Wylie, his kids, and his garage needed the money.

2

CAROL SCHMIDT SMELLED IT, TOO.

Schmidt was a birdlike woman, sixty-nine years old and wiry, a woman who kept active even when she didn't need to. Aside from her full-time job as a checker and bagger at Valley Foods, she crocheted afghans for hospitalized vets, attended both boys' and girls' games at Encampment High School, and was past president of the garden club.

She stood behind the storm door waiting for Bridger, her dog, to do his business in the snow in the small backyard. Bridger was an eight-year-old, eighty-five-pound, three-legged malamute/golden retriever cross. She watched him impatiently as he strolled through the shadows sniffing this and that, his white snout and legs picking up what little light there was, his tail straight up and swinging back and forth like a metronome.

There was no use rushing him. If she opened the storm door and hissed at him to hurry up, he'd obey and come running to get back into the house, but if he hadn't tended to his business, she'd just have to let him back out later. Not that she didn't curse him a little while she waited. "*Damn you, Bridger boy—hurry up.*"

She felt guilty about it. He was always so cheerful when he came through the back door that he cheered her up as well. She loved how something as simple as relieving himself made Bridger happy night after night, as if it were the first time that particularly wonderful experience had ever taken place in his life.

She envied him.

Bridger had been Paul's last dog. Her husband had brought the puppy home eight years before, after he'd found it on the side of Battle Mountain Road. Paul had been returning from his job as a lumberjack in the mountains and the puppy had been hit by a car or truck and left to die.

When Paul had come through the front door of their house with that whimpering little ball of beige-and-white fur and that look in his eyes, she'd known at that moment they would keep the dog, no matter what. No matter how much the vet bills added up for the surgery to repair the internal injuries or for removing the puppy's mangled right front leg. Paul had named the pup Bridger because, Paul said, the mountain man of the same name had had long hair just like their new dog. And Jim Bridger had once abandoned a man and left him to die.

Carol had never understood the analogy.

Now Bridger was her only company. It had been two years since Paul had died from injuries when his logging truck lost its brakes and missed a turn coming down Battle Mountain Road. The full load of green timber on the trailer had created such momentum that it had made it impossible for him to stop.

After the EMTs had cut him out of the cab with the jaws of life, Paul had lingered with severe head injuries in the Memorial Hospital of Carbon County in Rawlins for three days and nights before passing away. He'd never regained consciousness and she'd spent most of her time trying to recall the last conversation they'd had. She narrowed it down to:

Paul ***(putting on his coat before the sun was up)***: What did you pack me for lunch?

Carol: Two bologna sandwiches, Pringles, and string cheese.

Paul: Good. I like string cheese.

ONCE, DEEP INTO the second night at the hospital, his eyelids had fluttered and his grip tightened on her tiny hand.

He'd said one word.

Bridger.

Not *Carol.*

She hadn't held it against him. She figured he wasn't in his right mind and that his last thought was about the most vulnerable among them.

SO SHE STOOD behind the frosted glass that glowed orange from the light of the wood burner across the way and waited for Bridger.

She'd thrown Paul's old Carhartt logging coat over her nightgown. It still smelled of him: diesel fuel and pine sawdust. She also wore a pair of high-top Sorel pac boots over her bare feet. Even with the storm door closed, the cold night seeped in. The single inch of exposed bare calf between the hem of the coat and the top of the boots stung with it.

Despite that, she cracked the door and sniffed. She was used to the prevailing smell of wood smoke, didn't mind it at all. The odor seemed warm in itself and it reminded her of Paul. If their long marriage had an official smell, she'd thought, it would have been wood smoke.

But there was something else in the air and it reminded her of something unpleasant from her childhood. It had been so long ago and so repressed that she hadn't thought about it for decades. It bothered her that the older she got, the more she recalled from her early youth and the less she remembered from the week before. Schmidt was afraid she had a front-row seat to the early stages of her own dementia. So she put that recollection aside.

THE BURNER WAS HOT and glowing.

As she watched, the silhouette of a pickup passed in front of it, which was odd at that time of night. Because of her proximity, Carol Schmidt was a student of the mill across the road. She knew when the shifts changed, when the fresh-cut loads of lumber arrived from the mountains, when the sawdust and scrap were hauled down to the burner before dark.

And she knew that the only employee on the site was the caretaker of the burner itself and he wouldn't be driving around the yard in a late-model pickup with a camper shell on the back of it.

After a few minutes, the pickup turned and came down the access road with its headlights off, which was also odd.

Schmidt stepped back farther from the frosted glass of the storm door so she couldn't be seen. She could make out the outline of the pickup clearly because it was backlit by the orange glow of the mill.

The truck was silver or gray. She saw the heads of two men inside the cab.

The pickup slowed as it approached the service road and its lights came on and bathed the Schmidt house. Carol stepped back farther.

Of course, it was at that moment that Bridger finally lifted his leg and urinated and bounded back toward the house.

But she kept her eyes on the pickup.

It turned left and accelerated aggressively on the road behind her back fence and through the stop sign on the road toward the highway that led to Saratoga.

There was a screech of tires, a rapid *thump-thump*, and the yelp of a dog.

The truck had run over one of the neighbor's pack.

She watched as the vehicle stopped, the engine still running. Pausing like the driver didn't know what had just happened.

The dome light inside the cab came on as the passenger—a dark man in coveralls—opened his door and started to climb outside. She couldn't see the passenger's face because the light was behind him, but she could clearly see the driver. And she could hear him bark:

"Forget it. Leave the goddamn dog. It shouldn't be out running around anyway."

His voice was grating and it cut straight through the cold night air.

"You sure?" the passenger asked.

"Close the door before someone sees us," the driver ordered.

The passenger did as commanded and the truck lurched and drove away. One of the few streetlights in the town of Encampment was on her corner, and it cast a light blue glow in the night. She got a glimpse of the gray pickup and the logo and writing on its door, as well as the last three numbers of the license plate.

Six-zero-zero.

Bridger whined and did a clumsy dance on the other side of the door. He didn't like it when snow packed between his claws on his single front paw.

She stepped forward and opened the door and Bridger rushed in and sat down on the rug so she could remove the ice from his foot.

As she did, she thought *Six-zero-zero.* Her hands trembled from what she'd witnessed.

After Bridger padded off to go back to sleep, she called her neighbor. The phone rang eight times before a man with phlegm in his throat answered, "Do you know what time it is?"

"I do. This is Carol Schmidt next door. I don't know if you heard it, but I think one of your dogs got hit in the road."

"Who is this?"

"Carol Schmidt. Your neighbor."

She could hear him muffle the receiver and turn to someone and say, "It's that old lady next door."

A woman moaned and then he was back.

"Forget it," he said. "We've got too many dogs as it is."

"I could probably identify the truck and the driver."

"Carol, I'm asking you this politely even though you woke me up: mind your own business."

"I got part of the license number."

"Carol, my son went off to Alaska and he left us his three dogs. I never wanted any of 'em. I don't mind being down one."

"That's so sad," she said.

"Go to bed, Carol," he said, and hung up the phone.

SCHMIDT WAS HALFWAY to her bedroom with Bridger padding along beside her when she said "Dang it!" and turned back around on her heel and picked the phone up and dialed 911.

The twenty-four-hour dispatch center for the whole valley was located in Saratoga and she knew from experience that the woman dispatcher who pulled the late shift could be surly.

"I need to report a hit-and-run on a dog," Schmidt said. "I got a partial plate number."

She could hear the dispatcher take a long drag on a cigarette before asking, "Is this Mrs. Schmidt again?"

"Yes, it is."

"I thought I recognized your voice. You called about barking dogs last week, right?"

"Yes, I did," Schmidt said.

"And do you remember when you called that I told you this line is for emergencies?"

"Yes."

"Is it your dog?"

"No. I think it was my neighbors' dog."

"Would you consider that an emergency, Mrs. Schmidt?"

"Well, it is for the dog," Schmidt sniffed.

The dispatcher blew out a long stream of air. Probably smoke, Schmidt guessed. "We need to get off the line in case a real emergency call comes in," the dispatcher said.

"There is no need to take that tone."

Another sigh. "I'll tell you what. I'll make a report and send it on to the Encampment Police Department. Deputy Spanks should come by sometime tomorrow to follow up. That's the best I can do."

"Deputy Spanks has been no help at all with my previous calls," Schmidt said.

"I'm sorry you feel that way, Mrs. Schmidt."

"There's also an unpleasant smell in the air," Schmidt said. "It's coming from the mill."

"Is it wood smoke?"

Schmidt stamped her foot. "Young lady, I know what wood smoke smells like. This is different."

"I'll add that to the report," the dispatcher said dismissively.

"What about the dog out there?" Schmidt asked.

"I'm sorry I can't help you with that," the dispatcher said.

Shaken and angry with the state of the Saratoga and Encampment police departments and wondering how to file a formal complaint against the dispatcher, she cracked the back storm door again. The mill was empty of vehicles, as it should be. The burner roared. She could hear the dog whimper out on the road as it lay bleeding.

Tears froze on her cheeks as she crunched through the snow with the .38 she kept in her purse. No dog should suffer like that, she thought.

Then she got another whiff of the smell from the burner that had bothered her so.

And she tried to recall when, as a child, she'd first smelled the acrid odor of burning flesh.

3

THREE HUNDRED MILES NORTH OF ENCAMPMENT, WYOMING, GAME WARden Joe Pickett stood with his hands in the pockets of his down coat as he rocked back on his boot heels and watched the southern sky for the approach of Governor Colter Allen's state jet. He was the only person in the lobby of the Saddlestring Municipal Airport.

His green Ford F-150 pickup with the departmental pronghorn shield on the door was parked outside in the cold morning next to an ice-encased Prius rental with Utah plates that someone had apparently abandoned. Joe wondered what the backstory of the Prius might be, but he had no one to ask. The small carrier that had provided air service to Twelve Sleep County had pulled out due both to lack of customers and new federal regulations that had increased requirements for entry-level pilots hired by regional airlines. Ever since, the airport had become a lonely place that catered only to private aircraft. The six-person TSA squad was also gone and all that remained of their presence was fading posters and the half-full water bottles they'd left on top of the X-ray machine.

The loss of service hadn't changed the interior, though. Framed old photos of famous and semi-famous passengers deplaning still lined the cinder-block wall in back of him. Joe studied the shots of John Wayne from when he'd come to Wyoming to film *Hellfighters* in 1968. There were several photos of Queen Elizabeth carefully descending the stairs of her aircraft in 1984 on her way to visit a distant cousin who owned a polo ranch, as well as a photo of a different kind of royalty: the rock icon Prince in 1986 as part of an MTV promotion. After that, Joe noted, there had either been no celebrities flying in or the airport staff had lost interest in photographing them.

A hunched-over man in his sixties wearing horn-rimmed glasses and a three-day growth of beard tapped on a keyboard behind the counter that had once served as the check-in area for departing flights. Joe could see the top of his head and his startling comb-over. His name was Monte Stokes and there had recently been a feature about him in the Saddlestring *Roundup*.

Stokes had claimed that his employment contract with the airport board must be honored whether or not there was any commercial service, and he'd recently filed a wrongful termination suit against them. While the suit ground through the legal process, Stokes had maintained his job and spent forty hours a week sitting behind the counter and playing solitaire on his laptop.

"Waiting for *Air Allen*?" Stokes asked Joe without looking up.

"*Air Allen*?"

"Used to be called *Rulon One*," Stokes said. "Governor Allen changed the name of the state plane when he took over."

"Ah," Joe said.

"Surprised you didn't know."

"There are lots of things I don't know."

"I always heard you were pretty plugged-in when it came to the governor."

"Not this one," Joe said. He had no desire to explain to Stokes that he'd had a long and complicated relationship with Spencer Rulon, the previous governor. Rulon had at times asked Joe to be his "range rider" and investigate cases on his behalf. The arrangement had fallen just over the line of state personnel policy, but Rulon had been canny enough to work the system to his benefit. The ex-governor had always been careful to distance himself from Joe's investigations in case they went haywire.

Although Rulon had been mercurial and given to flashes of anger and impatience, Joe missed him.

Colter Allen was a different animal: a Republican, Yale-educated, Big Piney–area rancher who downplayed his Ivy League education as well as the fact that he not only owned a ranch but was also a wealthy lawyer and developer. Instead, Allen never failed to mention that he'd been a high school rodeo champion and U.S. Marine. Voters had gotten to know him when he'd campaigned across the state in a fifteen-year-old pickup that he drove himself. It wasn't until the general election was over that word leaked out that the pickup was usually hauled on an Allen Ranches, Inc., flatbed to within a few miles of each town and that Allen would then leave his aides in his eighty-five-thousand-dollar Land Rover LR4 and climb out of the backseat to take the old truck the rest of the way into town.

There were other rumors about Allen as well. Joe had heard from the Big Piney game warden that Allen's fortune had taken a big hit in recent years because of some bad investments and land deals that had gone sour. While he'd once been considered a multimillionaire, there were grumblings from local Sublette County businesses that for the past year Allen hadn't been paying his bills on time and that his excuses for payments due were slippery. The game warden also said that Allen had been propped up and financed by a couple of extremely wealthy benefactors whose identities were a mystery. The benefactors, according to the rumors, owned Governor Allen lock, stock, and barrel.

But there were always rumors like that about politicians, and Joe couldn't verify them, so he dismissed them as gossip.

Since Colter Allen had been elected, he and Joe had had two conversations and neither had gone well.

Stokes looked up and squinted at Joe through his glasses. "They're eight minutes out."

"Thank you."

Stokes's mouth formed a half smile. "Do you notice anything strange about the governor's arrival?"

Joe looked around. "Nope. What should I notice?"

"There's no ground transportation," he said with an impatient sigh. "That means he's just stopping over on his way to somewhere else. I'd guess Jackson or his ranch in Big Piney. Plus, the mayor isn't here to greet him or anything. I don't think they even know he's coming. It's just you."

Joe shrugged.

"What makes you so important?" the man asked.

"No idea," Joe said.

. . .

THE CALL HAD COME the night before, when Joe and Marybeth were at a Saddlestring High School performance of *Bye Bye Birdie* in which their eighteen-year-old daughter, Lucy, the youngest of three and the only daughter still at home, played the lead.

Although Joe had had his phone muted, he'd looked at the screen to see who had called, which annoyed Marybeth.

"Ignore it," she whispered.

"It's the governor's office," he whispered back.

"Lucy is about to sing. Call them back at intermission."

Joe nodded and put the phone in his pocket just as Lucy came onstage playing Kim MacAfee. He was stunned at how beautiful she looked and it made his chest hurt. Marybeth dabbed at her eyes with a Kleenex and clutched his arm as Lucy began to sing.

They'd heard her practice the song in her room for months and it was so familiar Joe could have sung it himself, although badly. But he couldn't have replicated Lucy's presence and poise. And unlike Joe, she could actually *sing*. It wasn't lost on him that he could recall falling deeply in love with Ann-Margret in the same role when he'd seen the movie as a boy, even though it was already an old movie at the time. The thought confused and confounded him. Would males in the audience think of Lucy *that way*? The way he'd thought about Ann-Margret?

If they did, he mused, things would get Western in that theater real fast.

At intermission, Joe let his wife go into the lobby of the high school to accept the compliments from other parents. He wasn't sure he could even talk to them through the lump in his throat.

He stepped outside into the icy night and breathed in deeply to clear his head. Ice crystals suspended in the air formed halos around the blue overhead lights in the parking lot.

The call went straight through.

"Hanlon."

Joe recalled seeing on a memo from headquarters in Cheyenne that Allen's chief of staff was a former D.C. operative named Connor Hanlon.

"This is Joe Pickett returning your call from Saddlestring."

"I can read the screen." Brusque. Joe could hear conversations in the background and the tinkling of plates and silverware. "Look," Hanlon said, "I'm at dinner with my wife and some important donors. I only have a minute."

So do I, Joe thought.

"Governor Allen would like to meet with you tomorrow. We're scheduled to land in Saddlestring at 9:10 a.m., according to the schedule. Are you able to meet with him?"

Although it was posed as a question, it sounded like a command. But Joe was more than available. January was the deadest time of the year for a game warden, and he'd been confined to his office and desk for the past ten days filling out bureaucratic paperwork—filing annual reports, making recommendations about local hunting seasons and quotas, and reviewing new regulations proposed by the Wyoming Game and Fish Department.

"I'll be there," Joe said.

"Of course you will."

"Can I ask what this is about?"

"You'll know tomorrow," Hanlon said. "Gotta go."

And the connection went dead.

. . .

GOVERNOR ALLEN'S SMALL JET, a twin-engine eight-passenger Cessna Citation Encore, touched down smoothly on the runway. As it rolled toward the terminal, Joe noted the bucking-horse logo on the tail as well as *Air Allen* painted above the windows in a frontier font.

The Cessna came so close to the windows that Joe could see the two pilots in the cockpit before it turned sharply to align the door of the plane with the vestibule that had once housed the TSA crew. The whine of the engines filled the building as they powered down.

"He's here," Stokes said unnecessarily.

The aircraft door opened and stairs telescoped down to the tarmac. Joe expected to see Colter Allen—with his wide shoulders, silver mane of hair, Western jacket, bolo tie, jeans, and cowboy boots—deplane first. Instead, a dark-haired hatchet-faced man in a suit and overcoat came down the stairs followed by the two pilots. The three men walked quickly toward the terminal, hugging themselves against the cold.

The hatchet-faced man pushed through the doors first.

"Are you Joe Pickett?"

"Yup."

"I'm Connor Hanlon. We spoke on the phone last night."

Joe nodded. Hanlon didn't extend his hand, but instead thumbed over his shoulder at the airplane. "The governor will see you now."

"He's not coming in?" Joe asked.

"What does it look like?"

Both pilots had found the men's room in a hurry, Joe noted. It was as if they wanted to get as far away from Connor Hanlon as they could.

"It looks like I'll go see him," Joe said.

"We're on a tight schedule," Hanlon said, shooting out his arm so he could check his wristwatch. "Where can I get an espresso?"

Joe looked to Monte Stokes, who shrugged his shoulders in response.

"Can you help him out?" Joe asked.

"What's an *ex*presso?" Stokes said.

THE WIND HAD COME UP since Joe had arrived at the airport and it cut through his jeans as he mounted the stairs of the Cessna. His boots clanged on the metal steps and he reached up and clamped his hat on his head so it wouldn't blow off.

He paused on the top step and leaned in.

"Come in and close the door, for God's sake," Governor Allen said from the back of the plane. "It's freezing in here."

Joe entered the aircraft, then turned and pulled the steps up and closed the hatch. Although the engines were off, a set of heaters hummed from a battery backup. The first thing Joe noticed was that the interior of the jet had been redone. Instead of three rows of single seats and a bench seat in back, there were now only two empty seats near the cockpit. The back of the plane had been converted into a flying office with a large desk, a television, a phone, an open laptop computer, and a small refrigerator.

Colter Allen sat in a high-backed leather chair behind his desk with both hands raised so he could drum his fingers on his chest.

"We got off on the wrong foot the last time we talked," Allen said. "Actually, *you* got off on the wrong foot with *me*."

Joe didn't know how to respond. Three months before, Allen had called him to say that he'd found several files from Rulon that mentioned Joe's involvement as an agent for the former governor. Allen had said he was intrigued by the concept and hoped Joe would continue his role as "range rider."

But before Joe could discuss it, Allen had asked that he travel to Campbell County in the northeastern corner of the state to gather intelligence on a group of unemployed coal miners who might be planning a protest of Allen's upcoming visit. The coal miners claimed that Allen had promised them their jobs back after he was elected, but it hadn't happened. The governor wanted Joe to disrupt their plans and save himself the embarrassment of bad press coverage.

Joe had refused by saying he "didn't do political."

Allen had huffed and disconnected the call. Joe hadn't heard from him since.

"Sit down," the governor said as he gestured to one of the two open seats. "They spin around so you can face me."

Joe sat and spun around. Allen beheld him with an amused grin.

"I don't have time for small talk because we need to get to Jackson Hole for lunch with the secretary of the interior."

He paused and Joe didn't respond.

"That would be the *secretary of the interior for the United States of America*," Allen said, enunciating each word.

Joe said, "I won't hold you up, sir," although he hadn't asked for the meeting.

Joe was well aware that for states in the West like Wyoming—where half of all the land was owned and managed by the federal government via a slew of agencies including the Bureau of Land Management, the Forest Service, the Fish and Wildlife Service, the National Park Service, the Army Corps of Engineers, the Environmental Protection Agency, and others—it didn't matter who the president was, because the secretary of the interior *was* actually their president. So a Rocky Mountains governor meeting with the new secretary was important but not unusual.

Joe had been in Rulon's office when the former governor, shouting over the phone, had challenged the secretary in the last administration to a "duel to the death with swords or handguns." *That* had both frightened and impressed Joe. Rulon had chuckled and explained that one of the highlights of his day was to "screw with our federal overlords."

Allen eyed Joe with suspicion and said, "I'd like you to go on assignment for me like you used to do for Rulon. I know you 'don't do political,' but this one isn't."

He said *don't do political* with a sneer, Joe noted.

"I mean, there are politics involved—there always is at my level," Allen said with a sniff. "But it's not overtly political. From what I understand, you've been fairly successful in the past with unconventional investigations. At least that's what Rulon told me before I took over his desk."

Joe blushed and looked away for a moment. Then he said, "I got lucky a few times by blundering around until the bad guys revealed themselves. You've got good law enforcement across the state and professionals at DCI who do a dandy job."

"Ah, the Division of Criminal Investigation," Allen said with a wave of his hand. "I asked them months ago to look into this situation, but all they do is whine about budget cuts and, quote, 'lack of resources.' I'm getting tired of their excuses."

Joe nodded, even though he really didn't agree. Due to a decrease in mineral-extraction activity within the state, there'd certainly been budget cuts to state agencies. The Game and Fish Department had not been spared.

"Plus," Allen continued, "those guys stick out like sore thumbs in a small town like Saratoga."

"Saratoga, sir?" Joe asked. He didn't know why Allen had specifically mentioned the southern-central community of Saratoga.

In fact, Steve Pollock, the game warden in the Snowy Range district that included Saratoga, had mysteriously moved on recently, and no replacement procedure had taken place. It was a puzzling development. Pollock had been with the agency nearly as long as Joe had been. Although he didn't know Pollock intimately, Joe thought he was well-liked and well-respected. He hadn't heard why he'd been terminated and that was odd in itself. Other game wardens throughout the state—and there were fifty—had been discreetly asking around for the reason for Pollock's demise, but Joe hadn't yet heard an adequate explanation.

"I'm getting ahead of myself," Allen said. "Have you heard of someone named Kate Shelford-Longden?"

"The name is familiar, but I'm not sure from where," Joe confessed.

"I wouldn't guess you spend much time reading the British tabloid newspapers, do you?"

"No, sir."

"Didn't think so," Allen said with a smirk. "But if you had, you'd know that Kate Shelford-Longden is the CEO of a high-powered English advertising agency. She's a very attractive woman and a real go-getter, from what I understand. Last summer she decided to come over here for a dude ranch holiday in Wyoming. She chose the most luxurious and pricey ranch in the state, which is Silver Creek Ranch near Saratoga."

Joe nodded for the governor to go on. He was familiar with the ranch resort because their oldest daughter, twenty-three-year-old Sheridan, had started working there after her graduation from the University of Wyoming. "Taking a year off before starting a career" was how she'd put it to Joe and Marybeth.

The governor said, "Between the time she left the ranch and when she was supposed to board her flight in Denver to go back to London she disappeared," he said. "She just never showed up.

"Anyway," Allen said, "it's been in the news over there, even though it hasn't been much of a story over here. They love that kind of stuff about good-looking blondes who vanish on vacation. Plus, her sister has made a bunch of noise about it. I didn't know much about the case until a few months ago, when my wife attended a cocktail party for our new president in Washington."

Tatiana Allen, the governor's wife, was ten years his senior, but had evened the age gap by remaining nearly skeletal in appearance and indulging in a good deal of hot yoga and cosmetic surgery. She was the heiress to a billion-dollar outdoor-clothing firm that had since gone bankrupt and she was known as Tatie Allen, a nickname chosen long before the title First Lady Tatie was thrust upon her.

Allen said, "At the event, Tatie was introduced to the British ambassador to the U.S. and his wife, Poppy. They have names like Poppy for people over there," he said as an aside.

Kind of like Tatie? Joe thought but didn't say.

Allen continued. "Tatie said the first thing the ambassador and his wife asked her when they learned we were from Wyoming was: What happened to Kate Shelford-Longden? Tatie didn't know what to say and she was embarrassed as hell. So she asked me about it and I didn't know any more about it than you appear to. We were busy with the transition at the time, so a missing British woman wasn't high on my list of to-dos at the moment."

"Why is it now?" Joe asked.

"Because Tatie promised them an answer," the governor said sourly. "She's on some humanitarian commission with Poppy, so Tatie presses me on it constantly. 'What about Kate?' 'Where could Kate have ended up?' 'Any news on the Kate inquiry?' Tatie reads all the British papers online every morning and then sends me a link whenever she finds a story about it."

Allen rolled his eyes and said, "Now the tabloids call her 'Cowgirl Kate' or something like that. It's ridiculous, if you want my opinion. But I'm in a bind, so I asked the DCI to get involved. And they came up with a whole lot of nothing.

"It's damned frustrating," Governor Allen said. "You would think that all a governor had to do was snap his fingers and his employees would jump in order to please him. But it doesn't work like that, I've found. It's harder than hell to find a good yes-man in state government. And when you cut their budget, they get all passive-aggressive."

Allen raised the tone of his voice to imitate and mock certain state employees Joe didn't know.

"They say, 'We'll get right on it, Governor Allen, just as soon as we get all these other things done that you've ordered. Too bad we don't have enough people or budget to do it, Governor Allen.' I'm sick and tired of it, so I'm asking you if you'll be my range rider like you were for Rulon. I want you to go down there to Saratoga and try to figure out what in the hell happened to Kate Shelford-Longden."

Joe took in a deep breath. He said, "I'm a game warden. I'm not a miracle worker. If the DCI couldn't find out anything and local law enforcement doesn't know either . . ."

"Are you saying you won't?"

"No. I'm saying I need more background."

"Joe," Allen said in a low tone, "this isn't exactly a request."

Joe looked up and his eyes locked with Allen's for a moment. "I understand," he said. "I do have a daughter who works there for Silver Creek Ranch. She might have some insight."

"There you go," Allen said, and did a single clap with his hands. "Hanlon has a file for you. We got it from DCI. Read it through and get back to me about how soon you can go down there. The way I figure it, you can take over the district temporarily and no one will know you're working directly for me or what you're working on. That might help you get some answers.

"I don't know why exactly," Allen said, "but in my experience people open up to game wardens. Maybe that's because they don't consider you Johnny Law. At least that's how it worked in Big Piney."

Joe nodded. He knew there was some truth to that. One of his best tactics for obtaining evidence was to knock on the door of a suspect and say, "I guess you know why I'm here." The answers he'd received in response to that ambiguous statement had led to multiple convictions over the years. Often the end result had had no relation to the crimes he had originally been investigating.

"And don't worry about Linda," Allen said, referring to Linda Greene-Dempsey, Joe's agency director, known within the agency as LGD. "I'll handle the transfer with her. She's afraid I may not reappoint her to her position, so she'll do anything I ask. In fact," Allen said with a grin, "she may be my best yes-man right now."

Joe said, “I’ll read the file.”

“I’d like your assessment by tonight,” Allen said. “Call Hanlon. He’ll be with me in Jackson.”

Joe nodded.

“Speaking of . . .” Allen said while pushing back in his chair to indicate the meeting was over, “we’ve got to fly or I’ll be late to my lunch with the secretary.”

Joe stood up.

“One other thing,” Allen said as he leaned forward on his desk and grasped his hands together. “Don’t let me down. State employees are a dime a dozen, if you catch my drift.”

Joe felt a surge of anger, but he suppressed it. Colter Allen’s approach was the opposite of Rulon’s. Rulon had had a way of making Joe *want* to work for him.

There was a knock on the door and someone shouted, “Governor, we’re ready.”

Allen nodded to Joe to let them in. The two pilots stood shivering outside and he pushed the stairs down for them. When they were on board, Joe glanced over at the governor before he left.

Allen had already turned his attention to his laptop.

HANLON STOOD HUNCHED OVER in the old TSA vestibule, smoking furiously on a cigarette. He was obviously waiting for Joe to come in. A thick file was clamped under his arm.

The vestibule was where passengers had sat after clearing security. It was ironic to Joe that Hanlon now used it as a smoking area.

“The coffee in this place sucks,” Hanlon said.

“Sorry to hear that.”

"I probably don't have to tell you how important it is to the governor that you find out what happened to this Kate Blah-Blah, whatever her name is," Hanlon said. "So don't screw it up."

"That's nice to hear," Joe said.

"I hope you don't plan to involve your friend. What's his name—*Romanov*?"

"Romanowski."

Nate Romanowski was an outlaw falconer with a Special Forces background who had pledged to protect the Pickett family years before. Nate carried two of the largest handguns in existence—a .454 Casull and a .500 Wyoming Express, both made by Freedom Arms of Freedom, Wyoming—and he'd disfigured men with his bare hands. He and Joe had had a complicated relationship as their lives had intertwined over the last nearly twenty years.

His friend had been recently released from a slew of federal charges that had gone back years, in exchange for taking on an assignment for a shadowy federal agency and for agreeing to testify against a multimillionaire hit man named Wolfgang Templeton, for whom Nate had once worked. Templeton had yet to be apprehended.

"Nate's gone straight and I'd like to keep him there," Joe said. "He's a legitimate businessman now. Have you ever heard of Yarak, Inc.?"

"No."

"It's a commercial falconry operation. He's much in demand, from what he tells me."

"You're going to keep him the hell away from this, I hope."

"I don't see how he'd be involved with this investigation," Joe said.

Hanlon looked up and his eyes flashed. "That area down there around Saratoga is really important to the governor, so I don't appreciate your attitude. We've got a lot going on in that valley, including the biggest wind farm this country has ever seen. The owner of the Silver Creek Ranch is one of our biggest contributors."

Joe wasn't sure where the chief of staff was headed with this.

Hanlon took a last drag of the cigarette before dropping it to the linoleum and crushing it out with the pointed tip of his shoe.

"What I'm saying is that as a state we don't need any bad publicity. Especially international bad publicity. We've got some big initiatives in the works regarding international trade. After all, *someone* has to buy our coal and oil since all the blue states have idiotic laws against it. But we've still got tourism, and Wyoming can't be known as a place where rich British women come on vacation and disappear, you get me?"

Joe nodded.

Hanlon said, "We've got to get those tabloids off our back before it starts to hurt us. So we—I mean *you*—need to make this thing go away for Governor Allen. Find her or figure out where she went. But when you do, make damned sure you call me before anyone else so we can spin it the right way. Then I never want to hear about Kate Blah-Blah again."

Joe felt like punching Hanlon in his temple. "Kate *Shelford-Longden*," he said.

"Whatever. I've found women with two last names are high maintenance. I don't have time for them."

Joe didn't respond.

"Read the file and call me," Hanlon said, handing him the two-inch-thick file and turning away from Joe to check messages on his phone. "Tell me some good news I can pass along to the governor."

"There might not be any."

“That’s not a good start,” Hanlon said. “You know, this might be helpful for your career if you do it right. Someday, your agency might need a new director who’s on the governor’s good side.”

“I’m not looking for that.”

“Everybody’s looking for that,” Hanlon scoffed. “What I’m saying is, if you solve this thing, it could go well for you.”

With that, Hanlon headed for the door and *Air Allen*. As he opened the vestibule door, Joe heard him mutter, “*Or really bad if you fuck it up.*”

4

STILL SEETHING FROM THE ENCOUNTER WITH GOVERNOR ALLEN AND his chief of staff, Joe drove his pickup from the airport into the town of Saddlestring with his Labrador, Daisy, on the passenger side and the file marked KATE SHELFORD-LONGDEN jammed down between the bench seats. Behind him, the roar of *Air Allen* thrummed through the air as the aircraft took off for Jackson Hole.

It was the worst of January: a rare overcast day with a steady twenty-miles-per-hour wind out of the north. Cattle in the meadows near town crowded together into black Angus gangs. A sheen of ice covered the streets, and the wind sculpted what was left of the last blizzard into razor-sharp drifts that clung to lawns and open spaces. A loose dog that looked like a cross between a hound and a hyena ran across the highway in front of Joe with a single severed mule deer leg in its mouth.

He turned on First into the parking lot of the Twelve Sleep County

Library and parked next to Marybeth's van. The sign near the grille of her vehicle read RESERVED FOR DIRECTOR.

"Take a breath," he said aloud to himself, although Daisy looked over from where she was curled up as if he'd spoken something interesting and wise.

"I DON'T HAVE a good feeling about this," Joe said to Marybeth as he sat across her desk in her office after explaining what had happened. "And I don't have a good feeling about our new governor."

"Well, that's a problem," she said, shaking her head.

Marybeth wore a dark wool suit with narrow lapels and a white blouse. A stray blond hair on her shoulder caught the light. Budget sheets covered her desk.

"The timing could be better," she said.

The last few months had been difficult for them. The state-owned home outside of town where they'd lived for years and raised their three girls had been burned to the ground in an arson fire. They'd lost one of Marybeth's horses in the blaze as well as their beloved Corgi/Lab mix, Tube—or so they'd thought.

The only good thing to come out of the disaster was when Tube had waddled down from the juniper scrub above the blackened debris a week later. His coat was singed and his pride wounded, but he'd apparently survived by catching and eating gophers. Marybeth and Lucy had been thrilled and they referred to the incident as "The Resurrection of the Tube."

Homeowners' insurance had helped them replace lost clothing, utensils, and other items, but the painful fact was that so much of their history had burned up. Boxes of artwork from Sheridan's grade school years, April's scrapbooks about rodeo and travel, Lucy's dancing costumes—things that could never be replicated.

Construction on a new game warden home was going as slowly as expected, given the red tape involved. Joe often drove the eight miles up Bighorn Road to see what progress had been made, and so far, the debris had been cleared away, but no new construction had begun. Seeing the property like that always filled him with a sense of melancholy.

So they were living in a rented condominium in a complex near the Twelve Sleep River with the department grudgingly paying the rent. That had its challenges as well.

The landlord allowed Daisy and Tube in the town house, but Marybeth had had to board her two remaining horses. They were at a stable owned by the county prosecutor, Dulcie Schalk, Marybeth's friend and riding companion, but still, Marybeth missed them acutely.

The move had been difficult for Joe, too. It wasn't lost on him that the fire had caused his family to move backward through time. Before the girls had been born, Joe and Marybeth had lived in a double-wide trailer outside Lovell, and they were in an apartment in town when he'd been given his first district to manage. They'd moved up to an actual home during his second stint outside of Meeteetse. Now, years later, he was descending the ladder again.

It rankled Joe, too, that his downward trajectory had long been predicted by Marybeth's mother, Missy Vankueren.

Missy despised Joe as much as she pined for Marybeth, whom she was convinced had married beneath her. Missy and Joe clashed often, and Missy's machinations to convince Marybeth to leave her husband had grown increasingly more desperate. Unfortunately, she had the means to support her efforts.

Missy had been married six times, each time to a man wealthier than the one she had left behind. Joe had thought she'd finally get her comeuppance when she was charged in the murder of husband number five, but no, she'd been found innocent, and then protected herself against further charges by marrying her defense attorney, Marcus Hand.

Luckily for Joe, Marybeth wasn't like her mother in any respect.

Even though, he thought with a grimace whenever he drove up to the rented town house, Missy had a point.

AND NOT EVERYONE liked the idea of a game warden living in the building. A divorced woman in her sixties who stayed home all day and occupied a condominium on the top floor of the building objected to looking outside and seeing Joe's truck parked in the lot with animal carcasses in the bed of it. She'd called the police, as well as the sheriff's department, to complain about it and had sent a letter to Game and Fish headquarters in Cheyenne. Joe had explained to her that retrieving and investigating dead game was a part of his duties, but that hadn't blunted her outrage and revulsion. Finally, he'd agreed to cover the carcasses with canvas and blankets in the future, and that seemed to have quieted her down.

Lucy's star turn in the high school production had been a wonderful break from all this, but now things were even worse than before.

"IT WASN'T AN OFFER," Joe said. "It was an ultimatum."

"How long would you be gone?" Marybeth asked.

He shrugged.

Joe had been assigned to other areas of the state multiple times and his absences had varied from a week to several months. Once, he'd been assigned to Jackson Hole too long and it had frayed their marriage. They'd promised each other it would never happen again, and when Joe was away now, he tried to call home every night.

"What can you tell me about the secret assignment?" she asked, genuinely intrigued.

"It's in Saratoga."

"Really? You'll get to see Sheridan, then."

"There's that. She might even have some insight into the matter."

"Maybe you can get an inkling of what she's planning next," Marybeth said with a sigh. "She really won't say. I can't decide if it's because she's keeping it close to the vest or she just doesn't know."

Sheridan was the oldest and had paved the way for her younger sisters, showing them how to be independent and to think for themselves. Of the three, Joe had probably spent the most time with her when she was growing up, because she was interested in his job and loved to ride along when he was in the field. She was comfortable outdoors and had become an apprentice falconer in her teens. Joe had always assumed she was destined for an outdoor job of some kind. Either that, or law enforcement. Instead, though, she'd declined graduate school and taken a job at Silver Creek Ranch while she sorted out her next steps.

"I think there's a boy," Marybeth said.

Joe winced.

"It's not that she's said it outright," she continued. "It's what she *hasn't* said. She's never said she's lonely, even though it has to get kind of lonely on a guest ranch in the winter when there are no guests. Her sisters probably know more because they text all the time, but they haven't spilled the beans."

Joe and Marybeth knew Sheridan had dated in college, but as far as they knew, she'd had no serious men in her life. Sheridan wasn't one to share her feelings until she was absolutely sure about them.

"If there's a boy, she probably doesn't want to see me around," Joe said.

"But you'll find out and report back, right?" Marybeth said with a smile.

"Of course."

"So what does the governor want you to do down there?"

"I'm pretty sure I'm supposed to keep it confidential," Joe said.

"With the public, sure. But I'm your wife."

"You sure are," he said.

"Damn tootin'."

"Have you heard of Kate Shelford-Longden?"

Marybeth's eyes got wide. "You mean Cowgirl Kate?"

"So you know."

"Of course I know about her. Cowgirl Kate—how *interesting*."

"Why?" Joe asked.

Marybeth said, "The British tabloids are obsessed with three things: reality TV stars, footballers—I'm talking about soccer players—and royalty. Kate ticked two of those boxes: TV and footballers. Both are clients of hers."

He shouldn't have been surprised. In general, Marybeth was better informed about the world than he was. When they were watching television together and a vaguely familiar face came on the screen and Joe wondered who it was, she not only knew the actor's name, but who he or she was married to, as well as who they'd been *previously* married to, plus their earlier roles. It was the same with questions about medical procedures, food, songs, politics, history, and even the royal family.

"So the governor wants you to try and find her?"

"Yup. Or what happened to her."

His wife cocked her head. "Does he suspect something bad?"

Joe shrugged.

"Do you want me to see what I can find out about her?"

Joe nodded. Marybeth had been invaluable to him on cases in the past. She had access not only to her vast library resources, but also to law enforcement databases. In fact, he thought, he should have told the governor that the main reason he'd solved the majority of his investigations was the research and background material supplied to him by his wife.

"I suppose Lucy and I can cope for a few weeks without you," she said.

He was puzzled by her reaction until she said, "Joe, every January you wander around the house grumping about all the paperwork you have to do. You're at your best when you're outside every day, and we both know that. Plus, this could be *really* interesting. It's an actual whodunit with an English twist. A real *Masterpiece Theatre* mystery right here in Wyoming. If we could solve it . . ."

"What?" he asked sourly. He noted the *we*.

"You might see your name in the British tabloids."

"That hasn't actually ever been a goal of mine," he said.

5

AFTER A QUICK CHEESEBURGER LUNCH AT THE BURG-O-PARDNER, JOE drove out to his temporary office in an unused room of the Department of Transportation building outside of town. It would have been more convenient to have an office space in town, closer to the condo, until the house was rebuilt, but a supervisor at Game and Fish headquarters had rejected the idea of paying rent at a commercial office building and worked out an interagency agreement with the Saddlestring DOT supervisor.

State agencies were tribes, and the DOT tribe didn't usually interact with the Game and Fish tribe. Joe credited highway patrol officers for the tension and he'd had several run-ins with individual troopers who'd muttered about how game wardens "drove around with their dogs all day in the woods looking for fishing spots and collecting a state paycheck." Not all the troopers were like that, by any means, he knew, but there were enough of them to keep the feud alive.

No more than a large closet, his office was at the end of a hallway with a view of fuel pumps outside in the icy yard. Headquarters had provided him with an old computer and printer, but he'd had to bother highway department staff to borrow a desk, a chair, empty filing cabinets, and a garbage can. He got stares from exhausted snowplow drivers for his occasional use of the break room. Using "shared" resources such as office supplies was such a complicated interagency procedure that he'd simply bought his own at the Walmart in Saddlestring.

While Daisy curled up on an old blanket in the corner, Joe sat down at the desk and opened the file marked KATE SHELFORD-LONGDEN.

The material inside consisted of a seven-page incident report written by a DCI agent, as well as photos, interviews, and statements obtained by other agents. The rest of the file included letters from the British Embassy to Governor Allen, printed-out email inquiries from reporters, friends, and relatives of Shelford-Longden, and over sixty items (most from online sources) from UK newspapers including the *Sun*, the *Daily Mail*, the *Evening Standard*, the *Mirror*, the *Daily Dispatch*, the *Telegraph*, and a couple of pieces from the *Times*.

It was a lot to review.

Rather than let himself be influenced by the incident report and summaries from the DCI, Joe placed that report facedown on the desk for later. Instead, he decided, he would read all the background material on the case first. It would be interesting to see afterward if the DCI agents had come up with theories on the situation that Joe agreed with.

He shuffled through all the material and divided it into four categories, making a pile for each: letters and correspondence, statements and interviews, photos, and newspaper clippings. Then he set about collating the documents by date. On a fresh legal pad, he wrote *Kate Timeline.*

The oldest document in the stack was a Silver Creek Ranch manifest of visitors for the week of July 23 to 30, Sunday to Sunday. The printout was extremely detailed and went on for thirty-six pages. He noted the dates of her stay at the top left of the legal pad.

Joe found the manifest fascinating because it was a glimpse into the world of an extremely exclusive resort as well as into the kind of people who could afford to stay there. The more Joe studied the document, the more he realized that the listing was not simply a guest list, but also a dossier that could be consulted by every employee at Silver Creek Ranch to cater to and better serve each customer.

Eighty guests had been at the ranch during the time period Kate—he was already thinking of her by her first name—had been there.

In the far left column of each page was the guest's name as well as a phonetic pronunciation of the name.

He flipped through the pages until he found her. Joe read on:

GUEST: Katherine Shelford-Longden
PREFERRED NAME: Kate
DATES OF VISIT: 23–30 July
TRANSPORTATION: Will hire car at Denver Airport and self-drive
ADDRESS: 1-5-107 Queen's Gate, South Kensington, London SW7 5LR, United Kingdom
EMAIL: KateSL@AthenaPR.co.uk
TELEPHONE: (W) 44 20 7496 5577 (Mobile) 44 7911 212545
OCCUPATION: Managing Director, Athena Public Relations

GROUP OR FIT: FIT
COMPANIONS: Traveling alone
AGE RANGE: 40–50
FITNESS RANGE: Good for a Brit (drink & smoke)
FOOD RESTRICTIONS: Would say bloody red meat, but I'm coming to Wyoming!
ALLERGIES: Ex-husband and Donald Trump
HOUSEKEEPING NEEDS: No telephone, television, or newspapers, please!
CELEBRATIONS DURING STAY (BIRTHDAYS, ANNIVERSARIES, ETC.): New Lease on Life
SPECIAL REQUESTS: Meet a real cowboy—ha!
FIRST RANCH EXPERIENCE?: Yes
OTHER FOUR-STAR RESORT EXPERIENCES: Laucala Island Resort, Fiji; Nayara Springs, Arenal, Costa Rica; Singita Sabi Sand, South Africa; Anantara Peace Haven Tangalle Resort, Galle, Sri Lanka; Borgo Egnazia, Savelletri di Fasano, Italy; and others.
ACTIVITIES:

- [x] Horseback Riding
- [ ] Fly-Fishing
- [x] Target Shooting
- [x] Upland Bird Hunting
- [ ] Yoga
- [ ] Hiking
- [ ] Whitewater Rafting
- [ ] Glamping
- [ ] Archery

- ☐ Spa
- ☐ Climbing Wall
- ☐ ATV Adventure
- ☐ Tennis
- ☐ Golf
- ☐ Culinary Classes
- ☒ Western/Cultural Experience
- ☐ Other

HOW CAN WE MAKE THIS THE GREATEST VACATION/HOLIDAY OF YOUR LIFE?: See "special requests" and "celebrations" answers above—ha!

Another column listed "Six Months," "Three Months," "30 Days," and "One Week." Each had been checked. Joe didn't know what the list meant.

It appeared from the dossier and her sometimes flippant and humorous answers that she had either filled out all the questions herself or someone had transcribed them from an interview or correspondence. He guessed the latter. He had no idea what an "FIT" was, and all the resorts she'd listed were completely unfamiliar to him, but they indicated she was quite a world traveler. He made a note to ask someone what "glamping" was.

He noted that she'd indicated she'd "hire" a car instead of rent one and that she referred to herself as "Managing Director" instead of CEO—both British terms. He keyed in on a couple of her responses, particularly "New Lease on Life" and "Meet a real cowboy—ha!"

The last item on the personal dossier was "Staff Liaison." The staff personally assigned to Kate were identified as "LR" and "SP^2."

Joe didn't know what those designations meant either, but he wondered if "SP^2" referred to Sheridan Pickett, his oldest daughter.

He turned next to the newspaper clippings, which was the largest stack of the four. He arranged the items in the order they had been published.

Joe noted the differences between the style of the articles he was reading versus the more familiar—but more stilted—style of the American press. The British stories had stimulating headlines and were written in a more vibrant and conversational tone.

The first item about Kate, from the August 4 edition of the *Daily Mail*, was titled PR HEAD REPORTED MISSING WHILST ON HOLIDAY.

Joe smiled at the word *whilst*.

It read:

> Katherine Shelford-Longden, 43, managing director of the leading public relations and advertising firm Athena, has been reported missing after not returning from a U.S. ranch holiday, according to a company spokesman.
>
> According to the spokesman, Kate Shelford-Longden was scheduled to return to the UK on the morning of July 31 but she never checked in or boarded BA flight 218 in Denver, Colorado, on July 30. The company grew concerned after calls, texts, and emails to her went unanswered.
>
> Founded in 1999 by Kate Shelford-Longden and her husband, Richard Cheetham, Athena has become one of the top-grossing PR firms in the UK with over £35m turnover and the only one headed by a woman. Cheetham left the firm in 2003.

According to the company mission statement posted on the Internet, Athena was named for the Greek goddess of "reason, intelligent activity, arts, and literature."

Most British readers know of Kate Shelford-Longden through her popular Instagram feed and for representing the notorious young bloods of football and reality TV. Rumours have arisen that her involvement with some of "her" footballers has not been strictly professional.

Photos posted to her Instagram account the previous week showed Shelford-Longden enjoying her stay at an exclusive ranch located in Wyoming. According to the spokesman from the Silver Creek Ranch, where she spent her holiday, Shelford-Longden departed the ranch on July 30 as scheduled. Airline personnel confirmed that she failed to arrive at Denver International Airport later that day for check-in.

"We're devastated," said Silver Creek Ranch General Manager Mark Gordon. "We treasure all of our guests and Kate was really special. We hope and pray that there is an innocent explanation for why she never got home."

Kate Shelford-Longden's ex-husband, Richard, said, "Kate has always been a free spirit and she's always been adventurous. Maybe this time the adventure caught up with her."

Local law enforcement in Saratoga, Wyoming, is investigating the disappearance . . .

Joe thought the quote from Richard Cheetham was less than sentimental and a little snarky. Under a category he titled "Suspects," he wrote down the man's name.

There were several photos of Shelford-Longden to accompany the story. The best one of her was from a press conference for the launch of a new nonprofit initiative to assist the children of immigrants to the UK, according to the caption. In the photo, Kate stood onstage with a massive screen behind her. She wore a slim wireless headset with a microphone bent under her chin.

Kate was tall and angular with shoulder-length blond hair that was swept back and stylish. She had blue eyes, high cheekbones, blood-red lipstick, and an open expression on her face. She wore a black pantsuit with heels and a single strand of pearls.

Other photos were more recent and credited to her Instagram account: Kate celebrating with "footballers" in a tent; Kate at Silver Creek Ranch wearing a touristy cowboy hat, on a horse with a big smile on her face; Kate cautiously holding up a small brook trout with a beaming guide over her shoulder; Kate aiming an over-and-under shotgun while wearing ear protection and safety glasses; Kate lounging in an Adirondack chair, hoisting a cocktail toward the camera in the golden light of dusk outside a stone-and-log lodge that Joe assumed was part of Silver Creek Ranch. The quality of light was familiar to Joe. It was Wyoming light.

He read on. Most of the stories were similar to the piece in the *Daily Mail,* with just enough differences not to be plagiarism, he thought. There was very little new information, other than quotes from Athena staffers saying they were getting more worried by the day that no one had heard from her.

A small feature in the *Telegraph* had a sidebar on the Silver Creek Ranch itself, with a scenic photo of a trail ride going into the mountains that had apparently been taken from the ranch website.

> Silver Creek Ranch in Wyoming is one of many ranch resorts in America and Canada that have seen a surge in British visitation in recent years, according to Malcolm Harris of Ranch-America, a tour operator specializing in ranch holidays.
>
> "Ranch vacations have become a very rewarding and exclusive kind of holiday," Harris said. "We're booking more and more Brits to them every year—especially successful businesswomen. Ranch holidays offer relaxation, comfort, and an all-inclusive holiday that really appeals to certain people."
>
> According to Harris, Silver Creek Ranch is the most exclusive and luxurious "ranch" in America, featuring stays that cost upwards of £1,200 per night . . .

There were scores of dude and guest ranches in the state, Joe knew, as well as in Montana, Idaho, Colorado, Arizona, and other Western states. In fact, the first-ever "dude" ranch had been established in the Bighorn Mountains less than an hour away.

He knew dude ranches were of three varieties: working, traditional, and ranch resort. Each was as different from the other as its management and ownership.

Guests on working ranches paid to do actual ranch chores such as branding and moving cattle, fixing fences, and clearing brush. They slept in bunkhouses and ate with the ranch family. Joe knew several working ranch owners who marveled at the fact that there were people who would actually *pay* them to do the work they had always paid laborers for.

Traditional dude ranches featured daily horseback rides, hearty food, fishing, a "night on the town," and campfire sing-alongs. They generally operated on a Sunday to Sunday basis with new guests—mainly entire families—arriving every week. The dude ranches tended to schedule different activities every day. Some featured children's programs. Most of the guest ranches in the region used this model.

Ranch resorts offered everything traditional dude ranches offered, plus an increasing number of amenities such as swimming pools, tennis courts, gourmet food, and a high level of service.

The Silver Creek Ranch, from what Joe could surmise, was a ranch resort in a category of one.

AS HE WENT through the pile, the stories got shorter and became a variant on NO NEW LEADS IN KATE DISAPPEARANCE–type headlines. The same photos were featured time and time again. Side stories began to appear, such as ATHENA CONTEMPLATES FUTURE WITHOUT MISSING DIRECTOR.

The exception to the NO NEW LEADS pieces was a series of articles in the *Daily Dispatch* written by a journalist named Billy Bloodworth. He seemed to have the inside track on all things Kate, and to relish it.

His pieces were accompanied by more personal photos of Kate than had appeared in the other newspapers. In them, Kate was shown celebrating her recent birthday at home, attending a wedding, and sailing—which suggested an inside source to Joe. The Bloodworth articles dove more deeply into potential motives for her disappearance. He was also the first to refer to her as Cowgirl Kate.

Although the headlines were provocative, the bulk of the stories themselves were primarily speculation. Each featured "experts" who, in Joe's opinion, were named only to bolster Billy Bloodworth's narrative in each story. They included:

**FROM INSTAGRAM TO INSTA-GONE!
DID COWGIRL KATE'S JET-SETTING
LIFESTYLE LEAD TO HER DOOM?**

. . . Since gaining prominence as managing director for one of the country's fastest-growing public relations firms, Kate Shelford-Longden's taste for unaccompanied exotic and expensive holidays abroad brought her into contact with hundreds of like-minded lovers of luxury. Did Cowgirl Kate meet someone at Silver Creek Ranch in America who saw an opportunity to do her harm?

"No one likes to think about it, because no one wants to ruin their holiday, but choosing an ostentatious resort and Instagramming your every activity also puts a target on the back of a wealthy person," said Miles Drood, an executive at a London private security firm . . .

**COWGIRL KATE: "SHE HAD ENEMIES,"
SAYS RIVAL**

Kate Shelford-Longden's rise from obscurity to one of Britain's most high-profile female executives may have created enemies along the way, according to a rival public relations executive who frequently tangled with her.

"When it came to acquiring new accounts or fighting for existing clients, Kate quite frequently had her claws out," said the executive, who asked to remain anonymous for this exclusive *Daily Dispatch* article. "I hope it doesn't sound sexist, but Kate would scratch your eyes out if she had her heart set on a new acquisition. She was known as a fierce competitor in the industry."

The executive went on to state that he wasn't suggesting that her recent disappearance was directly associated with the enemies she's made in the highly competitive industry . . .

"SOMETHING HAPPENED" AFTER COWGIRL KATE'S RANCH DEPARTURE, SAYS OFFICIAL

"Something happened" to Athena über-boss "Cowgirl" Kate Shelford-Longden in America between the time she left the American luxury ranch resort and her non-arrival at Denver International Airport for a flight home, said a high-level staffer within the Foreign Office.

"She left the resort in a car she'd hired on the day of departure and she had to drive four and a half hours to the Denver Airport, through the wilderness, to turn the car back in and check in for her flight," the anonymous staffer-in-the-know told the *Daily Dispatch.* "This is a huge expanse of wild country," he said. "There are thousands of square miles of woods containing grizzly bears, mountain lions, and other predators."

The staffer pointed out that there were perhaps human predators as well.

"Let's not forget this happened in America, in the West," he said. "Everyone there has guns."

He confirmed that Cowgirl Kate wasn't involved in any traffic altercations en route to Denver and that her car hasn't been recovered.

"You can draw your own conclusions . . ."

Joe rolled his eyes and thought that Billy Bloodworth was running out of angles on the story to have written that one. It was true that "Everyone there has guns," but . . .

COWGIRL KATE'S SISTER:
"SOMEONE HAS HER"

Sophie Shelford-Longden, the fashionable younger sister of missing PR boss Kate Shelford-Longden, thinks Cowgirl Kate was abducted and is being held against her will.

In an exclusive interview with the *Daily Dispatch*, Sophie said the investigation into her sister's disappearance has been inadequate and she blames both Foreign Office officials as well as American law enforcement efforts. Kate went missing after leaving a super-exclusive holiday compound in the state of Wyoming en route to the Denver Airport. No trace of her or of her hired car has been found to date.

"Kate didn't just vanish off the face of the earth on July 30 after she was done with her holiday," sophisticated Sophie says. "I just know in my heart that some backwoods redneck from the American outback is holding her captive. I have dreams where I can see her there in a small dark place with woods all around. It's like she's reaching out to me to let me know she's alive."

Sophie Shelford-Longden said there have been no ransom demands for the return of her sister.

"I seriously doubt that the troglodyte who has my sister even knows how to get in touch with us," she said. "And I doubt he has any idea who he's messing with. Kate is a

> fighter. Kate is a hero. And I'm not standing by idly myself. It's important that I have a voice in this."
>
> Sophie said that despite daily calls to the authorities there have been no leads on her sister's disappearance since it happened.
>
> "Maybe I'll go over there and find her myself!" fetching Sophie declared.

Accompanying the article was a photo of a woman who resembled Kate, except with red hair and a few extra pounds. In the picture, Sophie sat in a chair gazing plaintively out the window and clutching a framed photo of her sister. Joe thought the photo looked very staged.

Following the article was a boxed feature that got Joe's attention. It read:

NEXT WEEK: WHERE COWGIRL KATE DISAPPEARED

DAILY DISPATCH **JOURNALIST BILLY BLOODWORTH ACCOMPANIES KATE'S SISTER, SOPHIE, TO AMERICA TO INVESTIGATE THE DISAPPEARANCE.**

Joe checked the date. The item had appeared ten days before, which meant there was a very real possibility that Sophie and Billy Bloodworth were in Saratoga at the moment.

He flipped through the photos. Most of them were reproductions of what he'd already seen in the British press. There were a few shots of Silver Creek Ranch that looked like they'd been taken by a cell phone. The resort was sprawling and spectacular, with that huge central lodge of logs and stone that Joe had noted in the photo of Kate having cocktails.

The letters-and-correspondence stack wasn't revelatory, either. Most of the letters were reproductions of official-looking letterhead stationery from the British Embassy to Governor Allen, asking for his support and assistance in the case. The only exception was a plea via email from Sophie Shelford-Longden sent to the email address that appeared on Governor Allen's web page.

Honourable Governor Colter Allen:

I am Sophie Shelford-Longden writing to you from England. If the name sounds familiar to you, that is because my sister, Kate, disappeared in your state this past summer after going on holiday there.

I've heard from the authorities that they've been in touch with your office regarding this case, but I thought it important that you hear directly from a member of Kate's family. It has been months since we've heard anything at all.

Quite frankly, we're gutted. Kate was my older sister and only sibling. Our parents are distraught and barely able to function. This tragic situation is quite personal to us.

Although I'm a British citizen, and not a Wyomingan, I do implore you to please do all you can to find my sister, Kate. I miss her. We miss her. She has to be there somewhere.

Please help us.

Joe swallowed hard and put the email down. It got him. Kate was a real person, not just a case. She had a sister and parents. He wondered if the email had moved Governor Allen as it had him, even though Sophie had called Wyomingites "Wyomingans" as well as rednecks and troglodytes.

HE SCANNED THE STATEMENTS and transcribed interviews included in the file. The information was brief and more a series of notes than a full-blown report.

Mark Gordon, the general manager of Silver Creek Ranch, said that the last time anyone on the ranch had seen Kate was when she stopped by the main lodge to say good-bye to the staff on her last day:

> Asked about her state of mind when she left, Gordon said she was sad about leaving. She told the staff she'd had just the greatest time. She said she planned to come back to the resort the next year if she could. Gordon said it wasn't unusual for guests to be sad when they left and that KSL's demeanor was normal. He said KSL made no mention of making any stops between the ranch and the Denver Airport and that she was giving herself six and a half hours to get there (four and a half driving, two hours to check in for her flight home). According to KSL's registration doc (and confirmed with Hertz car rental in Denver), she was driving a metallic-silver 2017 Jeep Cherokee with Colorado rental plates AFR6967.

Carbon County Attorney Chia Schwartz told investigators that when her office was notified of Kate's failure to arrive in the UK an APB had been put out in both southern Wyoming and northern

Colorado, for the vehicle and any sighting of Kate. She said there had been several tips, but none that had proved worthwhile.

Staff members of the Silver Creek Ranch had been interviewed. Joe could tell by the very brief notes that the agents had focused on two things: relationships good and bad that Kate may have had during her stay, and her state of mind when she left.

The employees interviewed all said Kate had been friendly with everyone and well-liked by the staff and other guests, and they were unaware of any problems. She'd spent most of her days riding horses in the indoor arena, the outdoor arena, and on trails.

A ranch wrangler named Lance Ramsey said Kate was extremely enthusiastic about horses and a fast learner. Ramsey said the only time he'd heard Kate complain was when the day was over and she could no longer ride. He was aware of no close relationships Kate may have had with either guests or staff, nor any conflicts.

Joe sat back, closed his eyes, and mentally reviewed everything he'd just read. He was looking forward to turning the file over to Marybeth that night at home to see if she could find something interesting or unusual that he'd missed.

Nothing came to him. When he opened his eyes he saw two DOT crew standing outside in the hallway in orange coveralls. They were looking in at him on their way to climb into their snowplows. For all they knew, they'd caught him napping.

They shook their heads as they continued down the hall.

He sighed.

It was then that he read the incident report to see what theories the DCI had been pursuing before they'd been yanked off the case by Governor Allen.

The incident report was simply a clinical summation of everything he'd already read and looked at. Joe was disappointed. There were no leads to follow or angles to pursue.

Kate had come to Wyoming on a ranch holiday and left after a week for the Denver Airport. She'd never shown up. There were no suspects.

But something made his antennae go up. He reread the report. He'd seen DCI reports before, as well as incident reports filed by agency investigators. This one was too clean, he thought. There wasn't a single word of speculation and no summary of the investigation. It was the kind of report written by bureaucrats intending to cover themselves.

From whom? he wondered.

He flipped again to the last page to see that the report had been compiled and signed by DCI Agent Michael Williams in Cheyenne.

Joe booted up his computer and found Williams's contact information on the state of Wyoming website. He debated to himself whether to fire off an email or call the man direct.

Call, Joe thought. Emails could be ignored for weeks. It usually worked best to catch a man unaware.

He was reaching for his handset when his cell phone burred in his uniform breast pocket. No one usually called during the dead of winter except Marybeth. The other seasons, it could be a landowner, hunter, or fisherman.

The screen said NATE, and Joe arched his eyebrows. Nate Romanowski's name had come up just that morning from Hanlon and here he was. Nate had that quality about him.

"Nate," Joe said.

"Hey."

Nate's voice was low and whispery when he talked on the phone. It generally had a sarcastic edge to it.

Joe waited thirty seconds before saying, "What can I do for you, Nate?"

"I was hoping you could sort out a problem for me and a couple of friends of mine."

Joe waited again. Nate's phone etiquette was aggravating.

"Help you with what?"

"A falconry issue."

Licenses to hunt with falcons in the state of Wyoming were issued by the Game and Fish Department. Once an apprentice falconer had successfully passed a test based on the California Hawking Club exam—the California Hawking Club was the gold standard of falconry associations in the country—a permit to hunt with a falcon could be granted.

"So you're finally going to request a permit?" Joe asked. Nate had never bothered to get a permit. Joe thought part of the reason his friend had never requested one was simply to annoy him.

"No can do."

"Then what is the issue?"

"We need to talk to you in person about it."

"Who is we?"

"Two friends of mine. They're right here with me and we've been discussing a problem. It turns out they both have the same difficulty. When I heard about it, I thought of you. I told them I was friends with a game warden."

"Okay," Joe said.

"We can come to see you tomorrow."

"Tomorrow is no good. I'm going south to Saratoga. Can you just tell me the problem over the phone?"

"Nope. These falconers want to explain it to you in person. I'm just the facilitator of this meeting."

"So they're falconers."

"Good ones, too."

"So hand them the phone, Nate."

"Let me see if they'll talk to you."

Apparently, Nate covered the microphone on his set because Joe could hear a spirited but muffled conversation between Nate and the two men.

After a minute, Nate said, "Nope. They want to talk with you in person because you never know who might be listening in. They want to talk to you face-to-face to find out if you can be trusted to help them. I told them you could, but you know how falconers are."

"You mean paranoid?"

"Where will you be in Saratoga?" Nate asked, as if he had no intention of arguing with Joe's insinuation.

"I don't know yet."

"How long will you be there?"

"I don't know that, either. At least a week."

He heard another round of muffled conversation.

Then Nate said, "One of these guys needs to go down there anyway. So do I. So I'll call when we can meet with you."

"It may not be that simple, Nate," Joe said. "I'll be on assignment and I'll likely be in the field. I don't have an office there yet . . ." Then he paused. His phone was silent. Nate had punched off after he said *I'll call when we can meet with you.*

"You drive me crazy," Joe said to no one.

. . .

DCI AGENT MICHAEL WILLIAMS picked up on the first ring. He sounded cordial. Joe identified himself and said, "I've been asked to take a look at the Kate Shelford-Longden case and I was hoping, since you wrote the incident report, I could ask you a few questions."

Silence.

"I said I've been asked—"

"I heard you." Williams's voice was tight. "Who asked you to look into it?"

"I can't say."

"You don't have to. I can figure it out. Look, I don't have time right now to talk to you about it. I'm sorry."

Joe frowned. "Can I call you back later, then?"

"Not really," Williams said.

"So you can't talk about it because someone in your office might overhear you?" Joe asked.

"That's part of it. Hey, are you calling from your cell phone?"

"Yes."

"Then I have your number."

"So you'll call me back?" Joe asked.

"Thanks. Have a good day."

Williams disconnected the call and Joe stared at his phone.

6

TWENTY-THREE-YEAR-OLD SHERIDAN PICKETT TOPPED A SNOW-COVERED hill on the Silver Creek Ranch, driving a white company pickup with a dozen horses trotting behind her. The two-track road she was on had been recently plowed, but it had partially drifted in during the night. She turned the dial on the dashboard to switch the transmission into four-wheel-drive high. It engaged as she drove down the hillside and bucked snow toward the curve of the North Platte River. A bald eagle high in a riverside cottonwood tree watched her descend.

It was a cold and still morning. The truck tires squeaked on the snow as she drove. The meadows on the other side of the river blazed pure white in the sun beyond the trees and the thick willow walls of the riverbank stood like hedgerows. A large herd of bronze-and-white pronghorn antelope picked over the windswept open ground in the distance, and the surrounding mountains glowed azure except for their snow-covered peaks.

She parked the truck on the bank of the frozen river and pulled on a thick pair of work gloves before getting out. She shooed away the horses who'd followed her to the river so they wouldn't crowd her while she worked. They retreated into an impatient knot about twenty feet from the trees. Condensation clouded above their heads and their snouts bristled white with frost.

Sheridan retrieved a double-bladed ax, a shovel, and a stall fork from the bed of the truck and stepped out onto the ice wearing Bogs boots. She shuffled to the lip of the thick part of the ice and swung the ax blade down through the skin that had formed overnight on the wide hole they'd cut a month before with a chain saw. She cut the overnight ice into large plates that bobbed and clicked together on the open water, then moved them aside with the shovel and the stall fork. When she gathered her tools and shuffled back toward the pickup, she noted that the horses were again advancing so they could go to the river to drink.

"Get back."

The lead horse, a roan, turned on his back legs and the others followed suit.

SHERIDAN'S JOB IN THE WINTER was vastly different from the duties she carried out during the May-through-October guest season. After breaking the ice at six places along the river for the horses to get to water, and opening big bales of hay with a forklift so they could eat, she'd select five to ten horses a week to ride and tune up in the vast indoor arena until she'd ridden them several times—all one hundred and thirty mounts. Otherwise, they'd get "bronc-ey" and forget they were there on the ranch to provide safe and comfortable rides to guests of all skill levels. Horses were naturally lazy, and unless they were ridden hard and reminded of their jobs, they'd spend all their days grazing, sleeping, and standing around. Either that or figuring out unique ways to hurt and injure themselves.

But compared to her first season at the ranch that summer, winter was positively restful.

She'd been one of twenty-one full-time horse wranglers, most of them like her: fresh out of college and unready to commit to a full-time profession. Except for her supervisor—the tall, lean, handsome cowboy Lance Ramsey—all the wranglers were women. The reason, she'd been told, was that cowboys would rather work on the real cattle ranch that adjoined the property than at a guest resort. That, she learned, was partly true. It was also true that male guests were much more likely to participate in horseback riding—and listen to instruction—if their host was a young woman. Especially if the young woman wrangler looked good in a pair of jeans.

But the wranglers worked hard. Their mornings began at five when breakfast was ready in the chuckwagon tent. At six they called in the "jingle horses"—called that because they'd respond immediately to bells—who would lead all the other grazing horses to the barn and corrals. After grooming and saddling up to eighty mounts and matching them up with guests, the first session would take place, the guests riding with designated wranglers. Sessions lasted from one to three hours and included basic beginner training in the outdoor rodeo arena, personal lessons, and private rides, all the way to wilderness trail rides. A second session would occur in the afternoon after lunch and sometimes stretch into team penning and barrel racing for expert riders. Most guests were exhausted by four-thirty in the afternoon and ready for a cocktail at the saloon, but some requested evening rides, and the credo of the Silver Creek Ranch was to accommodate each and every guest no matter how outlandish their request.

Sheridan, like the other wranglers, worked six days per week from dawn to dusk. After all the riding sessions were complete, the horses were unsaddled, fed grain, assessed for injuries, and pushed off back to the meadows to graze. The next morning, with the ringing of bells, the activities would start all over again.

She'd learned a lot about horses—her mom had tried in vain to teach her while she was growing up—but even more about the hospitality business. As far as Sheridan was concerned, the jury was still out as to whether she liked it or not and as to whether it was something she wanted to pursue.

The people who came were generally wealthy visitors from the East Coast with a few internationals thrown in, and—with a few exceptions—most of them had not been to a guest ranch before. Although many had ridden horses, and a few of them were fine riders, most were spending their first time around horses and Western horse culture. A surprising number of the guests assessed their skill level at riding much higher than it actually was, so matching horses with them was a special skill in itself.

Until being hired by the Silver Creek Ranch, she hadn't spent much time around wealthy people before. She hadn't known what to expect.

During training, she'd been encouraged to engage with the guests, and to let them stay anonymous, even though some of them were well-known and used to special treatment. There were tech industry moguls, entertainers, old-rich bankers and new-rich hedge fund billionaires, even supermodels. But for the most part, nearly all of them were there with their families and they'd turned out to be surprisingly normal. She'd also learned very quickly that just because someone was extremely wealthy didn't mean he or she was extremely smart. And that despite their money, families were families in various shades of conflict, dysfunction, and love. It was a good thing to know.

In many instances, she heard from guests that their week on the ranch was the first time in years they'd eaten together as a family. Sometimes, the guests struck up friendships with staff employees and invited them to dinner as well.

Sheridan's favorite category of guests was twelve-year-old girls. That was the time in life when a special connection to a horse seemed to occur—after childhood and before the social pressure of dating. Young girls looked up to her and actually listened, and many became accomplished riders very quickly. It wasn't unusual for some of the girls to later text her or send a direct message to find out how their horse was doing. Sheridan always replied that the horse missed them as much as they missed their horse.

Just as there was a rhythm to each week from when new families arrived, unplugged, and settled in, there was a rhythm to the summer for the staff as well, she'd found. The first few weeks had been intense, especially for first-timers like herself. It was like some kind of super high school, with cliques, factions, and social circles that formed as quickly as they dissipated.

Hormones seemed to color the very air they breathed. Hookups happened—sometimes with remarkable speed—and breakups were found out almost at the same time as they occurred.

After staff and hospitality training, many of the employees went en masse to bars and saloons in Encampment, Riverside, and Saratoga. They played as hard as they worked and no one got enough sleep. Several new employees got into trouble when they crashed ATVs or were thrown off horses.

A month into the season, though, it had smoothed out. Sheridan found herself too physically tired each night after turning out the horses to do much of anything else. Each day was a new adventure, and the first couple of months on the ranch had gone by in a blur.

Of the one hundred and thirty employees at the resort, the wranglers were considered elite because horseback riding was the most popular activity. Sheridan had applied for the wrangler position as a lark, and was as shocked as her family that she'd gotten the job. She was even more surprised when she learned that there had been three hundred applicants for the ten open slots, and that she was the only Wyoming-born wrangler of the entire crew, which gave her a kind of special status among the other employees. Her boots, hat, and Cruel Girl Western clothing had all come via her sister April's employment at Welton's Western Wear in Saddlestring, so she looked the part. Wranglers from other states consulted her for fashion advice, and even male employees looked to her for what was "authentic" and what was not. That she'd been chosen to be offered a full-time position on the ranch—meaning her own apartment overlooking the indoor arena on one side and the Sierra Madre range from the other—was a point of pride.

She also secretly liked the fact that she knew her mother envied her.

And then there was Lance Ramsey, the boss of the equestrian division. Lance was twenty-six, single, tall, laconic, gentlemanly, and the most knowledgeable and experienced horseman she'd ever met. Nothing riled him, and both the wranglers and the guests admired and respected him. He was from Montana, which was practically Wyoming, and he had a way about him that relaxed even the most hyperintensive type A guest. Lance's name was atop the guest surveys nearly every week as the most personable and professional wrangler they'd met during their stay.

One of the most charming things about Lance, she thought, was that he seemed to have no idea that nearly every female guest had a crush on him. If anyone mentioned that fact, he'd blush and kick at the dirt with the point of his boot.

Lance had asked Sheridan to stay for the winter season over the other wranglers, even those who were more experienced. That meant a lot to her.

SHERIDAN FINISHED OPENING the last of the water holes by midmorning. As she walked back to the ranch pickup and twenty-one horses—most of them sorrels—rushed past her to get to the water, she caught a glint of light on the southern horizon.

The ranch itself was vast and the skeleton staff of twenty-eight people who worked there during the winter, primarily department heads and maintenance crew, kept pretty good tabs on one another.

So it was unusual to see a vehicle that was not from the ranch parked high on the summit of the foothills to the south. Hunting season was over, she knew, and if there were any outside contractors on the place, she should have been briefed. The ranch fleet consisted primarily of white pickups emblazoned with the Silver Creek Ranch logo on the front doors, like the truck she was driving. This truck was darker.

She tossed the tools back into the bed of the pickup and didn't stop to look directly at the trespassers. She'd learned from growing up riding along with her father that it was best to proceed with normal activities when being spied upon, so as not to alert the spy. In her dad's case, he was usually being watched by hunters who might be in the wrong hunting area, or who were poaching.

Sheridan opened the rear door of the pickup and found a set of binoculars in the seat back. She removed the caps from the lenses and raised the glasses inside the cab so she could see clearly through the rear passenger window.

The pickup on the horizon was gray and had a camper shell on the back. There was writing on the front door, but it was too distant for her to make out what it said.

She took in a quick breath when she focused on the cab itself because she could clearly see a pair of orbs side by side through the driver's-side window but not the driver himself. The orbs turned out to be the lenses of binoculars looking directly back at *her*. There was someone else in the cab, but she couldn't see who it was due to the sun's reflection on the windshield.

Cell signal strength varied depending on where she was on the property, but she was relieved to see she had one bar on her phone. The call went straight through to her boss. He was out of breath when he answered. She assumed he was on the back of a horse in the arena.

She said, "Lance, I'm down at the S-curve of the river and I see a truck over on the hills to the south. Two people, it looks like. Are you aware of any contractors on the place today?"

"Nobody told me about anyone working out there. Can you see a license plate?"

"No. The truck's in profile. And whoever is driving it is looking back at me with binoculars."

"How long has he been there?"

"No idea. But I know it isn't one of ours."

"Stay put," he said. "I'll get there as soon as I can."

It was almost as if the trespassers were listening in, because the truck moved forward and slipped out of view on the other side of the hill.

"They're gone."

"I'm still on my way."

Lance had been particularly anxious and jumpy of late, she thought. Coming to check on her seemed like an overreaction.

"Well, okay. But before you come, I need to ask you to clear out your things from my apartment just for the time being. You know, your toothbrush and razor. You've also got some clothes in the closet."

There was a long pause. Then a pained, "Why, Sheridan?"

"I've got a situation. My dad is driving down here tomorrow. He's going to be staying in town, but he might just show up here first. If he does . . ."

She heard him gasp, then recover.

"Okay," he said. "I understand, I think."

"Thank you, Lance."

"Don't go chasing those trespassers until I get there, okay?"

"Okay. I don't think I'd try to drive the truck across the ice, you know."

"Good. Now stay put and I'll get there as soon as I can. Get a license plate on that truck if you see it again."

"Right, boss," she said with a smile.

7

LATER THAT AFTERNOON, WYLIE FRYE KICKED OFF A PAIR OF CROCS and shed a heavy blanket as he neared the thick cloud of steam that was the mineral hot springs pool. He reached out through the steam to grasp the metal railing and muttered a curse before descending the moss-slick steps into the water itself.

Damn, it was cold outside.

The sensation, as always, was intense: below-zero air on the bare skin of his back and shoulders and burning-hot water below the surface. Both stung, but in different ways. He eased into the pool, felt the gravel surface beneath his feet, until he located the corner closest to the flow intake. He liked to think of this spot as "Wylie's Corner." It was close enough to the source of the geothermal spring, called "the lobster pot," to be extremely hot, but far enough away that his delicate skin wouldn't blister. He sat down slowly until the hot mineral water rose and washed over his shoulders. Only his head was not submerged.

It was so cold outside and so hot inside the pool that clouds of thick steam rose from the top of the water and he couldn't see a damned thing around him.

Within a minute, as the one-hundred-and-nineteen-degree water stung his skin and the heat began to penetrate into his fat, sinews, and muscles, he took a deep breath of the sulfur-tinted air and closed his eyes. Wisps of steam rose through his scalp into the air like a chimney. The mineral water dissolved the powdered gypsum dust on his skin from hanging drywall all day in his new-and-improved shop. Gypsum rose to the surface in a slick before it floated away and dissipated.

He had two hours. That was enough time to get in a hot soak, eat a big dinner at the Bear Trap or Duke's Bar & Grill, and show up for the night shift at the mill. Because of the extra money he was making, his ex-wife had stopped texting him for child support and his shop was insulated and almost completely dry-walled. He could envision spending a lot of time out there with a woodstove blazing and ESPN or rodeo playing on a wide-screen television.

Life was good for Wylie.

He wished, though, that he could get that acrid odor of burning hair and roast chicken out of his nose from before. It stayed with him in a way that he found disconcerting.

He tried not to think about it, but it came back to him at odd times and it was accompanied by a sharp pang of guilt. The owner of the mill was a good man who'd taken a chance on him and seemed to trust him. But it was more than that.

Wylie hated guilt. He'd had more than enough of it when his

marriage broke up. He blamed his mother because she was a devoted Catholic and she'd made him go to church with his sister as a young boy. Many of his friends and coworkers seemed to have no inkling of the concept of guilt, and he envied them.

WITH HIS EYES CLOSED, Wylie found that his hearing sharpened up. He could hear the lap of the river just outside the wall of the hot springs pool as well as contented clucking from wild ducks on the water. Every once in a while there was an errant shout from a guest who'd ventured outside from the Saratoga Hot Springs Resort across the river. The outtake grate at the other end of the pool sometimes made a slurping sound as hot water flowed through it.

There were rarely any other people in the hot pool at this time of night, he'd found, even though it was free and open to the public twenty-four hours a day. Locals sometimes brought their young kids earlier in the evening to tire them out in the super-hot water, and drinkers came later at night after they'd done their rounds at the bars. During the day, it was travelers and oldsters. Wylie avoided seeing all that wrinkled old flesh the best he could. He'd had enough of that to last him a lifetime when he'd visited his mother two years ago at her retirement village in Arizona. That's why he chose to stay here through the winter.

WYLIE HAD FOUND that twenty minutes in the hot pool was just enough. Twenty minutes heated up the core of his body so he'd stay warm for nearly an hour before he got to the mill shack. His bulbous milk-white body would turn crab red by the time he left. In fact, he would sometimes break into a sweat as he walked from the pool toward his truck when it was five below. Often he carried his blanket instead of wearing it. Wylie had a big gut and that belly fat heated up like an inner tube filled with hot water and it kept him warm. He often wondered how skinny people ever survived the winter.

Sometimes, when he felt adventurous, Wylie would lumber out of the hot springs, climb over the wall, and plunge into the North Platte River. There were several hot plumes of geothermal water out there as well, and sitting on a gout of hot water while the icy river flowed around him was a unique experience in itself.

WYLIE WAS SO COMFORTABLE ALONE in the hot pool with his eyes closed that he nearly fell asleep. But he was startled when he heard a particular voice, guttural and flat, that he recognized as the one he'd heard on the other end of his cell phone.

He couldn't see them through the steam, but he could hear and track them. The two men were talking low as they exited from the changing room and approached the hot pool. They were above and behind him and Wylie knew that even if the steam cleared, the men wouldn't be able to see him in there because of the sight lines.

"Jesus, how hot is it?"

The guttural voice said, "It's one-twenty-five at the source. That's what they say, anyway."

"That's too damned hot. Even in this cold, it's too damned hot."

The guttural man chuckled. Even his laugh was grating, Wylie thought.

"Well, do you swim in it or what?"

"Nah. It's too shallow for that. You just sit in it like it's a bathtub.

They say the Indians used to use it, but I don't know how true that is. They also say people with breathing problems used to come from hundreds of miles away to sit in it. I call bullshit on that."

There was silence for a moment, then a splash of water from the other side of the pool.

"Goddamn!"

"Told you," the guttural man said.

Wylie felt small wavelets lick his chin and jawbone as the two men entered the pool and sat down in the water.

"It stings like hell."

"You can get out anytime. I'll meet you in the truck."

"You have the keys." The other man moaned. The guttural man laughed again.

"It's getting better now, sort of."

The guttural man laughed again. "Yeah."

"How often do you come here?"

"Not often. I'm too busy most of the time. But when I do come, it's like three or four in the morning. I like to have it all to myself—like now."

Wylie remained still. They thought they were alone. He wanted to keep it that way. He hoped he wouldn't have a moment of flatulence, which sometimes happened when his guts got too hot.

There were a couple of minutes of silence. He could hear the ducks in the river again. They didn't quack so much as titter, as if engaging in pillow talk.

"It's a hell of a thing," the other man said. "I was kind of blown away by what you showed me today. Man—the scale of it!"

"It's mind-blowing. The amount of money that's gone into it is fucking crazy."

Wylie waited for more. *What thing?*

The two men changed the subject to talk about the waitress who'd served them that day at the Saratoga Resort across the river. The other man thought she might have been flirting with him. He went on to recount the signals he thought he'd received from her.

"In your dreams," the guttural man growled.

"You'll see."

"Forget that and get some sleep while you're here. We've got a long day ahead of us tomorrow. We've got a lot of work to do before the boss arrives. Everything needs to be cleaned up, like I told you. I don't want him asking any questions."

"Yeah."

"And I need to call that fuckin' rube to set up another delivery. Remind me to call him when we leave here."

"So it's back to the tipi or whatever you call it?"

"*Wigwam* burner. Not tipi. *Wigwam*."

"Wigwam," the other man repeated. "I knew it was some kind of Indian shit."

And Wylie realized that the fuckin' rube was *him*. His belly shuddered with a growl, but no bad bubbles appeared.

WYLIE WAITED FOR another fifteen minutes. He'd been in the pool much too long and was feeling faint. But he didn't dare move or speak before the two men left. Chances were the guttural man would recognize him. The two men continued to talk, but the subjects were football, gambling, and women they'd met and bedded in different parts of the country.

"I keep thinking about that one I told you about," the guttural man said.

"The blond one?"

"Yeah."

"Didn't you say she talked too much?"

"Find me one that doesn't."

"She's nothing compared to my little hottie waitress."

"Fuck you. You never saw her."

"True."

"So shut up about her."

There was a long pause.

"I didn't mean to hit a nerve. I was just fucking around, you know?"

"Don't fuck around."

"Believe me, I've got it."

"Good."

Finally, the other man sighed and said, "I'm getting out."

"Yeah."

"I feel like I've been fucking boiled alive."

"You have."

HE SAT STILL until he heard a car start up in the parking lot. Then Wylie crawled out of the water with the grace of a walrus. Although he knew the concrete walkway was freezing, it felt good against his skin. He hoped his wet body wouldn't stick to it when he was ready to get up.

At last, he raised himself to his hands and knees. The time he'd spent in the hot pool had taken away most of his strength. Plus, he'd jammed himself up for time and he'd have to grab a pizza or a hot dog at the Kum-N-Go instead of enjoying a sit-down dinner. He'd also get a six-pack of Gatorade to replenish all the sweat he'd lost in the hot pool.

When he shuffled to his truck, he checked his phone. No messages yet.

But he was sure now he'd get another call later that night.

The pang of guilt, like an icicle, stabbed at him just below the heart.

PART TWO

There is nothing more difficult to take in hand, more perilous to conduct, or more uncertain in its success, than to take the lead in the introduction of a new order of things.

—Niccolò Machiavelli

8

JOE BEGAN THE THREE-HUNDRED-MILE DRIVE FROM SADDLESTRING to Saratoga as the morning sun winked over the Bighorn Mountains. He'd packed his gear into his pickup the night before so he could get an early start.

After kissing Marybeth and Lucy good-bye at the breakfast table and unplugging the engine block heater outside in the parking lot, he paused at the door when Daisy padded along behind him. Tube stayed in bed.

"I'll see you a little later," he said to Daisy as he stroked her head, hoping that in her Labrador brain she wouldn't realize that he meant days or weeks. He didn't think he'd fooled her, though.

He'd left a complete copy of the Kate file for Marybeth to read and the original was clamped under his arm.

. . .

IT WAS NINETEEN BELOW ZERO. The springs and steering of the truck were stiff at first in the morning cold and it took nearly twenty minutes for the rock-hard frozen tires to become pliable. The streets of Saddlestring were snow-packed and slick. Residents had gone outside to start their vehicles and had left them in their driveways to warm up, creating rising columns of white exhaust.

The sun cleared the summit of the mountains and soon flooded the valley with cold light. The landscape was white and smooth for as far as he could see, with the exception of skeletal trees near the river and natural hedgerows of maroon buckbrush that caught the sunlight and held on tight. Angus cattle in the pastures had gathered into scrums to keep warm, and their exhalation condensed into miniature clouds.

Although he'd slept well, he'd arisen with his mind racing with what he'd learned about Kate's disappearance. There were plenty of gaps to fill and they could only be filled on the ground, by talking with people. He was intrigued to find out what Sheridan knew about Kate, since she'd ridden horses with her. Joe knew that, like fishing with someone, riding with a partner was often an intimate experience. There was time to talk while horses were saddled and tacked up, in the cab of the truck while they were being transported by trailer, and certainly over the hours on the trail.

Sheridan was a good listener and always had been, and wranglers were like bartenders: people felt drawn to talk to them.

Three aspects of the assignment bothered him, though. The first was the odd way Michael Williams had responded when Joe asked him about his work on the case. There was something Williams couldn't or wouldn't talk about and Joe didn't know what it was. Williams and the DCI's investigation appeared methodical and solid. There was a real question about why they'd been taken off the case by Governor Allen, and Joe had trouble believing it had to do with budget cuts and bureaucratic inertia, as Allen had said.

That led to the second concern in Joe's mind. Why him? Sure, Allen had found the old Rulon files where Joe had acted as the former governor's range rider. But with the entire DCI at his disposal, as well as local law enforcement on the scene, why had the governor chosen him? Something didn't make sense about it. Allen had no special feelings toward Joe. In fact, he seemed to distrust him, as Joe so far distrusted the governor in return.

The third unknown, and one that hadn't really been discussed, addressed, or documented, had to do with Saratoga game warden Steve Pollock. Pollock would have been the natural person for the governor to ask to help him surreptitiously. After all, Pollock was on the ground and knew the area, the people, and presumably the situation with Kate's disappearance. But he was gone and no one seemed to really know what had happened to him. There'd been no interagency gossip about Pollock's situation.

When a game warden quit or was fired, it was usually a big deal within the agency. Game warden positions were hard to get and there were hundreds of applicants for every opening. Not only that, but an open district meant that all the current game wardens had the opportunity to apply for it. Seniority was the major consideration to getting a choice district. New game wardens received districts no one else wanted.

Each game warden had a badge number whose order was based on how long they'd been employed relative to the others. Pollock had been badge number eighteen. Joe was now badge number twenty, meaning there were nineteen wardens his senior and thirty his junior.

Saratoga, like Saddlestring, was considered to be one of the best districts in the state. It had mountains on three sides, the North Platte River, which was a blue-ribbon trout fishery, and a large concentration of big-game animals. It was kind of a resort area like Jackson Hole, but without the high-priced housing and amenities and the crush of tourists. It was an attractive place to live. Joe had once suggested that he and Marybeth should apply for the district if it ever came open, and his wife had liked the idea—provided it could happen after all three girls were done with school.

Joe had seen no notices from headquarters about the open position yet, which was curious. It was something he wanted to learn more about.

Despite that, Joe had no idea if Pollock's termination was related to the Kate case or simply coincidental. But something about it nagged him. He doubted he would get a straight answer if he called headquarters. His director, Linda Greene-Dempsey, was rumored to be on thin ice with the new governor, and she'd bunkered in with the hope that Allen would forget she was alive. Therefore, she kept her head down and had ceased sending out directives that might call attention to her. She wasn't the right person to call and ask about what had happened to Steve Pollock—especially if he'd done something wrong. Director LGD would not want any bad publicity concerning game wardens to be heard by the new governor or his staff.

If that was the situation, Director LGD and her executive team would wait for the smoke to clear and quietly open the district for applications later.

. . .

JOE SLOWED DOWN north of Kaycee on Interstate 25 because the wind had kicked up. Ground blizzards like waves of thick-bodied snakes rolled across the blacktop and obscured the black ice underneath. He kept a tight grip on the wheel with the exception of an imaginary toast to Wyoming icon Chris LeDoux as he drove by the singer's hometown. He had toasted LeDoux countless times with Nate Romanowski as they passed through and he did it again. But when he was done, he concentrated on his driving.

The grille of a massive red Peterbilt tractor-trailer filled his rearview mirror and then roared around him in the passing lane. Joe glimpsed license plates from New Jersey. The bulk and momentum of the truck rocked his pickup and stirred up the ground blizzards. For a brief and terrifying moment, Joe could see only white through the windshield and he could gauge his progress only by glimpses of highway markers that shot by on the side of the road.

He eased off the accelerator and waited for the truck to get far enough ahead of him that the flurry of snow-smoke would clear and he could see again. For a second, he considered going after the driver with his lights and siren on because he could request the authority to cite him for driving too fast for conditions, but the thought of a high-speed chase on ice dissuaded him.

Eventually, the snow cleared and Joe could see the back of the red Peterbilt a quarter mile ahead of him. It kicked up snow like a powerboat kicked up a wake.

Driving across Wyoming in the dead of winter was always an adventure. It was the reason so many people never left their small towns or they wintered in Arizona. Joe didn't mind the winter. In fact, he perversely enjoyed how mortal and small it made him feel at times. Tough winters evened things out because everyone was in the same boat—as long as that boat was a four-wheel drive. He'd explained his reasoning to Marybeth once and she'd simply shaken her head.

Joe topped a long hill and looked out at the vast black-and-white ribbon of highway to the south to see that the Peterbilt that had roared past him, as well as another semi, were both lying on their sides in the borrow ditch ahead of him. They looked like two large animals that had decided to lie on their sides to rest for a while.

He pumped his brakes going down the incline and pulled in behind the red Peterbilt. The wind buffeted his pickup and the blowing snow stuck to the passenger window. Through the blizzard he could see a fireplug-shaped man hopping about in a black T-shirt clutching a cell phone. The man gesticulated wildly toward his truck. He apparently didn't have a coat.

Joe left his truck running and pulled on his parka and climbed out. The wind nearly blew him across the highway on the ice, but he bent over to make himself a smaller target.

The driver had a five-day growth of beard and food stains on the front of his T-shirt. He chattered at Joe in an unfamiliar language, Russian or something Eastern European, and gestured toward his truck as if he couldn't believe what had happened. The driver of the first truck was outside as well. He had a heavy red beard and he looked like he wanted a piece of the Eastern European.

Joe motioned for the red-bearded man—who also spoke a language unfamiliar to Joe—to go back to his vehicle, and for the Eastern European to climb back inside his cab to get out of the weather while he called for the Highway Patrol. A trooper who said he was eating breakfast at the Invasion Bar & Grill in Kaycee responded and said he was on his way.

"Anybody hurt?" the trooper asked.

"Doesn't look like it," Joe said. "Both the drivers are from somewhere else and I can't communicate with them. It looks like they had some kind of altercation on the highway and they slid around until the wind blew them over."

"Damn Russians, I'd bet. There's more of them on the road all the time. They're a pain in my ass," the trooper said with disgust. "You'd think they'd know how to drive in the winter. Don't they have winter over there, too?"

"Yup."

"Where is the crash?"

While Joe cleared a roadside mileage marker of snow so he could report the location of the crash, another call came through on his phone. He squinted against the driving snow and saw it was from an unknown number.

He punched it up and shouted, "Joe Pickett."

"What—are you standing outside?" The voice was familiar, but Joe couldn't place it.

"Yes. The wind is blowing."

"I can hear it. This is Michael Williams, but this isn't an official call."

Joe turned his back to the wind.

"Give me a minute," he said. "I'm talking to the Highway Patrol and I'll get right back to you."

"Don't take too long," Williams said, obviously annoyed.

. . .

JOE PULLED HIS DOOR SHUT against the wind and punched up Michael Williams on his phone. He'd told the trooper he would stay at the crash location until he arrived from Kaycee and took over.

Every few minutes, the dark-haired Russian in the T-shirt poked his head up out of the window of his cab and looked around. He appeared to be shouting. The red-bearded Russian in the other truck shook his fist at the driver of the red Peterbilt every time he saw him.

"Sorry about the delay," Joe said to Williams.

"That's okay, but I don't have long to talk to you. I'm calling from my personal cell phone and no one at DCI knows I'm making this call. You have to promise me it'll stay that way."

Joe agreed.

"I know who you are," Williams said. "I've seen your name around and I know you did some work for Governor Rulon. I'm guessing Allen has asked you to do the same thing for him."

Before Joe could respond, Williams said, "No need to confirm that. It just seems like something he would do."

Joe didn't confirm it.

"Whatever the circumstances, you've got a reputation for being a stand-up guy."

"Thank you. Why did he take you guys off the case?" Joe asked. "It seemed to me from reading the file you were building a good foundation to go forward."

"We were." Then a long pause. "I will only tell you it had nothing to do with the KSL case."

"Meaning the Kate Shelford-Longden case."

"Yeah."

"What do you mean when you say you were taken off the case for other reasons?"

"Look," Williams said, "I really can't get into why we were ordered off. I have two kids and another one on the way. I need this job and the bennies—especially medical insurance. You know how it is in the bureaucracy. If this call we're having ever got back to my agency or the governor, I'd be toast. Do you understand what I'm saying?"

"I think so," Joe said. But he didn't.

"I'm sure you have some questions about the investigation itself, so ask away. I'd like to see this case get cleared up one way or another, and if you can do it, I have no problem with that at all. The loose ends still nag me at night."

"What loose ends?"

Williams said, "Keep in mind I only have a few minutes until my break is over and I need to head back."

Joe nodded, even though Williams couldn't see him do it.

"Okay," Joe said. "There is plenty of good background in the report, but no conclusions or theories. Why is that?"

"You've got the redacted version," Williams said. "My original report listed suspects for further questioning."

"Who redacted—"

"I'm not going there. Do you have another question?"

"Yup," Joe said while he dug his spiral notepad and a pen out of the console box. "What were the names of the people you wanted to question further?"

"I've got 'em right here," Williams said. "The thing is, the Silver Creek Ranch really vets their people. They run background checks on everyone and they don't hire any sketchy types. You and I both know that just because someone doesn't have a record doesn't mean they're not capable of doing something wrong, but in this situation it didn't make much sense to me that a ranch employee had anything to do with the disappearance. They're just too busy and they all live with each other in housing right on the ranch. They've got a bunch of dormitory-like buildings there. Hell, they're a hell of a lot nicer than the dorms I stayed in at college.

"Anyway, if someone followed Kate when she drove away and did something to her, one of the other employees would have noticed that the guy was gone. At least that's the theory I was operating under.

"Plus," he said, "there are two hundred and fifty employees at that ranch in the high season. It seemed like a waste of time and manpower to question them all. That's not to say we might not have had to do it eventually, but at the time it seemed unlikely that an employee would be involved."

"Gotcha," Joe said.

"I mean, we had absolutely no leads to follow. Since the employees were clean, we thought, we looked at other people who might have been on the ranch while KSL was there, or other people who might have had it out for her. I was operating under the assumption that if someone grabbed her, it wasn't random. She was one of the few unattached guests that week, and she's attractive. The guy who grabbed her knew he'd have to get rid of the rental car she drove away in. So I operated under the theory that someone saw her there and made her a target. But I didn't think it was an employee."

Joe didn't ask the obvious question, because Williams was on a roll.

The DCI agent said, "Have you ever been there?"

"Not yet, but I've been to a few dude ranches."

"The Silver Creek Ranch is not another dude ranch," Williams said with a chuckle. "It's a world of its own. And it's a very controlled environment. Think of it as a cruise ship instead of a ranch. You've got a couple hundred employees and eighty or ninety guests all staying together on the same property. People don't just come and go, because the ranch is so big and it has so many activities going on that anything anybody might possibly want is right there."

"I understand." Joe declined to mention that Sheridan worked there. He thought it might take them on a tangent that would eat up the little time Williams said he had left to talk.

Williams continued. "So what I started to zero in on were the few people who came to the ranch that week who were *not* employees or guests. People who might not be as clean."

"Contractors," Joe said.

"Bingo. I got a list from the front gate of all the people who checked in and out that week, then I ran background checks on them. It turns out I got some hits on a couple of the names. Do you have a way to write these down?"

"Yes."

"Jack and Joshua Teubner," Williams said. He was obviously reading from notes and he spelled the names. "They own a private fish hatchery outside of Saratoga."

Joe was familiar with the facility.

"Father and son. They supply most of the guest ranches in the state and they operate into Colorado and Montana. Lots of private landowners use them to stock trout in their ponds, so they're the type of people who move through places like the Silver Creek Ranch with no one really noticing.

"Jack, the old man, has a couple of B&E's on his sheet and a DUI. Josh, his son, spent a year in Rawlins for stalking an old girlfriend."

"*Stalking*," Joe repeated.

"Yeah, that's what I thought, too. But I never got a chance to talk to either one of them."

"Who else?" Joe asked.

"Ben and Brady Youngberg," Williams said, and spelled their names as well. "They're farriers from Laramie. Brothers. They come to the Silver Creek Ranch every couple of days in the summer to take care of the horses. And we're talking, I don't know, *hundreds* of horses. There's a decent chance they saw Kate since she's a rider. Probably a better chance the Youngbergs saw her than the Teubners."

"I was just thinking the same thing."

"Well, from what I heard by asking around, the Youngberg brothers are the best farriers in the state. It's hard physical work, man. They spend the entire day bent over putting shoes on and taking shoes off. But these two are hound dogs. They work hard all day and party hard at night, wherever they are. Both have been charged with A&B—assault and battery—for bar fights. Brady spent a year in Rawlins for stomping some guy. They're rough customers."

Joe agreed.

"There's one more," Williams said. "And then I really have to go."

"Shoot."

"The ex-husband. Name's Richard Cheetham. I guess he and KSL had a pretty bitter and public divorce over in England. I couldn't really tie Richard to the case because I didn't get a chance to pursue that angle. But maybe he hired someone to follow her and take her out between the ranch and Denver. It's far-fetched, but you can never rule out the ex-husband, you know?"

"Right," Joe said, recalling that he'd also written down the name on his legal pad.

Outside, the trooper Joe had talked to cruised slowly by the pickup and pulled in behind the red Peterbilt. Joe waved at him and the highway patrolman waved back.

"I really appreciate you calling me," Joe said to Williams.

"Yeah, well."

"I'm not kidding."

"And I'm not kidding about you keeping this between us," Williams said. "But I would like to know what you find out."

"I'll keep you posted," Joe agreed.

"I don't like the idea of someone grabbing women tourists in this state," he said. "I've got daughters, you know?"

"Me too," Joe said.

"So I hope you find the bastard and put him away, even if the governor figures out a way to take credit for it."

Joe didn't comment. But before Williams punched off, Joe said, "Hey—there's one more thing I want to ask you."

"Do it fast."

"There was a game warden down in Saratoga named Steve Pollock. Did you ever run into him?"

At first, Joe thought he'd lost the connection. Finally, Williams said, "Yeah, I met him a couple of times."

"Do you have any idea what happened to him?"

"I'm not going there," Williams said with caution.

"So him leaving might be connected to the case?"

"I'm not saying that at all. He might be connected to why we were taken off, but not to this . . ." Williams stopped speaking and Joe strained to listen.

"Let's just leave it here," the DCI agent said. "I've already said too much. Gotta go."

And this time, the connection went dead.

. . .

JOE SAT BACK and watched as the trooper emerged from his cruiser in a heavy parka. He waved his arms at both drivers to indicate they should stay in their vehicles. The two Eastern Europeans gesticulated wildly and pointed at each other, each attempting to pin the blame for the accident on the other one. The trooper shook his head, uninterested in the dispute.

Even though Williams had ruled out the likelihood that the disappearance of Kate was a random act, Joe looked at the drivers and wrote down the words *Random stranger* next to the other suspects.

It was a lonely highway from Saratoga toward Denver, after all. A tractor-trailer driver with no ties at all to the state or region could have happened on Kate driving alone. The trailers of the rigs on their sides in front of him were certainly large enough to hide Kate's Jeep if they were empty or half-full.

He knew the possibility was a long shot, but so was everything else. He also knew that if a random predator had taken her he'd likely never find him.

Joe nodded at the trooper as he eased his pickup back onto the icy highway. The highway patrolman didn't look to be in a very good mood.

His last glimpse of the first Russian driver—with his wild eyes, stained T-shirt, and blowing snow now stuck to the side of his face—made Joe think: *That guy is capable of anything.*

ONCE HE TURNED OFF the interstate highway in Casper, Joe had a choice of traveling south on State Highway 487 over the Shirley

Basin to Medicine Bow or on Highway 220 through Alcova, Muddy Gap, and Rawlins. Either route would lead to Saratoga, and both were two-lane roads. He paused and checked his phone for the road conditions on the WYDOT website. Both routes were listed as "Wet, Slick in Spots with Dangerous Winds, and Blowing Snow—Advise No Light Trailers, Extreme Blow-Over Risk."

Six of one, half a dozen of the other. Both perilous. He chose 487 and within an hour he was high on the Shirley Mountains plateau where it seemed he was the only driver on the road and he got the feeling, like he always did when he was there, that he'd ventured on top of the world where the only inhabitants were pure white jackrabbits, pronghorn antelope, and the ghosts of winter drivers who'd slid off the highway.

The plateau was stark and there were no trees to cut the wind. Waves of blowing snow were forming small drifts across the road. He noted that the blades of the wind turbines that had been recently built on the flat were still. Joe knew that happened only in two conditions: when there was no wind at all or when the winds were so high that the speed of the turning blades would damage the equipment.

He recalled Chief of Staff Hanlon mentioning a massive new wind farm that was being built north of Saratoga and that the governor had a keen interest in the project.

JOE ATE A LATE LUNCH in the historic Virginian Hotel in Medicine Bow, the town where the classic Western novel had been set. He was the only customer in the restaurant and he went with the special: hot hamburger steak with mashed potatoes and brown gravy.

He left a twenty-dollar tip because the geriatric waitress called him "son" and she reminded him of a great-aunt he had once liked. Plus, he hoped the extra money would incentivize her to stay around on days when there were so few customers.

She thanked him for the tip while she rang him up. She said, "It's because of a game warden that my husband went to prison."

Before Joe could react, she winked and said, "It was the best day of my life."

Outside, he circled his pickup in the lot before climbing back in.

Snow and ice were packed in the wheel wells from the drive and had built up until the mass was less than an inch from rubbing against the tread on the tires. He turned with his back to the truck and kicked at the ice with his boot heel until it broke away and fell to the gravel in blocky chunks.

THE WIND FINALLY died away midafternoon as Joe crossed I-80 at Walcott Junction and drove south on WYO 130 toward the town of Saratoga. The area had gotten plenty of snow, but it was hard to judge the depth because of the drifts. Icy waves of it shone in the sun and it was so deep in places that only the top wire and tips of the fence posts were visible. Someone had used an earth mover to push the snow into barricades along the roadside hilltops to slow loose snow from drifting across the asphalt.

Elk Mountain and the Snowy Range rose sun-kissed and blue and the mountains dominated the view from the driver's-side window. The Sierra Madre range rose in front of him as well as out the passenger side.

He noted that the Upper North Platte River Valley, where Saratoga was located, was deceptively situated. The occupants of hundreds of thousands of cars and trucks using east-to-west I-80, where the terrain was high and windswept desert, would have no inkling that twenty-one miles to the south was a lush river valley with mountain peaks on three sides.

A herd of ninety elk were bedded down and sunning themselves on the top of a ridge to the east. Their forms blended in so well with the snow-and-sagebrush cover that he would have missed them if it weren't for the glint of afternoon sun on the antlers of the bulls.

He slowed down to let two bald eagles rise up clumsily from a road-killed rabbit in the middle of the highway.

There were snow-packed dirt roads on either side of the highway leading either to distant ranches or river access on the North Platte. And not a single oncoming car.

SARATOGA, POPULATION 1,671 SOULS, and elevation 6,785 feet, appeared spread out in front of him after he topped a long rise. The town was choked with cottonwoods and he could see a wide ribbon of river through the middle of it. The air shimmered over the hot stack of a lumber mill on the western edge of the town.

Joe took a deep breath and slowly expelled it. The drive across the state on winter roads had been long and tense. As he crossed the bridge into town, he smelled wood smoke from the mill and he saw hundreds of ducks and geese on the open water of the river. He loosened his tight grip on the wheel and let his shoulders relax.

Saratoga, to Joe, was a smaller and more intimate version of Saddlestring.

He turned right on West Farm Avenue and cruised up a snow-covered street. There were modest single-family homes on the left and a large pasture on the right. Within two blocks he found a brown two-story house with a sign in the front yard that read GAME WARDEN STATION. There were no tire tracks on the driveway or on the two-track path that led to a metal storage shop.

Joe pulled his pickup into the driveway and got out. The snow was ankle-deep on the way to the front door and he stepped over four editions of the weekly *Saratoga Sun* that were frozen to the concrete on the front porch. So it had been weeks since someone had retrieved them, he thought.

Next to the doorbell was a handcrafted sign listing Steve Pollock's official hours as well as telephone numbers for when he was off duty. The 800 "stop poaching" hotline was included as well. Joe had created a similar sign for the front of his house before it was torched. It didn't do much good. When citizens wanted to talk to the local game warden or report a violation, they didn't pay much attention to official hours of operation. That was part of the job.

Although the house looked dark and empty, Joe rang the doorbell anyway. He could hear the chime echoing through the empty rooms inside. Then he knocked on the front door with the same result.

Finally, he tried the knob. Locked.

As he stepped off the porch, he could see a woman watching him through the side window of the next house. He waved and she waved back, then stepped aside and closed the curtains.

Circling the house in the snow, Joe glanced through the windows. There were what looked like empty boxes in the front room as well as stray papers on the floor. He could see dirty dishes in the sink in the kitchen. Pollock's green Ford pickup, which was much cleaner than Joe's, was locked up in the garage.

It looked like Steve Pollock had cleared out fast and no one had been there to clean up since he left.

Joe shook his head as he trudged back to his pickup. He wondered if anyone in town had keys to the place or if he'd need to request a set to get in.

He placed a call to Casey Scales in Laramie, who was the Game and Fish Department district supervisor for the Snowy Range district. Scales had seven game wardens under him in southeast Wyoming. Joe had met him a couple of times and he seemed laid-back.

"Casey," Joe said. "I'm in Saratoga on a project and I was wondering if I could get the keys from you to our house over here."

"Steve Pollock's old place?"

"Yup."

"I haven't been over there yet. What kind of shape did he leave it in?"

"It looks like he just walked right out the door," Joe said.

"Hmmm."

"Can you tell me what happened?" Joe asked.

"I would if I could, Joe, but your guess is as good as mine. You know I keep a loose rein on my guys and I really don't get in their business unless I have to or LGD leans on me."

"Right."

"Steve didn't give me any warning at all about anything," Scales said. "He did his job as far as I can tell and he turned in his monthly reports on time. He had a lot of autonomy and he never gave me any reason not to trust him, so I just let him do his thing. He never told me he was dissatisfied with anything or gave me any reason to think he was going anywhere. And I haven't heard any evidence that somebody chased him off.

"When I heard he left, I called his ex-wife, Lindy, and it was real awkward because *she* didn't know he quit. I was the one breaking the news to her."

"Did she give you any reason why he might have left?" Joe asked.

"Well, she thought he might have taken up with a woman. There's some real fancy ones that come through Saratoga, you know. But she was just guessing, really. Steve had never mentioned another woman to her."

"Maybe the job just got overwhelming," Joe speculated. He made a mental note to himself to add Pollock's name to his list of suspects.

"Maybe," Scales said. "There's a lot going on around there and that's not counting all the new directives LGD and Governor Allen are pumping out. But I can't imagine Steve not just rolling with it. He's like me—he isn't a guy to get all worked up about things."

"About those keys," Joe said.

"Shouldn't be a problem at all," Scales said. "I think we've got an extra set at the office. I'll run them down and maybe even drive them over to you tomorrow if the roads are open."

"Thank you."

"What kind of project do they have you doing all the way down here?" Scales asked.

"Oh, you know," Joe hedged.

"Just more bullshit." Scales chuckled. "Kind of what they've got me doing. Let me know if you need anything or any info on the district. I might be able to help."

Joe breathed a sigh of relief that Casey Scales hadn't pressed him more.

And he knew he wouldn't be occupying the game warden house that night.

. . .

JOE THUMBED THROUGH the case file and found the name and number of Carbon County sheriff Ron Neal. Neal's headquarters was in Rawlins, which was forty-two miles away via Fort Steele and Sinclair. Carbon County was nearly eight thousand square miles and included most of the Red Desert, where Joe had been involved in a terrifying incident two years before.

It took a while to get through directly to the sheriff himself, but finally there was a brusque "Sheriff Neal."

Joe told him he was making a courtesy call to let Neal know he was in the county working on the missing persons case on behalf of the governor. Neal was silent for a moment.

"Does the governor think we can't do our job here?"

"Well, it's not that," Joe said. "He just wants another set of eyes on it, I guess."

"You're the fellow who was involved in that big mess out in the Red Desert, right?"

"Right."

"I was kind of hoping we wouldn't see you again."

"I understand," Joe said.

"Why'd he pull the DCI off the investigation?" Neal asked.

"I can't speak for the governor."

"He shoulda let them do their job. Just like he should let me do mine."

Joe took a deep breath and said, "Sheriff Neal, I really don't want to get crosswise with you. This wasn't my call."

"I appreciate that," Neal said after a beat. "It seems odd that he'd send a game warden, though. Are you taking over for Pollock?"

"Temporarily."

"That was an odd circumstance," Neal said. "Any idea why he just up and left?"

"No. I'd like to find out myself."

"If you do, please let me know," Neal said. "I liked that guy and I thought he was on the level. And keep me posted on what you find about that English gal."

"I'll do that," Joe said.

"Let me know if there's anything I can do to help. I don't like the idea of a woman vanishing in my county."

"Thank you."

"And try to keep a lower profile than you did the last time you were here, for Christ's sake," Neal said with a chuckle.

"I'll do that, too," Joe assured him.

HE DROVE BACK downtown and turned onto Main and slid into a diagonal space in front of the Hotel Wolf. The building was a three-story Victorian structure constructed of red brick with a covered front porch and lonely chairs and benches. The windows to the bar on the right side glowed warm yellow. He knew that the hotel rented rooms, although he hadn't made a reservation. He didn't figure it would be necessary in January and, judging by the few cars parked along the small downtown, he'd made the right guess.

As he reached down to open his door, the front door of the Wolf opened and three cowboys came out. Two wore wide-brimmed hats, Carhartt parkas, and Sorel pac boots. The third man, who looked older, pulled on a wool rancher's cap with earflaps. When they saw his mud-and-ice-encrusted pickup, the three of them paused for a moment and stared.

Joe waved hello through the windshield. They waved back and moved on, hunched over against the cold. He noted that the three of them gave him a second look over their shoulders before they entered the Rustic Bar down the street.

He knew that within hours the word would be out via the cowboys and the woman who lived next to Steve Pollock's former house:

There's a new game warden in town.

9

JOE STOMPED THE SNOW OFF HIS BOOTS ON A MAT ON THE WOODEN porch and entered the central hallway of the Hotel Wolf. To his left was the doorway to a dining room filled with set tables and a woodstove glowing red on the east wall. Straight ahead was kitchen access and restrooms. A wide staircase to the hotel rooms was buttressed against a west-facing wall. To his immediate right were a pair of batwing doors. He pushed through them into a lobby of sorts with a pool table in the center and a counter near his left elbow. Beside the counter was an opening with a side view into the adjacent bar and a cooler filled with wine bottles and six-packs to go.

The bartender looked up at him from where she was rinsing glasses. She raised a finger to indicate it would be a moment. He nodded back. There were two drinkers at the bar. One was a wide-faced man in his seventies with a bulbous nose who wore a polyester trucker cap that looked like he'd worn it long enough that it had come back into style again and a hipster-looking dude with sun-bleached hair who appeared to have parked his surfboard outside in a snowdrift. Both leaned forward on the stools so they could get a look at Joe through the opening near the beer cooler.

He nodded to them as well and they sat back out of view. He heard the old man mumble something and recognized the phrases *game warden* and *Steve Pollock*.

While he waited for the bartender, he checked out the room, which smelled of fresh popcorn from a half-full machine behind the counter. There were elk, mule deer, and pronghorn antelope mounts. He studied an old photo of the hotel looking exactly as it looked now except instead of Joe's pickup out front, there was a stagecoach pulled by a team of six white horses. The inscription on the bottom of the photo indicated it had been taken in 1893.

Joe liked the feel of the place.

The bartender approached the counter, drying her hands on a towel. She was short and compact and she wore a long-sleeved henley T-shirt and tight Western jeans. Her light brown hair was pulled back and tied with a red bandanna. She had wise brown eyes with gold specks in them and a full mouth. Joe thought she had the presence of a woman who was friendly enough but didn't suffer fools.

He placed his hand on the short counter. "Is this where you rent a room?"

"This is the place."

"I don't have a reservation."

"That's too bad, because we're booked solid until Christmas," she said. Then, flashing a sarcastic smile, she said, "I'm kidding. It's January in Saratoga. Except for the Ice Fishing Derby weekend, we're wide open. Just tonight?"

"Actually, I was thinking maybe a week."

She arched her eyebrows in surprise as she pulled out a large ledger and flipped through the pages. Joe smiled.

"We're updating our software so we're back to the old-fashioned method," she said by way of explanation. "What I'm looking for here is a room that's available for a week so we don't have to move you."

"Thank you."

She tapped on an open space on the page. "How about number nine? It's a deluxe room with a queen bed, a TV, a tub, and a handheld shower. Overlooks Bridge Street."

"Sounds good," he said. He liked the idea of being able to look outside onto the main downtown street to see what was going on—if anything.

"But I'll warn you," she said, "we don't have phones in our rooms."

"That's fine. Is there—"

"Internet?" she answered. "Yes. When it works."

"It's a deal."

As he reached for his wallet, she said, "Also, I need to tell you about the pedestal tub. It's old-fashioned, but it works perfectly. Just don't overfill it and thrash around. We had a very amorous couple here a couple of months ago who got a little excited"—she nodded toward toward the dining room—"and the bathwater dripped through the floor onto table number seven directly below."

"I'll try to stay calm," Joe said, handing her his state credit card.

"Don't worry about that for now," she said with a wave of her hand. "We'll settle up when you know for sure how long you're staying."

He thanked her and wrote *Joe Pickett, Saddlestring, Wyoming* on the ledger. He glanced over her shoulder at the two customers to confirm that they were perched on the edge of their stools so they could hear. They were.

"So," she asked, "what brings you to town?"

"Oh, I'm here on a project," he said.

"What kind of project?"

"I'm with the Game and Fish Department."

"That's obvious," she said with a sly roll of her eyes. "I don't mean to be nosy. I just asked because our last game warden just went away—literally. I assumed you were the replacement."

"Temporarily," he said. There was no reason to explain further and he didn't want to make something up.

"And my daughter works around here," he added. "I'm eager to see her."

"Good for you," the bartender said as she extended her hand. "I'm Kim Miller. Who is your daughter?"

"Her name is Sheridan Pickett."

Recognition flicked in Miller's eyes. "Silver Creek Ranch."

"Yup."

"Everybody knows everybody around here," Miller said. "She's a nice kid and I hear she's a good hand."

"Good to hear," Joe said. And it was. Reputation in a small community like this meant everything.

Kim Miller handed over a single key attached to a maroon plastic oval stamped #9.

"Take a left at the hallway at the top of the stairs. It's the first room on your left."

"Thank you."

"Can I get you something from the bar?"

"I'll wait."

"'I'll wait,'" she repeated. "Those aren't words I hear very much around here. Especially in the winter."

"Oh, I'll be back," he assured her.

Joe looked over her shoulder at the taps. Stella Artois, 312, Deschutes, Dale's Pale Ale, Bud Light, Coors Light, and two beers from Black Tooth Brewing Company in Sheridan.

"When I come back, I'd like a Saddle Bronc," he said. The brown ale was from the Black Tooth.

"Good choice," she said.

THE ROOM WAS SMALL, simple, and clean, and furnished to look like it might have looked when the hotel was opened. He hung up his uniform shirts and winter gear in a chifforobe and kicked his empty duffel bag under the bed. He touched the warm radiator with his fingertips while he looked around. The bed was covered with a floral comforter. A Samsung flat-screen television was mounted high on the wall in a corner. There were two reading lamps and an overhead light and fan. An ancient transom was painted closed over the entry door.

Joe texted Sheridan to tell her he'd arrived in town and that he could meet her in the bar if she was free. As he did it, he thought that he'd never before told any of his daughters that he'd meet them "in the bar."

She replied that she was just about done with evening chores and she'd meet him as soon as she could.

Excited to see you! she texted, followed by a string of happy emojis.

Joe was wary of emojis and texted back, *Me too.*

He rinsed his face in the antique sink, beheld the pedestal tub directly over table number seven, changed from his uniform shirt into a heavy chambray Cinch cowboy shirt, clamped his Stetson back on, and went back downstairs.

The Saddle Bronc was waiting for him in a chilled glass on the bar.

"Thank you," he said.

"Start a tab?"

"Sure."

He sat at a tall narrow table that faced the bar. The hipster was gone, but the old man in the trucker hat sat hunched with his back to Joe cradling a Budweiser in a bottle.

The saloon was narrow and intimate. There were more elk, mule deer, and pronghorn antelope heads on the wall, as well as University of Wyoming paraphernalia and historical photos of fly fishermen and community fish fries. Sawdust covered the floor and baskets of shelled peanuts were set on the top of the tables.

Two mounted televisions were tuned to basketball with the sound off. There were eight high-backed stools at the bar and a long high table that sat six and a smaller round table that sat four. Warm yellow light fused through the stems of wineglasses on the back bar. Cigars were for sale in a display case on the left side of the back bar and packs of cigarettes were available on the right. An errant blue marlin hung from the ceiling and arched over the length of the room.

Joe sat at the corner behind the long table and sipped the beer. It tasted good. He drew out his phone and sent a quick email to Allen's chief of staff that he'd arrived in Saratoga. Before he could text Marybeth to tell her the same thing, Hanlon replied:

Getting there and getting results are two different things.

Joe narrowed his eyes and did a slow burn.

When he looked up, the old man had spun around on his stool and was facing him. His Budweiser rested on his right thigh.

"If you're not here to take over for Pollock, what in the hell are you here for? We've got enough government types doing nothing around here as it is. Forest Service, Bureau of Land Management, Army Corps of Engineers—and that's not to mention the state government types like yourself."

Right to the point, Joe thought with a smile.

"Did you know Steve Pollock?" Joe asked, deflecting.

"I avoided him the best I could," the man said. "But yeah, I knew him. Everybody knows everybody around here, even if you don't want to."

"Got it. Do you have any idea what happened to him?"

"You don't?"

"No."

The old man raised his beer and drank it until it was gone. He ordered another over his shoulder.

"One more before rush hour hits," he said.

Kim Miller rolled her eyes for Joe's benefit while she dug out another bottle from the cooler.

"I got an idea, but I ain't sayin'," the old man growled as he reached behind him for the fresh bottle.

"Why not?"

"Because I ain't sayin'."

"What's your name? I'm Joe Pickett."

The old man froze for a moment and turned his head to the side without taking his eyes off Joe.

"I've heard of you."

"Only good things, I hope."

"Some of 'em were. Are you the one that got involved with the Cates clan up north?"

"Afraid so."

The extended Cates family in Twelve Sleep County, including rodeo champion Dallas Cates, had declared Joe their mortal enemy and they'd gone after his family. That had resulted in a slew of innocent and not-so-innocent deaths and with both Dallas and his mother, Brenda, in prison for what likely would be the rest of their lives. Joe still had nightmares about it.

"Dallas was a full-on asshat," the old man said as he slipped forward off his stool. "I had the displeasure of meeting him once. You done good on that one."

He extended his hand to Joe. His grip was still cold from cradling the bottle.

"Jeb Pryor," he said. "I own the lumber mill up in Encampment."

"Nice to meet you. Now, about Steve Pollock?"

Joe noted that Kim Miller was listening closely to the exchange while pretending not to do so.

"I got a theory, is all."

"Let's hear it. I haven't heard a reason why he's gone."

"He's got a lot of theories," Miller said. "Just don't ask him about 9/11 or the moon landing. Or the last election!"

Pryor ignored her. "I'll have to catch up with you later. I need to get to the mill before rush hour."

With that, he drained the bottle and placed it on the bar behind him, along with a wad of cash.

"See you tomorrow," Miller said to him.

Pryor pulled on a heavy parka and grunted that he'd be back.

When Pryor left, Miller pointed toward Joe's empty pint glass and said, "Another one?"

"Sure. What was that about?"

Miller shook her head and said, "We have a lot of characters around here. You just met one of 'em."

Again, a more compact version of Saddlestring, he thought. And he made a note to himself to interview Jeb Pryor when he got the chance.

RUSH HOUR WASN'T, despite what Jeb Pryor said.

Joe noted that there were a *few* more vehicles on the streets outside after five, and some locals parked out front and came in through the front door.

Winter darkness had come suddenly and the streetlights came on. He found that he'd inadvertently selected the catbird seat in the bar, where he could not only view all of the bar customers coming in but people going to the dining room as well for an early dinner. He could smell steak broiling from the kitchen. Kim Miller got suddenly very busy walking from the main bar to a service bar in an adjacent meeting room to take care of the dual crowds.

The bat-wing doors opened tentatively and Sheridan stuck her head through the opening. When she spotted Joe, she grinned. He felt his heart swell at the sight of his oldest daughter and he motioned her over and hugged her when she joined him.

Sheridan looked slim, fit, windburned, and lovely, he thought. She wore faded jeans, Bogs boots, a cowboy hat that looked surprisingly good on her, and a down coat emblazoned with SILVER CREEK RANCH on the front. Her blond hair was shorter than the last time he'd seen her. She smelled of hay and horses.

"I got here as soon as I could," she said. "My truck was due for an oil change and it's in the shop, so I had to hitch a ride into town."

"I'll be happy to buy you dinner," Joe said. "We can sit in the bar or go get a table."

"I'll be happy to eat it. I'm *starved*. It's good to see you, Dad."

"It's great to see you. You look like a ranch hand."

"I'm a wrangler," she corrected him. "Who would have thought, right?"

"I think your mother has wrangler envy."

Sheridan laughed and said, "I *know* she does."

His daughter shed her coat and took a stool to the right of him at the end of the table. Sheridan, like Joe, didn't like to sit with her back to the entrance.

"Let's eat here," she said as Kim Miller arrived and slid a glass of red wine to her.

"Thank you, Kim," Sheridan said.

Miller nodded and went back behind the bar.

Joe took a moment before he said, "She didn't even ask for your order."

Sheridan nodded and smiled. "I'm not exactly a stranger here, Dad. Kim knows I like shiraz. I usually come here on Friday nights."

Just like her mother, Joe thought. He had forgotten it was Friday, which, like in most towns in Wyoming, was a bigger night for socializing and going out than Saturday.

"I think she wonders how long you'll be a wrangler."

"You mean before I move on to a *real* job?" she asked with a sideways glance.

"Yup, I guess."

"You can tell her I don't know. Because I don't."

"That's what I'll tell her."

"I'm making good money and they give me a place to live on the ranch," she said. "I'm doing better than most of the kids I went to college with, in fact."

"You don't need to defend yourself," Joe said.

"I feel like I do. I grew up with Mom always wanting me to help her with the horses and asking me to go riding with her. When I showed up at the ranch, I had a skill set they really appreciated. So blame her."

"I'm not blaming anyone," Joe said. "So let's move on."

"Cheers to that," Sheridan said, and clinked Joe's beer with her wineglass and drank.

"This is a good place," Sheridan said, meaning the Hotel Wolf. "Especially on Friday night. Kim told me once that if you sit in here long enough, you'll meet everyone in Saratoga and everyone who comes through town. I thought she was kidding, but she wasn't. It's kind of like the heart of this valley."

Joe was used to having daughters—he'd never regretted not having any sons—but he was not yet used to having *adult* daughters. He looked at Sheridan sipping her glass of wine and saw her at seven years old hiding Miller's weasels from him in the woodpile.

She was obviously no longer that little girl, but her grit and determination were still hardwired. Marybeth and Sheridan were both strong-willed, and clashes between them were inevitable.

As Sheridan told Joe about her duties at Silver Creek Ranch and how happy she was there, more customers filtered in from the outside.

Sheridan seemed to know them all—or know of them—and she kept up a low-running commentary for Joe's benefit.

Of the three men in Carhartt coveralls who'd taken seats at the bar, she said, "They're construction workers on the Buckbrush—the Buckbrush Wind Energy Project going up north of town. It's the biggest wind farm in the country from what I hear. Those guys are semipermanent around here because they're building so many turbines."

Of the three ranch hands—two men and a woman—who clomped in and took a table near the back, she said, "Working cowboys just like we have back home. The woman with them used to be at Silver Creek Ranch for a while, but she got drunk one night and tried to run her boyfriend over with an ATV. She missed him and wrecked the four-wheeler in the trees. I think her name is Nelda."

Of the older man who sported a white mane of hair and who appeared to be arriving for dinner with his wife and older daughter, she said, "Ever heard of Klobasch Aeronautics? That's Dan Klobasch. He's a multimillionaire who owns a mega-house up on the hill and flies here in his Gulfstream jet. One of the women he's with is his wife and the other one is his mistress. Apparently, Mrs. Klobasch is okay with that."

Of the gruff man in winter outdoor gear who escorted a second man wearing a blazer into the bar, Sheridan said, "He's a hunting outfitter working on his client, trying to get the guy to commit to a hunt. There's a bunch of hunting guides and fishing guides in the area and they all compete for rich out-of-state clients. Tom there is one of the most successful guides around here because he knows how to wine and dine potential customers. Some of those other outfitters just have no interpersonal skills at all, you know?"

Joe turned his head to her and smiled.

"I guess you know all about hunting guides," she said with a roll of her eyes. "I don't know why I was going on and on about them.

"But you see what I mean, don't you? If you sit here long enough, you'll get to understand what makes this whole valley tick. You've got your ranchers, your multimillionaires, your lumberjacks, and your hunting-and-fishing types. They all just seem to blend together and get along around here, which I find kind of fascinating."

Joe agreed.

Kim Miller swooped over and asked them if they wanted to order food where they were in the bar or move into the dining room. Joe looked to Sheridan for guidance.

"We'll stay here," she said. "The scenery's better."

"What she said," Joe agreed, tacitly enjoying how his daughter had taken charge.

Joe ordered a steak sandwich and fries and Sheridan ordered a Kirsten's Roast Beef sandwich.

WHILE THEY WAITED for their food and Sheridan continued to point out new arrivals and regale Joe with gossip and stories about them, two large young men slipped into the saloon who didn't seem to fit any of Sheridan's earlier categories.

The men were big and raw-boned and they shambled across the floor in a loose-limbed way that sent off a signal that they were ready for anything, Joe thought. They had similar physical characteristics—heavy jaws, jug-ears, powerful arms that strained at the sleeves of their coats. One had jet-black hair and the other was a ginger. As they passed, the black-haired man assessed Joe coolly and shook his head with disapproval. The black-haired man led the other through the saloon into the meeting room and the two of them sprawled in chairs and waited for Kim Miller to take their order.

"There goes a guy who doesn't like game wardens," Joe said.

"Probably—but it's not that entirely," Sheridan said sotto voce. "We're sitting in their place."

"How was I to know that?"

"You weren't, but I do," she said with a sly smile. "And we aren't moving."

"Who are they? They look like brothers."

"Exactly," she said. "They're the Youngbergs."

Joe had heard that name before, and before he could recall it, Sheridan said, "Brady is the dark-haired one. He's the oldest by a couple of years. Ben is his little brother. They're farriers."

He nodded. They'd also been mentioned by DCI agent Michael Williams as suspects in Kate's disappearance.

"With all of the horses we have on the ranch, we need farriers to come out nearly every day in the summer," Sheridan said. "We've tried some other farriers from around the area, but there's no doubt the Youngbergs are the fastest, cheapest, and best. I kind of wish they weren't, because there's something about them when they're together that kind of makes me uncomfortable."

"In what way?" Joe asked.

"They look me over like I'm a piece of meat," she said. "And I've heard some things. Let's just say we actively try to keep them away from our female guests."

Joe felt a rise of anger in his chest. There was no doubt Sheridan was attractive, just like her sisters and her mother. But he didn't like the idea of two rough yahoos leering at her.

The food arrived just in time.

AS THEY ATE AND TALKED, more people came into the hotel. Soon, every seat in the saloon was filled, as well as most of the chairs in the adjacent meeting room. Kim Miller was slammed, but she moved into a higher gear and managed to keep up with demand. Joe nearly bolted from his stool when he saw Brady Youngberg make a grab for her hand when she delivered a third round of beer-and-shots to their table. Miller turned and said something fierce to Brady that made both Youngbergs blanch for a moment and then laugh it off as she returned to the bar. She was too fast for them, Joe thought.

His steak sandwich was perfect, and Sheridan ate her roast beef with determination.

"When you work outside all day . . ." she said defensively, and he smiled.

"So," he asked Sheridan after the next round of drinks arrived, "did you ever meet the woman from England who disappeared? Kate Shelford-Longden?"

"Oh yes, I met her. She was really nice and she loved to ride. And she wasn't one of those types who pretended she was an expert when she wasn't. I didn't spend as much time with her as my boss did, but she rode every minute she could and . . ."

Sheridan stopped talking and suddenly looked at Joe with suspicion in her eyes.

"What?" he asked.

"She's the reason you're here, isn't she?"

"I can't lie to you. I'd just ask you to please keep it to yourself."

She nodded, but continued to appraise him.

"Maybe I can help," she said.

"I was hoping you could. I have a lot of questions, but I don't want to talk about it here tonight."

"I understand. Does Mom know?"

"Yup. And she's probably more interested in this case than anyone else. She knew all about Kate's disappearance."

"I believe that," Sheridan said. "I can see Mom going all in on finding the missing British executive. That's right up her alley."

Joe agreed.

"Maybe we can get together this weekend," Sheridan said. "I need to work in the morning, but the afternoons are pretty open."

"Let's do that," he said. "I'll be in touch."

He watched her as she bent her head and finished her meal. Joe turned his plate so she could access his French fries, which she did.

He could tell she was intrigued by the whole thing.

"Do you remember when you used to ride along with me and we talked about working together to solve a mystery?" he asked her.

"I was just thinking the same thing," she said softly. Her eyes were moist when she said it.

"I always said someday we might do that, but I wasn't sure I believed it. But who knows?"

"I'll keep it to myself," she said. "But I'm warning you now: nothing stays a secret for very long in this valley. I won't say a word to anyone, but believe me when I tell you that everyone will know sooner rather than later that you're looking into the Kate thing."

He nodded. Just like Saddlestring.

THEY STAYED FOR ANOTHER twenty minutes as the bar got more raucous. It was crowded enough that it was difficult to have a conversation without being overheard by someone.

"I'd better get going pretty soon," Sheridan said. "I don't want to make my ride wait for me forever. And I know you're getting antsy with the crowd."

"You know me well," he said.

"I do."

"Who is your ride?"

Sheridan blushed. Then: "Let's just say he seems insanely nervous that you're here. He might have heard a little about you from me."

"Ah," Joe said.

She excused herself to use the restroom, and Joe waited for Kim Miller to deliver the bar tab. He planned to leave her a very generous tip because she deserved it, and he thought she might be a very good person to talk to about Kate's disappearance as well.

THE DENVER NUGGETS were hanging in there with the Golden State Warriors going into the half, when Joe heard a shout from the adjacent room and the crash of chairs being knocked to the hardwood floor. Through a gap in the crowd near the door, there was a flash of Sheridan's blond hair as she jumped back from the incident.

He leapt off his stool and slid through the onlookers while clamping on his hat. He cleared the people choking the doorway and guessed what had happened: Ben or Brady Youngberg had left their table and tried to intercept Sheridan as she returned from the restroom. She'd fought herself free and stood facing them both with her back to the service bar. Both brothers had risen from their table quickly enough that their chairs had fallen over backward. Brady, the black-haired brother, bent over slightly at the waist and grimaced with short breaths.

A tall slim young man with a clean-shaven face and silver-belly cowboy hat stepped out from the tables in the room and stood in front of Sheridan. The cowboy was outnumbered and outweighed by two hundred pounds if you combined both brothers.

"Get the fuck out of the way, Ramsey," Ben growled at the cowboy. "This doesn't have nothing to do with you. Brady just tried to talk to her and she kneed him in the nuts."

"I'll do it again if he tries to touch me," Sheridan said from behind the cowboy.

Joe instinctively reached down to his hip for the weapon that wasn't there and the movement caught Ben's attention. Ben was obviously not aware what a poor pistol shot Joe was.

"Everybody calm down," Joe said. He could see no weapons on either of the Youngberg brothers, and Brady was temporarily out of order. "Let's all just take a breath."

"Who the hell are you?" Brady asked through clenched teeth.

"He's the guy who sat at our table in the bar," Ben said.

"I'll let you have it now if you'll both just relax and step back," Joe said.

"It's okay," the cowboy said to Joe with a nod of his brim. "I've got this."

"Brady can break you in half," Ben said to the cowboy. The cowboy turned away from Joe and nodded his head as if he agreed with the statement.

"Maybe so," he said. "But I ain't moving."

Joe took a deep breath and walked over and stood shoulder to shoulder with the cowboy.

He heard Sheridan whisper, "Dad, don't get in a fight with them."

At the word *Dad*, the cowboy glanced over to Joe for a brief second before turning his attention back to the Youngberg brothers. His eyes settled on Joe's uniform shoulder patch and suddenly widened in reaction.

He *was* nervous; the expression on his face was a mix of alarm and fear.

Ben said to Brady, "You all right?"

"Getting there," Brady hissed.

"Brady's getting his breath back," Ben announced. "When he does, we're going to take you two apart."

They looked very capable of it, Joe thought. Both had removed their coats and their forearms looked like hams from the horse work they did every day.

A low growl came from the direction of the kitchen.

"Is everything under control in here?"

Joe looked up to see a human bulldog of a man in his early seventies filling the doorway. He recognized the owner of the Hotel Wolf from the photos he'd seen in the lobby of the building. The owner wore a bloody white apron and he gripped a meat cleaver in each hand. Apparently, he'd been cutting steaks in the kitchen.

"I think we're all right now," the cowboy said.

"Ben?" the owner asked as he waved a cleaver in the direction of the brothers. "Brady? I've warned you before that I'd eighty-six your sorry butts if you caused any more trouble in here."

"We're fine," Ben said, suddenly conciliatory. "We're completely cool."

"Brady?"

"Yeah, it's over," he grunted.

The owner nodded toward them, turned on his heel, and strode back into the kitchen to cut more beef.

"THIS IS LANCE RAMSEY," Sheridan said to Joe after the Youngbergs had left the building and gone down the street to the Rustic Bar. "He gave me a ride into town tonight."

Joe recognized the name from Williams's files. Ramsey had been interviewed because he'd been the prime liaison with Kate on the ranch. He was also the head wrangler and Sheridan's immediate supervisor.

Joe nodded and shook Ramsey's hand. "Thanks for standing up to them."

"My pleasure," Ramsey said with a shy grin. "I think they would've cleaned my clock without your help."

"They would have cleaned both of our clocks."

Ramsey blushed. He looked like a quiet, gentle, ramrod-straight caricature of what a shy but capable cowboy was supposed to look like. He could be Gary Cooper in his Helena, Montana, youth, Joe thought.

Joe looked to his daughter and she looked away.

"Nice to meet you, Lance," Joe said.

"Nice to meet you, Mr. Pickett," Ramsey said. "Sheridan talks a lot about you."

Which explained the look of alarm and fear he'd shown earlier, Joe thought.

Lance Ramsey was obviously more to Sheridan than her boss.

Marybeth, he thought, was right again.

10

"AS MUCH AS IT PAINS ME, I HAVE TO SAY I GOT A PRETTY GOOD FIRST impression of him," Joe told Marybeth on his cell phone, after saying good night to Sheridan and Lance Ramsey and going upstairs to his room to call her. "I wish you were here, because you're better at reading people than I am."

"I knew it," she said with triumph. "I knew she was seeing someone."

"And you were right. At least he's not a slacker or one of those hipster types."

"He's not a metrosexual?" she asked in a mocking tone.

"He's a cowboy," Joe said. "He looks like he walked in out of a movie. He really reacted when he met me—in a good way, I think."

"I can't believe you're sticking up for him already."

"Me either," Joe said. "He doesn't say much, but he was there for Sheridan."

He was always prepared to dislike any male who pursued any of his daughters. He'd been correct—in spades—when it came to April's choice of rodeo cowboy Dallas Cates. Joe wanted to dislike Lance Ramsey. He really did.

"You were there to protect her as well," she said. "I'm glad you didn't get into a bar fight on day one in a new place."

"Me too."

As they talked, Joe approached the window that overlooked Bridge Street and pushed the lace curtain aside. Sheridan and Lance Ramsey were on the sidewalk on the way to a white Silver Creek Ranch three-quarter-ton four-by-four pickup that was parked at an angle. Sheridan walked to the passenger door, but before she could get in, Ramsey jumped ahead of her and opened it for her. She slid in on the passenger seat. Then she turned and cupped Ramsey's neck with her hand for a moment and said something to him. Then she gave him a quick kiss on the mouth.

Ramsey blushed red in the glow of the dome light and stared at his boots for a moment afterward before gently closing the door and shuffling around the truck on the ice for the driver's side. Joe felt heat rush to his face as well.

Marybeth had been talking, but Joe hadn't heard a word. He wished he hadn't seen what he'd seen.

"Joe?" Marybeth said.

"Yup."

"Are you there? I asked you a question."

"I'm here. I just saw Sheridan give him a kiss in the street outside."

"Are you *spying* on them?" she asked, incredulous.

"Yup, and I wish I wasn't."

"She was probably thanking him for defending her in the bar. That's kind of a rare virtue these days."

"That's what fathers are for," Joe said as he watched the ranch pickup back out and turn onto the street. Before the dome light went out inside the cab, he saw a glimpse of his daughter's blond hair through the back window of the cab. She had her head turned and she was talking happily to Ramsey at the wheel.

When the light went off, the afterimage in Joe's mind was seven-year-old Sheridan sitting in the passenger seat of his Game and Fish truck during a ride-along sixteen years before. She of the ponytails and missing teeth.

"She's twenty-three," Marybeth said, reading his mind.

"So what was it you were asking me before?" he said.

"I asked how it was going so far."

"Complicated," he said.

TEN SECONDS AFTER HE SIGNED OFF with Marybeth, the phone lit up and burred. The screen read CASEY SCALES. Joe punched him up.

"Hey, I've got weird news for you," Scales said. "I went to my office to get the spare keys to the house over there—and I found out they're gone. I asked the receptionist about them and she said she sent the keys to Cheyenne about a week ago."

"To Cheyenne? You mean headquarters?"

"No. And that's where it gets even weirder. She said someone from the governor's office called, but she couldn't remember who it was."

"Why?" Joe asked.

"No idea."

“Someone from the governor’s office wanted the keys to a game warden house in Saratoga?”

“I know,” Scales said. “It doesn’t make any sense to me, either. Where are you staying while you’re there?”

“Got a room at the Wolf.”

“Ah, good place. If I was you, I’d stay there and send the bill to LGD.”

“Oh, I will. She can add it to my running tab. Still, I’d like to get in the house and see if I can figure anything out while I’m here,” Joe said.

“I’ll see what I can find out about those keys tomorrow and I’ll get back to you,” Scales said. Then: “Are you in *your* new house up in Saddlestring?”

“Not even close,” Joe said.

FOR THE NEXT HOUR, Joe lay on the bed with the reading lamp on and reviewed the Kate file again, hoping he would find something he’d previously overlooked. His eyes lingered on the names Ben and Brady Youngberg, and he circled them.

The brothers had been aggressive toward Sheridan in a public place. What, he wondered, would they be like if they encountered a lone blond British driver on the highway and thought they could grab her and get away with it?

HE STARTED TO GET READY for bed, when he realized he hadn’t signed off on his bar-and-food bill earlier. At the time, he’d been so flummoxed by the encounter with the Youngbergs and meeting Lance Ramsey he'd forgotten and walked out on his open ticket.

He closed the door to his room behind him and locked it, then took the staircase down to the first level and pushed though the batwing doors.

Kim Miller saw him and said, "Here for a nightcap?"

"Here to sign my tab."

"Don't worry about it," she said. "I'll keep it running until you check out. Besides, I know where to find you. Sure you don't need anything?"

"Maybe an ice water."

"Daredevil," she said, and winked.

While she filled a pint beer glass with ice, he noticed that the earlier crowd had largely dispersed and had been replaced with new faces. Four men wearing coveralls and with *Buckbrush Wind Energy Project* embroidered on the breasts of their coats sat side by side at the bar nursing draft beer.

Joe's gaze settled on a man and a woman at a table in the meeting area adjacent to the bar. While the room had been almost full during the confrontation with the Youngberg Brothers, the couple was alone in the empty room with their heads together, engaged in what looked like an intense conversation.

They were dressed almost entirely in black and they looked out of place in a town where denim jeans, sand-colored Carhartt canvas overalls, and puffy down jackets were the norm.

Miller handed Joe his ice water and noted where he was looking.

"*Ma'am,*" she mocked in a whispered British accent so the pronunciation sounded like *mom*, "*do you mind terribly if we smoke? And can I trouble you for a bar menu?*"

"Ah," Joe said, as much to himself as to Miller.

THE MAN AT THE TABLE looked to be in his early thirties and his skin was so pale it was nearly translucent. He had short spiked silver-flecked hair and a long pointed nose. He wore heavily scuffed black combat boots, tight black trousers, and a black peacoat over a black turtleneck. His long fingers were stained yellow from nicotine and he was scratching furiously on a steno pad while the woman spoke quickly in low tones. An expensive camera with a long lens was on the table, as well as a small digital recorder much like the device Joe carried in his own uniform breast pocket.

The woman had red hair the color of new rust and a round face with a full mouth and green eyes. A light peach-colored scarf was knotted loosely around her neck to break up the blackness. Her left elbow was on the table, but her right arm was held straight down at her side presumably to hide the cigarette in her hand from Miller behind the bar.

Both looked up and stopped talking as Joe approached. Neither looked enthusiastic at the prospect of an interruption, he noted.

Joe held out his hand and said, "Billy Bloodworth of the *Daily Dispatch* and Sophie Shelford-Longden. My name is Joe Pickett. I'm a game warden. Welcome to Wyoming."

Bloodworth and Shelford-Longden exchanged a long, confused look and Bloodworth said in a thick throaty accent that was nearly incomprehensible to Joe's ear, "Sorry, how do you know us?"

"I've read some of your . . . work," Joe said.

"You're shitting me," Bloodworth said, unable to keep the pride out of his voice.

"Nope."

"So you know about Kate," Sophie said. "We were starting to wonder if anyone around here knew about the story." She paused for a moment, then, "Or cared."

"They know and they care," Joe said. "It's not the sensation that it is in your country, but people around here would like to find out what happened to her."

She looked at Joe as if not sure to believe him.

"What does a gamekeeper do?" she asked.

"Game warden. Unlike England, our wildlife belong to the people of the state, not property owners. The state hires guys like me to enforce the laws and regulations and make sure there are plenty of healthy critters around. Most people in this state—and just about everyone in a town like Saratoga—have a freezer full of game meat for the winter."

"Barbaric," Bloodworth whispered to her.

She nodded to Joe and ignored Bloodworth. "Our hunting isn't like that."

"That's what I understand," he said.

"Our hunters are upper-class twits," she said with a curl of her lip. "They shoot birds raised on farms or they chase poor little foxes across the fields. They don't hunt to eat—they hunt for the sport of it. They're relics of the past, those so-called hunters."

Joe let it go. "Can I buy you two another drink?"

She nodded and Bloodworth said, "Finally, a man after my own heart."

Joe turned to see Miller was already on it.

"Do you mind if I sit down?" he asked. "It turns out we're here for the same reason: to try and find out what happened to your sister, Kate."

Bloodworth took a long breath and screwed up his face as if he were about to object, but Sophie nodded toward an empty chair. "We welcome any help we can get. It's bloody cold out there to be chasing around the countryside by ourselves."

Joe nodded and agreed.

"I thought I brought the right gear, but I could have used more heavy jumpers."

"Jumpers?"

"You call them *sweaters*," she corrected. Then: "What a horrible term."

He sat down as Kim Miller delivered a glass of white wine for Sophie, a pint of beer for Bloodworth, and another ice water for Joe.

When she was gone, Joe said, "Officials in Wyoming assigned me to this case along with my other duties. Right now, trying to fiqure out what happened to your sister, Kate, is my highest priority. From what I understand, you've been here in Saratoga for a while."

"Eight days," Sophie said. "Eight very long and jet-laggy days."

"Who are these officials?" Bloodworth asked with barely contained derision. "Are they the same people who didn't give Sophie and her family the time of day for months? Is one of them your Governor Allen, who acted like he didn't know anything about Kate when asked by the British ambassador?"

Joe ignored him just as Sophie had. Bloodworth, despite being a reporter, was not taking any notes. Joe turned his attention to

Sophie. "It seems to me there's no good reason for us to work at cross-purposes since we both want to find out the same thing."

"I find this area primitive but deceptively beautiful," she said as she took a sip. "We've seen elk, bald eagles, deer, antelopes, and mooses. And a *lot* of beef cattle. Today we took the wrong road to Silver Creek Ranch and we got stuck in the deep snow. Lucky for us, a local rancher happened by and pulled our car out with a chain he had with him. Otherwise we could have frozen to death out there."

"Fucking humiliating," Bloodworth grumbled into his beer.

Joe liked the way she said *antelopes*, *mooses*, and *RAHN-chers* in her British accent.

Sophie leaned forward and placed her hand on Joe's wrist. "The rancher looked at Billy and said, 'Who's the fop?'"

Bloodworth angrily looked away and Joe stifled a smile.

"'Who's the fop?'" she said again in a faux American accent.

"You're lucky I know how to drive," Bloodworth said to her. To Joe: "She doesn't have a driver's license."

"If I did, I wouldn't get us stuck in the snow, Billy."

He shook his head. "It's not like I've tooled around the countryside in a four-wheel-drive beast the size of my house before, Sophie."

"So," Joe said to them both, "I just got here this afternoon. Since you've been here a few days, have you come up with any ideas about what happened to your sister?"

She said, "We think we know who took her."

Joe sat back.

"Sophie," Bloodworth hissed. "We agreed to keep that on the QT until I broke the story. You agreed to that condition."

Sophie shrugged. "Billy wants a scoop because his tabloid sent him over here. I want to know what happened to my sister."

"We're a team, remember?" Bloodworth said. "We're fucking aliens in this world. We need to stick together like we talked about."

"We've actually got a snap of him," Sophie said as she rapidly scrolled though photographs on her phone. When she found the one she was looking for, she turned the screen toward Joe just as Bloodworth reached over and pulled her hand away.

"*Sophie*," he hissed.

But Joe had very briefly seen the blurry image of a man inside a home of some kind, the photo shot through a window from what looked like a great distance. The man stood in shadow in the background and seemed to be gesturing with his hands. In the foreground of the shot, near the bottom of the window itself, was someone's head. Long blond hair. She appeared to be seated with her back to the window as she watched the man inside. The shot was so out of focus that Joe couldn't see the man's face, only his lanky form.

"Let me see that again," Joe said.

"Absolutely not," Bloodworth said. He'd taken Sophie's phone from her and she looked away, half-embarrassed but completely resigned.

"Is that Kate?"

"We're sorting it," Bloodworth said.

"If you have evidence, you need to share it with law enforcement," Joe said.

Bloodworth looked suspiciously at Joe, then said to Sophie, "Something happened here to Kate. Right here, in this beautiful little valley. She didn't vanish on her own. Someone knows what happened to her and we think we know who it was. We're not ready to reveal our findings yet. We don't know who we can trust."

Joe said, "But if you've got proof that she's alive, wouldn't you want her rescued immediately?"

Sophie hesitated for a moment, and Bloodworth turned on Joe: "If these important officials are really trying to get to the bottom of this, why did they send a *gamekeeper*?"

"Game warden, Billy," Sophie said.

"Whatever," Bloodworth said. "The question still stands."

"And it's a good question," Joe said. He didn't want to get into the backstory, because there were too many things about his circumstance that seemed hinky and he knew they would sound that way if he tried to explain them.

"And why should we trust you?" Bloodworth asked. "Give us one good reason why."

"I'll tell you what," Joe said, pushing away from the table. "I'd rather earn your trust than beg you for it, so I'll leave the two of you alone. I need to get some sleep so I can get to work early tomorrow trying to figure out what happened to Kate. If I learn something, I'll let you know."

He stood and looked from Bloodworth to Sophie, then flipped his card down on the table. "But if you really do suspect somebody and that photo is real evidence, I hope you'll involve law enforcement right away. You may even want to call me."

His eyes settled on Bloodworth. "I hope this isn't all about a newspaper story, because people out here don't read the *Daily Dispatch*. Whoever you suspect probably has eight guns, because that's about average."

"Eight guns?" Sophie asked with alarm.

"Maybe more," Joe said.

"I've never even seen one except in movies," she said.

"Ignore him, Sophie," Bloodworth said. "He's trying to scare you."

. . .

JOE KNEW SOMETHING was wrong when he saw a band of light on the hallway floor emanating from the partially open door of room number nine. He knew he'd closed it tight and locked it when he left.

He instinctively reached for the Glock that wasn't there as he approached the door as quietly as he could. He paused to listen but could hear no stirring inside.

Then Joe shoved the door open and stepped back. Nothing.

The room had been tossed. Clothing was scattered across the floor and his duffel bag yawned open from on top of the bed. The chiffo-robe doors were open and his uniform shirts and civilian Cinch shirts were bunched on the floor where they'd been flung.

He sighed in relief that his weapon had not been taken from where he'd placed it on the nightstand. But it had been moved to the other side.

The Kate file was gone.

HIS BOOTS MADE A SOUND like thunder on the stairs and Kim Miller looked over at him from behind the check-in counter with her eyebrows arched in curiosity.

"Someone's been in my room," he said. "Did you give the keys to anyone when I was talking to the British couple just now?"

"Of course not," she said with heat. "We don't do things like that." She was offended.

He noted that from where he stood he could reach over the counter and access the board where spare keys hung. Anybody could have done the same.

"I'm sorry," he said. "Did you see anyone suspicious a few minutes ago?"

She shook her head. "I was washing glasses and keeping my eye on Sophie trying to hide her cigarette from me," Miller said. "I wasn't looking over this direction, because I didn't expect any guests this late."

Joe checked out the bar. Sophie and Bloodworth were gone. The four Buckbrush Project workers were still on their stools drinking beer.

"I know I locked the door," he said to Miller in frustration.

"No one locks their doors around here," she said with a shrug. "Maybe that was the problem."

FIFTEEN MINUTES LATER, after Joe had reorganized his clothing and gear and verified that the only thing missing from his room was the Kate file, he brushed his teeth, undressed, double-locked the door, and lay on his bed staring at the still ceiling fan. He doubted sleep would come quickly.

It would have been easy, he thought, for someone to snatch the spare key from the board downstairs, mount the stairs and enter his room, toss it, and depart down the stairs and straight outside while Joe was engaged in conversation with Sophie and Bloodworth.

Whoever had taken the file had been efficient and determined. They somehow knew who he was, why he was there, which room he was in, and what they were after. Random burglars would have left with his weapons and gear, after all. Those items had resale value. It was disconcerting.

He thought about all the people he'd seen in the bar that night, all the strange and unfamiliar faces, except for Sheridan. Word was already out, apparently, why there was a new game warden in town.

Someone who knew something about Kate's disappearance had been down there in the scrum and overheard his talk with Sheridan. Whoever it was was familiar with the Wolf, knew about the board with the spare keys, and knew Joe wasn't in his room for the fifteen or twenty minutes he'd been gone.

Kim Miller, the quarterback of the Hotel Wolf bar, seemed to be the most obvious suspect. His head told him yes, but his gut told him no. She'd seemed surprised and embarrassed that someone had entered his room, and he thought her reaction was genuine. She likely knew the secrets and agendas of her customers—including him—and no doubt she'd put two and two together when she saw him huddling in the back room with Sophie and Bloodworth. But she'd been behind the bar the entire time and within Joe's sight. Someone—probably not Miller—had been worried about what Joe was working on and curious how much he knew.

Either that, he thought, or something else was going on in the valley that he didn't yet grasp. Maybe the person who'd broken in wasn't involved in Kate's disappearance at all, but was involved in something else. Maybe the presence of a new game warden—for whatever reason—was a threat to them. Whoever it had been was now in possession of everything Joe knew about the case, including his notes.

If Billy Bloodworth had excused himself to use the restroom earlier, Joe would know where to look for his file. But Bloodworth was so worried that Sophie would divulge his scoop that he hadn't dared move an inch from the table during their introduction to each other.

Was the blurry photo he'd see on Sophie's phone legitimate? Could that blond head actually belong to a still-alive Kate? He wished he could have studied it. No doubt Bloodworth had other shots in his camera that might be more clear.

Then there were the missing keys to Pollock's game warden house. Keys that were requested by someone in the governor's office, according to Casey Scales.

And the question Bloodworth had asked that Joe couldn't answer with confidence: *If these important officials are really trying to get to the bottom of this, why did they send a gamekeeper?*

Joe dreaded the conversation he'd have to have at some point updating Connor Hanlon or Governor Allen on the progress of his investigation thus far. Explaining that the case file had been pilfered before his investigation really began would be . . . painful.

That's when he heard footfalls outside in the hall.

He turned his head when the footfalls stopped outside his door. There were four shadows of boots, meaning two people.

Then a sharp knock.

His first thought was that two men had trashed his room and stolen the file and they'd come back. The security lock prevented them from entering this time.

He reached across his body and grasped the handgrip of his weapon and pulled it free from the holster. There was no need to rack the receiver because there was a round in the chamber of his .40 Glock, and of course no safety to thumb off.

Joe rose and padded to the door and squinted into the peephole. He held his weapon muzzle-down alongside his thigh.

When he saw who it was, he grunted, unlocked the door, opened it, and stepped aside.

Nate Romanowski chuckled as he came inside, followed by a thin man with gaunt eyes whom Joe thought looked familiar from somewhere. They both carried daypacks.

Nate was tall and broad-shouldered with a blond ponytail and blue eyes the color of lake ice. There was a sense of calmness about him that was disarming. He flicked his eyes around the room like a raptor.

"What were you going to do with that gun of yours?" Nate said. "I know you can't hit the broad side of a warehouse with it."

Before Joe could respond, Nate said, "The hotels in this town are already closed for the night, so we figured we'd bunk with you."

"Nate . . ."

Nate gently pried the weapon out of Joe's hand and tossed it on the bed. Then he grasped Joe's hand inside both of his. As he did, Nate's heavy canvas Yarak, Inc. coat gaped open and Joe noted the grip of his friend's heavy .454 Casull in a shoulder holster inside.

"It's been a while, my friend," Nate said. "It's good to see you even in your underwear."

"Nate . . ."

"This is Jeff Wasson," Nate said, gesturing toward the gaunt man. "He's a master falconer from Riverton and I've known him for years, so you can trust him. He's the guy I told you about."

"Nate, why are you here?" Joe asked. The room seemed suddenly very crowded. Wasson didn't make eye contact with Joe and he seemed to find the walls and fan very interesting.

"We've got a problem and I told Jeff you were the man who could fix it," Nate said. "I don't need to remind you that you owe me a couple of favors."

"I do, but I've got problems of my own."

Nate snorted. "You always do."

Joe said, "Maybe we can help each other."

11

AS JOE AND NATE CAUGHT UP, CAROL SCHMIDT WAS WRINGING OUT her mop in aisle seven of Valley Foods and she thought she heard someone else inside the grocery store. That was odd because the store closed at ten and it was nearly eleven-thirty.

Schmidt often traded with other employees for the last shift of the night when they'd been assigned to it. She didn't like that last shift any more than they did, of course, but she figured most of the others were young with families at home and all she had to worry about these days was Bridger, her dog. She'd fed him and let him out before she left Encampment to drive the eighteen miles north to Saratoga to start her shift. He'd be fine. All he did was sleep, anyway.

After the store closed and the lights above the doors were turned off, she dimmed the lights inside and locked up. It was the responsibility of the last employee to clean the place up before they left. In the winter it was an especially onerous responsibility, because every customer who came in tracked snow and mud on the floors. It was an easier job in the summer when all she had to do was sweep.

Because it took so long to mop the aisles, she tried to get a jump on it by starting early, like she had tonight. The only customers in the last hour the store was open on Friday night were single men buying frozen pizzas to take home or teenagers reeking of weed loading up on pastries and candy. She'd pause her cleaning, check them out, and go back to it when they left. The good thing about the teenagers was there was no need to bag up multiple sacks of groceries and take them out to waiting cars in the freezing night. The bad thing about them was they were obviously high on drugs. It bothered her that she recognized a couple of basketball and football players from her attendance at high school games.

She'd considered dialing 911 and reporting them, but she knew from recent experience that the dispatcher refused to take her complaints seriously. Carol Schmidt was getting sick and tired of not being taken seriously.

Seven aisles were clean. Only one more to go in the meat department.

Then she heard the scuffle of feet in heavy boots two or three aisles away.

VALLEY LIQUOR STAYED OPEN until midnight and it was directly adjacent to the grocery store. It was possible, she thought, that the liquor store manager had simply neglected to close and lock the steel accordion door between the two at ten o'clock when he was supposed to do it. He might have forgotten, and perhaps a liquor customer had wandered down the steps into the grocery.

If so, she'd need to find whoever it was inside and shoo him out. And, in all likelihood, mop up wet boot prints after he left.

"Hello," she called. "Whoever is in here—the store closed at ten."

Probably more teenagers, she thought.

She shoved her mop into the bucket and walked to the front of the store near the registers. There was a lone pickup in the lot. It was parked about twenty feet from her ancient Toyota 4Runner. She could tell the pickup had been left running because she could see exhaust rising from the tailpipe.

In the ambient light from inside, she could barely make out the front license plate.

It ended with *six-zero-zero*. Schmidt gasped and raised her tiny closed fist to her mouth.

She took a long breath and summoned her courage before calling out, "This is the night manager and you shouldn't be in the grocery store after hours. You need to come up to the front and I'll let you out."

Technically, Schmidt *wasn't* the night manager. But she thought using the title might give a more authoritative impression.

"On my way." The grating male voice came from halfway down aisle two. She recognized it immediately from the night the dog was run over on the road next to her house. It was the same voice that had said, *Forget it. Leave the goddamn dog. It shouldn't be out running around anyway.*

She quickly took her place behind the counter at the middle checkout stand where she'd worked earlier in the evening. She felt safer there than if she sought out the man in the aisle.

He came from aisle two, around the endcap, with an armful of items. He was big with white hair, a square jaw, thick lips, and pale blue eyes. She was surprised that his face was familiar to her, but it wasn't from that night she'd encountered him. She recognized his face from a photo in the *Saratoga Sun* newspaper.

He walked up to her register and opened his arms and the items he'd gathered up spilled onto the counter. Bags of pork rinds, individual energy drinks, jerky, a package of extra-large rubber gloves.

"We're closed," she said, thinking about the .38 in her purse that was tucked away in a cubby near her feet. There was also an alarm button under the counter near the cash register, but she'd heard from another checker that the day manager had turned it off because it was too easy to accidentally lean into.

"Yeah," the man said. "I didn't know you were closed. I'll just pay for these few little things and be on my way."

His eyes stayed on her face while he spoke in a way that made the hairs on the back of her neck prick up.

"Do you know who I am?" he asked.

She squared her shoulders and said, "Everybody does." She said it even though she couldn't think of his name or who he was with, just that he'd been in the *Sun*. God, she resented not being able to instantly recall things anymore.

He chuckled.

She said, "I also know you're the man who ran over that dog in Encampment. I saw you do it that night. What kind of person runs over a dog and just leaves it there to suffer?"

He arched his eyebrows and tilted his head a little to the side, as if he was amused by her. Although she was frightened by him, the hot resentment of not being taken seriously took over.

"I told the neighbor who owned the dog," she said. "Then I called the cops on you."

"I'm aware of that, Mrs. Schmidt. I wish you hadn't done that."

"I'll do it again if I have to." She thought, *Especially if you have something to do with the smell that's been coming out of the mill burner.*

And it suddenly all came back to her: the incident she hadn't been able to recall earlier. She looked down so he couldn't read her face.

"Do we have a problem, Mrs. Schmidt?"

His words chilled her to her soul, but she didn't dare look up at him.

He was big and he looked fit. There was no way she could run away from him. If she bent down to dig out her purse, he could reach over the counter and pick her up like a twig and snap her in half.

"The groceries, I mean," he said. "We have a problem that I've picked them out and you haven't rung them up."

Then he grinned.

She realized she was trembling. She gestured to the items. "You can get all those things down at the Kum-N-Go. You don't need to buy them here. Except for the rubber gloves. I don't know if the Kum-N-Go has them."

"No, I'd rather pay for them now and be on my way."

She shook her head quickly. "The register's turned off. I don't have a key to open it up after hours."

"So now you want to lie to me?" he asked, arching his eyebrows again. "Why would you do that, Mrs. Schmidt?"

"Because I want you to go away. It's after hours and you're not supposed to be here."

"But I am."

"I guess I'm scared of you," she said.

He reached out and grasped her hand with both of his. When she tried to pull back, he tightened his grip. His hands were rough and enormous.

"You don't need to be scared of me, Mrs. Schmidt," he said in a near whisper. "You just need to learn to mind your own business. You need to just enjoy your little home there across from the mill and you need to not be so quick to grab the phone and call 911 anytime you feel like it. You need to be a little more trusting and not always assume the worst about people—even if they're newcomers to the valley. Do you understand what I'm telling you, Mrs. Schmidt?"

She nodded, barely. She could no longer meet his eyes.

"Was that a yes?" he asked. His voice was gentle.

"Yes."

"Then I guess we're done here," he said. "So can you ring me up or do you want me to put these things back on the shelves?"

"Just take them," she said.

"That wouldn't be right, would it?"

"Just take them and get out."

He stood there, hulking above her. He still had her hand.

"I'm not going to let you talk me into stealing, Mrs. Schmidt. Then you really would have something to tell the police, wouldn't you?

"Tell you what," he said, finally letting go. He reached behind him for his wallet and withdrew a fifty-dollar bill from it and placed it on the counter. "You take the cost of the groceries out of that and keep the rest. That way we're square."

"I can't do that," she said.

"Sure you can," he said, gathering up the items. "Now, I'd appreciate it if you'd please unlock the door so I can get out of your store. I can tell you're quite rattled and I'm sorry I'm responsible for that."

She could barely feel her legs as she walked from behind the counter to the double doors. He was right behind her. She expected a blow to the head any second. The key rattled around outside the lock until she finally got it in and turned the bolt.

A gust of freezing air washed over her as the door opened.

"You have a pleasant night, Mrs. Schmidt," the man said as he passed by her. "Remember: mind your own business and everything will be fine."

She watched his wide back as he walked toward the pickup. There was no one else in the cab.

Before he opened the door and the dome light came on, he turned and looked at her and gestured for her to turn around. She did.

As she locked the door from the inside, she glanced up to see the truck back up and turn for the highway.

Schmidt didn't have a cell phone. She had to go all the way to the rear of the store to the manager's office to call 911 and report what had just happened.

SHE WAS STILL SHAKING and she was angry with herself as she drove toward Encampment on the dark highway. She was extra-cautious, as always, because there was ice on the road and the eighteen-mile distance was famous for deer, antelope, and elk at night.

The dispatcher had been alarmed at first when Schmidt told her someone had been in the store after hours and refused to leave. But with every question the dispatcher asked, Schmidt's confused answers made the situation sound more and more benign.

"Did he actually threaten you?" the dispatcher asked. "Or did he say the two of you had a problem because he wanted to buy some items and you didn't want to turn the register on?"

"Both," she'd explained. "But it sounded like a threat. It *felt* like a threat."

"Did he grab you physically or just reach out and hold your hand?" the dispatcher had asked.

"When he was standing there in front of me, I remembered that smell, all right. The same smell as my daddy's field that time."

The dispatcher said, "What smell?"

"From the mill burner."

"Now I'm really confused," the dispatcher said. "I thought this was about someone in the grocery store after hours."

Her words came rushing out. "My daddy was a cattle rancher over by Yoder and I grew up on the ranch. When I was little—maybe ten or eleven—he discovered a dead body out in the irrigation ditch.

"You see, there used to be a lot of hobos around in those days. We didn't call them homeless like we do today. They were just hobos who would show up at the front door and work a day or two on a ranch and then go on their way. My daddy recognized that dead hobo as one who had worked on our place the week before. Daddy figured that hobo had taken the money we paid him and bought cheap alcohol and stumbled into the irrigation ditch.

"Daddy didn't trust the local sheriff and he didn't want any of us involved in finding a dead body on our place. Especially because it would raise suspicion and questions, I guess. So Daddy pulled that body out of the ditch and built a big pile of branches and boards. Then he put that hobo on top and lit it up.

"I'll never forget the smell of that burning hobo, but it didn't come back to me until he was standing there in front of me. It was the same smell that came from the mill burner that night."

"That's quite a story, Mrs. Schmidt," the dispatcher said.

By then, Schmidt knew she'd lost the conversation. That everything she said made her sound more batty and disoriented.

"Come in tomorrow and talk to one of the officers," the dispatcher counseled. "Maybe after some rest you'll be able to make a little more sense."

WHEN HER REAR WINDOW suddenly filled with headlights, Schmidt naturally eased over to the side of the highway so the speeding vehicle could pass her. She clicked her tongue at whoever would drive so fast and so recklessly on a snow-packed roadway with deer and antelope lurking just off the shoulder in the dark brush.

When she glanced up, there was a pair of headlights so close to her Toyota she could actually see the bulbs and the license plate.

Six-zero-zero.

The impact was bone-jarring.

12

"SO YOU CAME ALL THE WAY DOWN HERE TO ASK ABOUT . . . FALCONRY permits?" Joe asked Nate and Jeff Wasson with suspicion at breakfast at the Saratoga Hot Springs Resort. He looked at Nate. "Why didn't you just call me?"

"There's not a lot going on in the nuisance bird abatement business in January," Nate said. "Besides, I have other business here."

Joe waited for more that didn't come. Nate was like that. Joe had long given up trying to penetrate his cryptic pronouncements.

Wasson said, "Nate told me you'd want to hear my story. When he said he was driving down here, I figured I'd come along for the ride and meet you in person."

Joe shot Nate a disapproving glance, and Nate smiled back with mischief.

Serious master falconers were a different breed, Joe knew. They ate, drank, and slept falconry. Their lives were shaped around it and their outlook on life came from a severe perspective in which the practice of falconry was tantamount to everything else. When they had problems or disagreements, falconers often had a tough time believing that their concerns wouldn't be shared by those outside their world if just given enough explanation. Falconers were passionate, willful, and obstinate.

"I've got a lot on my plate right now," Joe said to Wasson.

"Nate said you always do, but I was hoping you'd give me a few minutes. This is important."

They were in a high-backed booth in a space just off the darkened bar-and-lounge area, where the barstools were metal saddles with pointing six-guns for armrests. The sprawling complex on the bank of the North Platte River featured private hot springs and had been known as the Saratoga Inn for so many years that locals still referred to it as "the Inn." They were the only guests in the restaurant and even a crackling fire in the fireplace couldn't warm it up yet.

Joe had slept in his bed, and Nate and Wasson had unrolled sleeping bags on the floor of his room. Joe recalled that he hadn't been in a similar situation since college when friends and acquaintances had crashed in his dorm room for the night. This was nothing unusual for Nate, who sometimes slept in the crook of a tree or in a cliff-side cave while waiting for raptors to return to their nests. But Joe thought, *I'm getting too old for this.* Wasson snored, and Joe didn't get much sleep because of his guests as well as the incidents the night before. While he hoped that he could make more sense of the situation in the morning, he found that his head was fogged up.

A waitress wearing a down vest and fleece-lined boots approached the table and asked for their order. As they studied the menu, she said, "Did you hear about that accident on the highway last night?"

"What accident?" Joe asked.

"A dear old lady who works at the grocery store slid off the road into a deep ditch. They found her this morning and from what I hear she's probably not going to make it. Can you imagine being trapped in a wrecked car all night with it this cold outside? It's really awful."

"I'm sorry to hear that," Joe said.

"Mrs. Schmidt," the waitress said, shaking her head. "I'm in the garden club with her. She was, I mean *is*, such a sweetheart.

"Let's hope she makes it," the waitress said.

WASSON WAITED IMPATIENTLY for the waitress to take their order to the kitchen and then he leaned across the table toward Joe, his eyes lit up from the inside.

After explaining that both he and his wife were former schoolteachers who'd recently been laid off due to budget cuts in Riverton, he began: "I'm one of a handful of falconers in the country who is licensed to possess and hunt with a golden eagle. My wife and I both have federal permits we obtained years ago through the Wyoming Game and Fish Department. We used our eagles to hunt jackrabbits, showshoe hare, and pheasants, but we knew our birds were capable of much, much more. It was like taking an F-16 fighter jet out to hunt deer, you know?"

Joe knew. Male golden eagles weighed up to ten pounds and had wingspans exceeding eight feet. The gripping strength in their talons could bring a strong man to his knees.

Wasson said, "Do you know that falconers in Mongolia use eagles to hunt fox, wolves, and deer? It's amazing. It's like the kind of falconry you're used to but blown up to a whole different level. You can find clips of it on YouTube."

Joe nodded. His longtime friendship with Nate had taught him plenty about the lethal capabilities of falcons and hawks. He was aware that falconry was the sport of kings in the Middle East and that American and British falconers had adapted the practice to better suit the more egalitarian cultures of the Western world.

"Mongolian falconers sometimes use two birds in tandem to take down large prey," Wasson said. "So we know it's possible. But as far as I can tell—and believe me I've talked to every falconer in the country with an eagle permit—it's never been done over here. But even though I have the license and I've studied falconry with eagles for thirty years, I can't get permission to try it here."

"You're getting ahead of yourself," Nate said to Wasson. "He won't understand what you're asking unless you go back to the beginning."

"The beginning?" Joe said with caution. He figured he only had enough time for them to have breakfast together before he resumed his investigation into Kate's disappearance.

Wasson said, "You probably know about the Bald and Golden Eagle Protection Act that was passed in the 1940s to save both birds. It was a, quote"—Wasson made quote marks with his fingers in the air—"*good thing*, but like all good things there were unintended consequences when politicians and bureaucrats with no wildlife experience decide to play God. Think about when the feds introduced Canadian gray wolves into Yellowstone where Canadians had never been before. Or . . ."

"Stay on topic," Nate commanded.

Wasson blinked from the rebuke, but didn't take offense. Joe assumed Nate often had to ask Wasson to get to the point. Falconers did tend to go on.

"Anyway," Wasson said, "the eagle population increased at the same time herds of sheep were growing across the state. That's when the prices of wool and meat were high—before the Australians entered the picture. Eagles figured out that lambs were really good to eat. Lambs are easy prey. They have lots of meat, and ewes don't try very hard to defend them. Sheep ranchers all over the West were getting hammered by eagles, and a few bad ranchers tried to fight back by poisoning eagles, hunting them from the air, and cutting off their legs and letting them fly away."

Joe nodded. He'd heard the stories.

"In 1972, the Act was amended. The fines for unlawfully killing an eagle were increased significantly and the law specified that ranchers could lose their federal grazing leases if they got caught killing an eagle. At the same time, the Act was fixed to allow falconers to obtain eagles associated with depredation of livestock or other wildlife. Eagles are great creatures, but they're eagles. In addition to killing lambs, they also like to kill bighorn sheep lambs. Oh, and golden eagles are the number one aerial predator of adult sage grouse."

The mention of sage grouse made Joe sit up. Sage grouse were radioactive when it came to state politics and policy. The survival of the chicken-sized bird was a massive topic of controversy in Wyoming and other Western states and it affected energy exploration and land use regulations in general. He'd been involved with a case in which someone had slaughtered an entire population—called a lek—and the incident's far-reaching consequences had swept in multiple federal agencies and nearly shut down the energy economy in northern Wyoming.

"Now I've got your attention," Wasson said with triumph. Nate looked on with an amused expression. Joe ignored his friend.

Their breakfasts arrived. Three orders of biscuits and gravy with bacon on the side. Joe dug into his, while Wasson ignored his plate and continued on.

"After the falconry amendment was added to the Act, it took a typically long time—about twenty years—for the feds to finally write the regulations for it. Finally, *finally*, falconers like me who'd obtained a license could hunt with an eagle. We're not talking about hundreds of birds, either. We're talking about just a few one-to-three-year-old eagles. It was an absolute win-win-win for all concerned," Wasson said. "If woolgrowers were getting their lambs slaughtered, they could call the U.S. Department of Agriculture Wildlife Services agency and the state would allow falconers like me to go to the ranch and trap the birds for hunting. That saved lambs. It also saved countless sage grouse and other wildlife. And it allowed me and other master falconers to advance the art of falconry with eagles.

"That lasted until 2009," Wasson said. "That's when the last administration suspended the program without any notice. We could no longer trap and fly eagles. So unless you had a pre-2009 eagle in your mews, you were shit out of luck."

Joe was puzzled. "Why did they do that?"

Wasson slammed the table with both open hands and did it hard enough that the silverware danced. "Someone needs to find out," he shouted. "Someone needs to rattle the cages of those federal bureaucrats to start up the program again. If you've noticed, ranchers are raising sheep again and lambs are getting killed again. And who knows how many of the state's precious sage grouse are getting slaughtered?"

Before Joe could respond, Wasson gestured to Nate. "We all look up to this guy, as you know. Some of us falconers have been involved with some kind of shady stuff in the past, like growing premium weed or selling trapped peregrines to Arab interests and things like that . . ."

Joe narrowed his eyes and Wasson backed away from the topic so quickly it was if his hands were singed. Joe figured Wasson must have been warned by Nate that he was a by-the-book law enforcement officer who wouldn't hesitate to arrest Wasson. And it was true.

Wasson said, "I could have gone back to that after the school district let me go. But I saw how Nate went legit. He left his old life behind and he's raking in money hand over fist with Yarak, Inc., helping out farmers and ranchers with problem birds—many of them invasive species. In a lot of cases, all he has to do is deploy his Air Force and the problem birds see what they're up against and just go away."

Nate referred to his growing arsenal of red-tail hawks, prairie falcons, peregrine falcons, and gyrfalcons as his "Air Force," Joe knew.

"So I contacted half a dozen sheep ranchers a while back," Wasson said. "They told me coyotes had replaced eagles as the number one killer of their lambs. Coyotes are exploding in numbers, as you know. My idea is to hunt two eagles at a time to take out coyotes on the ground, the same way the Mongolians use two eagles to kill wolves. These ranchers will hire me directly to trap eagles that are killing their lambs and use them to kill coyotes that are doing the same thing. Another win-win-win. But it's January and spring is a few months away. I can't get anyone in D.C. on the phone to help me get permission to trap an eagle or two. And I'm not the only one.

"No licensed falconer has been allowed to trap an eagle to fly since 2009," Wasson said again. "It's not against the law. It's not wrong. It helps ranchers and saves sage grouse. Coyotes are predators and they breed like rabbits. The eagles aren't harmed. *But I can't get permission to hunt with an eagle.*"

"Which is where you come in," Nate said to Joe. "You can do the right thing and get involved."

Joe shrugged. "I don't have any connection with the feds in D.C. who could issue the permits. That's above my pay grade."

"*Which is where you come in*," Nate said again, this time emphasizing every word.

Then Joe got it. "You want me to talk to Governor Allen."

"Bingo," Nate said.

Joe sat back. "I'm not sure I have any influence with him."

Nate said, "You know him. You work for him. He's the reason you're down here."

"To be honest, I'm not sure why I'm here," Joe confessed. "It doesn't feel right."

"But if you manage to do whatever it is he's asked you to do, won't he owe you a favor?" Nate asked.

"Nate, he's the *governor*."

"He's a politician," Nate said. "And I think he's a certain kind of politician. The kind who operates in the world of favors."

"Maybe," Joe said. "But that's not the kind of thing I want to get involved in. I don't do political."

Nate smirked and Joe felt his face get hot. He hated the idea of feeling compromised, but he wasn't sure he could make a cogent argument to the contrary.

Nate said, "I took a job this fall around Big Piney and I learned a few things about our governor. I think that if you pull this assignment off, he'll owe you in spades."

"I don't understand."

"Look," Nate said. "I have nothing to do right now. Liv is back in Louisiana visiting relatives for the month. Yarak, Inc. is dormant until spring. I can help you out with your assignment and maybe the governor will owe you one."

Wasson kept nodding his head and looking between Nate and Joe. It was obviously going the way he wanted it to go.

Joe thought about it. "I've got a lot of ground to cover in a short time. Not to mention that someone stole the case file from my room last night and whoever it was knows why I'm here."

"Nowhere to go but up," Nate offered. "Give me the names of the people you want me to talk to. As you know, I can be persuasive when it comes to getting information."

Joe snorted. "None of that, Nate. This needs to be a clean investigation. We can't have broken bones and ears ripped off."

"I'll keep my head down and I'll behave," Nate said. "I don't want to get crosswise with the new governor or the feds again."

"The governor's chief of staff doesn't want you involved in this," Joe said.

"He's an ass." Nate grinned. And Joe realized he'd all but accepted his assistance.

He was grateful for the help.

"This is your cue to leave," Nate said to Wasson. "Eat your breakfast and then go back to Riverton. I'll let you know how things work out."

Wasson looked from Nate to Joe and back again. Joe didn't encourage him to stay either.

"I guess I gave it my best shot," Wasson said. To Joe: "Thanks for listening to me."

"I haven't done anything yet," Joe reminded him.

. . .

WHEN WASSON WAS GONE, Joe looked long and hard at his friend across the table.

"What?" Nate asked.

"I know you. There's something going on besides getting Wasson and his friends eagle licenses."

Nate didn't react. "Wasson is a master falconer. There aren't many of us and we're brothers."

There was no tell on his face, but Joe still suspected there was more than eagles on Nate's mind. His mentions of "other business" as well as information he was holding close about the governor seemed to indicate he had a private agenda, Joe thought.

"Look, I know how much you enjoy conspiracy theories," Nate said.

"I don't."

"So I'm not going to burden you with another one right now. Not until I know more."

"I appreciate that."

"But you have to admit I've been more right than wrong over the years."

Joe started to object, but caught himself. Nate took to conspiracy theories in a natural way, like he'd taken to falconry. Nate had a unique, unvarnished way of looking at the world without preconceptions or faith in institutions—especially government institutions. Most times, Joe didn't automatically ascribe evil intentions to men and women with power and authority. Nate was just the opposite. He'd told Joe more than once that Joe was the only person in law enforcement that he trusted.

"But you'll let me know if you come up with something legitimate?" Joe asked.

"I will."

JOE BRIEFED NATE on the Kate Shelford-Longden disappearance and tried to recall as many of the names and details as he could without the case file. As he talked, Joe scribbled down bullet points and specific suspect names on the back of a Saratoga Hot Springs Resort napkin.

Next to each name he assigned which of them would be responsible for making contact.

"I'll take Steve Pollock," Joe said. "There's something really hinky about him leaving the agency with no notice. I'm just waiting for a set of keys right now so I can get into his house."

"Who needs keys?" Nate asked.

"I do," Joe said with a sigh. "I'll also take Mark Gordon. He's the GM of the Silver Creek Ranch. I don't consider him a suspect and neither did the DCI agent, but he's a good place to start. I'll quiz Sheridan and head wrangler Lance Ramsey about what they recall about Kate and who she hung out with during her stay."

Nate raised his eyebrows. "Sheridan is here?"

Joe explained the situation. Sheridan had once been Nate's apprentice in falconry and the two of them had a special relationship. The apprenticeship had been postponed for years while Sheridan attended college and Nate was on the payroll of Wolfgang Templeton as well as in and out of federal custody.

"I want to catch up with her," Nate said.

"I'm sure you'll have that opportunity."

"And she's got a thing going with this Lance guy?"

"How did you know?" Joe asked suspiciously.

"By the way you said his name. *Head wrangler Lance Ramsey.* Like he's in *your* head a little."

"Maybe he is."

Nate smirked. "Is he a suspect?"

"I've got no reason to put him on that list."

"Maybe to get him to stop seeing Sheridan?" Nate suggested.

He shook his head. "He seems like a good guy."

Joe said he'd follow up with farriers Ben and Brady Youngberg since they'd tangled the night before, and he gave the names of the fish hatchery owners Jack and Joshua Teubner to Nate to check out. He explained DCI agent Michael Williams's theory that it was more likely a ranch contractor who took Kate than an employee.

He wrote down the name *Richard* on the napkin, and next to it the initials *MBP*.

"Richard Cheetham is Kate's ex-husband," Joe said. "She kept her maiden name. We always have to look at the ex. And because he's in England, I'll ask Marybeth to get online and check him out."

"Smart," Nate said.

"I'll take Jeb Pryor, the Encampment lumber mill owner," Joe said. "I might be wrong, but I got a vibe off him last night that he knows something he wants to tell me."

Then Joe described what he knew about Sophie and Billy Bloodworth.

"My guess is you'll run into them without even trying," Joe said. "They stand out. Like I said, I've talked with them and Sophie flashed a blurry photo on her phone that indicated they think they've determined a suspect. No names, though, and Bloodworth is protective of the information. I couldn't get any more out of them and they wouldn't let me look closely at the photo."

"Bloodworth is the fop, right?"

Joe grinned. "Yup, he's the fop. I was thinking that if you had a chance to have a conversation with them and they didn't know you were connected to me or the investigation . . ."

"They might tell me something," Nate said, finishing Joe's sentence. "Maybe I can get ahold of that photo."

"Sophie might find you interesting," Joe said. "If you could get her away from Bloodworth, that is. She's single and a little playful."

Nate arched his eyebrows again. Joe didn't say more because he didn't need to. Nate's effect on some women was well-known to them both. Marybeth had said as much and Joe tried not to think too much about that.

"I'm serious about not busting any heads," Joe said.

"I agreed."

"So you have to promise me that if the situation gets dangerous, you'll back off and call me. I know how you are. Can you do that?"

Nate grinned in a way that made Joe uncomfortable.

"Nate?"

"Okay, okay. But I might have to use my judgment at some point."

As he said it, Nate opened the left side of his jacket so once again Joe could see the butt of his .454 Casull revolver in a shoulder holster. The five-shot weapon made by Freedom Arms was one of the most powerful handguns in the world and Nate was deadly with it. Wyoming had few restrictions when it came to the open or concealed carrying of firearms in public, so Nate wasn't breaking any laws.

"Keep it in the holster," Joe said.

"It never comes out unless I need to use it."

"You know what I mean."

"Yeah."

"You've got your phone, right?" Joe asked.

Nate patted his breast pocket with annoyance. He'd once eschewed the use of cell phones, but with Yarak, Inc., and Liv in Louisiana, he was now married to it.

"Does it still read 'Dudley Do-Right' on the screen when I call you?" Joe asked. Not only that, but a cartoon image of the big-chinned Canadian Mountie also appeared.

"It does."

"You wouldn't want to change that, would you?"

"No. It fits."

Joe sighed and turned back to his napkin. For the first time since he'd spoken to Governor Allen about Kate's disappearance, he felt that he had a solid plan of action, with or without the case file.

Nate had helped give him that confidence.

"Thank you," he said.

Nate shrugged. "It's good to be doing something. Maybe we'll even find out what happened."

Joe laughed.

"One thing, though," Nate said as they got up from the booth. "Why you? Why would Allen send you down here when he has hundreds of government lackeys working for him?"

Joe shoved his hands in his front pockets as he walked toward the lobby. "Trying to figure that out myself," he said.

"Ah," said Nate. He said it in a way that indicated Joe had just confirmed something Nate had been thinking.

13

ACROSS TOWN AND ACROSS THE RIVER, TED PANOS CLIMBED OUT OF his four-wheel drive in the parking lot of the JW Hugus & Co. restaurant. He'd parked next to a late-model pickup with a camper shell.

Steam rolled from the open ovals on the otherwise frozen river, which made the ducks and geese on the open water look like carnival booth silhouettes. The openings were created by thermal springs within the river, he'd been told.

His boot soles squeaked on the icy surface and he thrust his hands into his coat pockets and cursed. It was so cold it took you by surprise, he thought. The sky was cloudless and the morning sun lit the buildings and dormant river trees with such vibrant light that it made his brain think it was warm out—but it wasn't. The cold pinched your skin between icy fingers and gave it a sharp twist. He'd never get used to it and he was starting to wonder if spring would ever come.

The thick file was clamped under his right arm so he pushed through the door with his left hand. The door was made of steel and it bit his bare hand.

Inside, he stood still on the mat for a moment because his eyeglasses had fogged up. When they cleared, he saw Gaylan Kessel sitting by himself in the corner booth he always took. Kessel was looking up at him coolly, a pair of readers pushed halfway down his nose. An empty breakfast plate was pushed to the side, with a crumpled napkin on top of it.

A waitress came out of the kitchen to greet Panos, but when she recognized him right away, she gestured toward Kessel's booth. She knew the routine.

"Cold one out there, isn't it?"

"No shit."

"My car's got vinyl seats," the waitress said. "When I climbed in this morning to come to work, they *cracked*. And when I got it started up, two geese flew out from underneath it."

"That's cold," he said.

"It's got to warm up soon, don't you think?"

"I have no idea," he said ruefully. "This is my first winter here. I hope it's my last."

"Oh, I like it," she said. "It keeps the riffraff out."

Panos cursed under his breath. Kessel shifted in the booth with impatience.

"I'll have my usual," Panos said. He liked the chicken-fried steak and eggs with a side of biscuits and gravy in this place, and ordered it nearly every morning.

"Coming up," the waitress said, and retreated into the kitchen to tell the cook.

There were no other customers in the restaurant. Panos knew Kessel liked it that way.

"YOU GOT IT," Kessel said, as Panos slid into the booth next to him. He meant the file.

Panos nodded and slid it across the Formica top to him.

"Anybody see you?" Kessel asked.

"No."

"You're sure?"

"Yes. The keys were right there where you said they'd be. And I tossed the room to make it look like a robbery just like you asked. The game warden was in the bar talking to those foreigners the whole time."

Kessel nodded, but offered no praise. He never did. Panos had learned that Kessel simply expected excellence at all times, and as long as he did exactly as he was told and offered no excuses for failing, they got along all right. Panos dreaded the consequences when he screwed up, as he had a few weeks ago when he'd been instructed to keep watch on a subject and had lost him. It hadn't been Panos's fault. Kessel told him to watch the house and see where the guy went in his company truck. The company truck remained parked in the driveway. He hadn't told him about a back door or that the subject had a second car back there.

When he explained that to his boss, Kessel had tensed up and balled his fists, and for a moment Panos thought he was going to beat him.

Panos knew he wouldn't be able to defend himself. Kessel seemed to be constructed of cinder blocks. His arms were the size of Panos's thighs and his fists were like two hams. When he'd seen Kessel shed his shirt that afternoon at the Saratoga hot pool, it confirmed that he'd be no match for the man. Plus, the scars from one or more knife fights looked like pale zippers across Kessel's broad chest. His snow-white hair was deceiving, because Kessel was younger and more fit than he looked at first glance.

For the rest of that day, Kessel didn't say a word to him. Finally, as they parted in the evening, Kessel said, "Ted?"

"Yes?"

"Don't ever fuck up again. Do you understand what I'm saying?"

"I do."

Kessel had driven away. And Panos hadn't screwed up again.

Since that day, Panos had tucked a two-barreled Bond Arms .45 derringer into his boot top. He'd bought it at Koyote Sports in town. It was a tiny weapon, but it packed a wallop. He never revealed the presence of the weapon to Kessel. If the man did attack him, he hoped he could get to it in time. He'd aim for center mass with the first shot. A point-blank .45 round would stop even a bear like Kessel. Then he'd finish the man off with a shot to the head. He'd *have* to finish him off.

A wounded Gaylan Kessel was more terrifying than a living Gaylan Kessel.

PANOS KEPT SILENT AS KESSEL read through the file page by page in front of him. The waitress delivered his breakfast and he ate quietly.

Panos knew very little about Kessel except for a few side comments he'd heard him make. He knew he'd been in the army during Desert Storm and he'd liked it so much he hired on after his deployment with a mercenary outfit. As Kessel put it, he "got to see the world and kill men of every hue." He had a low grating voice that made everything he said seem menacing. Kessel was from Minnesota, which he once referred to as "Minne-so-cold." The cold didn't seem to bother him at all, Panos noted. Kessel often went outside without a coat and Panos had to beg the man to turn up the heat when they rode together in the pickup with the camper shell. Kessel always drove.

Panos was from Las Vegas, New Mexico, originally. It had been cold down there, especially in the mountains, but nothing like *this*.

After a stint in the air force, Panos had taken a job as a correctional officer at the New Mexico state penitentiary in Santa Fe. It was dangerous work and the general population was filled with gangbangers both domestic and illegal, Aryan supremacists, and various reprobates of every stripe. The authorities who ran the place were so spooked not to repeat the infamous New Mexico prison riot of 1980—where thirty-three men had been murdered, some by having lengths of steel rebar shoved through their heads—that they'd urged the COs to ruthlessly clamp down on violators. Panos had been an enthusiastic practitioner of the edict, and he'd never had a problem with cracking heads.

There was one inmate in particular, a lifer who'd participated in the riot and considered it a badge of honor, who caused trouble as a matter of course. His attitude was, *What more could they do to him*?

Panos and a few other COs decided to teach the prisoner a lesson. They'd held the miscreant down so they could pry his closed eyes open for a point-blank blast of pepper spray. When the scumbag went blind and later sued the Department of Corrections and won, Panos as well as four other experienced COs had lost their jobs. Panos was still bitter about it.

He'd bounced around after that, taking any security officer job that paid a few dollars more per hour than the one he currently had. He couldn't even imagine not being in law enforcement of some kind, even if the jobs barely rated over mall cop. It was a miserable existence without the state insurance, perks, and pension he'd had for two decades. His wife, Gabriella, had left him and taken their three kids.

So when Gaylan Kessel interviewed Panos a few months before and said that blinding a perverted loser might be a recommendation instead of a detriment, Panos leapt at the opportunity. He'd encountered men like Kessel in the military and on the inside and he admired them. Men who lived their own lives, stood up for themselves, and administered justice to those who deserved it. When Panos learned how much he'd be paid and that the position came with benefits that surpassed even what the state of New Mexico had offered, it was like icing on the cake.

Of course, that had occurred in the early fall, when the temperatures during the day were in the sixties and seventies and trees were just starting to turn color near the river. He had welcomed the still cool and crisp nights, which was when he and Kessel did most of their work, and he had had no idea what it would be like in January during a historic cold snap.

KESSEL CLOSED THE FILE and sighed. He said, "Nothing to worry about here."

"Really?" Panos asked as he sopped up the last of the sausage gravy with the last of the biscuit.

"Naw."

"Good."

"We have to keep an eye on him, though. We can't let him get too close. But right now he's on the wrong track."

Kessel, Panos had learned, had a lot of duties in addition to overall security. One of them was combing the Upper North Platte River Valley for additional wind tower locations as well as ranch property for company executives who might want to visit or live there eventually. They'd even found themselves on the back roads of a high-end dude ranch known as the Silver Creek Ranch. Unfortunately, a female employee had made them at the time.

Panos didn't ask which particular track the game warden was following because he knew Kessel wouldn't elaborate. Kessel leaned forward to make sure the waitress was back in the kitchen gossiping with the cook and couldn't overhear them.

"You know that old lady who called the cops? The busybody?"

Panos felt a cold pang of fear shoot through his chest. He nodded.

"She's not going to be a problem anymore," Kessel said.

Panos tried not to react. He didn't want Kessel to know how scared he was of being implicated.

"An accident," Kessel said. "She slid off the highway on her way home last night."

"I'm sorry to hear that," Panos said.

"Yeah, me too," Kessel said with the slightest grin. "Because soon we need to make another run."

"Already?"

"Something about the weather," Kessel said.

"I'll dress warm."

"You do that," Kessel said with a smirk.

14

AFTER BREAKFAST, JOE DROVE TO STEVE POLLOCK'S OLD HOUSE AT the top of the hill and bucked a deep snowdrift in the back driveway that nearly launched his pickup into the garage door. Luckily, he was able to stop the truck three feet away.

He got out and looked around. The garage was attached to the back of the house. From where he was parked, he couldn't be seen from the street or from the neighbors' homes, which was the idea.

Joe crunched through the snow to the garage door and tugged up on the handle with no luck. Then he tried the knob on the back door and confirmed it was locked as well.

The house was state property, not Pollock's. Joe could either wait for Casey Scales to come up with a spare set of keys and get them to him, or authorize a local locksmith to get inside, provided there was a locksmith in Saratoga. Both would take time Joe didn't think he had and involve procedures that could get back to Connor

Hanlon—who would rightly question why Joe wanted to poke around inside the house of an ex–state employee rather than investigate the disappearance of Kate Shelford-Longden.

Which was a good question, he thought. Almost as good as why he'd been sent to Saratoga in the first place.

But Pollock's sudden absence was, to Joe, as puzzling as Kate's.

He had to try and figure it out, he thought. And he could partially justify it because there was the remote but possible chance that the two disappearances were somehow related. Had Pollock encountered Kate while on patrol? Had they possibly met at a bar when Kate was in town? Was it even credible that a sophisticated British executive would fall for . . . a game warden? The thought made Joe shake his head.

Did Pollock have a dark side that might have led him to grab Kate as she left the ranch? Could his guilt about the incident have led him to flee his job?

The door itself was made of cheap laminated wood with a four-pane window in the center of it. He thought about knocking out one of the glass panes so he could reach inside and unlock it. He decided instead to simply shoulder his way in.

Joe glanced around again to make sure no one was watching, then threw himself toward the left side of the door. The doorjamb splintered free on the inside and he stepped quickly inside and shut it. There were tools on a workbench and a pile of scrap wood in the corner of the garage. He knew he could remount the lock plate and fix his damage before he left.

POLLOCK'S PICKUP TRUCK was open and the keys were in the center console. Joe climbed inside and looked around. The Ford F-150 was a newer model than the one he drove, and it was remarkably neat and clean inside. Even the floor mats were clean.

This is the kind of vehicle you get, Joe thought, *when you don't have the dubious reputation of destroying more state vehicles than any other employee.*

He dug around and found Pollock's citation book in a seat pocket and thumbed through it. Pollock had issued his last ticket two weeks before to a couple of ice fishermen on Saratoga Lake for fishing without licenses. There were no major incidents or arrests for the past three months that caught Joe's attention. What he was looking for was the type of violations that might result in bad blood between a game warden and a violator. Something serious enough that Pollock had felt threatened by sticking around.

But he found only standard stuff: hunting in the wrong area, taking a buck pronghorn antelope in a doe/fawn-only area, failing to adequately tag elk. The book contained citations going back eighteen months. Joe recognized none of the names of the perpetrators, but made a list of them in his own notebook. He replaced the citation book in the seat pocket where he'd found it.

There were flex-cuffs in the glove box as well as a package of jerky, an unopened can of Copenhagen chewing tobacco, and a field first-aid kit.

But as he went through the truck, Joe became more and more puzzled. Not by what he found, but by what he didn't find.

He climbed out and opened the utility box in the bed of the truck and looked inside. There were extra coats and vests, a sleeping bag, ropes, chains, come-alongs, a shovel, winter overalls and extra Sorel pac boots, a Handyman jack, road flares, as well as gloves, ice-creepers, and a satellite phone. But no briefcase that might have contained paperwork, maps, and other items.

Game wardens lived in their vehicles. Their pickups were not only their means of transportation, but they also served as their offices in the field and holding cells when necessary. Every nook and cranny of Joe's truck was used to store or cram something. There were topo maps wedged between the bench seats, evidence bags including tooth envelopes for determining the age of carcasses, ballistics pamphlets, seizure tags, a necropsy kit, and reams of printed departmental memos, edicts, and reports. Every warden pickup Joe had ever ridden in was in the same condition, and many were much worse when it came to clutter.

Either Steve Pollock was the neatest and tidiest game warden in the state of Wyoming, Joe thought, or someone had already been through his truck and removed most of the contents.

Whether that was Pollock himself or someone else was the question Joe couldn't answer.

THE DOOR INTO THE HOUSE from the garage was unlocked, so Joe didn't have to force it open. It also meant that Pollock probably entered his house primarily through that door. Pull into the garage, shut the garage door, and go inside.

It was a good procedure for a game warden, Joe knew. Saratoga, like Saddlestring, was a hunting-and-fishing community. Locals kept close track of where the game warden patrolled—especially potential violators. If the Game and Fish vehicle was parked at home out front, it served as a green light to poach or commit other crimes. But if the vehicle couldn't be seen from the street—if it were parked in the garage—it meant the game warden could be anywhere.

The door opened onto a small vestibule that served as a mudroom. Boots lined the floor, hats and caps were lined cheek-by-jowl on a high shelf, and over a dozen coats and parkas hung in between.

Joe spent a few minutes going through the pockets of the coats and found nothing of interest except a few spent cartridge casings, gum, and empty Copenhagen tins.

It was cold inside. Joe walked through the kitchen and found the thermostat mounted on a hallway wall. He turned it up to sixty-eight and heard the sound of electric baseboards hum to life. He was grateful the department had continued to pay the electrical bill even though the occupant was gone.

The kitchen had the look of one used by a single man. Pollock had been divorced for a while and apparently he'd had no partner at the time he vanished. There was one plate in the sink and one set of silverware. One glass had been turned upside down on a folded towel next to the sink.

There were still items in the refrigerator. When Joe opened the door, he caught a whiff of spoiled milk. The freezer compartment was crammed full of locally packaged elk steak and burger.

As he'd guessed the day before, it appeared that Pollock had simply walked out of the house. There were still clothes, including uniform shirts, in the bedroom closet. A suit hung still sheathed in clear plastic from a dry-cleaning shop in Rawlins. Two of the dresser drawers were empty. He'd taken his underwear.

Joe pushed the clothes aside to check out the corners of the closet, then he did the same in the two other bedrooms. He looked for Pollock's agency-issued weapons: an M14 carbine chambered in .308, a .40 Glock like the one Joe had on his hip, a .22 revolver loaded with cracker shells to scare off game animals, a scoped .270 rifle, and a Remington 12-gauge shotgun that held seven rounds.

He got down on his hands and knees and looked under the bed and found only dust bunnies. There were no weapons.

Joe found it curious. If Pollock had taken the weapons, he'd committed the crime of stealing state property. Guns of every kind were easily available to anyone in Wyoming who wanted to buy them. It made no sense to Joe that Pollock would take that risk.

AS JOE GRUNTED to his feet, his phone vibrated. It was Marybeth.

"What are you up to?" she asked.

"I'd rather not say right now."

She knew better than to ask by his tone, so she changed the subject.

"You called this morning?"

"Yup."

He told her about the missing file and Nate's arrival after they'd talked the night before.

"So how is Nate?" she asked.

"He's Nate," Joe answered.

"And we wouldn't have it any other way, would we?" she said with a laugh.

He asked her to find out what she could about Richard Cheetham and she agreed to do that.

"Anything on Kate?" he asked.

"I'm still looking," she said. "She had a Facebook page and was on Twitter, but she was very cautious. She only seemed to post things that were related to her clients and her company. No personal stuff at all. And of course there's been no activity since July."

POLLOCK HAD USED a spare bedroom as his home office and Joe sat down behind the desk. When he jostled the mouse, the monitor of Pollock's computer came to life. The screen saver was a photo of Pollock digging his pickup out of the mud and glancing toward the photographer with a frustrated look on his face.

Joe smiled. One of the features of the annual Wyoming Game Warden Foundation dinner was photos taken over the previous year of game wardens digging their pickups out of mud, rivers, and snowdrifts. It was the kind of gallows humor they all seemed to identify with and hoot at. Joe himself had been in several of the photos over the years, once when he'd broken an axle on a rock.

But he couldn't get into Pollock's hard drive because he didn't know the password. He tried *password*, as well as *GF-18*, Pollock's warden designation. Neither worked.

Joe looked around on the desktop and in the drawers for a hidden sticky note that might reveal the password. He found nothing. He'd have to wait for a department investigator to officially enter the home and send the computer to the crime lab. That could take weeks or months. But he had no choice other than to leave it be.

If he took the computer with him now, it would be an admission of breaking and entering the house.

Frustrated, Joe opened Pollock's file drawer on the side of the desk. Pollock was neat and organized, and the files were hung alphabetically inside. Behind the *A* tab were manila file folders with headers including ANTELOPE LICENSES, ANTELOPE NUMBERS, ANTELOPE HAR-

VEST, and so on. Behind the *C* tab were Pollock's old citation books that went beyond the one Joe had found in the truck. *D* was for DEER and *E* was for ENDANGERED SPECIES. The records were voluminous and Joe spent nearly an hour thumbing through the tabs for anything out of the ordinary.

Which he didn't find.

HE CHECKED HIS WATCH. On the way to Pollock's, he'd called Mark Gordon, the general manager of the Silver Creek Ranch. Gordon had agreed to meet with him, but said he had to do it at one o'clock before he drove to Denver for a flight. He sounded like a very busy man.

Joe pushed back in the office chair and stood up. The heat had been on since he adjusted it, but he could still see his breath. He wondered what he was missing and if he should consider coming back when he had more time.

As he turned for the door, he stopped.

Again, it wasn't what he had found but what he hadn't found.

He walked back to the file drawer and double-checked. There was no file for the Silver Creek Ranch under *S* and not a single folder mentioned Kate Shelford-Longden. It seemed to Joe that a man as fastidious as Pollock would have kept records on the premier dude ranch in the area that included vast hunting and fishing opportunities, as well as a bizarre missing persons case that had occurred within his own district.

But the files didn't exist.

Then he realized that the entire *B* section was missing as well.

The only explanation Joe had was that whoever had cleaned out

Pollock's pickup had also gone through his files and removed some of them.

Had Pollock taken them along with his weapons?

But which ones, and why?

JOE WAS A LITTLE EMBARRASSED by the poor patch job he did on the inside of the back garage door, but he was pressed for time. He'd resorted to securing the lock plate back into the jamb using a couple of lengths of lathe and he'd screwed them in using Pollock's electric screwdriver from his workbench.

He stepped outside and closed the door. He put a little pressure on it to make sure it held and he was pleased with the result.

As he climbed into his pickup and backed out through the drift, he glanced through his side window at the road, just in time to see a light-colored pickup with a camper shell pulling away from the curb and driving toward downtown.

He didn't recall seeing it when he'd arrived at Pollock's.

PART THREE

We are chameleons, and our partialities and prejudices change place with an easy and blessed facility, and we are soon wonted to the change and happy in it.

—Mark Twain

15

"I'VE ALREADY TALKED TO LAW ENFORCEMENT SEVERAL TIMES ABOUT all of this," Silver Creek Ranch general manager Mark Gordon said to Joe from behind his desk. He appeared to be trying not to show his impatience with Joe's arrival. "Don't get me wrong. I'd like to find out what happened to Kate as much as anyone on earth. Maybe more. This thing has been hanging over our heads for months and I'd really like to see it get resolved."

Gordon's office was surprisingly small for such a massive operation, Joe thought. It was located adjacent to a receptionist desk in the administration structure—the latter was a renovated log cabin that from the outside looked like it had been constructed for a single man in the 1950s.

The office cabin was on a hillside tucked away in a copse of fat bell-shaped spruce and could barely be seen from the ranch complex itself, which was both vast and understated at the same time. Within the sprawling complex below was a massive lodge, the Activity Center, barns and outbuildings, an indoor shooting range, a saloon, the largest indoor riding arena Joe had ever seen, and dozens of well-appointed cabins for guests. Although most of the buildings had been built in recent years, they'd been constructed to blend into the folds and contours of the exposed granite boulders of the terrain like natural outgrowths of the landscape itself.

Even under eighteen inches of snow, the Silver Creek Ranch at first sight took his breath away.

GORDON WAS LARGE, fit, and anxious. His dark hair was pasted back and he had a fashionable three-day growth of salt-and-pepper whiskers framing a thick reddish mustache. He had intense hazel eyes and a habit of drumming the eraser end of a pencil on the top of his desk while he talked and thumping it hard on the wood to emphasize a point. He wore a fleece vest over a button-down shirt with *SCR* embroidered on the breast. His manner indicated that he had a lot to do and not enough time to do it, even though it was January and there were no guests at the facility.

"This winter has been absolutely brutal," Gordon said to Joe. "We've got a five-month season and seven months to update, maintain, and improve the ranch. Three of those months have been like this." He indicated the heavy snow outside his window. "The clock is ticking," he said.

A huge whiteboard covered the wall inside his office and a long list of projects to be completed was written on it in colored scrawls.

Renovate Bridger, Owens, Saddlehorn units
Complete ropes course
Test all 32 wells
Update 4-wheeler fleet
Wind turbine project
Order wine for cellar
3,000 pheasants for upland game bird farm

And on and on.

"I realize you've gone over much of this ground before," Joe said. "I really don't want to waste your time. But it would be helpful to me if you gave me some background on the ranch as it pertains to Kate. The governor has asked me to look into this case while I'm here."

"Governor Allen?" Gordon asked, suspicious.

"Yup."

"I've already talked to his chief of staff. Hanlon was his name, I think. He called to ask if there had been any developments."

Joe tried not to show his surprise. Hanlon hadn't told Joe that he'd talked to Gordon directly. Once again, the governor's office had come up in a circumstance that seemed odd.

"When was that?" Joe asked.

"Oh, I think it was a month ago. He also wanted me to invite our owners to the Governor's Antelope Hunt next fall as his guests."

"Ah."

Joe knew that this year the invitation had been made only to Allen's biggest political contributors. Allen's predecessor Governor Rulon had invited ordinary Wyoming citizens. It said something about both of them, Joe thought.

"So can you give me some background on the ranch, even though you've done it before?" Joe asked.

Gordon glanced at his wristwatch, then said, "This ranch is like no other property I've ever managed, and that includes the thirty-five hotels and resorts I've opened up around the world. This place has special challenges and every day is a new adventure. Last week, the pipes froze and burst in the main lodge and we're trying to find master plumbers to come in and fix them. There are so many existential factors working against us here. We've got the weather, the distance from a major airport, and the lack of a nearby population center to draw contractors and employees. Not to mention that creating a super-luxury resort in the least populated state in the country brings its own challenges.

"Not that I'm complaining," Gordon said. "I wouldn't trade it for anything else in the hospitality industry. My owners have put hundreds of millions of dollars into this property to make it the best in the world—and it is. It's a privilege to make this place hum. We've reached out to the entire world to tell them about us, and we've been rewarded by nearly one hundred percent occupancy.

"Our market isn't the one percent," Gordon said. "It's one percent of the one percent. Those people who can choose to holiday anywhere in the world. Convincing them to come out here to the Wild West and get dusty may sound to some like a crazy idea. But we did our research."

While Gordon talked, Joe scribbled in his pad and nodded to encourage him to keep going.

"We hire over two hundred employees to serve ninety guests," the GM said. "That's an astounding level of service. Our guests include household names in entertainment, politics, and business. We've hosted the president's son-in-law."

He went on to fire off a laundry list of celebrity names. Even Joe had heard of a few of them. He knew his daughter Lucy would know them all and be impressed. Sheridan had let a few names slip in phone calls with her mother.

"They come from around the world for a seven-day ranch experience like no other," Gordon said. "These are people who are used to being treated like kings and queens and they come here to be cowboys and cowgirls for a week. Our research showed that in the back of many men's minds is the desire to be a cowboy, and that many women want to play cowgirl as long as they can retire to a luxury cabin at night and enjoy the finest food and wine available anywhere. Once they know that . . ."

He continued. "We're in contact with our guests at least six times from their first inquiry to when they show up. We know as much as we possibly can about every guest in order to make this the best vacation they've ever had in their lives."

Joe recalled the questionnaire he'd seen of Kate's.

"Why a week minimum?" Gordon asked before answering his own question. "Because it takes a full three days to get our guests to unplug and disengage from their phones and the rest of their busy lives. You can actually watch their protective armor melt away on day three. Then they become real people, which is why they came here in the first place. There are no categories of guests, no special status for anyone. They're all our guests and they're all treated with courtesy and respect equally, whether they're celebrities or newlyweds on a once-in-a-lifetime honeymoon.

"Our staff sign nondisclosure agreements promising not to publicize our client list on social media and not to talk about them in town. That guarantees privacy. Our guests really appreciate that.

"You know," Gordon said, "we do a lot of good in this valley."

Joe looked up for more.

"We're one of the biggest employers in the county. We contribute hundreds of thousands of dollars to the community and endow even more to ensure top-tier medical facilities. Every year, we host inner-city kids to experience nature for the first time.

"So," Gordon said, thumping his pencil on the desktop like the tail of an excited puppy, "this is why it's so disconcerting to have a guest just *vanish*. And for that incident to become a news story in our biggest overseas market. So if you can help solve this thing, we'll be eternally grateful. And you can bet we'll show our appreciation to Governor Allen."

"Two hundred and fifty employees are a lot to keep track of," Joe said. "How are they vetted?"

"Thoroughly," Gordon said. "More thoroughly than any other resort I've ever worked at. Every one of them has to have character references before they go through two background checks. If they sail through, there's fairly intense hospitality training. We get the best of the best. Like your daughter Sheridan."

Joe blushed with pride, but kept to the task at hand.

"Not that there is never any drama," Gordon said with a bemused grin. "You can't take two hundred single twenty-somethings from around the country and put them into one place and not have some drama. June is the first round of employee romance and it's inevitable. Many of the breakups occur the first of July. Some go on. Our Human Resources Department calls that period *As the Wagon Wheel Turns*."

Joe smiled, thought of Sheridan and Lance Ramsey, and frowned.

Joe said, "No one who's looked into this case before me has suspected any of the staff."

"And neither do we," Gordon said. "We did our own internal investigation as well."

Joe looked up. "What did you conclude?"

"We concluded that something happened to Kate *after* she left the ranch. And that whatever happened to her had no connection to her week here.

"This isn't like a normal company where the employees show up and do their shift and go home," Gordon said. "It's like one huge extended family during the season. Our people stay together here in one place, they work hard together, and they're with each other twenty-four-seven. Nothing that happens in one corner of the ranch isn't known by everybody else that night. There are no secrets, is what I'm saying. If one of our staff had something inappropriate going on with Kate, we all would have known about it.

"Look," Gordon said, leaning forward at his desk and lowering his voice, "I'll give you a glimpse into how we operate, so you'll know why it doesn't make sense to suspect anyone here."

"Okay."

He continued. "Unlike the vast majority of resorts, we encourage our people to interact with the guests and treat them like normal people. Our guests are a little surprised at that the first three days and then they understand the purpose of that is to set them all at ease. And that happens ninety-five percent of the time. Our guests enjoy our staff and sometimes invite them to dinner with them, or even extend an invitation to visit in the off-season. We don't discourage that. But we absolutely draw the line at any kind of fraternizing. Like between a guest and his or her wrangler or fishing guide."

"So it's never happened?" Joe asked.

"Most of our wranglers are beautiful girls," Gordon said. "Your daughter included. I see how one could assume that male guests might proposition them. I see that. But our wranglers are a tight-knit group and they look out for one another. They go to church together. They just don't entertain that sort of thing."

"So it's never happened?" Joe asked again.

"It's extremely rare," Gordon said. "And if it does, that staff member is immediately dismissed. That's only happened one or two times in the whole time I've been here. We've let go a housekeeper and a fishing guide."

"And nothing like that happened between an employee and Kate?"

"Absolutely not," he said, thumping his pencil so hard it popped out of his grip and he had to retrieve it. "Every morning during the season, we have a daily standup."

Joe scribbled *daily standup* in his notebook and Gordon picked up on it.

"While our guests are at breakfast, all of our departments get together for a briefing," Gordon explained. "They talk about what's on the schedule for the day, but they also talk candidly about guest satisfaction. They play psychologist to unlock the desires of every guest so when our customers leave this place they're raving about it. But they also discuss problem guests—there are a few here and there—and how to deal with them. If Kate were creating any issues, we would have known about it and addressed it. But our investigation found that Kate was very popular among the staff. Our head wrangler, Lance Ramsey, spent the most time with her and he said she'd fallen head over heels for the place. Especially riding."

Joe asked, "Is it unusual for a single woman to book a week here?"

Gordon nodded. "It's not the norm, but we get a few every year. Most of our guests are families."

"Anything odd take place with the other singles?"

"Of course not. They all returned home safely."

He said it definitively, but Joe noted a flutter of his eyelids as he said it. It was a tell. Joe waited a moment for Gordon to continue, but he didn't finish whatever thought had entered his mind.

So Joe prompted him. "Are there any similarities in personality or circumstances with the single guests? I ask this because you guys obviously know a lot about your customers."

"Well," Gordon said as his neck flushed slightly, "we do and there are."

As he said it, the GM slid his chair back and opened a file drawer on the right side of his desk. He withdrew a folder and placed it on his desk.

"They're all British women," Gordon said, not quite meeting Joe's eyes. "All successful British women, many professionals like Kate. Some married, some not."

Joe raised his eyebrows with interest.

"This is how *we* market our property," Gordon said.

He slid a Silver Creek Ranch tourism brochure across the surface of the desk to Joe, who picked it up. It was printed on heavy paper, and as he thumbed through it, he was impressed by the high quality of the scenic photography. There were deep orange Western sunsets, big skies, guests on horseback or fly-fishing. He'd seen many of the images on the SCR website and in the missing case file before, but he was struck by how atmospheric and well-done the photos were.

"This is how our exclusive tour operators in the UK market the property," Gordon said, withdrawing two glossy brochures from the file.

Rather than a sunset or a horseback ride, the cover of the first brochure, from a tour operator called Western Dreams, was a dusky photo of cowboys lined up on a fence with their backs to the camera. Joe recognized that they were watching a rodeo rider inside the arena, but the rider himself wasn't shown.

What *was* shown in sharp detail were eleven backsides in tight Wrangler jeans.

He thumbed through the brochure to see more of the same. Rugged young wranglers on horseback, cowboys adjusting the flank straps on saddles while older women looked on, a stoic horseman leading a herd of horses toward the camera.

"Different approach," Joe said.

Gordon had a slightly embarrassed grin. He said, "Certain British women come over here for a different reason than our American family guests. Our UK tour operators have figured that out and they market directly to them. It seems some British women really want to be around young cowboys."

Joe had some familiarity with the phenomenon. It wasn't unknown among the dude and guest ranches in the Bighorn Mountains near his base. In fact, he'd once been in the Stockman's Bar in Saddlestring on Wednesday night—the night a local dude ranch sent its guests to town as part of their weekly activity schedule. He'd witnessed a lone woman dude ranch guest in her fifties—in fact, she was British—seduce a young local cowboy with multiple Coors Lights and shots of

Jim Beam and then leave the bar with him. Joe had been struck by how young the ranch hand was and how predatory the woman.

And Joe had once encountered two faux cowboys from the East who dressed up in Western wear solely to attract older women dude ranch guests and later fleece them.

"It's simply a market niche," Gordon said somewhat defensively. "Different markets have different niches. We provide the same experience to all of our guests and we don't cater to anything untoward. But it is what it is."

"Was Kate on the prowl, then?" Joe asked.

"We have no information at all that she was. We would have known. You're welcome to talk to Lance or Sheridan, in fact. They spent the most time with Kate while she was here."

"Was Kate disappointed by all the female wranglers?"

Gordon huffed a laugh. "Not that she indicated. We ask all of our guests to complete a thorough exit survey on their last day while the experience on the ranch is fresh in their mind. I'll give you a copy of her exit survey, as I did with the other investigators, if you'd like. You can believe me when I tell you Kate didn't even mention the gender of the wranglers. Her only comment was that they were all excellent."

Joe asked, "Have you met Kate's sister, Sophie, and Billy Bloodworth?"

Gordon's face twitched involuntarily. Another tell.

"Unfortunately, I have," Gordon said. "They came out here a few days ago and one of my maintenance guys pulled their vehicle out of a snowdrift. They were snooping around, but they didn't want to admit it, I guess.

"I told Sophie how sorry we all were about her sister. She seems like a sincere person. That Bloodworth guy, though."

"What about him?"

Gordon sat back and crossed his arms across his chest. "He kept pumping me for the names of famous people who'd stayed here. He was very persistent and even rude. But I didn't give him a single name. Even when he listed some of our actual guests, I wouldn't confirm the names. I thought he was a pain in the ass looking for some kind of sensational angle for his cheap tabloid."

"Did they mention they might have a suspect?" Joe asked, recalling the photo on Kate's phone the night before.

"No, but Bloodworth acted like he blamed me and this ranch for Kate's disappearance," Gordon said. "As if this place had lured her here to be kidnapped. He kept calling the ranch 'posh,' as if there was something wrong with that. I think it was more about his own class anxieties, if you want my personal opinion."

He adopted an English accent and said, "*What kind of people can afford a posh place like this when the homeless are starving?* Questions like that."

"What did you tell him?"

"I threw them the hell out of here," Gordon said. "I don't have time for that. And I called our security guys and asked them to escort them off the property so they wouldn't take any more photos of the buildings."

"Ah," said Joe.

Gordon glanced at his wristwatch again. "Anything else, Mr. Pickett?"

Joe read through his notes. He could tell that Gordon wanted to move on.

"On Kate's registration, she was marked as an 'FIT.' What's that mean?"

"It's travel industry terminology for 'Foreign Individual Traveler,'" Gordon said. "It means she booked direct through a tour operator. It means she didn't come as part of a group."

"Thank you. What's 'glamping'?"

"Glamorous camping," the GM said. "Guests stay in tents or tipis, but with all the comforts of our lodge as well as great food."

When Joe looked up, puzzled, Gordon shrugged and said, "It's a thing."

Joe nodded toward the whiteboard.

"What's the 'wind turbine project'?"

"We were approached by representatives from Buckbrush about constructing fifty turbines on the property. They tried to sell it to us as a way of making the resort green—which they claimed would attract socially conscious guests. They might have a point, but we weighed that against spoiling the view shed with those monstrosities and decided against it. Not that they've given up on it, though. There have been reports about Buckbrush vehicles sneaking around this winter."

"Interesting," Joe said. Then: "Which employee is SP^2?"

"Sheridan Pickett," Gordon said with a rare smile. "I believe you know her. Steve Pringle is our head chef, so he's SP^1."

"Contractors," Joe said. "How are they vetted?"

"Unless they're directly involved with an activity here like a celebrity wedding, they aren't," Gordon said with hesitation. "We simply can't do background checks on every vendor or contractor we work with. Think about it. We're talking food suppliers, mechanics, construction companies, and all the specialty people associated with the operations of a large-scale ranch. It would be a daunting challenge. But understand that contractors have little or no interaction with guests."

"The DCI agent you spoke to listed two particular contractors for follow-up interviews," Joe said as he found the names in his notebook. "He thought I should talk to Ben and Brady Youngberg as well as Jack and Joshua Teubner."

"Our farriers and our fish hatchery guys." Gordon nodded. "I can see why they're worth talking to. I don't know a lot about either of them myself, but their names came up when we did our internal investigation. We didn't interview them ourselves."

"I met the Youngbergs last night," Joe said. "Things almost got Western."

Gordon squinted at Joe, not comprehending.

Joe moved on. "Could I get a complete list of your outside contractors?"

Gordon sighed and said, "Sure. I had a list compiled a couple of months ago. I've handed it over to Sheriff Neal and your DCI. Like I said, I've answered all of these questions before."

The GM pushed back and left his office to ask the receptionist to print off the list as well as to make another copy of Kate's exit survey.

While he did, Joe slipped his cell phone out of his uniform breast pocket and took several shots around the room, particularly the tasks listed on the whiteboard. He didn't suspect Gordon of withholding anything, but he wanted to be thorough.

ON THE FRONT PORCH of the administration cabin, Gordon swept his arm to take in the enormity of the Silver Creek Ranch below while Joe clamped on his Stetson.

"You should see it in the summer," he said. "It's a magnificent place."

"It looks pretty good now."

"Are you going to see your daughter while you're here?"

"Yup."

"You'll find her at the arena," Gordon said. "She's a good one. You and your wife should be proud."

"We are."

"I wish we had a hundred more like her," Gordon said. Then: "I'm sorry, but I've really got to get going to Denver to catch my plane."

With that, he mounted a four-wheel ATV and roared through the snow to the employee parking lot.

JOE WANTED TO FIND SHERIDAN. He also hoped Lance Ramsey would be there.

But he had the nagging feeling that he was covering the same ground that Sheriff Neal and DCI Agent Williams had already trod.

Except for his missing file and the glimpse he'd had of the photo on Sophie's phone, it seemed like he was getting nowhere fast.

At the same time, he couldn't get rid of the thought that he was missing something in plain sight. If only he could figure out what it was.

16

FOR NATE ROMANOWSKI, THE TEUBNER FISH HATCHERY WAS THE SEC-ond strange sight he'd taken in after leaving Saratoga that morning. And as odd and incongruous as it was—a fish hatchery located in the middle of nowhere—it didn't even compare to the first.

After driving north from Saratoga that morning after breakfast with Joe, he'd left the ice-covered state highway for the more familiar feel of an improved gravel road that ran straight and true east through a vast sagebrush-covered plain directly toward the Snowy Range in the distance.

Although Nate drove his four-wheel-drive GMC Yukon XL, he found that the drifts across the road had been plowed that morning and it was clean and clear. Someone—not the county, for sure—had spent a lot of money constructing such a wide and heavy-duty road, he thought.

But it wasn't the mountains that dominated the horizon. It was hundreds of white wind turbines, their blades rotating against the deep blue sky as if propelling the scudding clouds along and out of their way.

The turbines were so high and massive that it took twice as long as he thought it would to arrive at the Buckbrush Wind Energy Project. As he got closer, Nate was stunned by the scale of it. Towers in different stages of construction stretched as far as he could see, with improved roads connecting each concrete base. He was reminded of an epic prairie dog town, but upside down.

Many of the turbines were already operational and he'd never seen so many in one place. But it wasn't the number of functional turbines that stunned him. It was the fact that the project looked only about ten percent complete.

Vehicles and machinery moved over the network of roads taking parts of the wind turbines from one place to another for assembly. A single blade on the trailer of a flatbed tractor trailer dwarfed the vehicle itself.

He'd read about the project, but it had been hard to comprehend without seeing it with his own eyes:

—*The largest wind energy facility in the world.*

—*One thousand 250-foot turbines placed within the largest footprint of land—two thousand acres—ever designated for a wind farm.*

—*Situated on land with consistent Class 6 and 7 winds.*

—*Each turbine is designed to produce three megawatts of electricity.*

—*The electricity produced is a result not of market forces but a combination of federal tax incentives and mandates imposed by state and local governments; the mandates were that a significant portion of their power come from renewable sources including solar and wind even though it is more expensive than traditional methods of electricity generation.*

—*Once complete, the project will power one million homes in California via transmission lines.*

—*Also on the plus side are the hundreds of high-paying construction jobs the facility produced in a county where the coal mines have been shuttered.*

NATE STAYED ON THE ROAD and saw that a half mile ahead it was blocked by a high chain-link gate. He noticed how the air pressure within the Yukon changed the closer he got to the working turbines. It seemed to push down on his head and shoulders. There was also a steady low hum from the spinning blades that replaced the sound of the wind through the sagebrush. It was a kind of subsonic whooshing that made Nate's stomach clench.

He braked to a stop at the gate in front of a sign directing him to do so. On the other side of the fence was a single-wide trailer, and a figure emerged from it zipping up a heavy parka and pulling a hood up and over his head. He moved in a jerky way that conveyed he was annoyed by the intrusion.

The man swiped a key card across a unit mounted on the fence and a walkway gate opened. Nate couldn't see the man's face because his head was covered by the hood. Embroidered on the breast of the parka was *Buckbrush Security*. The security guard circled the Yukon and noted Nate's license plate number on a clipboard before coming up to the driver's-side window. He stood there until Nate powered it down.

"This is private property and you're not on my vendor list. Do you have business here?" the man asked. The hood was long and conical and all Nate could see of his face were yellow teeth framed by dark rubbery lips. "And what the hell is Yarak, Inc.?"

"I run a commercial falconry operation," Nate said.

"Where are your falcons?"

"At my headquarters. I don't drive around with them inside."

"Falcons, huh?"

"Yeah. The kind these turbines chop up."

The security guard said, "I have no idea what you're talking about."

"Right."

"If you've got a grievance, you can file it with the bosses."

"I don't have a grievance, but I'm sure I could find one," Nate said.

"Then what are you doing here?"

Nate peered down the length of the high fence to his right and then his left. It was so long it literally vanished from sight in both directions.

"I'm trying to get to the Teubner Fish Hatchery. My map said it's dead ahead. But . . ."

"So you're a falconer without falcons looking for a fish hatchery in the middle of the winter," the guard said with sarcasm.

"Exactly."

"This used to be the road to get there, but this is as far as you can go now. You've got an old map," the security guard said.

He vaguely gestured to the north. "You'll have to go around."

"How far is that?" Nate asked.

Although the parka was bulky, it didn't hide the shrug.

"Not my problem," the guard said, starting to turn back to his trailer.

"Thanks for all your help," Nate called after him. "Those people in California should feel good that a man with your social skills is helping them keep their lights on and their air conditioners running so they don't even have to think about where their power comes from."

The guard stopped and turned, the tube of his hood pointed at Nate like a gun muzzle.

"What the hell is that supposed to mean?" he asked.

Nate powered his window up and backed away. He'd seen what he wanted to see, and it confirmed his worst fears. Anger coursed through him and he found himself gripping the wheel so tightly he couldn't feel his fingers.

The security guard, and Joe for that matter, didn't have any idea that an important piece of Nate's conspiracy theory had just snapped into place.

IT TOOK TWO HOURS to circumnavigate the Buckbrush Project on a service road that paralleled the chain-link fence, in order to find a road that took him east again. As he drove, he glanced out the side window to get different perspectives on Buckbrush. The westbound transmission lines were strung from structure to structure until they merged with the horizon and vanished out of sight. The afternoon winter sun reflected on the lines and they looked like frozen steel ocean waves lapping toward California.

He couldn't recall ever seeing such a sprawling man-made facility and it made him feel small.

Nate relished feeling small in nature. He despised feeling small next to a thousand windmills. If he were king, he thought, he would require every California politician who mandated "green" energy as well as every resident who would be the recipient of the electricity produced at Buckbrush to come see the massive complex where their power actually came from. He'd make them walk the steel perimeter and look inside the fence at what they'd built on top of a wild game migration corridor. And he wouldn't allow them earplugs to protect them from the punishing *whoosh*.

It was a good thing, he decided, that he wasn't king.

THE TEUBNER FISH HATCHERY was located in a most unlikely location, Nate thought. Rather than being situated near a river or stream, the cluster of long metal ramshackle structures rose out of a sagebrush-and-snow-choked bench fourteen miles from the nearest paved road. There wasn't even a tree on the property.

The cluster of buildings looked as if they'd been assembled over several decades. In addition to the long metal buildings was a two-story home, a huge metal barn filled with vehicles, and what looked like an outhouse. He slowed to a stop on the two-track road and consulted the topo map on the passenger seat to confirm it was the correct location after all. Having to go around Buckbrush to get to the hatchery had thrown off his bearings.

Snow-capped Elk Mountain rose from the plains in the background and dominated the eastern skyline. High-altitude wind picked up loose snow on top and carried it away so it looked like there was a thin flag unfurling from the summit. The ever-present wind had also cleared much of the snow from the two-track roads on the bench that led to the hatchery, although he'd had to gun his four-wheel-drive GMC Yukon through several drifts that blocked the road. Fish hatchery owners didn't take care of their roads like Buckbrush did.

As he neared the hatchery, he saw a man exit one of the buildings and stride toward another. The man leaned against the wind and walked quickly to get out of it. He froze when he saw Nate's Yukon coming up the road. Then he broke into a run and disappeared into the longest metal building, as if Nate's arrival had spooked him.

It was the behavior of someone guilty of something. Which was odd.

Nate felt a rush of adrenaline. His senses sharpened and he locked in on the five ramshackle buildings like a falcon at two thousand feet locking in on an earthbound rabbit.

Was Kate confined in one of them?

He kept in mind Joe's admonition not to bust any heads, and to back off if things got hinky.

Nate thought, *The hell with that.*

HE CRUISED SLOWLY into the hatchery yard toward the house. He noted that the barn was filled with trucks mounted with round plastic tanks behind the cabs. He assumed the tanks were filled with water and hatchery fish to be delivered to private ponds and lakes. It was obvious none of the vehicles had been used for a while, though, because there was a knifelike snowdrift across the front of the open building that had not been breached.

A hand-painted sign on the side of the front door of the house read:

TEUBNER FISH HATCHERY
OFFICE
RING BELL

Nate climbed out of the Yukon and zipped up his heavy coat against the wind and to conceal his weapon. The wind blew hard and it was filled with tiny ice crystals that stung his face. This location, he thought, made more sense for a wind farm than a fish hatchery.

He pushed on the bell, waited, and pushed it again. When there was no response, he reached down and found the door unlocked.

Inside was a large room cluttered with plastic tubs and coffin-sized concrete tanks. Water burbled and the smell was dank and earthy: fish food.

"Hello?"

His voice echoed through the room.

Nate walked among the tanks and looked down inside. Thousands of tiny slivers moved away from him as if they were a single organism.

"Can I help you?"

Nate turned and involuntarily reached up for the tab of his zipper in case he needed to get to his gun. A squat man in his late fifties or early sixties stood up from a desk in a small office in the back corner of the room. He wore stained coveralls and knee-high rubber boots. His head was large and he had jowls that trembled when he talked.

"I rang the bell," Nate said.

"It don't work."

"I figured that."

"You the fish inspector?" the man asked. He eyed him suspiciously.

Nate paused. *Fish inspector?*

"You're not the fish inspector, are you?" the man said.

"Do I look like a fish inspector?"

"I don't know what you look like. Are you a fish buyer?"

"Let's say I was. What would you tell me?"

The man took a deep breath. "I'm Jack Teubner. This is my place. We supply catchable trout to nearly a hundred ponds and lakes across five states. Rainbows, browns, cutthroats, cutbows, and tigers. This is the incubation room.

"Are you looking to buy some?"

"Maybe," Nate said. "But these are too small."

"They're fry," Teubner said. "They'll be two to three inches long by this summer and then we'll move them out to the raceways. In a year they'll be big enough to stock. Meanwhile, we'll start the whole incubation process in here again. You can see it takes a while, so if you want to make an order, you need to do it soon. Like now. Otherwise, you'll be shit out of luck."

Nate nodded. Jack Teubner seemed oddly stiff and discouraging for a fish salesman.

"Where do you get your water?" Nate asked.

Teubner tapped his foot on the concrete floor. "You're standing on top of a natural spring. We built the hatchery right on top of it. The spring produces twenty-five hundred gallons of water per minute. It's pure, too, not like the water that comes from lakes or the river. No particulates or bacteria. That's why our fish are so healthy."

"Is this a two-man operation?" Nate asked. "I saw someone outside when I drove up."

"My son, Joshua," Jack said.

"He ran like he was scared of me."

"He don't like fish inspectors any more than I do," Jack said. "Either the state guys or the federal guys. Those idiots could shut me down in a minute if they thought they found something wrong, and I don't trust their methods. They take samples of our water and our fry and I worry they'll get cross-contaminated with fish from some other place but blame me."

"I'm not a fish inspector," Nate said.

"Didn't think so. Are you a buyer?"

Before Nate could come up with a good answer, a door opened and the man he'd seen earlier—presumably Joshua—strode in. Joshua looked from his father to Nate and back to his father again.

"What's going on?" he asked.

"We're talking fish," Nate said.

"Fish?" Joshua said with a smirk. "Just fish?"

Joshua was thin and gaunt with sharp hawk-like features and unkind narrow eyes. Even from across the room and despite the pungent fish food, Nate could smell the reek of marijuana from his clothing.

"Looking for something to help get you through the winter?" Joshua asked Nate. "I figure that's why you're here."

Nate nodded his head slightly. Now he got it: the reason for Jack's strange reticence and Joshua's behavior when he saw him on the road.

"I want to see what I'm buying first," Nate said.

"Before you go out there," Jack said, indicating to Nate the door Joshua had used, "I've got to ask you something. Are you law enforcement?"

Nate turned back to him. "No."

"Are you affiliated with any state or federal agency?"

"No."

"Prove it."

In his peripheral vision, Joshua moved so that an unused concrete fish tank was between them. What was in the tank? A gun?

"How do I prove it?" Nate asked. He'd never been mistaken for a cop before and he thought Jack probably surmised that.

"I'm going to pat you down," Jack said.

"No, you're not."

Nate unzipped his coat and opened it so Jack could see the butt of his .454 Casull. "Jack, if you put hands on me, this will turn out to be a really bad day for you."

He turned his head toward Joshua. "You too."

Rather than reach inside the tank or get angry, Joshua grinned.

"I don't think we need to worry about him, Dad. I've been expecting him."

Jack nodded his agreement.

Nate thought, *You have?*

"Follow me," Joshua said.

"HE GETS PARANOID EASY," Joshua said to Nate as they crossed the yard toward the nearest long metal building. "He don't trust nobody."

"I don't blame him," Nate said. He noted that the right side of Joshua's heavy Carhartt parka sagged more than the left. *Gun in there*, Nate thought.

"He mentioned a raceway," Nate said.

"That's what we call where we raise the mature fish. You'll see."

Nate followed Joshua through a metal doorway into the building. It was one long open area with six separate lanes where water coursed through. Trout were stacked in each lane with their noses aimed at the inflow. Some rose and kissed the surface with their dorsal fins.

It was colder in the raceway building and the fish smell was much stronger than in the incubator room.

"I was starting to think you wouldn't show up," Joshua said as he dug a stubby pipe and a baggie of marijuana from his pocket. He lit the pipe, inhaled deeply, then handed it to Nate.

Nate wiped off the mouthpiece and took a deep drag. It was a test, he knew, to ensure he wasn't a cop.

Joshua obviously thought he was someone else, though. Nate decided to play along.

He could feel it immediately.

"Good shit, isn't it?" Joshua said.

Nate agreed.

"I used to grow it, but the market dried up. Fish shit is great fertilizer. But when Colorado legalized weed just across the border, my customers went south."

Nate nodded to the raceways and slowly expelled the smoke from his lungs. "I would have thought it would freeze in the winter," Nate said.

"Naw. The water from the spring stays at forty-five degrees summer and winter. It's the perfect temp to keep them healthy and feeding. Lower than that, they don't grow fast enough; hotter than that, they get sluggish."

"So why cover it?" Nate asked, indicating the roof.

"To keep out the critters that like to eat fish," Joshua said. "Mink, raccoons, blue herons, osprey. People."

"People?"

"You'd be surprised how many idiots have come out here with

their fishing poles. We lock the buildings at night so they can't get in, but they still try."

Nate followed Joshua on a metal grated walkway that spanned all six of the raceways. He half-listened as Joshua explained that males were confined to one lane and females to the other, except for spawning season, and that brown and rainbow trout matured at two to three years. One lane was filled with massive two-foot-long trout used strictly as brood stock.

The grate led to a steel door at the end of the building.

"Now you'll see where the magic happens," Joshua said. "Now you'll see how we get through the winter."

Nate stayed behind Joshua's shoulder while he dug a key out of his pocket and unlocked the door. Before opening it, he grinned.

What if Kate was kept inside? Not likely, but . . .

The smell from inside was a mix of paint thinner and ammonia and it was so strong it made Nate's eyes tear up.

And they entered the Teubner meth lab.

THE ROOM WAS made of concrete and it had no windows. Fifty-five-gallon drums sat in the middle of it and a bench was filled with Pyrex containers, mason jars, and rolls of hoses. A tall anhydrous ammonia gas cylinder with a blue-colored brass valve stood near the drums, and in the corner of the room was a loose bundle of red-stained bedsheets that were used for straining. The odor was nearly overpowering, and as if in response Joshua hit a switch that turned on a fan to vent it outside.

Nate stepped back through the open door until the air in the room cleared.

"What we got here," Joshua said, "is a fucking perfect setup for making high-quality crystal. I get the pseudoephedrine through my old man's industrial chemical accounts because he buys a lot of different stuff to keep this place disinfected. The fish smell disguises the meth cooking, so as long as I keep the door closed, even the smartest cop or fish inspector wouldn't notice it."

He refilled his pipe and lit it again.

"I've doubled my product in the past year and I could do it again. You'll never have to worry about supply," he said.

"So you've got a lot of customers around here?" Nate asked.

"Oh yeah," Joshua said with a wide grin. "I go along when Pop delivers fish and sell hits to the ranch hands and shit. You'd be amazed how many Crystal Cowboys there are around here.

"But let's talk business," Joshua said. "Let's talk territory."

"Okay."

"I'm thinking I want you distributing in the northern half of the state. From Casper up, but I get Casper. Casper's a fucking gold mine with all those unemployed energy workers. I keep the south. That means you get Jackson Hole, Sheridan, Gillette, Cody. That ought to keep you busy and make you rich. Gillette's a gold mine, too, but you have to compete with asshats from Rapid City and Sturgis. But my product is better, though. You'll do fine," Joshua said.

"And make you even richer," Nate said.

"That's how it's supposed to work," Joshua said with a stoner smile.

He said, "You can charge fifty dollars or more for a quarter gram because this is really good meth. You set the price—I don't want anything to do with your business. But don't set it too high and scare off customers. If I was you, I'd start low and build up your clientele, then gradually increase the price. That's what I did down here and it worked out just fine for me."

"How much?" Nate asked.

Joshua looked at Nate with a hint of suspicion. "I thought we talked about that. I'll sell you each quarter gram for twenty-five dollars. A hundred dollars for a gram and you'll clear a hundred for your pocket. Or," Joshua said, waggling his eyebrows, "you can get that half kilo we talked about for fifty grand. Did you bring the money with you?"

"In my Yukon," Nate said. He hoped the person Joshua had been expecting wouldn't show up while they were talking in the lab.

"Cool, cool," Joshua said. "You want to sample the product?"

Nate's head was still clouded from the single inhalation of Joshua's marijuana and he shook his head no. Nate wasn't used to how strong weed was these days.

"I trust you."

"You should. This is high-quality shit. So go get the money and I'll measure out that half kilo. You can watch if you want, so you know you're getting what you paid for."

Nate didn't want to be rushed into revealing himself, so he asked, "So you go on fish runs with your dad and sell on the side. That gives you cover."

Joshua nodded.

"Do you have customers at the Silver Creek Ranch?"

"I've got a few customers there, sure." He'd answered quickly, impatiently. Joshua wanted to see the money.

"Do you recall a British woman last summer? Blond?"

Joshua narrowed his eyes. "Are you talking about Kate?"

Nate felt a jolt go up his back.

"What about her?" Joshua asked with suspicion.

"Did you sell to her?"

"*Who the fuck are you?*" Joshua asked, suddenly alarmed. "Why would you care about her?"

He reached into his coat and pointed a 9mm Charter Arms semi-auto at Nate's nose. It was a cheap handgun, a favorite of drug dealers, and Nate had no respect for people who carried one. Joshua held the weapon sideways like gang-bangers did in the movies. That also irritated Nate.

But he cursed himself because he'd let it happen. His head had been too clouded to react.

"You need to put that away," Nate said.

"I asked who the fuck you were," Joshua said, spittle forming on his lips. "You're not Hargrove."

"My name is Nate. Hargrove sent me in his place."

Joshua processed that, and as he did, his face screwed up quizzically. But the muzzle of the gun stayed up.

"I'm gonna call him and check that out," Joshua said, nodding his head and finally deciding on a plan. "He didn't say nothing about sending another guy. But you need to get rid of your piece."

"Okay," Nate said.

"Don't try nothing."

"I won't."

Nate pulled his coat aside with his left hand and slowly reached for the grip of his revolver with his right. Joshua's eyes followed Nate's right hand. Those eyes didn't track that Nate had leaned his upper body a few inches to the side so that if Joshua's weapon went off the bullet would miss his head and slam into the concrete wall behind him.

In one lightning motion, Nate drew the .454, cocked it while he raised it, and shot Joshua in the right shoulder. The concussion was thunderous in the closed room and Joshua's body spun a hundred and eighty degrees from the impact. The 9mm clattered on the floor.

Nate closed the distance between them with two long steps and grabbed Joshua by the back collar of his coat and dragged him out through the meth lab door. The exit wound had spattered the wall with blood and the slug had penetrated the concrete, leaving a neat O in the wall. Joshua cried out for help and he didn't stop screaming until Nate plunged into the raceway used for brood stock and pulled him in after him.

In the cold waist-high water, Nate holstered his gun and plunged Joshua's face into the water as most of the big trout in the lane fled for the inlet end in a rush that made a froth on the surface.

After holding him down long enough that Joshua began to panic and thrash his legs, Nate pulled him back up. A ribbon of red from his shoulder wound streaked the lane and curled toward the outflow grate.

"I told you to put that gun away," Nate hissed.

Joshua gasped for air and said, "You shot my arm off."

"Not completely," Nate said. "But I'll rip it out of the socket if you don't tell me what you know about Kate."

"*I don't know anything*," Joshua yelled.

"You knew her name."

Joshua's eyes pleaded with Nate. "I knew her name and that's all. I saw her out there and thought I'd really like to hit that, you know? But I didn't do nothing. I never made a move on her."

"Was she a customer?"

"No!"

"Do you know what happened to her?"

When Joshua hesitated too long, Nate dunked his head under the water again and held it there until the man kicked at the surface of the water in a panic. Then he pulled him back up.

As he did, a ball of brood stock trout that had retreated to the outlet end of the lane decided as one to muscle past Nate to join the others on the far end where they'd pooled together. As the brown trout went by, Nate reached down and grasped one just in front of its powerful tail. It was about four pounds.

"I asked if you knew what happened to her," Nate said while swinging the trout. He smacked Joshua in the side of his head with a wet slap.

"I heard at a bar that she's still around," Joshua gasped.

"Who told you that?"

"I overheard it at the Rustic from a couple of old guys. I don't know them. I really don't. I was texting a buddy of mine at the time—making a deal. I kept my head down."

"What did they look like?"

"Old, I told you. Like my dad."

"Who do they work for?"

"I don't know. Shit."

Nate smacked him with the trout hard enough that the fish spasmed and died after the blow.

"Stop hitting me with that *fish*," Joshua said. "I was out of it at the time."

"When was this?"

"Last fall. October, November—I don't know."

"*Think*. What can you tell me about them?"

"That's all I can remember," Joshua pleaded. "I thought I heard

’em say they saw her and she was hiding out. But I ain’t even sure that I didn’t imagine it. Like I said, I was testing out my own product at the time.”

Nate studied Joshua’s face, which was twisted from pain. Then he let him go. Joshua dropped into the raceway and scrambled back to his feet while sputtering. He’d swallowed a lot of water. His right arm hung straight down and he pinned it to his body with his left hand.

“It’s a through-and-through meat wound,” Nate said to Joshua. “You’ll recover if you don’t bleed out. Go get your dad to clean it out and bind it up.”

“It hurts really bad,” Joshua said in a little-boy voice.

“It’s supposed to,” Nate said.

In his Yukon on the way back toward Saratoga, Nate watched his cell phone until it finally found a signal. Joe had called, but not left a message. Probably checking on him, Nate thought.

As the Teubner Fish Hatchery receded in his rearview mirror, he saw a jacked-up four-by-four with Campbell County license plates coming through the snowdrifts Nate had bucked to get there. Nate pulled over to let the vehicle pass by and saw it was driven by a nervous-looking skinny guy with a pointed nose and a wisp of beard.

“Sorry, Hargrove,” Nate said as the car went by.

The large brown trout lay on the passenger-side floor mat. It was a beautiful fish and Nate felt guilty for braining it. Joe liked a fish dinner and maybe he’d approve.

He wouldn’t approve of Nate’s interrogation methods, however.

17

JOE FOUND SHERIDAN RIDING LONG FIGURE EIGHTS ON A SORREL gelding on the loose sand surface of the indoor arena. Although the arena was heated with forced-air furnaces the size of pickup trucks in each corner, it was cold enough outside and the arena was so massive that the gelding puffed clouds of condensation as it loped.

Sheridan looked good in the saddle, Joe thought. Better than he ever had. Her movements were fluid and she guided the horse by leg pressure rather than tugging on its bit with the reins. She saw him come through the door and she tipped her hat as she rode. He waved back.

There were five horses in a stall on the far wall. Three had the sweaty imprint of a saddle still on their backs.

After completing the pattern, Sheridan rode up to Joe and pulled the gelding to a sliding stop.

"Now you're just showing off," Joe said with a proud grin.

"Got to keep 'em all tuned up so they remember they're horses," she said. "I've got one more to go today and then I'll dry them off and turn 'em out."

"Don't let me rush you," Joe said.

"Have you had lunch?"

"Nope."

"How about a late afternoon snack? Soup okay?"

"Yup. Your mom would love to do your job. So would April."

Sheridan grinned. Her face was flushed red from the exertion of saddling and riding four horses, one right after the other. "I think about that. I kind of feel bad about it sometimes."

With that, she clicked her tongue and the gelding spun away.

SHERIDAN'S APARTMENT was located on the second floor above the arena itself. There was a small kitchen, a bathroom, a fabric couch and matching chair, a desk with her laptop, and a wall filled with family photos that tugged at his heart. The room was neater than Joe would have guessed it would be, judging by the state of her room when she lived at home.

The apartment overlooked the empty arena on one side and the vast white winter landscape on the other. Outside, with the sun reflecting off the snow, it was so bright it hurt his eyes.

He sat at a small table while she emptied condensed tomato soup into a pot and added water. She'd hung up her jacket on a rack near the door and kicked off her cowboy boots.

"Grilled cheese?" she asked.

"That would be great," he said.

Joe excused himself to use the bathroom while she prepared the food. He couldn't recall her ever having done that for him before. Sure, his oldest daughter had helped Marybeth with some meals, usually during holidays, but it used to be that Joe was often the cook when his girls were growing up—especially breakfast. He could tell she was thinking similar thoughts about the role reversal as well.

In the bathroom, he glanced at the shower—generic and exotic hair products, a loofah—and looked hard at the mirrored medicine cabinet but decided not to open it. He didn't want to find any men's items, and thought it best not to look, even though he guessed Marybeth would have if given the same opportunity.

"THANK YOU," HE SAID as he spooned the last of his soup. "It was delicious."

She looked at him to check out his sincerity. "It came out of a can."

"Still, it was good."

She gathered up the dishes and told him that her apartment was one of the few reserved for senior staff and she was lucky she didn't have to share it with anyone. Most of the employees spent the summer season in dorm-like buildings located about a quarter mile away and had to bunk together.

"This is a good place," she said, sitting back down. "I never thought I'd want to work at a guest ranch."

"How much of it is because of Lance Ramsey?" he asked.

"*Dad*," she said, blushing.

"So tell me about Kate," he said, changing the subject for the benefit of both of them.

Sheridan said, "Well, some guests really like to stand out while they're here. It's strange. You've got these rich and famous people trying to impress all of us nobodies. But Kate wasn't like that. She blended in and just seemed to enjoy herself. I'd say she was a perfect guest."

Joe nodded for her to go on.

"She was hungover most mornings," Sheridan said, with a knowing smile. "She was English, after all, so it's not unusual. But there's no doubt riding was her thing. It was her passion.

"We're encouraged to accommodate the guests as much as we can, so if we have one who wants to ride outside of the scheduled rides, we do our best to make that happen. By the end of the week, she wanted to go on early-morning rides and evening rides after the rest of the guests had turned their horses in."

"Did she go alone?" Joe asked.

"We can't allow that," Sheridan said. "That's against policy and it should be. For the safety of our guests."

"So you accompanied her?"

"A couple of times, yes. But she mainly went out with Lance. It's kind of a big deal for a guest to ride with the head wrangler and she really liked that."

"When you were with her, did she talk to you about anything?"

"Mostly horses and scenery," Sheridan said. "She said she tried fly-fishing and shooting, but that wasn't her thing. Really, what we talked about was her, even though she asked me about my background once. She was really interested to hear how I grew up and that I wasn't as crazy about horses as my mom and my sister were. She really didn't get the concept of you being a game warden, I don't think. But we didn't talk about me much."

"Did you find that odd?"

"Not at all," Sheridan said. "It's part of the training here. We have to keep in mind that this isn't about us. That's hard for some of the staff, because they're naturally so self-centered. A lot of kids my age have grown up being told they were the center of the universe—I get that. But if they don't learn to put that aside for the sake of the guests, they don't last long around here."

"I approve," Joe said.

Sheridan laughed and said, "I thought you would."

"What kinds of things did she tell you when you rode together?"

"Stuff I've heard before, but she was really intense about it. She talked a lot about the contrast between the ranch and her life at home. It weirded her out at first not to be connected all the time. She said the first time she turned off her iPhone and left it back in her room she nearly had an anxiety attack. That kind of thing.

"I got the impression that her life back in England was really high pressure and that just getting from place to place was a major hassle. Kate loved the natural beauty of the ranch and she said the slower pace made her crazy at first until she got used to it. She said it took a lot of getting used to just to enjoy herself and soak it all in—to realize that people around here weren't going to demand anything of her."

Joe noted that.

"Kate did once say that she'd never felt more free in her life," Sheridan said. "She told me I didn't know how lucky I was to live with such freedom. Of course, she didn't have any idea how many hours we work while the guests are relaxing.

"I know that the last couple of days she was here she said she *really* didn't want to go back. Kate seemed to love this place even more than most guests, and you could see a troubled look cross over her face when she talked about going home."

"Interesting," he said. "Any idea what troubled her?"

"Not really. A lot of guests say that. In fact, most of them. This is kind of a fantasy camp for some people and they don't want to go back to their real world once they get used to it."

Joe asked, "Did she talk about any of the staff or any of the guests while you were with her? Did anyone interest her or annoy her?"

"Not that I can remember," Sheridan said, then paused. "She did mention that she didn't like the way the Youngbergs looked at her when they were shoeing the horses. But she sort of rolled her eyes when she said it, like it was no big deal. I think I told her those two yahoos look at every female that way."

"As we know," Joe said.

Sheridan rolled her eyes in agreement. "That would have been really something if you and Lance fought them last night."

"Luckily, we didn't. But I was impressed how Lance stood up for you."

"So was I," Sheridan said, with a wistful smile that told Joe more than she probably wanted to.

"By the way, where is Lance? I wanted to ask him some of the same questions."

"He'll be here by Monday," she said. "He's got the weekend off and he went up to his cabin. He usually comes back Sunday afternoon."

"Is it here on the ranch?"

"No—it's about twenty miles away up in the Snowy Range. It's been in his family for years and he really likes to go up there whenever he can. We can drive there in the early summer, but in the winter it's really hard to get to and he has to snowmobile in."

Joe noted the *we* and Sheridan realized at the same time what she'd revealed.

"Oops," she said.

"He seems like a good guy," Joe said. "I hope he knows better than to do my daughter wrong."

Sheridan flushed and shook her head. "The things you say . . ."

"So what do you think happened to her?" Joe asked. "You must have thought about it and talked about it with other people here."

"There were a million theories, as you can guess," she said. "You've probably heard most of them already. That she got kidnapped on the highway, that somebody on the staff here grabbed her, that a ranch contractor targeted her and took her after her stay."

"I've heard all those," Joe said. "What do you think?"

Sheridan sat back. "You really want my opinion?"

He nodded. "Next to your mother, you're the smartest person I know. Plus, you've got a unique perspective on the whole case."

"I think it was something else," Sheridan said thoughtfully. "I just don't know what."

"Why do you say that?" he asked. But he'd felt the hairs rise on the back of his neck because he thought the same thing.

"Because in each of those scenarios, her car isn't accounted for," she said. "Kate drove a 2017 silver Jeep Cherokee with Colorado rental plates. It couldn't have just vanished from the face of the earth. Somebody around here would have seen it if any of those three things happened."

He said, "I'm going to tell you something, if you can keep it confidential."

"I can."

"Kate's sister is here with a British newspaper reporter. I met them last night and they let it slip they think she's still here—alive. They think some local has her locked up somewhere. In fact, I got a glimpse of a photo they took that could be her, but they wouldn't let me get a good look at it."

Sheridan's eyes got large. "You've got to be kidding me."

"Nope."

"If they think they've found her, why didn't they go get her out?"

"I was wondering the same thing," he said. "There's more to this, but the journalist wouldn't let Sophie talk to me about it."

"Does Sophie have red hair?"

"Yup."

Sheridan shook her head. "I haven't seen them myself, but I heard they harassed our GM the other day. And Lance told me he helped a maintenance guy pull them out of a snowdrift after they'd left. They'd trespassed here on the ranch and they got stuck because they didn't know how to drive in the snow."

"That's them."

"Do you know what they drive?" she asked.

"No," he said, thinking that he *should* know that. "Why?"

"I saw a strange vehicle a couple of days ago and I called it in to Lance. There were two people in the truck and I had the feeling they were watching me from across the river. Could that be them?"

"Describe the vehicle."

"It was a four-wheel-drive pickup with a camper shell," she said. "It was light colored—maybe off-white or gray. I didn't get a very good look at it and I couldn't see any license plates from that distance."

"It sounds like the truck I saw this morning," he said.

Before he could continue, his phone went off in his pocket and he pulled it out and looked at the screen.

"Nate," he said to Sheridan. "I need to take this."

"Nate's here?" she asked.

"He's helping me," Joe said. "I *think*."

SHERIDAN WATCHED HER DAD take the call. She felt both thrilled and disconcerted. The man who used to cook her breakfast and take her out on ride-alongs was speaking to her as if she were an equal. She wasn't used to it and she wasn't sure what she felt about it. She thought she liked it, that it meant she'd matured and he recognized that, but at the same time she had a feeling that something special was now lost between them.

But maybe in a good way.

And she felt guilty not telling him more about how she felt about Lance. That the head wrangler was her sun, her moon, her stars. That he'd carefully cleared all of his things out of her apartment before her dad had arrived. That he'd gone to his cabin in the snow for the weekend because he had nowhere else to go.

"What do you mean you shot him and then hit him with a fish?" her dad said, his voice rising.

Sheridan was confused at first, but then again it was Nate he was talking with.

If there was anybody capable of shooting a man and then hitting him with a fish, it was Nate Romanowski, her master falconer. Even if she couldn't imagine the scenario. Where did Nate get a fish in the middle of the winter with the rivers and lakes frozen?

"What if he calls the sheriff?" her dad asked Nate.

. . .

JOE COULD FEEL Sheridan's eyes on him as Nate said, "Come on, Joe. What's he going to say? Is he going to tell them a guy came out and shot him inside his meth lab? He's not going to involve law enforcement in this at all."

"*I'm* law enforcement."

Nate didn't respond.

"What if he bleeds out?" Joe asked.

"Then there'll be one less scumbag in the world."

"Nate."

Nate said, "I figure he'll end up in the hospital using some lame excuse for the gunshot wound. His dad won't let him die."

"Good."

"Hey, do you want a fish for dinner? I bet you could ask them to cook it up for you at the Wolf."

Joe took a deep breath and expelled it slowly while he tried to stay calm.

"Tell me exactly what he said when you were torturing him."

Nate snorted at the word *torture*. Then: "He said he was in a bar texting someone to make a drug deal and overheard these two old guys talking about Kate—that she was still alive and in the area. Teubner said he listened but kept his head down, and he's not even sure what the two guys looked like. He was high on his own product at the time."

"Which bar?"

"The Rustic."

"That's it?" Joe asked. "Did he tell you when it was?"

"He said he couldn't remember but he thought it was in October or November but he wasn't sure."

"So two months or three months ago," Joe said. "This makes the second time it's come up that she might still be alive."

"What about the fish?" Nate asked. "You know I don't kill things for sport."

"Meet me here," Joe said. "I'm at the Silver Creek Ranch with Sheridan."

"I thought I was supposed to interview Sophie and the fop."

"I can't afford any more casualties," Joe said, and punched off on Nate in mid-chuckle.

"**SO WHERE DID** he get a fish in the middle of the winter?" Sheridan asked Joe.

"From a fish hatchery," he said.

Sheridan grinned at the absurdity of it, and Joe had to agree.

The phone was still in his hand when a text message appeared from Marybeth. It read: *Check out this link and call me.*

"Your mom found something," he said to Sheridan as he stabbed the hyperlink on his screen with his index finger and waited for it to load.

What appeared was the online home page of the *Daily Dispatch*. Under a headline that read IS THIS KATE? was the grainy photo Joe had glimpsed the night before on Sophie's phone.

"Oh, no," he said.

"What is it?" Sheridan asked.

"The fop strikes," Joe said.

He expanded the photo to fill the screen. It was presumably taken from a long distance and it was more out of focus than he recalled, but there it was: the back of a seated person with blond hair, seen through a window, the figure of a man looming in shadows in the background as if approaching her. Joe noted snow on the outside windowsill and weathered log walls that he hadn't noticed previously.

The byline of the story was credited to Billy Bloodworth.

> Is this a photo of missing Kate Shelford-Longden being held captive by a mountain man in the wilds of Wyoming, an area where primitive gun-toting Trump-voting "individualists" still occupy the mountains?
>
> The single photo appears to show Cowgirl Kate, the British PR MD long thought dead, being menaced by an unknown male while she cowers near a window. The photo was taken within the last week and obtained exclusively from a source by the *Daily Dispatch.*
>
> The exact location of this den of depravity is unknown at press time. Kate's fetching sister, Sophie Shelford-Longden, who is on location in Wyoming to search for her sibling as part of a *Dispatch* investigative team, said she was cautiously optimistic that her sibling was still alive and being held against her will.
>
> "This is a remarkable development," she said. "I can say within eighty percent certainty that the woman in the photo is my sister, Kate. It's like my prayers have been answered."

> Prior to the revelation of this photo, U.S. law enforcement authorities have been stymied thus far into the investigation into Cowgirl Kate's disappearance, leading many to wonder if a thorough effort had even been made . . .

"What a weasel," Joe said to Sheridan. "He's a lot more interested in headlines than actually finding her."

"Can I read it?" she asked eagerly. He sent her the link and speed-dialed Marybeth.

"That story just appeared on their website," Marybeth said. "They're seven hours ahead of us, so it's midnight there and likely very few Brits have seen it yet. But when it comes out in print tomorrow morning over there, you'll have a full-blown tabloid scandal on your hands."

Joe grunted.

"I wouldn't be surprised if more reporters start showing up now," she said. "They're really competitive over there."

"That's all we need."

She said what he was thinking: "I can't imagine Governor Allen and Hanlon are going to like this news."

"Nope," Joe sighed.

"Maybe you should brief them before they find out on their own."

"If I get a minute, I will."

He filled her in on developments since he'd last talked with her.

"A fish?" Marybeth asked. "He beat a man with a fish?"

"Yup."

"What's with this Billy Bloodworth guy?" she asked.

Joe said, "It's obvious he has an agenda of his own. He's been uncooperative with us, to say the least. I can't tell if Sophie trusts him or whether she was duped to get involved in his trip over here."

"So there is no investigative team?"

"*He's* the investigative team. I wish I knew where that photo came from."

"Maybe Nate can visit him and bring his fish," she said.

Joe didn't laugh.

"I was kidding," she said.

MARYBETH CHANGED THE SUBJECT by telling Joe what she'd learned about Kate's ex-husband, Richard Cheetham. Although he'd given a few pithy quotes on her disappearance when it happened, she said, he'd stayed out of the story ever since. Apparently, he'd moved from London to an estate in the countryside in the Midlands and had recently remarried. Marybeth had found records of their divorce settlement and a few small news stories about the proceedings—enough information to indicate that he'd gotten a pretty good deal. He still owned nearly half the shares in Athena, and if Kate continued to shepherd the company well he received a steady income. Marybeth confirmed that the PR company had been profitable the last two years.

Unless Richard had some other reason to harbor a murderous resentment toward Kate, she said, it seemed he had no transparent motive to hatch a scheme to go after his ex-wife while she was on vacation in another country.

Marybeth's conclusion was that Richard's name should be moved to the very bottom of the suspect list, but not yet crossed off.

He realized Sheridan was talking to him as well and he looked up.

"Tell Mom hello," she said.

"Sheridan says hello."

"Tell her to call me tonight and we can catch up."

He said he would.

"It sounds like you're going to be busy," she said. "At least it's not snowing there today and you can get around easier."

He agreed, but said, "How do you know it's not snowing?"

"I checked the webcam," she said.

"What webcam?"

"There's a single webcam for Saratoga. It's on the home page of the radio station there."

Joe hadn't noticed a single closed-circuit camera around town when he arrived, which wasn't unusual for a community that small. He'd apparently missed the webcam unit.

"What can you see?" he asked.

"The main street," she said. "Including the porch of the Hotel Wolf."

"Can you see the Rustic Bar? It's at the end of the block."

After a few seconds, she said, "Yes, I can see it."

For a minute, he didn't speak.

"Joe?"

"I'm here."

"What's going on?"

"I'm thinking."

"I hope my phone battery holds up long enough," she joked.

"Can I ask you to do something else?" he said, oblivious.

"Of course."

"Find out who owns the radio station and see if they have a way of accessing their computer archives for the last couple of months. I don't know if a webcam even has archives, but please check. We need to know whether or not we can find out who entered and exited the Rustic Bar in October and November. Maybe even December? I know it's a long shot, but maybe it'll help."

"Can you give me a specific date?"

"I wish I could." Then he went silent again.

"Joe?"

"I think I know how we might be able to determine the date," he said. "But if you could make contact with the owner or his tech guy in the meanwhile, I'd appreciate it."

She agreed and said she'd call him back when she learned more.

"Can this be true?" Sheridan asked Joe, after reading the *Dispatch* article.

"I doubt it," Joe said.

"I'm not so sure," Sheridan mused.

"Do you recognize the cabin?" Joe asked.

Sheridan's eyes flared. "If you're asking me if it's Lance's cabin, it's not."

"Sorry," he said.

THERE WERE FOOTFALLS on the stairway outside Sheridan's apartment, followed by a heavy rap on the door.

"Nate," Joe told Sheridan.

Her eyes got large and she rushed to the door to open it.

"There she is," Nate said to Sheridan. "She's a cowgirl."

"I'm a falconer first," she said. "I'm playing cowgirl until my master falconer finally decides to show up again."

He smiled at her. "Every time I see you, you're in the middle of some kind of trouble and we never get around to falconry."

Sheridan gestured toward Joe. "Blame him this time."

Nate turned serious. He said, "Falconry, as you know, is Zen. You can't rush it. We need some uninterrupted time to resume your apprenticeship."

"Did you bring any of your birds with you?" she asked.

"Not this time."

While Sheridan and Nate talked falconry, Joe called the Memorial Hospital of Carbon County. The receptionist made it very clear that she could not give out any information on patients other than to confirm they'd been admitted.

"His name is Joshua Teubner," Joe said, spelling the last name.

The receptionist confirmed that he was there. Alive. Joe thanked her and cleared his throat to get Nate's and Sheridan's attention. Nate was telling her about recently seeing the gyrfalcon he'd hunted with two years before in the Red Desert.

"I hate to break this up, but we're going to Rawlins to visit Joshua Teubner in the hospital," Joe said. "I need to look at his cell phone if I can."

"I'll bring my fish," Nate said. It made Sheridan cover her mouth so she wouldn't laugh out loud.

"Leave the fish here," Joe said. "While we're in town, I'll brief Sheriff Neal on where we're at."

"I'd like to tag along," Sheridan said to Joe. "I'm pretty much done for the day."

He started to object, but didn't have a good reason to do so.

"Maybe you can keep an eye on him," Joe said, indicating Nate.

"I'll be happy to do that," she said with a full-wattage smile.

. . .

NATE AND SHERIDAN went down the stairs and Joe was a beat behind them when his phone lit up in his hand. He glanced at the screen. Hanlon.

He considered letting the call go to voicemail, but he punched it up instead.

"What in the fuck is going on over there?" Hanlon asked. Joe could hear traffic sounds in the background and assumed Hanlon was racing from place to place in Cheyenne in his SUV.

Before Joe could respond, Hanlon said, "I just got off the phone with Governor Allen. The British Consulate called him and said there's a photo of Kate Blah-Blah on the front page of an English rag. They said there's evidence that she's being held against her will in our state right now—right under your nose."

Joe said, "It's unconfirmed. I was going to tell you about—"

Hanlon cut him off: "*When?* This is not the way things should work. I shouldn't be calling you to find out what the hell you're doing. You're supposed to keep me up to speed on your investigation. I never again want to learn about something from the governor or from a British tabloid. So are you going to confirm that photo and find her?"

"I'm on it," Joe said, tight-lipped. He knew he should have briefed Hanlon earlier as Marybeth had suggested.

"Governor Allen is not happy about this development, Pickett."

"Neither am I."

"But there's a difference," Hanlon said with faux calm. "He's the governor and you're a nobody."

"I'm well aware of that."

"We've called a press conference for tomorrow where the governor will announce that Kate has been rescued. I'm going to ask the British Consulate to send a representative. It'll be a big deal and it'll be great for us to get this stupid issue off our plate and we'll finally have a win."

Joe sat up straight. "I'd really advise you not to do that until we know for sure we've got her."

"I tell you what: you do your job and I'll do mine."

Hanlon terminated the call before Joe could ask about the keys to Pollock's house.

"TROUBLE?" NATE ASKED outside as Joe strode around him toward his pickup.

"Politics," Joe said.

"This is the life you've chosen."

"Not really," he said while climbing behind the wheel and turning the key in the ignition.

THEY DROVE NORTH on WYO 130 toward Walcott Junction with Nate in the passenger seat and Sheridan crammed into the back amidst discarded winter clothing and other gear. Shadows were starting to nose west on the snow from exposed sage and buckbrush in the late-afternoon sun.

Joe told Nate about Billy Bloodworth's scoop and Sheridan let him read it on her phone.

"That photo could be from anywhere," Nate said about the shot. "It could have been taken two years ago or it could be staged."

"Maybe," Joe said.

"Or maybe she's still here," Sheridan said from the backseat.

"DID YOU KNOW William Shakespeare was a falconer?" Sheridan asked Nate.

"Yes, I did," he said.

"It's true," Sheridan said to Joe, who was obviously unaware of the fact. "He used falconry terms in his plays that have become part of the English language—only people don't know where they came from.

"'Fed up' is from when a bird has eaten too much of his kill and doesn't want to hunt or do anything for a while," she said. "And 'under my thumb' and 'wrapped around his little finger' are from holding a falcon tight to your fist by its jesses so it can't fly. Those terms were in Shakespeare's plays and until then they weren't common usage."

She said, "'Haggard' is a falcon that's difficult to fly, and 'hoodwinked' is from putting the leather hood on the bird so it can't see to fly away."

"Interesting," Joe said. He meant it.

Nate recited:

"My falcon now is sharp and passing empty;
And till she stoop she must not be full-gorged,
For then she never looks upon her lure.
Another way I have to man my haggard,
To make her come and know her keeper's call."

"That's from *The Taming of the Shrew,*" Sheridan told Joe.

Joe looked skeptically at his friend and then at his daughter. He'd never heard Nate recite poetry before and was unaware that Sheridan had that much familiarity with Shakespeare.

"You two make me feel stupid," he confessed.

Nate shrugged. "We're falconers," he said.

Sheridan giggled.

TWO MILES SOUTH of Walcott Junction and I-80, Joe speed-dialed Sheriff Neal's private number.

The sheriff answered immediately.

"Sheriff, Joe Pickett. I'm on my way to Rawlins right now to brief you on some new developments."

"Where are you now?"

"I can see the interstate."

"Well, hold tight," Neal said. "In fact, pull over and wait for us."

"Why?"

"We've got a man in custody on a DUI rap who claims he took the picture of Kate and sold it to the English reporter two days ago. He's agreed to show us where the cabin is, so we're headed your way. We're about ten minutes out."

Joe pulled over.

"Here we go," he said.

"What's going on?" Sheridan asked.

"Break in the case."

His heart raced. Joshua Teubner's phone records would have to wait—and might not even be necessary.

18

THREE CARBON COUNTY SHERIFF'S SUVS WITH LIGHTS FLASHING TOOK the Walcott Junction exit, followed by a three-quarter-ton pickup hauling a trailer topped with six snowmobiles.

Joe powered his window down as the caravan approached and slowed to a stop on the highway. Neal was in the lead and he climbed out of his Chevrolet Tahoe and lumbered over to the pickup. Neal was heavyset and stoop-shouldered. He had a thick mustache threaded with gray and large brown cop eyes that took in everything he looked at. As he neared Joe's truck, he could see Neal assessing Nate and then Sheridan.

The sheriff zipped up his heavy parka against the cold as he approached Joe's window.

"Why can't this stuff ever happen on a nice summer day?" he said.

"I see you brought snowmobiles," Joe said, nodding toward the three-quarter ton.

"I called a snowmobile outfitter I know and rented his whole fleet," Neal said with a shake of his head. "That'll do some damage on my budget."

"So where are we going?"

"All the way up the Snowy Range Road until it ends," Neal said.

Joe knew that the Snowy Range received so much snow every winter that the highway department didn't bother to plow it until spring, and even then they had to use rotary snowplows to cut through the ten to twelve feet of accumulation that blew off the roadway into huge plumes. He'd noted that the snow got so deep that highway workers attached fifteen-foot lengths of wood to the steel mile markers so the plow drivers could discern where the road was located.

"Who is your informant?" Joe asked. He could see the silhouette of a head in Neal's backseat. The man had a round face the shape of a pie tin and a scraggly beard.

"Name's Eli Jarrett. We know him."

He said it in a way that meant, *He's familiar to law enforcement and not in a good way.*

"Eli used to work in the mine in Hanna before it went bust. Picked him up a few times for DUI. Likes meth, too."

Joe heard Nate grunt with recognition from the passenger seat.

Neal thumbed over his shoulder toward Jarrett. "He collects sheds in the mountains and sells them to dealers. He said he knows of a couple of open meadows up there where the wind blows them clean in the winter. He took his snowmobile and sled up there last weekend to try and get a jump on his competition."

Joe knew that "sheds" were elk antlers that naturally detached and dropped to the ground each winter from bull elk. The price for them from Asian pharmaceutical representatives, artists, and furniture makers had climbed to over fifteen dollars per pound, meaning that a massive set could go for over eight hundred dollars. It was tough work, but it could be lucrative.

There was a big run on sheds in the late spring and early summer when the snow melted to reveal them where they'd dropped. "Shed wars" were so named because collectors sometimes got into disputes with others over territory, and there were very few rules or regulations about gathering them. There were shed wars in other Wyoming mountain ranges, including Joe's Bighorns.

"That's where Eli bumbled onto a cabin," Neal said. "He said he was surprised it was occupied, because the road to it is snowed in."

"Do you know who the cabin belongs to?" Joe asked.

"Trapper by the name of Les McKnight," Neal said. "He's a mysterious old coot who sometimes works for the Fish and Wildlife Service, but mainly he works for himself. Gets badgers, beavers, coyotes . . ."

"I've seen him," Sheridan said urgently from the backseat. "He put some traps by the river last summer at the ranch."

"Silver Creek Ranch?" Neal asked her.

"That's where I work," she said.

"Well, there you go," Neal said to Joe. "That puts McKnight on the ranch where Kate disappeared."

Suddenly, Billy Bloodworth and Sophie's theory sounded more plausible, Joe thought.

"Eli had his phone with him and he took some pictures of McKnight's cabin," Neal said. "It wasn't until he got home and looked at them that he noticed the blonde in the window. He ran into that English feller in the bar and sold him the photos for a couple of hundred dollars apiece. He didn't know what the reporter was going to do with them or how fast they'd show up on the Internet."

The sheriff used the word *Internet* as if it were some strange new trend in technology, Joe noted.

Neal sighed. "That's his story, anyway. The photos *are* still on his phone, so he's not lying about that part."

The sheriff squinted against the icy wind and looked at the mountains to the east.

"We better get going if we hope to get up there by dark," he said.

"Lead the way," Joe said.

"Remember when I told you trouble always follows you around?" Neal asked.

"Yup."

"Maybe it worked out in our favor this time."

JOE MADE A U-TURN and joined Sheriff Neal's entourage headed toward Saratoga.

"Yes, I remember him," Sheridan said. "He's a creepy guy and we had to throw him off the ranch because he didn't have permission to put traps there. Mr. Gordon was worried that one of our ranch dogs would get hurt, you know?"

"Is it possible," Joe asked, "that McKnight was on the property the same week Kate was there? July 23 to 30?"

"I'm thinking," she said. "I can't say for sure. I know he was there in the middle of the summer, so it's possible. Mr. Gordon might remember."

Joe called the Silver Creek Ranch office, but Gordon wasn't in, so he left a message asking the GM if he could recall the specific week when McKnight was ordered off the property.

. . .

A FEW BUNDLED-UP pedestrians on the sidewalk in Saratoga paused to watch the five-vehicle law enforcement caravan pass through town and out the other side.

"Tongues will be wagging before we get there," Sheridan observed.

THEY TURNED LEFT at the junction of Highways 130 and 230 and started the climb to the Snowy Range. The sagebrush and rock formations in the foothills gave way to a long willow-choked flat where Brush Creek meandered and two cow moose and a yearling calf watched them go by. The snow on either side of the road got deeper with every mile.

Joe checked his rearview mirror to discover that an additional four-wheel-drive vehicle had slipped into the convoy behind the truck pulling the snowmobiles. He couldn't see who was inside until he took a turn into the trees and got a better angle.

"Oh no," he said aloud. "Billy Bloodworth and Sophie have joined us."

He reported the interlopers to Sheriff Neal on the radio.

"He's the English reporter?" Neal asked.

"Yup. And Kate's sister."

"That son of a bitch should have turned those photos over to us instead of putting them on the Internet," Neal said, with the typical disdain cops had for the media in general. "Did you know it's common for those UK types to pay people for stories and photos? I didn't know that until today."

"He's gonna want to go along with us," Joe said. "He wants an exclusive before any other reporters show up."

Neal grunted and signed off.

Joe realized Nate had said nothing since they'd spoken to Sheriff Neal and joined the procession south.

"What are you thinking?" he asked his friend.

"I'm thinking this new development really doesn't work in my overall conspiracy theory," Nate said.

"Aha," Joe said with a hint of glee.

A LARGE TURNAROUND had been plowed at the end of the highway so that unsuspecting drivers could easily loop around and head back to Saratoga instead of going over the top of the mountain toward Centennial and Laramie. There was enough room to use the alcove as a staging area for the snowmobiles. Joe parked next to Neal's vehicle.

Joe watched Billy Bloodworth erupt from his rented SUV as soon as he parked it with the others. Sophie stayed inside. He was at Sheriff Neal's Tahoe as Neal climbed out. Joe left his truck running while he got out to join them.

"I must go with you," Bloodworth said to the sheriff. His voice was unusually high-pitched and frantic.

"Not possible," the sheriff said affably. "I'm not risking the safety of a civilian."

"I beg your pardon, sir," Bloodworth said as his eyes bulged. "I'm not a *civilian*. I'm media and therefore I have a right to report the news under the First Amendment."

"So you're American?" Neal asked him.

"I'm a British subject."

"Then have your queen send me a note," Neal drawled.

Joe looked away so he wouldn't laugh.

"You don't understand," Bloodworth pleaded. "This is my narrative. This is my legacy."

Neal stared at Bloodworth for a moment. "Show me in my mission as the sheriff of Carbon County that it's my job to help you with your legacy."

Bloodworth turned to Joe. "Tell him this wouldn't even be happening without my reporting."

"He's the sheriff," Joe said. "It's his call."

Neal said, "You're welcome to stay here, though, and see what we find."

"This is fucking *outrageous*," Bloodworth said. Then, as if it had just occurred to him, he hugged himself and said, "It's cold as fuck!"

"Put on a coat," Neal said sourly. "And try not to curse every time you open your mouth. What's wrong with you people?"

Bloodworth turned toward his rental, but stopped short when he saw Eli Jarrett being escorted by a deputy from the back door of the SUV.

"Mr. Jarrett," Bloodworth said with venom. "We had a deal to keep this information confidential until I could finish reporting the story."

Jarett flushed and said, "I don't even know what that means."

"*Fucking idiots*," Bloodworth spat, and pulled himself quickly inside his car and shut the door. Joe could see but not hear Sophie admonish him, and Bloodworth go on a rant with dancing hands and spittle flying on the inside of the driver's-side window.

"He's a little too tightly wound to go along," Neal said to Joe. "And I doubt he's ever driven a snow machine."

Joe agreed.

TWILIGHT IN THE MOUNTAINS brought a special kind of cold. It crept out from the darkness of the lodgepole pine forest where it had spent the daylight hours and it slithered across the top of the snow to sting every inch of exposed human skin. Sounds became sharper and the snow itself became a different texture that squeaked like nails on a chalkboard with every footfall.

While the snowmobile-rental owner backed each machine off the trailer one by one, Joe and the sheriff's crew pulled on snowmobile suits and exchanged their footwear for heavy snowmobile boots. Joe was grateful his coveralls had been in the backseat and they were still warm from Sheridan's body heat. His helmet, though, had been in his gearbox in the bed of his pickup and it was as cold as a block of ice when he pulled it on. The plastic face shield fogged up instantly.

He approached Neal as the sheriff struggled to fit into his suit with SHERIFF written in yellow across the back.

"Do you have a spare for my partner?" Joe asked, nodding toward Nate in his truck.

"I might have," Neal said. "Who is he?"

"He's a guy we'd rather have along with us," Joe said.

"We're running out of machines."

"He can ride on the back of mine."

Neal gestured to the snowmobile-rental operator. "Check with him," he said. "Tell him to put it on my quickly growing tab."

"Thanks," Joe said.

. . .

"WHAT ABOUT ME?" Sheridan asked as Joe handed Nate an extra-large black snowmobile suit that had *Snowy Range Sleds* embroidered over the breast pocket.

"Call your mom and let her know what's going on," Joe said. "She's going to want to know."

Thinking: *So would Hanlon.*

But he'll be even more pleased, Joe thought, *with a call that tells him we've solved the case.*

THE STILL AIR filled with the acrid fumes of six idling snowmobiles. Sheriff Neal and his three deputies waited for everyone to straddle the machines and nod their helmets that they were ready to move out. Joe took a Polaris 550 WideTrak LX because it was extra-long and could seat two people. Nate settled in behind him. Snug, but not embarrassingly snug, he thought.

Eli Jarrett sat alone, revving his engine. He was bookended by two deputies on their snowmobiles.

Joe had spent hundreds of hours patrolling on sleds and although he wasn't an expert, he considered himself competent. He could tell when he watched the deputies, by the way they took in the gauges and got the feel for their hand throttles, that they were far from experts themselves.

Sheriff Neal rode up beside Joe and raised his face shield.

"Keep a close eye on Jarrett," he said. "Keep right on him. This might be a ruse to get us up here where he knows the mountains and the trails so he can get away from us and hightail it out of here. I don't think my guys could keep up with him, and I damn well know I can't."

"Gotcha. What is our plan when we get to the cabin?" Joe said.

"I'm workin' on that," Neal said, and slid his mask down.

19

AT THE SAME TIME, WYLIE FRYE ARRIVED AT THE ENCAMPMENT LUMBER mill for his overnight shift wearing insulated coveralls, Sorel pac boots, and his wool rancher cap. It was eight below zero and falling by the minute. He parked his pickup facing the warm wall of the conical burner to keep the motor warm through the night, and he grabbed his "lunch" from the passenger seat to take inside so it wouldn't freeze solid.

As he lumbered toward the burner shack, he felt his phone vibrate in his shirt breast pocket and he stopped to check the screen.

UNKNOWN NUMBER.

The second time that night. He ignored it and quickly put his phone back and zipped up the coveralls so the temperature wouldn't make the zipper lock up.

Even though management would disapprove, Frye wanted to start up the front-end loader as soon as he could after he arrived to transfer the waste and sawdust from the mill itself and shove it into the burner all at one time. Management had told him to feed the fire incrementally every couple of hours throughout his shift. But it was a pain in the butt to put on his coveralls and walk up to the mill itself three or four times a night when he could do it all at once. This way, he had more leisure time in the shack and he could maybe even get in a nap, he figured.

Sure, the temperature of the burner might exceed its recommended threshold. Frye knew that. But he also knew it was supposed to get to twenty-five below after midnight and some extra heat *probably* wouldn't damage the inner workings of the structure. And it would keep the shack toasty warm.

He placed his lunch on a shelf next to the steel burner wall so it would keep warm. As he did so, his phone went off again.

He cursed and chose to punch it up. If nothing else, he could tell the UNKNOWN CALLER to fuck off.

"Who is this?" he asked.

"Answer your phone. You know who it is." The gravelly voice was unmistakable.

"I didn't answer because I didn't recognize the number."

"I've got a new phone. I'd suggest you get one, too. In fact: do it. Get more than one."

"I've got a phone," Wylie said.

"Jesus, you're dense. What I'm saying is I want you to get a couple of prepaid disposable phones to have on hand in the future. We can't have anyone pulling up a record of calls from me to you, got it? So go out and get a new phone and text the number to me. I'll call that number the next time."

"You want me to get a burner?" Wylie asked.

"Yeah. I didn't say burner because I didn't want you to get it confused with where you work."

"I'm not stupid."

The man chuckled at that. Wylie ignored it.

"Where am I supposed to get burners?"

"Try the Kum-N-Go. They've got a rack of them. If you don't want to do that, go to the Walmart in Rawlins."

Wylie hesitated, said, "I guess."

"Do it."

"Okay, okay."

After a beat, the man said, "We'll be ready to make another delivery run tomorrow night, so have that new phone handy."

"Tomorrow?" He asked only to stall for time and screw up his courage for what he was about to ask.

"That's what I said."

"Well, I wanted to talk to you about that. I think I need more money if we're going to keep doing this."

The silence on the other end made the hair on the back of Wylie's neck prick up.

Wylie said, "I'm running a big risk here. I've got kids with medical bills."

It was a lie. If his kids got sick, his ex took them to the free county clinic. But Wylie had his eye on a new long-distance rifle: the HAMR. Chambered in .375 CheyTac and manufactured by Gunwerks in Cody, Wyoming, it weighed nearly twenty-one pounds and could hit a target over two thousand yards away. Wylie had watched the video on the Gunwerks site dozens of times and it gave him an erection. Plus, the look of the rifle itself with its bipod, Nightforce scope, and folding stock was completely badass.

And it cost over twelve thousand dollars.

"You don't know who you're dealing with, do you? I'm not a man who negotiates after we have a deal," the man said finally. "That's not how I operate."

"I thought at first it was a onetime thing," Wylie said, his voice rising in register. "You didn't tell me you'd be calling me every ten days to two weeks."

More silence. It made Wylie nervous. He realized he was sweating inside his coveralls.

"Look," he said, "how about we go with what you've been paying, but just for tomorrow night. After that, if we go forward, we need to have better terms."

"Is that right?"

"Just think about it, okay?"

Wylie knew how lame he sounded.

"We'll be there between two-fifteen and three-thirty as usual," the man said. He didn't even address Wylie's proposal. "In the meantime, delete your phone records and my old contact number from your phone."

"Seriously?"

"And not just that. I need you to reformat your phone completely so it looks like it did when you took it out of the box."

"I'll lose everything," Wylie complained. "All my contacts and my game apps . . ."

"Do it or you're gonna wish you did. And leave your old phone on your desk tomorrow when we show up. I want to make sure you did everything right."

"What's going on? Why are we going through all of this if you don't have hazardous materials?"

"Shut the fuck up, Wylie," the man snapped. "Just do what I tell you."

"I'll text you my new number tomorrow," Wylie said with a sigh of resignation. He could put up with the abuse if it meant he could get closer to that HAMR.

The call dropped and Wylie stared at his phone for a moment. He took his hat off and ran his fingers through his hair. His scalp was moist.

He didn't have a good feeling about the conversation.

From behind him, Jeb Pryor said, "I overheard some of that, Wylie. What the hell do you have going on the side at my mill?"

Wylie turned slowly. Pryor, the owner, had come into the shack and shut the door behind him. Wylie hadn't noticed him because he'd been so focused on the call itself. He didn't know how long Old Man Pryor had been there or how much he'd heard.

"Nothing," Wylie lied. "I've got nothing going on."

Pryor looked him over. Wylie just stood there, his sphincter contracting. He knew his face was flushed.

"I think you and me need to have a little talk," Pryor said.

20

THE SUN DROPPED BELOW THE SUMMIT OF THE SIERRA MADRE RANGE at their backs as the snowmobiles tore across a long meadow toward the forest. Joe glanced at his watch—a half hour left of daylight. He wished it didn't get dark so early in the winter.

Eli Jarrett roared up an untracked logging road on his snowmobile followed by the two deputies assigned to him, then Joe and Nate. Sheriff Neal and his undersheriff trailed them all and fell farther and farther behind. The two deputies behind Jarrett were struggling to keep up with him on the flats, Joe thought. Once the old road started to climb and twist through the forest, he didn't know if they could stay with him. Joe goosed the Polaris and it responded with a leap forward to close the gap.

Jarrett was an aggressive snowmobile driver who knew how to use his weight and the power of the machine itself to get farther and farther ahead. Joe didn't see the man look over his shoulder once to see if the others were still with him.

"Stay in his track," Nate shouted from behind Joe.

Joe knew what he meant. Jarrett had been up the road the weekend before and had packed down and groomed a path. Although that path had been obscured by several recent snowfalls, it was still down there as a base for the snow machines. Just a few feet to either the right or the left was several feet of pure powder snow. The hidden but groomed path served as a kind of land bridge through the fluffy snow. Joe hoped the deputies knew that.

The deputy directly behind Jarrett apparently didn't, though, and when he took a turn too wide, he went flying off the road into the meadow, where his snowmobile immediately bogged down. The front sleds of his machine nosed into the sky and the back sank down.

The second deputy saw what had happened to his colleague and slowed to assist him.

Joe whipped by him and closed the gap behind Jarrett. He couldn't tell if the man was intentionally trying to leave the others behind, as the sheriff had suggested, or if he just naturally rode like a bat out of hell.

Jarrett had to slow down once they were in the shadows of the lodgepole forest, because the narrow road took several sharp turns. Joe stayed with him, aided by Nate on the back, who also knew when to use his weight to keep the machine on track. The high-pitched whine of the snowmobiles was muted by his helmet, but it reverberated through the crowded trees and enveloped him in a halo of motorized buzz.

The forest was dense on both sides, with baseball bat–like trunks so close together Joe wasn't sure he could leave the road and maneuver his machine through the trees even if he wanted to. He knew that if he tried to do that, he'd need to relocate the shotgun that straddled his seat. There wasn't enough space between the trees for the length of the weapon from muzzle to butt.

The beam of the headlamp on his Polaris strobed through the trees with each turn and he caught glimpses of Jarrett's red taillight up ahead of him.

Despite the suit and helmet, he could feel icy fingers of cold creeping in through his collar and cuffs. The heated handles of the machine beaded with melted snow that had sifted down through the branches like fine flour.

Before they broke out of the thick stand of trees, Jarrett decelerated suddenly and Joe nearly ran him over. He was able to turn slightly at the last moment so that his left ski missed the back of Jarrett's machine by inches.

"What?" Joe asked him after he turned off his motor. Jarrett had as well. It was so cold that when Joe breathed the raw air in, he felt ice crystals form in his nostrils.

After being pummeled by the high-pitched whine of the Polaris and the reverberation in the trees, the sudden quiet seemed awesome. But it wasn't totally silent. Joe could hear the remaining machines getting closer.

Jarrett lifted his face shield and pointed a gloved finger a half mile ahead through an opening toward where another dense pine forest began. The light was so low that the tree wall to which he was gesturing looked black.

"The cabin I saw is right in the middle of that timber," Jarrett said. "Straight up the road we're on."

Joe couldn't see any lights from an occupied structure, but he thought he caught a whiff of wood smoke, and perhaps a cooking smell.

"Let's wait until the sheriff gets here," Joe said.

"If he ever does," Nate grumbled.

WHEN NEAL FINALLY joined them, he pulled in behind the other five machines and killed his motor. The snow was so deep on both sides of the trail that no one had climbed off their machines for fear they'd sink down past their thighs and have to climb back on.

"What do you think?" Neal asked Jarrett. "Are we close enough to walk in if we stay on the groomed part of the trail?"

"I guess." Jarrett shrugged.

Joe thought he didn't seem very enthusiastic about the idea.

Joe said, "Sheriff, these sleds are *loud*. If he's still up there with her, he's likely heard us coming. I think we can assume we've lost the element of surprise."

Neal nodded in agreement. He said, "Let's bull-rush the son of a bitch."

His deputies all seemed to agree.

Neal said, "Safety first, gentlemen. I don't want anybody getting hurt—including McKnight. He's armed because everybody is, but we don't know if he's desperate or dangerous. Remember—we have probable cause to ask him some questions, but we don't have a warrant for his arrest. Got that?"

"Got it," his men grumbled, even though Joe could tell they were spoiling for a confrontation after coming all this way up the mountain to rescue Kate.

Neal said, "We want to avoid a standoff or a hostage situation if we can. But I don't want him getting away, either. Just remember your training, officers. We don't want an incident."

He rose on his machine so he could see Jarrett in the dying light. "Eli, is there a door in back of that place?"

Jarrett took a minute to think. "I don't think so. Just windows. But don't hold me to that."

Neal pointed to one of his deputies and said, "You go around back when we get there and make sure no one comes out and runs."

Then, to the rest: "We'll all fan out when we get to the cabin. Remember to get behind your snowmobile and use it as cover or find a tree or something. I'll do the talking."

To Jarrett, Neal said, "Stay here and don't even think about running. If you do, we'll track you down like a dog."

Jarrett nodded.

Neal looked at everyone else to make sure they were paying attention, then tipped his head forward so his face shield slid down. Then he unzipped his snowmobile suit so he could access his weapon.

The deputies unsheathed M4 rifles and shotguns and armed their weapons. Joe racked a shell into the chamber of his Remington Wingmaster 12-gauge and checked to make sure the safety was engaged. Behind him, Nate drew his .454 and placed it casually on his thigh.

"Start your machines and mount up, boys," Neal said. *"Go, go, go."* His voice was muffled and tinny because of his closed face shield.

Joe tried to swallow, but his mouth was too dry with anxiety.

SINCE JARRETT HAD been ordered to stay back, Joe led the charge to the cabin. He kept his front skis squarely in the middle of the old road where the trail was and hoped the others behind him stayed in the track he made.

His headlight lit up the trunks of the stand of trees and he plunged into them. The road started a slow bend to the right.

"They're still all with us," Nate shouted.

Joe didn't know how far the cabin was within the forest but he felt its presence dead ahead.

And it was. He saw it all at once: a small dark box-shaped structure opening up on a clear meadow that glowed with ambient moon- and starlight. There was a dim yellow light in one of the front windows and a curl of smoke from the top of a stone chimney. Snow was tramped down around the cabin itself and a path with three-foot walls led to a detached outhouse.

Joe shot by an open loafing shed filled with animal hides stretched and mounted on plywood sheets and on the interior walls. He thought, *A trapper lives here.*

When he turned straight toward the cabin his headlight swept across the front window. He got a glimpse of blond hair near the bottom of the sill. Just like the photo, he thought.

Exactly like the photo.

"See that?" he hollered over his shoulder to Nate.

"Saw something," Nate responded.

Then he felt Nate's hard grip.

"There he goes," Nate yelled.

Joe looked to the right in time to see the headlight of a snowmobile flashing through the stand of trees headed the direction from which they'd all just come. He couldn't get a good look at the driver.

There were two orange star-shaped flashes followed by sharp

cracks. McKnight was firing at them as he fled. Joe had no idea where the rounds had ended up.

Nate's weapon thundered and Joe felt the recoil rock the Polaris. The slug missed the driver but smacked into the trunks of several trees and a shower of snow from the branches turned the grove into a man-made blizzard.

"Missed that bastard," Nate hissed.

Suddenly, Neal was beside Joe as his men raced around them toward the cabin as ordered. Two of the deputies bailed off their snowmobiles and hunkered behind them as they aimed weapons toward the structure. The third raced around back to make sure no one escaped through a window.

"What the hell happened?" Neal asked Joe.

Joe nodded to the grove of trees. "McKnight heard us coming and took off. He shot and Nate returned fire."

"It sounded like a cannon."

"McKnight is behind us," Joe said. "He's headed back down the mountain."

"Did he have Kate with him?"

"Not that I saw. I think she's still inside."

Neal reached into this saddlebag and withdrew an extra-long five-cell MagLite. He flashed the beam on the front of the window and choked it down to reveal the back of a blond head.

"She's not moving," Neal said.

"Not good," Joe said.

Neal accelerated past him and ordered the two deputies in front to chase McKnight and arrest him. Joe couldn't hear the words over the burbling snowmobiles, but he could tell by the sheriff's actions and the reaction of his men what had just occurred. The deputies climbed back on their machines and drove them across the meadow. They entered the stand of trees where McKnight had fired at them to cut McKnight's track.

GUNS DRAWN, Joe and Nate followed Sheriff Neal and his undersheriff onto the rough wood porch of the cabin. They covered him as he shouldered through the front door.

"Oh," he heard Neal say from inside. Then: "Oh, shit."

Joe entered and his initial impression of what he saw at the other end of Neal's flashlight beam was that it looked like a corpse.

She was seated in a hard-backed chair with her back to the window and her long bare legs spread out straight. She wore spiked heels and lacy black lingerie. Her arms hung limp down at her side.

The beam paused on her face: billowing blond shoulder-length hair, large blue eyes, a pert nose, and a wide-open O-shaped mouth.

Neal said, "We came all this way to find McKnight's damn sex doll."

Joe lowered his shotgun and briefly closed his eyes. The tension he felt morphed into humiliation.

"They're going to be talking about this one for years," Neal said.

They meant everyone, Joe knew. Locals, voters, the media, other law enforcement people. Not to mention Chief of Staff Hanlon, Governor Allen, and the British Consolate.

"Well," Nate said, "at least my conspiracy theory is back on the table."

"What theory is that?" Neal asked. His voice was suddenly weary.

Nate ignored the question, but shot Joe a knowing look as he expelled the empty cartridge from his five-shot revolver and replaced it with a live round.

SHERIDAN HAD HEARD SHOTS several minutes before as they echoed through the mountains.

Crack-crack-BOOM.

She turned the fan down on the truck heater so she could listen better, but there were no follow-up gunshots. She glanced over at the other occupied vehicles in the lot.

The snowmobile operator was sitting in the cab of his truck, but she could tell by the blue glow on the side of his face that he was talking on his phone. There was no indication he'd heard anything.

Sophie and Billy Bloodworth were still in the middle of an argument and hadn't heard it either. Their interior light was on. She could see Sophie pointing her finger at Bloodworth and jabbing the air. Bloodworth theatrically covered his ears with his hands for a moment and rolled his eyes toward the sky.

Sheridan cracked the driver's-side window an inch and felt the cold stab into the cab. The whine of an approaching snowmobile was faint at first, but it grew stronger.

Just one snowmobile returning?

Her dad's pickup pointed toward the wall of snow where the sheriff and his team had departed. She assumed whoever was coming was using that same trail.

After a minute, she saw a yellow glow flash through the treetops. Then a single headlight appeared over the embankment of snow and the snowmobile descended into the parking area. The driver paused at the sight of all the vehicles, then apparently made up his mind. The machine launched forward and was coming right at her.

The snowmobile-rental operator opened his door as the machine and driver shot by him. The interior light from his truck gave Sheridan a glimpse of the driver. She recognized McKnight's face through his plastic face mask. He looked angry and determined.

She raised her hand so the bright light wouldn't blind her as it got closer. McKnight seemed to sense that if he got through the parked vehicles he'd be home free.

The roar grew, and Sheridan could see that the man was going to attempt to squeeze through the opening between her dad's truck and Sheriff Neal's SUV. It was a narrow chute.

She unlatched the passenger door and waited until he was almost beside her before she kicked it wide open.

With a *bang* that rocked the pickup, the door took out McKnight's windshield and threw the man to the ground. His machine continued on for fifteen feet behind them before foundering in a drift.

She scrambled outside. McKnight lay motionless on his back with his arms flung out as if making a snow angel. His face mask was spiderwebbed with cracks.

A semiautomatic pistol lay on the packed snow a yard from McKnight's outstretched hand. She lunged forward and picked it up. The steel was cold in her bare hands.

TWO OTHER SNOWMOBILES appeared on the trail. She was grateful they were being driven by deputies.

McKnight was starting to recover from the impact and he groaned and writhed in the snow. She pointed his pistol at him and told him to be still.

Billy Bloodworth's camera flashed repeatedly somewhere behind her.

One of the deputies shut off his motor, climbed from his machine, and said with admiration, "*Damn*, girl. That was a good trick."

21

"THIS'LL BE FUN," JOE SAID SOURLY AS HE PUNCHED IN HANLON'S cell phone number.

It was an hour and a half after they'd all descended from McKnight's cabin and Joe had finally been cleared by Sheriff Neal to depart from the parking lot at the end of the road. Joe and Sheridan had agreed to drive to the sheriff's office in Rawlins the next day to give formal statements. Nate didn't commit.

An ambulance with flashing lights was ahead of them on the highway with McKnight inside. The preliminary diagnosis from the EMTs was that the trapper had a broken jaw, a cracked clavicle, and upper-body contusions.

As he examined McKnight, one of the EMTs had said simply: "Lawsuit."

The call to Hanlon went straight to voicemail, for which Joe was grateful.

He said, "The lead about the cabin turned out to be a dry hole. It wasn't Kate. It wasn't even a person in that photo. I can explain when we talk, but we'll close down that channel of the investigation and start fresh in the morning."

Joe ended the call and dropped the phone to his lap.

"I bet you regret that choice of words," Nate said. *"Dry hole."*

Joe glanced up at the rearview mirror to see Sheridan looking away. She pretended she didn't know what Nate meant.

"I could have phrased it better," Joe said.

Despite the heater running full blast, it was cold inside the truck. The passenger door had been dented by the impact of McKnight's crash and it wouldn't close tightly. Joe had secured it to the doorframe as best he could with duct tape, but the icy wind whistled inside the cab.

THE SCENE IN THE PARKING LOT had been barely controlled chaos once Sheriff Neal and his colleagues returned from the mountain. They were drawn to where Sheridan stood over McKnight in the snow by the flashes of Billy Bloodworth's camera.

Joe wouldn't soon forget the image of Sheriff Neal barking out orders to call for an ambulance with the blow-up doll pinned horizontally under his right arm. Bloodworth took several shots of that, too, and the sheriff ordered him to "get the hell out of my crime scene."

Bloodworth and Sophie sped away toward town, but not before the reporter got quotes from a couple of the deputies about what had happened at the cabin and what they'd found.

Joe assumed Bloodworth was on his phone dictating the scoop to his editor in London. He'd likely upload the photos he'd taken as soon as he got back to Saratoga.

. . .

JOE PARKED NEXT to Sheridan's company pickup at the Silver Creek Ranch so she could go back to her apartment. He said, "You were great up there."

She rolled her eyes. "I injured an innocent pervert."

"Don't forget that he took a couple of shots at us," Joe said. "Sheriff Neal will probably charge him with using deadly force against a law enforcement officer. McKnight's not exactly home free."

"Will he sue all you guys?"

"Probably."

"Will he win?"

"Probably."

"What a night," Sheridan said.

As she climbed out, she patted Nate good-bye on his shoulder and said to Joe, "For what it's worth, I still think Kate is alive."

"You do?"

"Love you, Dad."

"Love you. Call your mother."

"FOLLOW ME IN TO THE WOLF," Nate said as he pushed through the tape holding his door closed so he could get to his vehicle. "We'll dump your truck and you can get in with me. There's something I want to show you."

Joe raised his eyebrows. "Does this have something to do with your conspiracy theory?"

Nate nodded.

. . .

FIFTEEN MINUTES LATER, as the glow from Saratoga smudged the northern horizon and Nate's taillights were ahead, Hanlon called back.

Joe took a deep pull of icy air and answered.

"A fucking doll?"

Joe didn't say, *Literally*. Instead, he said, "Word travels fast."

"A dispatcher at DOT listened to the whole thing on the radio and informed the governor of your latest screwup." He didn't sound enraged, Joe thought. He sounded cold and businesslike.

"I tried to call you earlier," Joe said.

"I was on the phone with him at the time," Hanlon said. "We're trying to decide if we're going to cancel the press conference and come out looking like we're idiots or have it anyway and come out looking like we're idiots. Plus, it sounds like we'll get sued by the innocent trapper you attacked."

"We didn't attack the trapper," Joe said, while trying to keep his voice calm. "If you'll recall, I advised against the press conference until we could confirm the photograph."

"I don't," Hanlon snapped. "Do you remember when I told you the governor wasn't happy with you? Now he just wants you gone. You are officially a non-person as far as this administration is concerned."

Joe let those words sink in, but before he could reply, Hanlon continued. "This is going to make us all look as stupid as you are when it gets out. And it will, thanks to the reporter on the scene. It'll go viral. Governor Allen and law enforcement in the state of Wyoming will be the subject of jokes, thanks to you."

Joe cut in. "When you say he wants me gone, he means I can go back to my district?"

"He doesn't give a shit where you go, as long as he never hears your name again. You're fired, Pickett. We'll send over the paperwork to Game and Fish first thing tomorrow."

Joe was stunned. Images of Marybeth, Sheridan, April, and Lucy flashed before his eyes.

"Maybe we'll change the focus of the press conference," Hanlon said, apparently thinking out loud. "The governor can announce that he's canning the incompetent investigator leading the search for Kate and redoubling his efforts to find out what happened to her. That way, he comes out looking like a determined man of action. Yeah, I *like* that."

Then to Joe: "Lose my number. If you call again, I won't pick up. You've done enough damage already."

"We aren't done," Joe said, suddenly angry. "You need to answer a couple of questions first."

Hanlon scoffed. "You don't get this chain-of-command thing, do you? Ten seconds. You've got ten seconds."

"Why did your office clean out Pollock's house and take his keys after he left?"

"Five seconds."

"What did you do to Pollock to make him leave?"

"Two seconds."

"Why did the governor send me down here?"

"We're done. Have a nice life."

And the line went dead.

22

NINETEEN MILES NORTH OF SARATOGA, JOE SAW THE SEA OF BLINKing red lights as they emerged over the horizon. There were so many of them that the stars faded in the night sky and the untrammeled snowfields in the foreground glowed pink.

Nate eased to the shoulder of the highway and then turned at a ninety-degree angle into the deep snow. When the front end of his Yukon began to bog down, he switched it to four-wheel drive and it lurched forward until the headlights illuminated the top three of a four-strand barbed-wire fence.

Joe didn't ask what they were doing. He was still too numb from the conversation he'd had with Hanlon to focus.

"Look away as I break the law," Nate said.

His friend climbed down out of the vehicle with a well-used fencing tool he'd stashed in the driver's-side door compartment. Joe watched without comprehension as Nate strode through the knee-high snow and pulled the staples from four posts until the wires sagged down. Then he reentered the Yukon, dropped the staples into the ashtray for later, and drove over the top of the fence.

After he cleared the wires, Nate accelerated and the Yukon lurched forward. Joe braced himself as they broke through snowdrifts and ground over tall sagebrush that scraped along the undercarriage of the SUV. After a few minutes, they began to climb a steep hill that had been blown nearly clean of snow. The red lights had vanished from the horizon, but the illuminated sky was dead ahead.

Finally, Joe asked, "Where are we going?"

"To the top."

Joe nodded.

"What's wrong with you, anyway?" Nate asked as they powered up toward the summit. "You haven't said anything since you got in. You didn't even give me a hard time about taking that fence down like you usually do."

Joe had trouble saying the words. He cleared his throat. "Hanlon found out about the botched raid and he fired me. He said the governor wants me gone."

"I'm not surprised."

Joe turned to him. Nate was concentrating on driving the Yukon up the hill and avoiding boulders. He didn't even glance over.

"You're not?" Joe asked.

"It was a matter of time."

"What are you talking about?"

Nate said, "Sometimes you get so close to the case you're working on, you can't see what's going on around you. I don't say this to insult you, but it's something I've observed over the years. It can be an asset that you're so bull-headed, but sometimes it works to your disadvantage. One might think that after you being in the government for so many years, you'd be more cynical. But that's why I like you, Joe: you aren't cynical."

"What I am is confused."

"That, too."

"Where are we going?"

"Up. Until we can't go up any farther without going down."

Joe paused for a second. "Have you ever considered talking like a normal human?"

"*Nyet*," Nate said.

BEFORE HE COULD ASK Nate to explain further, the Yukon broke over the top of the summit and the windshield filled with the blinking red lights. They were more intense than they'd been before because Nate had chosen a location where they could see . . . everything.

The Buckbrush Wind Energy Project stretched across the vast valley as far as Joe could see. The blinking lights on the top of each two-hundred-and-fifty-foot turbine made him wince. Wind buffeted the Yukon and rocked it, and the interior of the vehicle filled with a kind of low subsonic hum from the turbine blades that spun in the dark.

Below the blinking lights, spread across hundreds of acres, were the lone yellow lights from line shacks and maintenance buildings. They were tiny compared to the steel structures that rose before them.

"You're looking at the largest wind energy construction site in the world," Nate said. "It cost five billion dollars' worth of tax breaks and government subsidies to build it, and it exists to fulfill other government mandates about using a certain percentage of 'green energy' thousands of miles away. It's being built so the beautiful people in California can keep their houses cool and their swimming pools heated. Plus, they won't have to get all stressed out about creating their own electrical power and impacting the planet—that they can see, anyway. Out of sight, out of mind. As long as the lights stay on."

Joe smiled and shook his head. "Don't beat around the bush, Nate. Tell me what you really think about it."

Nate actually growled in response.

But Joe couldn't believe the size and scope of the construction in front of them. The moon and the starlight lit up an immense grid of roads that linked up the bases of hundreds of turbines, and the roads glowed pink as well. A single vehicle miles below drove slowly down one of the roads.

"See that truck down there?" Nate asked while he pointed.

"I do."

"Watch what it does and where it goes." He handed Joe a pair of binoculars and Joe focused in. He didn't know why. The truck was too far to see clearly. It was light colored and it moved slowly.

"What am I looking for?" Joe asked.

"You'll know it when you see it. Watch what it does when it goes from the base of one turbine to another."

Joe watched. The truck kept going straight and didn't turn toward the base of the nearest turbine. It drove straight past the second turn-off as well.

"Crap," Nate said. "We picked the wrong night."

"The wrong night for what?"

"The wrong night for my theory to fall into place right in front of your eyes. That's not the truck I was looking for. It looks like they're not out tonight."

Joe lowered the binoculars to his lap. "Your theory?"

"I'll get to that," Nate said. "But first let's talk about you and Governor Allen."

"Go on."

"I told you I'm acquainted with a few falconers around Big Piney, right? Guys who knew Colter Allen when he was a rancher and before he became a politician?"

"Yup."

Nate said, "They knew the guy when he was filthy rich and arrogant. And they knew him when the bottom fell out of all of his investments, but he didn't want anyone to know that fact. When it happened, he'd already decided he was going to run for governor, and all of a sudden he didn't have the money to pull it off on his own. No one could know, though, or it would have destroyed the illusion of his candidacy. Who would vote for a financial failure, especially when the whole idea behind the guy was that he was a winner?"

Joe nodded for Nate to go on.

"So Allen needed backers with enough money to fund him and maintain the illusion. He needed backers who would stay in the background."

Nate paused, and said, "He found two of them. And you can bet he owes them now."

"Who are these people?"

"When you find out who one of them is, you'll know why you were sent down here to Saratoga to fail. It isn't easy firing state employees. There has to be a good reason."

Joe sat up. "What do you mean I was sent down here to fail? The governor said he wanted me to be his range rider like I was for Rulon."

"Don't be naive, Joe," Nate said cruelly. "Allen wants to get as far away from Rulon as he can. He doesn't want anyone comparing him to the last governor, because deep down Allen is insecure. He wants to get rid of anyone who might be loyal to the ex-governor—but he has to do it in a way that doesn't get his hands dirty."

Joe started to rebut what Nate said, but it hit him.

The strange disappearance of Pollock and the looting of Pollock's records. That cleared the deck and prevented Joe from knowing what the former game warden was working on.

The robbery of the case file from his room at the Wolf let someone know for sure why he was down there.

The planned press conference even though Kate could not be positively identified.

The pressure from Hanlon.

The fact that he'd been sent out of his district to take over the case from the DCI in the first place.

All had contributed to the debacle that had occurred at the trapper's cabin, and all had helped establish a pattern of incompetence and failure if spun properly.

Joe said, "Even if what you say is true, that's an awful lot of trouble to go through just to get rid of one game warden."

"It is," Nate said. "And my guess is that Allen didn't figure it all out by himself and then set it into motion. He's not that smart. He turned to a guy who knows how to work the system to do his dirty work."

"Hanlon," Joe said.

"Bingo. He's been pulling the strings like a puppet master."

Joe sat back. He was hurt and tried not to show it. "But why me? Other than I worked for Governor Rulon?"

"Think about it, Joe. Think about the backers. One of them asked for a quid pro quo. Something that backer insisted on before a check was written."

Joe started to ask *Who?* but then it all made sense.

"Missy," Joe said.

"Your mother-in-law," Nate said. "She has the means and she wants you to fail. That way, Marybeth will finally see the light: that she married a loser."

Joe moaned. It was insane, but it fit. Missy Vankueren was nothing if not diabolical.

"How do you know it was her?" Joe said, while the Yukon rocked in a sudden burst of wind.

"My falconer friends saw the two of them together a week or so before he formally announced his campaign. All they knew was that she was some rich lawyer's wife from Jackson Hole. They didn't make the connection, but I did. She's always wanted to bust up your marriage so Marybeth and the girls can live with her in Jackson Hole high-style."

"It won't work," Joe said. "I know my wife. Missy doesn't appreciate or understand her and she never has."

"True, but that won't stop her," Nate said. "Missy wants to finish you off. She's relentless and she's getting crazier by the year."

Joe knew that to be true. Nevertheless, he felt a chill roll through him. "I'm a forty-eight-year-old soon-to-be ex–game warden with one girl in college and the other about to start," he said. "How am I going to support my family? I don't have a Plan B."

Nate nodded and pursed his lips. He didn't disagree.

"Why didn't you tell me?" Joe asked.

"You asked me not to."

Joe rolled his head back and moaned.

. . .

AFTER A FEW MINUTES of silence, Joe asked, "Who was the other backer?"

Nate chinned toward Buckbrush. "You're looking at it."

After that sunk in, Joe winced and asked, "So what's your conspiracy theory?"

"Do you really want to know?"

"That's why I asked."

"Are you sure?"

"Nate, I'm not in the mood."

Nate said, "You know all the elements. They're right in front of you. You just haven't put them together yet."

"Enlighten me," Joe said, trying to keep his annoyance with his friend tamped down.

And for the next twenty minutes, Nate laid it out.

WHEN HE WAS THROUGH, Joe said, "That's pretty crazy."

Nate conceded that. "Do you have a better one?"

"No."

"So how should we proceed?"

Joe thought about it for a minute, then said, "We keep going with the investigation as if nothing had happened tonight—as if I never even talked to Hanlon and you didn't tell me about Missy's role in this. We just keep moving ahead, because that's the last thing Missy or Hanlon or the governor or whoever has been following me will expect."

"How do we do it if you've been fired?" Nate asked.

"It won't be official until they notify my director and they send me the paperwork. It's Saturday night, so the administrative staff at HQ won't be in the office until Monday morning. Plus, I'm not sure they know exactly where to send it. My town house in Saddlestring? The Hotel Wolf? The wheels of state government turn really, really slow. That can work in our favor."

A grin spread across Nate's face. "I like it," he said. "And we'll come back here every night until we've got them?"

"Yup."

"When we nail them, all bets are off," Nate said. "I'm going to go Yarak on their ass. After all, how much more trouble can I get you in?"

"Not much, but let's not talk about that now," Joe said cautiously.

Then: "Maybe we can break everything wide open. If we do that, everything might change."

Nate nodded and his smile remained intact.

"Plus," Joe said, "it's the right thing to do."

Nate laughed. "And just when I was starting to think you were getting more cynical, you come back as Dudley Do-Right after all."

IT WAS EASIER to drive to the highway in their tracks because Nate didn't have to break through the crust of snow.

Nate said, "When you step back and look at everything going on around here, it's more than coincidence that three things happened in this little community at the same time. Kate vanished as they were starting to put up the first turbines of the wind energy project. Then the local game warden just vacates his house and no one knows where he is. Have you thought about how that is?"

"Not really," Joe said. "I don't see the connection at all."

"Do you want me to see how I can work the game warden's and Kate's disappearances into my theory?" Nate asked.

"Not really."

"So you think all three events were random? That each has nothing to do with the others?"

"That's what I think."

"We'll see," Nate said, arching his eyebrows in a conspiratorial way.

Nate gathered his fencing pliers to pound the staples back in as they approached the downed fence. He said, "I'm guessing your talk with Marybeth will be eventful."

"Yup."

But Joe wasn't yet thinking about that. He was recalling the missing files from Pollock's drawer.

Was *B* for Buckbrush?

23

JOE WAS PLEASED TO FIND OUT THAT A ROOM HAD OPENED UP AT THE Wolf for Nate, who got his keys and went upstairs. Kim Miller handed Joe a Saddle Bronc brown ale.

He said, “Thanks, but I didn’t order this.”

“It’s on me. I heard you had a rough day.”

Joe didn’t respond. How much did she know? Was the word already on the street that he’d been fired?

“I’ve never actually seen a blow-up sex doll,” she said, by way of explanation. “Are they as gross as I think they are?”

“Oh, that,” Joe said, relieved. Then: “Yup.”

“It doesn’t surprise me that McKnight had one of those disgusting things. He never seemed to like real people.”

“So you know him,” Joe said.

“I’m the bartender,” she said with a grin. “I know *everybody*.”

“Of course you do.”

"That doll of his looked pretty ridiculous in the picture," she said. "And so does our sheriff."

"The picture?"

Miller swiped at an iPad until the home page for the Daily *Dispatch* website came up. She handed it over to him.

The headlines read: COWGIRL KATE FOLLY: NOTHING BUT HOT AIR!

Followed by: PLASTIC FANTASTIC? *LOVE IN A COLD CLIMATE.*

Joe winced. The article—which of course had Billy Bloodworth's byline—was written in a campy and derogatory style designed to portray the Carbon County sheriff's office in the worst possible light. He referred to the raid as undertaken by "Countrified Keystone Kops." The lead photo was of Sheriff Neal barking out orders while clutching the doll under his arm. The flash from Bloodworth's camera highlighted his fleshy jowls. The flesh-colored vinyl of the doll stood sharply out against the dark background.

There was also a shot of Sheridan standing menacingly over the prone figure of McKnight in the snow. Joe was grateful her back was to the camera so her face wasn't shown. The caption of the photo read:

Cowgirl Tough: This unidentified local female was an eager participant in the Keystone Kops debacle and stands proudly over the injured body of the innocent trapper. Photo by Billy Bloodworth.

Nowhere in the story was it mentioned that the reason for the raid in the first place was the photo on Bloodworth's phone or his claims that he and Sophie had identified the kidnapper and were closing in. The press had its privileges, apparently.

Joe was furious. He would have been less angry if it were a photo of *him*. But his daughter?

He considered chasing Bloodworth down on the highway but the reporter and Sophie had too much of a head start. They were well into Colorado and Joe not only didn't have jurisdiction, he wasn't sure he officially had a job in law enforcement anymore. And the damage was done. He knew it would be only a matter of time before Hanlon and the governor saw the story and used it for their press conference the next morning.

"When I run into this Bloodworth guy, things are going to get real Western," he growled.

"Too late," Miller said. "He and Sophie checked out a couple of hours ago. I heard him say they were driving to the Denver airport."

"Tonight?"

"They checked out in a hurry. She was yelling at him for making her pack up in a rush.

"And they stiffed us," she said while shaking her head. "The company credit card he gave me was rejected and won't go through."

"Oh, man," Joe said.

"It's bad," Miller agreed. "That article makes us all look stupid. I don't think Billy likes us very much."

"No," Joe said. "I don't believe he does."

"Your daughter looks fierce, though," she said while jutting out her chin. "She looks like a warrior."

Joe handed the iPad back to her, but left the beer on the counter. He told her he'd be back for it in a minute.

He climbed into the freezing cab of his truck.

Game wardens in Colorado used the same mutual-aid radio frequency Wyoming wardens used. He'd met several northern Colorado wardens and found them to be just as hardworking, professional, dedicated, and underpaid as their Wyoming brethren.

When the dispatcher responded, Joe said, "This is GF-24. I'd like to request a BOLO in southern Wyoming and northern Colorado for a rental vehicle being driven by two suspects."

He described Bloodworth's four-wheel-drive and gave a brief description of the reporter as well as Sophie. He told the dispatcher the persons of interest were suspected of defrauding an innkeeper, and "possibly other violations."

Joe didn't feel very virtuous about his actions as he went up the icy porch steps into the Wolf.

But what could they do? Fire him again?

HE HAD GATHERED UP his beer and started to mount the stairs when Kim Miller said, "Oh, there's something else I need to tell you. I nearly forgot about it."

He paused.

"Earlier tonight someone called and asked if you were staying here and he asked if he could talk to you. He wouldn't identify himself, and it's our policy not to give out that kind of information."

"Thanks."

"I could hear lots of voices in the background and glasses clinking together. I think he was calling from a bar. I do know what a bar sounds like, you know."

"Any idea who it was?" Joe asked.

"I would swear it was Steve Pollock. I said, 'Steve, is that you?' He just got real quiet. Then I said, 'Steve, this is Kim. I recognize your voice,' and he hung up."

"Did he leave a callback number?"

"No."

Joe said, "Why would he call here and not on my cell phone?"

"Maybe so you *won't* be able to track him down," she said. "He used to come in here all the time. He knows our phones don't have caller ID."

IN ROOM 9, it took nearly a half hour for Joe to recount all the events of the day to Marybeth. She was aware of Sheridan's involvement because she'd talked to her daughter earlier, but she was silent when he told her about his call with Hanlon. Then he told her about Nate's theory about Missy being behind it all.

Marybeth responded with a string of curses unlike anything Joe had ever heard from her before.

"She's really crossed the line," Marybeth said about Missy after she'd calmed down. "I'm absolutely done with her this time. She's gotten so evil and bitter that she doesn't realize how going after you hurts us all. Do you want me to call her out on it?"

"Would it do any good?"

"No. She'd just deny it," Marybeth said. Then wearily, "What are we going to do?"

He knew she was talking about his job.

"I don't have an easy answer." It killed him to admit it. "I'm still a game warden until I get the termination notice in writing from LGD," he said. "Who knows—maybe she might not agree with the governor?"

"Are you kidding me?" Marybeth scoffed. "Linda Greene-Dempsey will do anything to keep her position. Do you really think she'd take some kind of stand on principle?"

He didn't hesitate. "Nope."

"I'll have to sleep on it," she said. "Not that I'll sleep."

He understood and said so. Joe appreciated the fact that Marybeth didn't panic, though she had every reason to do exactly that. Together, they had maybe two months' of savings to cover them without his income. And they didn't even have a house to move into.

He knew there were grievance procedures for wrongful termination in place within the state personnel system, but he was unfamiliar with them. The very idea of pleading his case before a table of bureaucrats filled him with loathing. And deep down, he wasn't sure he could prove that Hanlon and the governor had set him up to fail.

Which he absolutely had so far.

After a long pause, she said, "So you're going to just press ahead as if nothing has happened?"

"Yup." Thinking, *That's all I know how to do.*

"You don't owe those people. Plus, it isn't like we knew Kate and she's important to us. You could just pack up and come home."

"I know that," Joe said.

"But you can't, can you? You're like a dog with a bone. I know you. You won't quit."

He didn't respond. She knew him better than he knew himself.

"In that case," she said, "I do think I'm onto something with Kate, but I can't confirm it a hundred percent yet."

Joe sat up.

She said, "I was able to get into her Facebook timeline even though I'm not her friend and she had privacy settings on."

"How were you able to do that?" Joe asked warily.

"There are ways. I learned this one from Lucy."

Their youngest daughter was adept at using social media and it came naturally to her. Joe didn't realize she was capable of hacking into a private account, though.

Marybeth continued. "It appears Kate liked a group called Cowboys Are My Weakness. The group is made up of like-minded women from all over, but most are from the U.S. or UK.

"They're cougars, Joe. Wealthy women who travel to pursue young cowboys. They have memes like 'Wrangler Butts Drive Me Nuts' and that sort of thing. They post photos of cowboys they've been intimate with, or at least they claim they've been intimate with. I think Kate posted a few of the photos, but I can't confirm it yet. If she did, it was under the alias 'Miss Kitty.'"

"Miss Kitty?" he asked. "Like the *Gunsmoke* lady?"

"That's right," Marybeth said, warming to it. "The redheaded one with the beauty mark. Anyway, Miss Kitty liked a lot of the photos posted on the group page. Kate wasn't the most prolific user on the page by any means, but it's obvious she spent time on that site. And she posted a few photos of her own."

"You're good," Joe said with admiration. "This is new. DCI missed that, and so did Billy Bloodworth and the British tabloids."

She said, "Maybe it takes a woman to have a feel for what other women want."

He agreed without saying, *I never know what women want.*

Instead, he asked, "Is there anything on the site about her stay at the Silver Creek Ranch?"

"Yes. I can't confirm Miss Kitty is absolutely Kate, but there are a few photos posted on the page that correspond to the July dates when Kate was there. I recognize some of the buildings from the Silver Creek Ranch in the background. And there's one photo in particular you'd recognize. I just sent it to your phone while we were talking."

"Hold on," Joe said. He activated his email and found it. It was a shot of wranglers saddling up horses in the golden light of early dawn. Sheridan could be clearly seen throwing a saddle on the back of a roan.

"See her?" Marybeth said.

Joe didn't respond, because although Sheridan was identifiable, it was obvious the photo wasn't specifically taken of her. She just happened to be there.

"Do you see your daughter?" Marybeth asked again.

"Yup."

In the foreground, pulling on the cinch strap of a saddle, was a young cowboy. Marybeth hadn't recognized him because she'd never met him before.

But Joe had.

"The cowboy in the photo is Lance Ramsey," he said.

"You mean . . ."

"That's what I mean. What does Miss Kitty say about Lance?" he asked.

"She wrote, *Yippee-Ki-Yay*," Marybeth said glumly.

"Is that it?"

"Yes, but it's clear what she meant."

He said, "She must have played that really close to the vest, though. The GM of the ranch wasn't aware of that and neither was Sheridan, who has good instincts."

"Almost as good as mine," Marybeth said.

Joe asked, "Why would she post it, unless . . ."

"Let's not jump to conclusions, Joe," Marybeth warned. "There might be a good explanation. Maybe Miss Kitty—I mean Kate—was trying to put one over on the other cougars in the group. Or maybe not. Either way, Sheridan will need to know at some point."

Joe nodded, even though Marybeth couldn't see him.

"She's not going to like this new development," Marybeth said.

"I don't either," Joe said.

"It might break her heart."

"I might break his head."

"Joe . . ."

"I'M STILL RESEARCHING Richard Cheetham," Marybeth said. "I'm not finding much and certainly not anything to implicate him."

"I'll keep him ranked low on the suspect list," Joe said.

"There is something interesting, though. When I did an image search on his name, I found several photos of Richard and Sophie together. The most recent one was of them leaving some kind of formal charity shindig in their finest clothes."

"What's interesting about that?" he asked.

"The photo was from a month ago. Supposedly when Sophie was distraught about finding her missing sister. Doesn't it seem odd that she'd go to a formal event with her ex-brother-in-law?"

"Didn't he remarry?"

"Yes, he did. It lasted a few months and he's back on the market again."

"Hmm."

"There may be a simple explanation for it," she said. "I'll keep digging."

THEY TALKED FOR another twenty minutes until his phone was nearly out of power and he had to sign off, find the charger, and plug it in.

He realized he'd forgotten to tell her that Steve Pollock had resurfaced and had inquired about him.

Joe lay fully clothed on his bed and stared at the inert ceiling fan. It wasn't spinning like his mind was. He visualized Marybeth doing exactly the same thing in the town house. He wished she were here.

Finding out about "Miss Kitty" framed Kate's disappearance differently, and in a way that he'd really need to think about.

Coincidences began to harden into connections under the Miss Kitty light.

Sunday morning couldn't come soon enough, he thought. It was a matter of time before his walking papers came through and he could no longer continue the investigation in an official capacity.

Yippee-Ki-Yay.

PART FOUR

The difference between the new managerial elite and the old propertied elite defines the difference between a bourgeois culture that now survives only on the margins of industrial society and the new therapeutic culture of narcissism.

—Christopher Lasch

24

THAT SAME HOUR, GAYLAN KESSEL SWUNG HIS COMPANY PICKUP INTO the outside lot of the Memorial Hospital of Carbon County on West Elm Street in Rawlins. He drove to the far back row, where the overhead lights wouldn't reach, and he backed the vehicle into a slot and killed the headlights but not the engine. There were fewer than ten cars in the lot, and Kessel's pickup was the only one in the last row, which was backed by a frozen wall of plowed snow.

Ted Panos glanced down at the large envelope that lay on the front seat between them. It had been there since they left Saratoga, but the contents were a mystery to him. Also unexplained was why Kessel had texted Panos to dress in a sports coat and slacks instead of his usual Carhartt overalls and pac boots. The term Kessel used was *business casual.*

Panos had replied, *ur kidding, right?*

When Kessel hadn't responded, Panos had closed his eyes and

tried to keep his heart from racing. Going out late at night wasn't unusual, but going out "business casual" certainly was. Something bad was going to happen. Panos had felt it inside when his heart started to race.

Before pulling on his too-tight dress slacks and brushing a coat of white dust from the shoulders of a suit jacket he'd last worn to a funeral—it still had a folded-up memorial card in the pocket—he riffled through his shaving kit and found the plastic container of bootleg Percocet that had helped him get through similar situations before. He couldn't recall if he was supposed to take one or two five-milligram tablets, so he swallowed two whole and put two more in his pocket for later.

The medication began to rise through him like an internal blanket of calm even before Kessel arrived in the hotel parking lot.

NOW KESSEL POINTED a stubby finger toward the entrance marked EMERGENCY.

"That's where you'll go in," Kessel said to Panos as he handed him a short-brimmed fedora. "Put that on and walk in there like you do it every day of your life. Don't go in looking suspicious and sneaky. And don't look up directly at any of the closed-circuit cameras. Keep your head down."

Panos clamped the hat on his head. It fit.

"Do you remember everything I told you on the way here?" Kessel asked. He said it in a clipped, disinterested military way. It was Kessel at his most annoying, Panos thought.

"Of course I do." The second word came out *coursh.*

"Why are you slurring?"

"I'm not slurring."

Kessel glared at him and his eyes reflected the distant red light from the EMERGENCY sign.

"Ted, you better be clean for this. Have you been drinking?"

"No, sir."

"Are you sure you're okay?"

"Yes, sir."

In fact, Panos felt more relaxed than he had in quite some time. So relaxed that he fought back a wide smile that would only enrage his boss.

"Tell me who you're looking for?" Kessel asked.

"Carol Schmidt."

"Where will she be?"

Panos had to concentrate to remember what Kessel had told him on the drive there. He'd feigned attention at the time because he was basking in the Percocet calm. It reminded him of a warm bath but from the inside out. Or cloudy pillows floating through his entire body and into his brain. He didn't dare tell Kessel.

"Carol Schmidt will be located in the critical care unit," Panos said. "That unit is located to the right of the reception desk down a hallway."

Kessel continued to stare at Panos as if he could see his thoughts, but he didn't correct him or interrupt. Apparently, he'd passed the quiz.

What Panos *could* remember clearly was how in awe of Schmidt Kessel seemed to be. He couldn't believe she'd lasted the night after she went off the road and was transported to Rawlins. He'd called her a "tough old bird."

And there was something about a head injury, a medically induced coma, and that she may or may not emerge from it with the ability to recall what had happened to her on the highway to Encampment.

That was why they were there in the parking lot. Carol Schmidt was the reason for business casual.

KESSEL OPENED THE ENVELOPE and handed Panos a lanyard with a plastic Memorial Hospital of Carbon County badge with Panos's driver's license photo on it.

"Whoa—where'd you get this?" Panos asked, meaning the photo.

"I know some people who work here," Kessel said, meaning the hospital. "That's where I got the intel that she's here and where she's located."

Panos didn't follow up on the misunderstanding because deep in his brain he knew that the more he talked, the greater chance there'd be he would say something foolish or ridiculous. The Percocet was now playing sentimental show tunes in his ears.

"Don't do anything stupid or obvious," Kessel said. "Don't hit her over the head or choke her out, I mean. It's got to look like she passed in her sleep."

"So what do I do?" Panos asked. He was amazed how cool and calm he sounded.

"Size up the situation and make a decision," Kessel said. "Look for machines to shut off, or tubes to disconnect. If nothing else, use a pillow. Just don't leave her so anyone suspects anything. Use your best judgment. Got that?"

"Got it," Panos said.

"Remember, you need to walk into that hospital like you've been in there a hundred times before. You're a pharmaceutical rep who usually makes calls on docs during the day shift, but you left an important file in one of the offices and you didn't realize it until you got back to your hotel. The receptionist won't know you because she's only there at night. You're there to retrieve your file."

With that, Kessel handed Panos the envelope from the seat of the truck. "Stick that down the back of your pants so no one sees it when you walk in. Make sure it's in your hand on the way out."

"What's in it?" Panos asked.

"What does that fucking matter?" Kessel asked, his teeth flashing in the red light. "It's a ruse."

"Right," Panos said.

"Her name will be written outside her room on a whiteboard," Kessel said. "Get in and get out. Don't take any longer than it would take to retrieve a file."

"Got it." Then: "Why am *I* the one doing this?" Kessel got still. Panos regretted the question immediately. But he was feeling his oats. The drug had flattened his first line of caution.

"Because. Ted." Kessel said, saying each word as if it were a sentence in itself, "*People. Around. Here. Fucking. Know. Me.* They don't know you. If I went in there, someone would say, 'Hey—I saw him in the newspaper, or Hey—he spoke at my Rotary Club.'

"Use your fucking brain, Ted," Kessel said. "Now, go."

"I didn't sign up for this kind of dirty work. Especially against an old woman I don't even know."

Kessel lowered his chin slightly, but kept his eyes wide open and probing. "You signed up to do what's necessary, same as me. I did my part, but somehow she lasted the night. Now it's up to you to finish the job.

"It's for the greater good," Kessel said. "That old woman could stand in the way of . . . *everything*. She doesn't know how much she knows, but she recognized me. If she wakes up and starts yammering, it's all over. I explained this to you. Didn't you listen?"

Actually, no, Panos thought. He'd zoned out during that part of Kessel's monologue on the way there.

Panos grasped the door handle, but didn't yet open it. "Will I get a bonus for this? This is a lot to ask. I better get *something*."

"You'll get something," Kessel said. "I promise."

Panos wasn't sure he could believe him. But in his medicated state, he wasn't completely sure what he was hearing for certain and what he *thought* he was hearing. So he let it drop. But he was glad he was numb. He could never do what he was about to do in his right mind.

He opened the door and the cold hit him right away. Sobered him up a little, which was good.

He fumbled for a minute getting the file into the back of his pants and it almost got embarrassing. Finally, though, he managed to slide it inside his waistband. He covered it fully when he buttoned his ancient trench coat and walked from Kessel's truck toward the hospital doors.

Panos could feel his boss's eyes on his back, so he moved slowly, deliberately. It wouldn't be good if he slipped on ice and fell.

He wished the trench coat was lined, because it barely kept him warm.

But it was the only thing he owned that was business casual.

A WOMAN WITH a carrot-colored bouffant and glasses looked up from her game of computer solitaire as Panos pushed through the double doors. A sign on the counter in front of her read MAGGIE WHITE.

He reminded himself that he had been inside the building a hundred times, even though he hadn't.

"Evening, Maggie," he said with faux familiarity, as he flashed his lanyard. "I'm Phil with Pfizer"—it was the only pharmaceutical company he could come up with on the fly—"and this afternoon I left a file I need down the hall. It'll just take a minute."

He didn't make eye contact with her. Just kept moving.

Don't stop and chat. Was it left or right at the counter?

He turned on his heel and strode on. To the right.

"Sir?" she called after him. "Phil?"

He kept going. He was suddenly sweating and his vision blurred.

Panos made himself slow down, calm down. Maggie White wasn't pursuing him down the hallway and he didn't hear her call for security. She'd be there when he came back with the file in his hand, he figured.

Head down. Don't even glance up to see where the cameras are.

Look for the whiteboard that says Carol Schmidt is inside the room.

Her name was scrawled on the outside of a door halfway down the hallway.

IT TOOK LESS than a minute. Panos opted for using a pillow since the machines that were attached to her looked complicated and the tubes were filled with clear liquid that he figured she could likely do without.

It was dark inside the room, although the screens and monitors put out enough ambient light that he could see. One of the machines issued a rhythmic *click-click-click.*

She was older than he thought she'd be and smaller than he'd imagined. Her eyes were closed.

Her feet fluttered under the blankets and she reached out with a small bony hand to try and grasp his wrist, but she couldn't find it. He held the pillow firmly on her face until she went limp, then placed the pillow back under her head when she was gone. He refused to look directly at her gape-mouthed face.

Panos stepped back and took a breath that filled his lungs. As he did so, he realized he'd lolled his head back. He quickly lowered it, but not before eyeing the single red light in the top corner of the room that may or may not have been a closed-circuit camera.

He put that out of his mind.

Streams of sweat poured down his collar. He fumbled the envelope again as he pulled it from his waist and he dropped it on the linoleum floor. Papers scattered and he shoved them back in the file.

In and out, like Kessel had said.

Would there be alarms going off now that she was dead? Buzzers?

But there was nothing. Maybe some nurse at a different station could see the monitor flatline, but Panos wanted to be out of the hospital by the time someone had the chance to react.

"Thanks," he said to Maggie White as he passed by the desk and turned away from her.

"You forgot to sign in," she called after him. It wasn't threatening or unfriendly. More like, *You know the drill.*

But he pushed through the double doors and was outside.

The cold actually felt good on his skin for once.

He was halfway across the parking lot when he saw that Kessel was no longer there.

Panos stopped and said, "*Fuck me.*"

He turned and nearly lost his footing on the glazed-over snow. His arms windmilled, but he was able to regain his balance.

He could see Maggie White stand up through the double doors. The receptionist was witnessing a nurse in green scrubs jog from left to right in front of her. Obviously, the nurse had seen the monitor, Panos thought. He hoped it was one of the life-monitor machines and not a closed-circuit video feed.

Because the nurse didn't turn her head to see where he'd gone, he guessed it was one of the machines.

He looked around. Rawlins was dark, cold, and absolutely lifeless. The cold was freezing his face and inching up his cuffs and pant legs.

He thought, *Why would . . .*

A pair of headlights flashed on and Kessel's pickup appeared on the street he'd just crossed. Kessel had left the lot and was waiting outside somewhere on the street while Panos had gone inside. Panos figured the man had probably chosen a different location to observe so he could make a fast lone getaway if Panos was caught inside.

His boss leaned over in his seat and pushed open the passenger door.

"Get in," he said.

Panos scrambled in and sat back while Kessel drove away toward I-80.

KESSEL DIDN'T SPEED or do anything to attract attention from hidden cops. They caught a break when the few stoplights on Cedar Street were blinking amber due to the late hour.

"It's done," Panos said.

"How?"

"Smothered."

"She go quietly?"

"I guess."

Panos recalled her kicking feet beneath the blanket and it affected him more deeply in retrospect than it had when he'd been in the room.

"Texas," Kessel said. "You're going to Texas."

"Texas?"

"It's warmer there. You'll do down there what I do up here. It's a promotion, and a big one."

Panos thought about it. "So *that's* my reward?"

"Yes. Either there or Iowa."

So Kessel had been talking to the big bosses about him. He wondered if he'd talked to them before he picked him up in Saratoga or while he was inside the hospital. Not that it mattered.

Panos had never been to Iowa and he sometimes got it confused with Idaho or Ohio. But he knew Texas.

"Okay," he said.

"Good. But we're not done here. We've got a lot to do before the end of the week."

Panos nodded. He realized that the emotion he'd felt about recalling the final moments of the old woman might be the result of the Percocet wearing off. He fished in his pocket for the remaining two and swallowed them dry. He did it in a furtive movement when Kessel's eyes were on the road.

"There's a couple of snoops down here we need to take care of," Kessel said. "It's high priority and it might get a little hairy."

Panos sat back and waited for the warm bath to wash through him once again. Obviously, Kessel had obtained some new information about these "snoops."

He hoped he had enough medication to last through whatever came next.

BACK IN THE HOSPITAL, the emergency nurse approached Maggie White at the desk and sighed, "She's gone."

White shook her head. "I'll call the tech."

The technical administrator was in charge of securing the room until the morning shift arrived. The body would remain there until the next of kin was notified and the body moved downstairs into the morgue.

The nurse said, "Make sure you note that someone forgot to change the patient's name on the whiteboard after we moved Schmidt to the second floor this afternoon."

"I'll do that," White said as she checked the patient roster on her monitor. "So it was Mrs. Alvarez who passed?"

"Yes. Pneumonia in a woman that age . . ."

She thought about telling the nurse about Phil with Pfizer, but didn't. He'd only been there for a minute and he was gone.

25

SHERIFF NEAL LEANED BACK HEAVILY IN HIS CHAIR AND TOSSED A folded copy of the *Rawlins Daily Times* across his desk toward Joe and Nate.

Joe didn't open it. He could see the photo of Neal clutching the blow-up sex doll that had first appeared in the *Daily Dispatch.* It was on the front page.

"We all look like a bunch of damn fools," Neal said. "*I* look like the biggest fool of all."

Joe said, "Yup."

"You don't have to agree with me. It's gonna be a long nine months until the election."

Nate shifted next to Joe. He was eager to get going. They'd both given their statements and Nate didn't want to spend another minute in the Carbon County sheriff's department office than he had to. Nate, Joe knew, was uncomfortable in these kinds of surroundings.

"What about Les McKnight?" Joe asked.

"He's got a busted nose and cheekbone and a concussion," Neal said. "Your daughter clocked him a good one. The hospital said he'll have to stay there a few days before they can release him. Word is he's taking calls from lawyers looking to sue the department. You and especially your daughter will probably be safe, though. They'll go after the deep pockets.

"We're gonna bargain with him," Neal said. "After all, he did take a couple of shots at us. We might be able to get the suit dropped in exchange for making the attempted assault charges go away."

Joe winced. The negotiations would be messy and he hoped he could stay out of them. After all, McKnight could claim quite credibly that he was defending his home at night from attackers who'd not identified themselves. And owning a doll wasn't probable cause for an all-out raid.

"I didn't go to morning coffee today," Neal said. "I thought I might end up saying something I'd later regret."

After a beat, he said, "What a mess."

"Yup."

"Trouble does seem to follow you around, doesn't it?" Neal asked Joe.

"Seems to."

Joe turned his head. Neal's office was on the second floor of the county building and his window overlooked a brick building across the street. In a scene that looked like something out of the Depression, a line of men stood outside in the cold waiting to go inside. They shuffled their feet and clouds of condensation rose from their mouths. Blue-collar workers, Joe thought. He noted heavy boots, Carhartt coats, and insulated overalls.

"What's going on over there?" he asked.

"Hiring for Buckbrush," Neal said. "The company leased out that empty building a month ago as their headquarters for hiring. We've had guys show up from all over the country trying to get on with that outfit."

Joe heard Nate snort with derision but ignored him.

"Construction jobs are hard to come by," Neal said. "Some of those guys were laid off for a couple of years. It's gonna be a real good thing for the county, that wind farm. Good for the tax base while they build it. After that, the workforce will be fairly small. But we'll deal with that a few years down the road. We're used to boom-and-bust cycles around here."

"Are there any new leads on Kate's disappearance?" Joe asked. "I mean, good ones?"

"I think I'm out of the Kate business for a while," Neal said with a heavy sigh. "Maybe you should be, too."

NATE STAYED IN JOE'S PICKUP with the heater running, in front of the Carbon County hospital.

Inside, the front desk confirmed to Joe that Joshua Teubner had been admitted the day before for an accidental gunshot wound to the shoulder. His prognosis was good.

As he walked back to his truck, Joe realized that in the last two days, at least three people had been sent to the hospital building behind him: Joshua Teubner, Les McKnight, and the older woman from Saratoga who'd slid off the ice on the road. At this rate, he thought, the hospital would be full and Saratoga empty within a short time.

Trouble does seem to follow you around, doesn't it?

. . .

HIS PHONE BURRED as he climbed into the cab. It was another unknown number.

Joe punched it up. The connection was filled with static.

"Is this Joe Pickett?"

"It is."

"This is Jeb Pryor."

It took Joe a few seconds to recall the man. "Yes?"

"I'm the owner of the Encampment lumber mill. We met the other night at the Wolf."

"Gotcha. What can I do for you?"

"I've got something I need to talk to you about. I think you'll have an idea what to do about it."

"What is it?"

Pryor started to speak when Joe's phone chirped and the call dropped. Cell service was as unreliable in Carbon County as it was in Twelve Sleep County. Joe lowered the phone to his lap.

"Is Josh Teubner in there?" Nate asked, glaring at the hospital.

"Yup."

"Want me to go talk with him and get his phone?"

"Nope."

"Maybe he'll recall a little more about that conversation he overheard if he's got a clear head for once."

"Nate . . ."

The phone lit up again with UNKNOWN NUMBER.

"Mr. Pryor?" Joe said.

The line was clear this time. So clear, he could hear someone breathing.

"Joe?" It was a familiar voice.

"Yes."

"Steve Pollock. I hear you've been asking about me."

Pollock spoke softly, as if he didn't want anyone near him to overhear.

"Where are you, Steve?"

"I'm in Cheyenne, but I'm on my way to Arizona. I find that I can't stand this cold and wind anymore now that I don't have to be out in it."

Joe had the feeling that Pollock was making the call with reluctance. And that he might disconnect at any second.

"Steve, I think you know I'm in Saratoga. What happened over here?"

"Shit. Shit happened."

Pollock sounded resigned and morose.

"Would you like to talk about it?" Joe asked.

"I'm not sure."

"I'll come to you."

Pollock laughed a bitter laugh. "Yeah, there's no way I'm coming back over there."

"I'll come to you in Cheyenne. How long are you going to be there?"

Pollock hesitated so long, Joe looked at his phone to make sure they were still live. They were.

"I'm leaving early tomorrow," Pollock said. "I don't plan to be back."

"I'll meet you this afternoon."

"Man, I don't know if this is such a good idea after all."

"One conversation," Joe said. "Game warden to game warden. It'll just be between us. No one at headquarters needs to know we talked."

After another long pause, Pollock said, "I can trust you, can't I, Joe?"

"Yup."

"Alf's Pub on Nineteenth. I'll be at a booth in the back. Leave your recorder in your truck and don't bring anybody else, okay?"

Joe agreed and Pollock killed the call.

"Going to Cheyenne?" Nate asked.

He nodded.

"Bad things happen there."

Joe didn't want to start an argument. He knew Nate's experiences in Cheyenne—his confinement to an off-the-books federal lockup facility for nearly a year—were much different from his own encounters at the state capital.

Nate said, "While you're gone, I'll circle back on a few things and keep my eye on Sheridan."

"Are the few things Kate-related or conspiracy theory–related?" Joe asked.

"Maybe both," Nate said. "Drop me at the Wolf so I can get out and switch over to my outfit. Yours is too cold inside with this crappy door."

Joe agreed. Then: "Nate, we really don't want another interrogation that results in another local going to that hospital, if you know what I mean."

Nate grunted.

JOE TOLD HIM about the call he'd received from Jeb Pryor.

"You could save me some time if you went and talked to him. Maybe find out what he was calling about and why he thinks I'd be interested in what he has to say. Give me a call after and we'll figure out our next move."

"I'll do it. I've got some business that direction anyway."

Joe nodded. He said, "I can't really ask you to do this in any official capacity, because I'm not sure I even have an official capacity anymore. What I do know is I don't have much time left to pretend I do."

"I'm taking my fish," Nate said, after turning in his seat to confirm it was still in the back of the pickup.

"If you have to," Joe said.

AFTER CHECKING THE WYDOT APP on his phone to find out that I-80 East between Elk Mountain and Laramie was once again closed due to high winds and blowing snow, Joe turned south toward Highway 230 to Laramie and beyond that to Cheyenne. It was the only remaining west-to-east route that was still open.

No interstate highway was closed as much as I-80 through southern Wyoming. The locals still complained that the feds should never have built it where they did, and there were still postcards available along the route that read: *I survived the Snow-Chi-Min Trail.*

Two-thirty was a lonely two-lane highway with narrow shoulders surrounded on both sides by endless white punctuated by distant ranch buildings. Blowing snow had glazed the blacktop shiny with ice and he slowed down and guided his pickup from milepost to milepost on the far-right side of the lane, where there were a few dry patches. Several times, he stopped dead while the ground blizzards smoked across the road and he waited for them to clear up so he could see. As he drove, he was careful not to clip the posts with his exterior mirrors.

Oncoming traffic consisted of three vehicles total. The drivers looked over at him furtively as they passed, then resumed their concentration.

The route wound up into the heavy timber of the Medicine Bow Forest and dipped into northern Colorado before re-crossing the Wyoming border. Thick lodgepole pine trees slowed down the blowing snow from drifting across the highway, although acres of beetle-killed timber did little to help. He saw a herd of brown and beige elk with ice crystals imbedded in their thick fur trudging single file along the borrow pit with their heads down as if on a forced march to slaughter. In one mountain meadow, he saw the forlorn heads of sage grouse poking just above the surface of the snowpack as if looking around for relief from the weather.

Snowmobilers raced around on groomed and ungroomed trails near WyColo Lodge and he eyed them warily to make sure none of them darted out onto the road in front of him.

Wind whistled inside the cab because of the damaged door, and his heater, even on full, couldn't compete with the cold. He turned on the radio to distract himself from the fact that his fingers and toes were getting numb.

He caught the middle of the hourly newscast from KOWB out of Laramie.

". . . In the case of missing British public relations executive Kate Shelford-Longden, Governor Allen said in a rare Sunday-morning press conference this morning that the state would be redoubling its investigation after purging the effort of what he referred to as 'incompetent state employees' . . ."

He quickly turned it off.

. . .

ON GOOD ROADS, it took a little more than two hours to drive from Saratoga and Cheyenne. Joe was approaching hour three as he finally rolled through snow-blasted Laramie. He hoped Pollock's resolve would hold until he could get to Alf's Pub in Cheyenne.

The snippet he'd heard on the radio from the governor's press conference had planted a dark seed of defeat in Joe's belly. Despite what Pollock might tell him—if he was there at all—Joe doubted it would get him any closer to unraveling Kate's disappearance.

He felt very alone on the highway and in his own head. Although he still had his badge, pickup, and uniform shirt, he wasn't sure he was even acting in an official capacity anymore. His end as a game warden and state employee was approaching fast. They'd cut off his state gasoline credit card and delete his email account. Rent would stop being paid on his temporary housing in Saddlestring.

Joe would be adrift and he'd be dragging his family along for the ride.

His mother-in-law, Missy, had finally exacted her revenge, and she'd done it in a sophisticated way from the comfort of her Jackson Hole compound and likely using her most recent husband's fortune. And she'd done it in a way that provided her cover.

Joe knew he could probably never prove that she was behind his sacking, unless Governor Allen admitted to the quid pro quo, which was highly unlikely. Allen took no responsibility for his bad choices and decisions. He admitted to nothing and never apologized. If something bad happened, it was because of the actions of others and their lack of loyalty to him.

There was a lot of that going on these days, Joe thought.

Missy's involvement in sending Joe into a no-win situation made a perverse kind of sense to him only because he knew where her motivations lay. With Joe unemployed and adrift, she thought Marybeth might have to turn back to her for financial assistance and possibly even housing. Library directors in small towns didn't make much money, and mortgages and college tuition didn't pay for themselves.

Plus, he thought, Missy could claim that she'd been right about Joe all along. In the end, he couldn't provide for his family.

Marybeth was too smart to fall for that and she was tougher than Missy ever gave her credit for.

Still, though . . .

HE NEVER SHOULD have agreed to be Allen's range rider, he thought, even though he hadn't seen it as a choice at the time. Allen was not Rulon and never would be. Rulon had always maintained plausible deniability when sending Joe out on an assignment, in case he screwed it up, but Rulon never threw him under the bus when things went pear-shaped.

Rulon's motivations had come from a lofty place, even if they were sometimes misguided. Politicians like Allen, with a fake biography and a recent pasted-on ideology, came from a different place altogether.

Joe was conflicted. He no longer wanted to be on Allen's team even if he hadn't been fired, but at the same time he couldn't simply walk away from Kate's disappearance without knowing what had happened to her.

Kate Shelford-Longden was a real person made up of flesh and blood. What if she were Marybeth or one of his own daughters?

. . .

JOE PARKED HIS PICKUP at the back side of Alf's Pub and Package Liquor so it couldn't be seen from the street. Green Game and Fish pickups were easily identifiable, especially in the capital city where the headquarters was located. He didn't want Director LGD or any of her toadies seeing the vehicle parked in the lot of a bar in the middle of the afternoon and stopping to roust him.

He paused after entering, and the door wheezed closed behind him. It took a moment for his eyes to adjust from the bright white ocean of snow outside to the darkness of the bar.

Neon beer signs, television monitors, a longhorn bull skull above the bar all emerged from the gloom.

And there in the back, seated behind a small table in a brown faux-leather chair, was Steve Pollock. Pollock was out of uniform and wearing a thick University of Wyoming hoodie and jeans. Next to him was a wide-shouldered man in a jacket and tie. He looked nervous.

Joe walked up and tipped the brim of his hat to them.

"I thought it was just going to be us," Joe said to Pollock.

"Joe, meet Michael Williams of DCI."

Joe shook his hand and sat down.

Pollock said, "We thought we'd all have plenty to talk about, since the three of us have all been disappeared by the governor."

26

ON HIS WAY SOUTH FROM SARATOGA TO THE ENCAMPMENT LUMBER mill, Nate took a once-familiar turnoff from the highway. It was a ranch access road a mile past the frozen North Platte River. He noted there was already a set of tire tracks in the snow ahead of him.

Dr. Kurt and Laura Bucholz had sheltered him two years before when he'd been hiding out from federal charges. The ranchers had allowed him and Liv Brannon to hide out in a small log cabin near the river and stay off the grid. They'd allowed it even though the two of them were patriotic and law-abiding people who could have been arrested for harboring a fugitive.

The feds had eventually located him on the ranch and they'd offered him a devil's bargain: work with them on a secret mission in Wyoming's Red Desert or be prosecuted. Additionally, the agents had threatened Liv and the Bucholz couple with arrest. He'd jumped at the deal because he didn't have a choice. But he'd never really said good-bye to the ranch couple or properly thanked them for all they'd done for him and Liv.

When he made the turn through the stark river cottonwoods, he didn't expect to find the ranch house empty and all the vehicles and ranch equipment gone, including the stock trailers. Or the single new-model company pickup backed up to the front door of the ranch house with a pile of clothing, furniture, and artwork in the back. He recognized the possessions as having belonged to the Bucholzes.

He narrowed his eyes and felt a tremor of rage roll down his back.

Nate drove his SUV up to the grille of the company truck so the bumpers were nose to nose and he leapt outside without turning off the motor. His right hand was on the grip of his .454 inside his coat.

A man came out of the house with an armful of clothing, but didn't see him standing there because the pile blocked his vision. He tossed the items into the bed of the truck.

Only when he heard the *snick-snick* of Nate's weapon being cocked did he look up quizzically.

He was a young man, early twenties. He wore a stocking cap pulled down over his ears and he had a long bushy ZZ Top–style reddish beard sequined with ice. He looked to Nate like what he was: an employee of Buckbrush Power. The company name on the outside of his jacket and the logo on the door of the pickup confirmed it.

"Who are you and what are you doing?" Nate hissed. The front sight of the gun fit neatly between the Buckbrush man's widening eyes.

"I'm Earl Wright. Don't shoot me. *Don't—don't shoot me.*"

He was stammering.

"Where are Kurt and Laura?"

"Who?" Wright asked, genuinely confused.

"The people who used to live here."

"Oh, is that who they were?"

Nate's finger tightened on the trigger and Wright saw it.

"I never met them," Wright said quickly. "I'm just doing what I was told to do. I don't know anything about no Kurt and Laura. From what I understand, they moved out a few weeks ago."

"Then why are you here?"

"My company bought the place," Wright said. "I guess one of the executives wants to live on a ranch. I don't know much more than that. I was told to come out here and clean the place out. I just do what I'm told. If you have an issue with it, I'm not the guy to talk to."

Nate believed him. He lowered the weapon to Wright's belt buckle.

"Hell," Wright said, "I'm a coal miner. I live in Hanna and I didn't have a job once they closed the mines up there. This is the only thing I could find. Buckbrush is the only outfit hiring right now. When I'm told to do something, I don't ask too many questions about why."

The possible scenario made some sense. The Bucholz ranch was kept afloat by Dr. Bucholz's medical practice, not by the income generated by the cattle operation. Nate knew that. It was a similar story on most small family-owned operations.

The good doctor was getting old. The only day a small ranch was successful financially was the day it was sold.

"So Buckbrush bought them out?"

"I guess so," Wright said. "I wasn't privy to any of the details."

Nate said, "Are you telling me they left this house without taking all their stuff?"

"They took some, all right," Wright said. "I'm just getting the rest."

"Where are you taking it?"

Wright hesitated for a moment. "The dump."

Nate felt his anger spike again. Despite the difficult financial circumstances they were in, Nate couldn't see the doctor leaving his ranch in such a rush unless pressure had been applied.

"If you want this stuff, you can have it," Wright said, gesturing toward the items in the back of the truck. "Take anything you want."

Nate felt like shooting him, but he didn't. Earl Wright wasn't the problem.

"Who are you, anyway?" Wright asked.

"A friend of theirs. Do you have any idea where they moved?"

"Not a clue. But I hope somewhere warm," Wright said.

"Is Buckbrush going to take over this entire valley?"

Wright hesitated before saying, "Probably." Then: "Believe me, mister, I don't like it either. I'm from a coal family, third generation. Do you think I like working for a wind outfit that helped put the mines out of business and pays me half of what I used to make? If I didn't have a wife and rugrats to feed . . ."

"Enough," Nate said.

FIFTEEN MINUTES LATER, Nate rolled into the icy parking lot of the Encampment lumber mill. He parked in a slot between two pickups that apparently belonged to workers. When he opened his SUV door, the cold air was filled with the high whine of a vertical saw blade and it smelled of sweet cut pine.

He had to mouth the words *Jeb Pryor* to a sawyer inside who was wearing a hard hat, safety glasses, and ear protection. The man pointed toward a door in the interior corner of the mill. Nate felt the eyes of mill employees on him as he traversed stacks of fresh-cut two-by-fours and waded through ankle-high piles of sawdust. Obviously, they didn't get many visitors.

Because the scream of the saw was so loud that it would be unlikely anyone inside the office could hear a knock on the door, he opened it a few inches and stuck his head inside.

"Jeb Pryor?"

An older, powerfully built man with a wide face and thick white hair looked up from a stack of orders on his desk. His face was wrinkled and weather-beaten and his meaty hands were scarred from years of hard outside labor. His arched eyebrows indicated that yes, he was Jeb Pryor.

Nate stepped inside the small office and closed the door. It muted the sound of the saws and machinery, but didn't completely block them out.

"Joe Pickett asked me to come," Nate said. "He said you called him."

"Who are you and why didn't he come himself?"

Pryor didn't talk so much as boom. Nate attributed it to years of hearing loss and trying to make himself heard over chain saws and heavy equipment.

"He had to go to Cheyenne today."

"And you are?"

"Nate Romanowski."

"Romanowski," Pryor said, while pointing Nate toward a chair in front of the desk. "I used to work with some tough old Polacks up in the timber. We called 'em the 'ski' bums because all their names ended in 'ski' like yours. Hard workers, though. One of 'em cut his own hand off at the wrist with a chain saw and he picked it up with his other good hand and pretended to wave it at his pals.

"After that they all quit and went to work in the mines in Kemmerer. Are you related to any of them?"

"Not that I know of."

"Because they were crazy, those Polacks."

"Sounds like it."

"You kind of have that crazy look in your eye, I'd say."

Nate said, "I'd call it 'deliberate,' not crazy."

Pryor grinned. "So you're working with the new game warden."

Nate nodded.

"What are you—his deputy?"

"Of sorts."

"I did a little research on him after I met him the other day. He's got a reputation, you know."

"I'm aware of that."

"Is he as trustworthy as he seems? I ask because I've run into a few game wardens who weren't. And don't even get me started on the feds."

Nate said, "He's the most trustworthy man I know. He's a straight arrow. Sometimes to a fault."

"That's the impression I got when I met him," Pryor said. "Did he really arrest the governor of Wyoming once for fishing without a license?"

"That was him."

"Damn."

"You called him this morning," Nate said, trying to get on track.

Pryor nodded. He said, "I've got a knucklehead working here named Wylie Frye. He's my night man in charge of the burner out there. You know, that tipi-looking thing?"

"Yes?"

"Wylie's been letting somebody on my property at night. I just found out about it."

Nate raised his eyebrows, urging Pryor on.

"I'll get right to it," the lumber mill owner said. "I think Wylie has allowed somebody to cremate bodies in my burner and I think they're bringing another one here tonight. You think your Joe Pickett would be interested to find out about that?"

NATE FOLLOWED PRYOR out of the mill and through the parking lot toward the conical burner on the far edge of the mill property. There was no wood smoke coming from the stack. A rusty metal shack was next to it.

Nate asked, "Why haven't you called the local cops about this?"

"For one, I just got suspicious about it because I overheard Wylie talking on his cell phone last night. He wouldn't fess up to who was on the other end or what he was talking about.

"Second, our one local cop is a peckerwood named Spanks. He's the type who would screw up a train wreck."

"What about the county sheriff?"

"Neal?" Pryor said. "He's a good egg. But he's got some people in his department I'm not so sure about. This is a small isolated valley, Romanowski. Everyone knows everyone. There are some powerful people here. I have no doubt if I called the sheriff's department, somebody would make a quick call to whoever is bringing the bodies here and tip 'em off.

"We might never find 'em, or they could shut my mill down while they investigate. I can't afford to have the mill shut down. My bankers are just waiting to move in and take it over as it is. I think they want to sell out to the Saratoga mill."

He paused near the base of the burner and turned to Nate.

"If my saws shut down, my cash flow stops. I'm leveraged to the hilt and I'm competing with those big boys in Saratoga. If I can't pay my loans, all those men you saw up there in the mill will be on the street. Not to mention the lumberjacks up in the mountains and the truckers who deliver our raw material.

"I could have just fired Wylie Frye and kept my mouth shut," Pryor said. "But I just couldn't live with that. So I thought maybe Pickett could look into it with a fresh set of eyes. Didn't Governor Rulon give Pickett assignments outside of his game warden duties?"

"Yes."

Pryor said, "I loved Governor Rulon, even though he was a damned Democrat. If Rulon trusted Pickett, then I do, too."

Nate nodded. There was no reason to tell Pryor about Joe's recent experiences with the new governor.

"Follow me," Pryor said, as he turned the metal handle of the burner hatch door and stepped inside.

EVEN THOUGH THE FIRE inside had been out for hours and the temperature outside was below zero, the interior of the burner was close and warm. Cold white light filtered down from the steel mesh cone directly above them and lit up tiny particles of ash hanging in the air. The ash on the floor of the burner was fine, white, and ankle-deep.

Pryor said, "Every other week or so, I've gotten a couple of calls from Mrs. Schmidt—her house is about three hundred yards away—

that the burner was overheating and putting out too much smoke in the middle of the night. I asked him about it, but Wylie Frye assured me that he was following the procedure and that there wasn't anything to worry about. Mrs. Schmidt is a nice old lady and all, but she's known for complaining about things."

"Schmidt?" Nate repeated.

"Carol," Pryor said. "The poor old lady is in the hospital in Rawlins. She went off the road and was trapped in her car all night. I don't know how she lived through it."

"I heard about that," Nate said, recalling what the waitress had told them.

"Anyway," Pryor said, "when this burner is really cranking with sawdust, it can get to nearly a thousand degrees in here. We try not to ever let it get that hot, because I worry about the structural integrity of the steel."

As he said that, he knocked on the interior wall with his knuckles.

"Do you know how hot a crematorium gets in order to dispose of a human body?" Pryor asked. Then he answered his own question. "Between fourteen hundred and eighteen hundred degrees. Hot enough to make the bones break down into sand. It doesn't take much imagination to figure that a guy could get this burner about that hot."

Nate wished Joe were there. Joe was better at connecting dots and he'd talked to more people in the valley. Nate committed what Pryor was telling him to memory.

"Do you know what a burned corpse smells like?" Pryor asked.

"Yes."

"Military?"

"Special Forces."

"I thought so," Pryor said. "You have that special operator thing going. I was an Airborne Ranger."

Nate nodded. Pryor had that thing as well.

Pryor said, "Take a whiff."

Nate did. The odor of the burned pine sawdust was overpowering. But within it there was just a trace of something acrid and sweet, like burned hair or pork.

"Mrs. Schmidt complained about that, too," Pryor said. "She said she thought we were burning garbage."

As his eyes adjusted to the darkness, Nate shuffled his boots through the ash on the floor. It was powdery and light, but there was grit on the bottom of it.

He said, "I wonder if a forensic scientist could sift through this and find something besides wood ash?"

"I wonder that, too," Pryor said. "We use the Skid-Steer to clean it out when the ash gets above ten inches, then we spread it on the field out in back of the mill. The material is so fine it's absorbed by the soil or it blows away in the wind. But it's possible if experts went through it after our visitors come, they could find some kind of remains, I suppose."

Nate looked up. "The remains of Kate Shelford-Longden, for example?"

Pryor groaned. He said, "I guess it's possible. But I don't think that lady is really missing. I think she'll show up somewhere."

Pryor, Nate thought, was echoing what seemed to be the prevalent theory in the area. Nate wasn't sure there was enough room inside the burner for more than one conspiracy theorist.

"Where could the bodies come from?" he asked Pryor. "Are there a lot of missing people around here?"

"A few, I suppose," he said. "Or maybe someone's bringing them here from a long distance. There's all kinds of crap with gangs and such going on in Denver and Phoenix. Maybe they're driving up and getting rid of bodies here."

"Maybe."

"I was also thinking Pickett could take a look at the funeral homes in the area," Pryor said. "Maybe one of 'em cut a deal with Wylie to do cremations on the cheap. Most folks wouldn't know the difference between ash from a body or from a wood burner, would be my guess."

Nate continued to shuffle his feet through the ash. Then he felt something larger than grit under the sole of his boot.

He bent over and plunged his hand into the material. The warm ash was cloying and still warm. He felt something solid and grasped it.

"What did you find?" Pryor asked, moving in.

"I'm not sure," Nate said as he blew on his hand and the object to clear both of the ash. He used the illuminated screen of his phone to look closer.

The intense heat had discolored and elongated it, but there was no doubt he was holding what looked like a band or a ring. It was several times thicker in width than a wedding band and lighter in weight.

Nate didn't want to tell Pryor just yet that he thought he knew where it came from.

Instead: "Is Wylie Frye still in town?"

"As far as I know," Pryor said. "I wasn't going to fire him outright until I could train his replacement. He doesn't seem like the type to have anywhere else to go."

"Let's go find the son of a bitch," Nate said.

. . .

NATE POCKETED THE RING and jabbed Joe's cell phone number on his phone. The cartoon image of Dudley Do-Right appeared on the screen, but Joe didn't pick up.

As he followed Jeb Pryor across the yard toward their vehicles, Nate left a voice message.

"Call me back."

27

JOE TOOK A SEAT IN A CHAIR DIRECTLY ACROSS THE TABLE FROM Steve Pollock, who listed to his side as if slightly deflated. Pollock, who to Joe had always looked well-groomed and put together for a game warden, had a three- or four-day growth of whiskers on his cheeks and neck, and his hair was unkempt. His eyes were so bloodshot that Joe felt his own eyes tear up with some kind of odd empathy.

Michael Williams was perched on the far-left end of the booth seat as if he might spring from it and run toward the door at any second. Either that, or he wanted to get as far away from Pollock as possible but still be in the booth. The ex–game warden smelled of musk and stale whiskey.

The waitress arrived before a word was spoken between any of the three men. Joe and Williams ordered black coffee. Pollock said, "You know what I want," and she smiled and strode back to the order station at the bar.

"Do you two know each other?" Joe asked.

"We met over in my district," Pollock said as his draft beer and a shot of Wyoming Whiskey were put down in front of him. "Mike asked me if I knew anything about that disappearance of Kate what's-her-name."

"Kate Shelford-Longden," Williams interjected.

Joe nodded.

"Mike and I aren't friends or anything," Pollock said. "We hardly know each other besides that. Just a couple of state employees."

His voice was lazy and a bit slurry. Joe guessed that the order in front of Pollock wasn't his first of the day.

"What did you tell him about Kate?" Joe asked. "I don't remember any interview notes in the file."

Williams sat up. He was more than a little defensive. "That's because there was nothing to write up. Pollock said he'd never seen her or met her and he had no intel to share with me."

Pollock said, "That's true. There were lots of fancy people coming and going at the Silver Creek Ranch. I'd rarely see any of 'em except if they decided to come to town at night, like at the Wolf or something. Occasionally I'd see a bunch of them riding nose-to-tail on ranch horses pretending to be cowboys, but I never really talked to them.

"That place runs a really clean operation," Pollock continued. "I never had any trouble with them over the years. Mark Gordon is tightly wrapped, but he doesn't want his guests breaking any Game and Fish rules or regulations. I hardly ever got called out there, and if I was, it was to help shoo away elk from their haystacks. But that was the winter, when they didn't have guests.

"I remember one time there was a moose just walking right

through their fence lines. That bull was dragging about a hundred yards of barbed wire behind him and didn't even act like he knew it . . ."

Williams shot out his hand so he could see his watch below his jacket sleeve. He said, "I'm sure it's a good story, but I can't stay long. My supervisor doesn't want me working on Sundays and racking up overtime hours."

Pollock paused in midsentence and looked over, amused.

"You're kind of wrapped tight yourself," he said to the DCI agent.

"Look," Williams said to Joe and Pollock. "I shouldn't even be here. I can only stay as long as my normal lunch break and I can't spend the whole time listening to elk and moose stories from a couple of game wardens."

"I'll keep mine to myself," Joe said.

Williams lowered his voice and bent forward across the table. He obviously didn't want to be overheard by the waitress or the bartender. "Pollock asked me to come here and meet you before he left the state. I agreed because there's something going on over there and I thought maybe if the three of us traded notes, we could figure out what it is."

Joe wondered if Williams or Pollock knew of his own circumstances. Could the news of his firing be public knowledge in Cheyenne already?

"I hope you found my notes helpful," Williams said.

"I did," Joe said. "They saved me weeks of plowing the same ground. But somebody broke into my hotel room and took them."

Williams said, "That's *exactly* what I'm talking about. Things like that happen over there. The whole time my team was investigating Kate's disappearance, we had the feeling that we were being watched and observed. We reported everything we were doing to the Carbon County sheriff's office and I think there's a couple of leakers there. My guys said they saw strange trucks parked down the street in the morning when they went outside—things like that."

Joe recalled the same experience outside Pollock's former home.

Williams said, "When we didn't get any immediate leads in and around the ranch, we did our job and expanded the search. We were methodical about it. But it seemed like the farther we got away from the immediate area, the more we were being monitored. And when we were pulled off the case, we puzzled over it for weeks. We asked ourselves: Who did we offend? Who wanted us gone?"

Joe was interested in the answer. It didn't come.

"I know the governor is an impatient man," Williams said. "To pull us out of there like that was humiliating. We've never worked for a governor so quick to piss inside his own tent. But I guess you know a little about that."

Joe felt his neck flush hot. "I do," he said.

"I heard the press conference this morning. It sounded familiar. If I were you, I'd keep my head on a swivel," Williams advised.

Joe concluded that his firing hadn't been publicized yet and he was grateful.

Joe turned to Pollock and arched his eyebrows.

Pollock's vague smile turned sour.

"Well?" Joe asked. "Why did you quit the way you did?"

THE STORY WAS LONGER than it needed to be and Joe was aware of Williams fidgeting as it went on and on. Pollock gave the background: his wife, Lindy, left and took the kids because she said he worked too many hours and was distracted when he was home. Then the divorce. Then the state froze all salaries and he was looking at ending his career eventually without ever building a nest egg or owning any real assets like a home of his own. He felt trapped, and the bureaucracy was getting worse by the month.

He didn't get along with agency director Linda Greene-Dempsey, and the department had cut his district down from a three-horse district to a no-horse district. He could see the writing on the wall, he said.

"They were putting the squeeze on me," Pollock said. "Hoping I'd quit eventually. LGD isn't comfortable with us old-school game wardens. She wants to replace us all with younger, greener versions. You know that, Joe."

Joe nodded, hoping Pollock would get to the point.

"I was doing my job," he said. "The Kate investigation was going on in the background. Then all of a sudden I got a visitor at my office.

"His name is Ted Panos," Pollock said. "Do either of you know him?"

Joe said he didn't. Williams said he thought he might have heard the name, but he couldn't place it.

"From what I understand, he works for Buckbrush," Pollock said. "I really didn't check him out at the time and the reason is he offered me a hundred and seventy-five thousand dollars to hit the bricks."

Joe sat back, stunned.

"A hundred and seventy-five K is a hundred and seventy-five K more than I had in the bank," Pollock said. "He couldn't have timed it better, because I was sick and tired of life at the time. All I could think about was being on some beach in the sun instead of bucking snowdrifts every day. I said yes and he delivered it in three suitcases the next morning. I packed some clothes and that was about it: I was gone. It was an impulsive decision on my part, I know. But I'm still gone. I ain't ever going back."

Joe was disgusted at Pollock's decision to abandon his district like that, but he tried not to show it. He measured his words carefully. "What did he ask you to do for that kind of money?"

"Nothing," Pollock said. "Just leave."

"Just like that?"

"It was an easy decision at the time," Pollock said. "Tell me you wouldn't do the same."

Joe tried not to think about his own circumstances at the moment and how he might be tempted to take a quick buyout for the sake of his family.

"Did you take any of your files with you?"

"No," Pollock said. "I left all my official records in place for the next poor son of a bitch who takes over."

"Let me ask you," Joe said, "did you keep a file on the Silver Creek Ranch?"

"Sure."

"Some of the files are gone now," Joe said. "Including that one."

"Really?"

"I was in the old house and I went through your desk. There are missing files, including the ranch records. Also, the *B* files are missing."

Pollock sat back and rubbed his chin, trying to recall what was gone.

Williams asked, "Was there a Buckbrush file?"

Pollock nodded. "Of course there was."

"Not anymore," Joe said.

At that moment, his phone lit up and started to skitter across the table. It was Nate. Nate *never* called. But Joe couldn't interrupt the conversation to take it and he let it go to voicemail.

Pollock said, "Are you thinking what I'm thinking? That Panos went back and took a bunch of stuff from my office after I left?"

"There wasn't anyone to stop him, was there?" Joe said.

He withdrew his notebook and opened it to a fresh page. On the top line, he wrote the name *Ted Panos*. On the second line, he wrote *Buckbrush*.

Joe noticed that Williams had gone silent since he'd asked Pollock his question. The man was recalling something.

Williams said to Pollock, "Did you ever run across a guy named Gaylan Kessel?"

"Sure," Pollock said. He said it in a way that indicated he didn't like him.

"Who is Gaylan Kessel?" Joe asked.

"The point man for Buckbrush Power," Williams answered.

"More like a security specialist of some kind," Pollock said. "He bigfoots his way around the county like he owns the place. People suck up to him because of who he works for."

Williams placed his hand on Pollock's arm to quiet him for a moment. "As we were casting our net wider on the Kate case, we got farther and farther away from Silver Creek Ranch. You know, we were thinking that maybe when she left, she took a wrong turn for some reason. That maybe she went north instead of south. As you know, the entire north is the Buckbrush Power project.

"We thought maybe—and we knew it was a stretch—she got lost and maybe ended up on the project. Or maybe she was taken somewhere else and her body dumped up there. So I made a request to interview the man in charge."

"Gaylan Kessel," Joe said.

Williams nodded. "He was a prick about it. He said he didn't want anyone thinking her disappearance had anything to do with the project—that it was bad PR for the company. I told him I'd be discreet, but he said he was in charge of keeping Buckbrush's public image safe. He said it was his job to make sure the company was seen in a positive light given their five-billion-dollar investment, and that us even associating a missing woman with the company was outrageous."

Joe wrote the name *Gaylan Kessel* on his page.

"We never had the interview, because later that week the governor pulled the plug on the investigation," Williams said.

Joe asked, "Are you thinking your contact with Kessel and Buckbrush was the reason you were yanked?"

"I never made the connection until now," Williams said. "I'd kind of forgotten about it. But when Pollock said they paid him off, it just clicked."

Pollock winced at the phrase *paid him off*, Joe noted.

Williams said, "I wouldn't be surprised if Panos worked for Kessel."

Joe turned to Pollock. He said, "Steve, you need to think. Why would they want you gone? Did someone call in a violation up on the project that you were planning to check out?"

Pollock shook his head. "I honestly can't think of anything like that. There was lots of grumbling about the size of the project and how the company was able to skirt around all the environmental impact studies because they represent clean energy and that's what the feds want. And because the project is all on private property, I'd need permission from them to even go there. So I steered clear of that mess."

Joe nodded. "But there had to be something," he said. "Something in another of the missing files. Something related to either Kate or Buckbrush—or both."

Pollock reached for his beer and Joe slid it away before he could grasp it.

"Think," he said. "Then drink."

Pollock sat back and closed his eyes. It went on for over a minute. Joe and Williams exchanged looks.

Then Pollock's eyes shot open. "You said there was no Silver Creek Ranch file in the *S*'s."

"Correct."

"Was there a file that said 'Eagle Permits'?"

"I don't recall one," Joe said. "I think I would have remembered, because I talked to a falconer the other day who was complaining that he can't get the feds to grant him a permit to hunt with eagles."

Pollock slapped the table with his palm. He said, "That might be the connection."

Williams looked over, obviously puzzled.

Pollock said to Joe, "I had a whole file of complaint letters from pissed-off falconers who aren't allowed to use the eagle permits they've earned. They've got this big conspiracy theory about how the feds are granting take permits to wind energy companies, and even the governor's office is looking the other way."

Joe said, "I've heard it."

He didn't say he'd heard it from his friend Nate just the previous night.

"What's a take permit?" Williams asked.

Joe said, "It allows wind energy companies to kill up to a certain number of golden and bald eagles legally without penalty."

"What?"

"It's true," Pollock said. "There's a company up by Glenrock, Wyoming, that killed over forty golden eagles last year and those are just the birds we know about. The falconers think the feds are denying them eagles to hunt with because so many birds are being slaughtered by wind turbines."

"I thought eagles were an endangered species?" Williams asked.

"Not for renewable energy companies," Pollock said. "Their take permits exempt them from the law. Those falconers who complained said the general public would go ballistic if they knew about all the dead eagles, and they're probably right. But few people know, and our government makes sure the take permit program stays below the radar. The worst part of the program is that the companies are asked to self-report the eagle deaths. How many of them do you think are likely to do that once they've exceeded their take permit?"

Joe said to Pollock, "Were you going to follow up on those complaints with Buckbrush?"

"Eventually," Pollock said. "I was waiting for the dead months in the winter between big-game seasons. When I had some time."

"That's when Ted Panos came a-calling," Joe said.

"I guess so," Pollock agreed.

Joe said, "A hundred and seventy-five thousand is a lot less than millions of dollars in fines if Buckbrush got caught exceeding their take permit. And that doesn't include the cost of massive bad publicity. It was a business decision."

Pollock closed his eyes. He said, "I came cheap."

"Yup."

"I'll see if I'm able to live with myself."

Joe eyed him with disdain. He was disappointed by Pollock, and Pollock knew it.

To Williams, Joe said, "Kessel probably didn't want you to go up there to his project because you might see something he didn't want you to see."

"Dead eagles," Williams said. "But what about Kate? Do you think it's possible she went there?"

Joe had no answer. He circled the name *Gaylan Kessel* on his pad so many times the ball point of his pen nearly cut through to the next page.

Then the three men simply looked at one another for a few minutes, absorbed in the revelations and their own thoughts.

As Williams got up, he put his hand on Joe's shoulder.

"I gotta go," he said. "But be careful. It seems like if you get too close to Buckbrush like Steve and I did, something bad might happen to you."

Joe said, "It already has."

JOE FELT A WEIGHT crushing down on him as he went outside toward his pickup. And he felt duplicitous.

He hadn't told the two men that he'd been fired by Hanlon, that he was there with them at the table under what could be deemed false pretenses. He'd had several opportunities to do so, but he hadn't taken them.

The fact was he was ashamed and embarrassed by being taken off the job. It was what defined him, as well as being a husband and a father. The news of his canning would get out. It would be a matter of days or even hours. He was operating on borrowed time, and he'd implicated both Williams *and* Pollock in his deception.

The only answer was to try and end this thing before word got out.

Joe decided to return Nate's call once he got back on the road to Saratoga. But first he needed to think about what he'd learned.

The governor's two biggest campaign contributors, Missy and Buckbrush, had both gotten what they wanted.

Things were falling into place and not in a good way.

28

SHERIDAN PICKETT WAS GETTING ANXIOUS.

After spending Sunday morning chopping water holes in the ice and gathering the guest horses she'd ride and exercise later that day, she'd returned to Silver Creek Ranch to find that Lance Ramsey hadn't shown up for work.

She'd zipped up her coat against the cold and looked for signs of him with a rising sense of dread.

His truck and snowmobile trailer weren't in the lot in front of the indoor arena nor in the pull-through of the Activity Center. She couldn't remember when he'd been so late to work before.

There was no cell service where his cabin was located and no way to reach him. He'd told her he *liked* being off the grid for a few days at a time, that it gave him a sense of calm, and she'd not been able to convince him otherwise.

As she checked for his truck at the employee housing units and the outdoor rodeo arena, unwelcome scenarios played out in her head.

She thought:

His snowmobile wouldn't start this morning and it's seven miles from the parking area.

Or:

He's gotten his snowmobile or his truck stuck in the snow getting out from the cabin.

Or worse:

He's gotten stuck on the way there two days ago and he is stranded.

Or even worse:

An avalanche swept through the little valley where the cabin is located and buried him beneath several tons of snow.

Or maybe:

He's deathly ill and is trembling and feverish in his single bed with no way to call her for help. Sick in that same iron-framed bed where they . . .

SHERIDAN HAD STARTED the morning with anticipation. She couldn't wait to tell him about the raid on the mountain and how she'd clocked the fleeing subject with the door of her dad's truck.

Or that her image from the back standing over the injured man had appeared in newspapers and on websites all over the world. She didn't like the photo because it looked like she was threatening the poor man, but nonetheless it was her.

Sheridan didn't want General Manager Mark Gordon to know Lance hadn't made it back from the weekend because she didn't want him to get in trouble. But if he didn't show up soon, she might have to. The ranch had a fleet of snowmobiles and she could use one of them to go up into the mountains and try to find him. Her dad was in Cheyenne and Nate was in Encampment, so she'd have to go by herself if it came to that.

Plus, she missed Lance. She missed him more than she wanted to admit to herself. The ranch in the winter was a lonely and hollow place without his shy smile and his steady presence.

AFTER LOOKING EVERYWHERE she could think of, Sheridan finally went to the office. Gordon sat at his desk with his back to her, answering email on his computer.

"Mark, have you heard anything from Lance? He hasn't shown up today from his cabin and he's usually back by now."

Gordon wheeled around, concerned. "He hasn't let us know he was coming back late, if that's what you mean."

"I'm starting to get worried."

"I don't blame you. There's a lot of snow out there. Do you want me to call the sheriff's department?"

She shook her head. "To ask them to do another blind raid on a mountain cabin? They might not be real excited to do that again."

"I see your point."

"If it's okay with you, I'd like to borrow one of the snowmobiles to see if I can find him."

Gordon enthusiastically agreed. He said, "Take a satellite phone and call me every hour to check in. I don't want two of my people lost. Do you know where his cabin is?"

She looked down at her boots. "Yes."

"*Oh*," Gordon said simply.

He handed the keys over without further comment and she took them and trudged back through the snow toward the Activity Center.

So now Gordon knew. She hoped he wouldn't remind her of what a bad idea it was for senior employees to fraternize, because she and Lance were well aware of it. Both of them had counseled junior employees against it.

Still, it had happened.

It was important to her to know that her dad seemed to genuinely like Lance. The next test would be to see what her mother thought of him. That time would come.

But first she had to find him.

SHERIDAN STUMBLED A BIT when she saw that a beige three-quarter-ton GMC pickup was parked outside the Activity Center. Large opened gearboxes filled the bed of the truck. Stenciled on the driver's-side door was YOUNGBERG FARRIER SERVICE. She knew they often used the old stalls in the building for putting on new horseshoes in the winter, but she hadn't heard they were scheduled for today.

In any other circumstance, she would have turned on her heel and walked back to the arena to wait them out. But this wasn't any other circumstance and she put her head down and kept going.

Inside the long building was a central walkway with storage room doors on both sides and horse stalls at the far end. Cold white winter light poured down through the overhead skylights inside and lit up the floating dust from the farrier activity. She could see Ben and Brady in silhouette outside the stalls. Ben was bent over an iron anvil, holding up a horse's leg clamped between his knees, and tapping nail after nail through the shoe into its hoof. Brady was preparing to do the same procedure with a different horse when he saw her come in.

"Well, look who's here," Brady said.

"Who?" Ben asked through a mouthful of nails. He put them there for easy access.

"Little Miss," Brady said.

Ben paused in mid-swing of his hammer and looked up.

"*Li'l Miss,*" he mumbled through the nails.

She didn't know they called her that. She said, "I don't want any trouble with you two. I'll only be here long enough to get a snowmobile and trailer out of here."

"She don't want no trouble," Brady said. "Little Miss don't want no trouble."

His tone was mocking and amused.

She narrowed her eyes at them and vowed to herself not to say anything that would provoke them. Not now.

Brady asked, "Do you have your daddy with you? And where's Lance Romance, your bodyguard?"

So they had names for them both.

"I seen your picture on my phone," Brady said. "Were you standing over that poor guy in the snow telling him he better watch out or your daddy and Lance Romance would come beat him up?"

Ben laughed and several nails fell out of his mouth into the dirt. His whole body shook when he laughed.

She could still hear him laughing when she went through the door into an oversized storage garage and closed the door behind her. Then locked it.

Ten Polaris snowmobiles were lined up on individual trailers. Eight were 550 WideTraks for getting around on the ranch and two were 800 Titans big enough for two or three riders. Shallow tubs were attached to the Titans for hauling junk and equipment from place to place on the ranch in the winter.

She filled a pack with emergency blankets, a first-aid kit, and a handheld GPS unit and a satellite phone that both sat in charging stations.

The keys Gordon had given her were for the lockbox mounted on the wall where the keys for each machine were hung. She selected keys for one of the Titans, thinking that if Lance were injured she could bring him out in the tub and call ahead for the EMTs to meet her.

Sheridan was grateful that there was an overhead garage door on the far side of the room. That way, she could back her truck in and drive away with the snowmobile without having to confront the Youngbergs and their taunting again.

But the first thing she saw when she began to raise the door to the outside were four heavy boots in the snow.

The door rolled up smoothly and there they were. Brady wore his sloppy grin and Ben stood with his hands on his hips and his chin raised. There was a dribble of brown tobacco juice hanging from his chin.

"Do you need some help hooking that trailer up?" Brady asked.

"No."

"Are you one of those 'I can do anything a man can do' type of gals?"

"One of them feminists?" Brady added.

"No."

"Which one of these snow machines do you need?"

She nodded toward the Titan. "Please step aside. I need to go get my truck."

To her surprise, they did. But she could feel their eyes on her backside as she made her way to her pickup. There was a lever-action .30-30 just inside the door if she needed it.

She didn't.

BEN GUIDED HER as she backed up to the open garage and Brady was strong enough to lift the snowmobile trailer and roll it forward on its wheels so they could hitch it up easily.

"Thank you," she said out her driver's-side window.

"Anything for you, Little Miss," Brady said to Ben's laugh.

She kept waiting for the other shoe to drop.

It did as she started to pull away, when Brady jogged alongside her open window and waved for her to stop.

She did, but she kept her finger poised on the button that would close it.

"Maybe when you find him you'll figure out why we call him Lance Romance," he said.

"What are you talking about?"

Brady didn't answer. Instead, he looked over at his brother and the two of them exchanged wide smiles as she drove away.

Then she thought: *How did they know Lance was missing?*

29

WYLIE FRYE LIVED IN A TWO-STORY WHITE CLAPBOARD HOUSE ON THE corner of Freeman and 8th Streets in Encampment. The streets weren't paved, but they'd been plowed to their frozen gravel surface and the excess snow bordered the lanes like tall white cornrows. The Sierra Madre range loomed blue and sharp over the entire town to the south and west.

Pryor pulled his truck parallel to the left-side wall of snow and got out. Nate pulled in behind him.

Wood was obviously the heating fuel of choice in the little town, Nate observed. A layer of smoke hung above the houses at treetop level.

A curl of it emanated from Frye's chimney, and Pryor pointed it out.

"Looks like he's home," Pryor said in a near-whisper.

"You knock on the door," Nate said. "I'll go around back."

Pryor hitched up his jeans and waited to give Nate time to go around. Condensation from his breath hung about his head like a thought balloon.

Nate high-stepped it through knee-high snow across the front lawn and around the large garage. It was obvious the garage wasn't used to store Wylie's vehicle, which was parked on the side of the building with an extension cord plugged into the engine block to keep it warm. Nate glanced through a window on the side of the structure to see inside.

The interior was a work in progress; a shop, den, and man-cave rolled into one. There were big-game mounts on the walls, a pool table covered with loose plastic, a woodstove, a bar that looked like it had just been installed, a seventy-inch Vizio television, an overstuffed lounge chair. Stacks of two-by-fours and wood scraps on the floor indicated that Frye was still working on the room.

He peered around the corner toward the back of the adjacent home. There was no back fence but Nate could see a porch and back door. He unzipped the front of his parka so he could access his weapon.

In a moment, he heard a heavy rapping from the front of the house and Jeb Pryor shout, "Wylie, it's Jeb. Open up. I need to talk to you."

Nate waited. He could feel the cold of the deep snow start to seep into his boots and through his trousers. Then he heard footfalls inside the house and the sound of the back door being opened.

The secondary storm door pushed out toward the porch and Nate saw a rotund man with a heavy beard come out and step heavily down the concrete steps. He wore an insulated Carhartt coat and a Stormy Kromer cap with earflaps and he turned toward where Nate was located near Frye's pickup.

Nate stepped out from the corner of the garage and leveled his .454 at Wylie Frye's chest.

"Where are you going?" Nate asked.

Frye stopped so quickly he nearly toppled over forward. His eyes widened on the large O of Nate's muzzle.

"Aren't you going to invite us inside?" Nate asked.

Frye straightened up and sighed. Nate hoped the man wasn't stupid enough to reach for a gun of his own. No doubt he had one. Everyone in Encampment did.

"Do I have a choice?" Frye asked.

"Nope."

"I ain't done nothing wrong," Frye said. "You're on private property, you know."

"Turn around," Nate said. "That's quite a workshop you've got going here. It's hard to believe Jeb pays you enough for all of that."

"Are you some kind of cop?" Frye asked.

"The worst kind," Nate said. "The kind without a badge or rules."

Wylie Frye started to say something, but apparently thought better of it. He turned and shambled toward his back door.

Nate followed him inside and found himself in the kitchen. The place was a mess; dishes piled in the sink, a tall garbage can overflowing with empty beer bottles, a linoleum floor caked with dried mud and snow so thick the original design was obscured.

"Don't tell me," Nate said. "You live alone."

"Ever since Ginny left with the kids," Frye said. "It's hard to maintain the place with the hours I work."

"Yeah, yeah."

Nate stepped around Frye, but kept his eye on him as he opened the front door.

Jeb Pryor entered, along with a blast of cold air from outside. Pryor closed the door and stood off to the side of the doorjamb, indicating it was Nate's play. He looked like he was unsure of the situation he was now in.

"Take off your coat and let it drop to the floor," Nate told Frye. "Then your gun."

Frye hesitated for a second before removing the coat and doing what he'd been instructed to do. The grip of a semiautomatic was shoved into the front of his waistband.

"Take it out using your thumb and index finger and lower it to your coat. I don't want it going off by you dropping it on the floor."

Frye grunted as he placed his weapon on his jacket. He wasn't flexible enough to bend all the way over.

"Okay," Nate said. "Thank you."

He stepped forward and pinned the sleeve of Frye's coat under his boot and slid it and the gun toward him. It was a shiny new Smith & Wesson model 1911 in .45.

"This is a thousand-dollar pistol," Nate said. "Jeb must be paying you pretty well."

Frye and Pryor exchanged glances. Frye looked guilty.

Nate handed the pistol to Pryor, who looked it over.

"Not *this* well," Pryor said. There was disappointment in his voice. He lowered the muzzle to the floor.

Nate riffled through the pockets in Frye's parka and found two cell phones—a Samsung smartphone and a cheap prepaid flip-phone.

Frye said, "You've got no business going through my coat."

"Call the cops," Nate said.

Frye didn't move.

"Why do you need two phones?" Nate asked.

Frye didn't answer.

"Why do you need a burner?" Nate asked, flipping the device open and turning it on.

"Please, mister," Frye said. There was desperation in his voice. He turned to Pryor. "You can't just let him do this, boss."

Pryor shrugged.

Nate found a single text thread on the flip-phone with a lone text that read: *He knows*. It had been sent the day before to an unknown number.

"Who knows?" Nate asked Frye, who screwed up his face like he was going to cry.

He simply glared at Frye. Nate often found that silence was the best way to get someone to talk.

Finally, the man nodded toward Pryor. "He knows," he said in a near whisper.

"I know *what*? You never fessed up what was going on," Pryor boomed. He couldn't help it.

Frye looked helplessly toward his boss, then to Nate. He said, "These guys scare me."

"I'm going to scare you worse," Nate growled. To Pryor: "Hold him here."

Nate went out the front door to his SUV and found the brown trout. It had frozen solid into the shape of a four-pound club. It looked like an oversized prehistoric billy club. Nate grasped it in front of the tail and took it back inside.

Frye was saying to Pryor, "I don't want to be involved with them anymore."

Nate raised the trout club and swung it at Frye like a baseball bat. It landed hard on his rib cage and Frye's knees buckled and he dropped to the floor. Pryor stepped back as if to distance himself from the act as much as he could.

Nate swept Frye's hat off his head with a backhand, then grasped the man's left ear. He was so close Nate could smell wood smoke on Frye's clothing.

"Sometimes, I pull these right off. They make a popping sound."

"Please, mister . . ." Frye begged.

"So you told them the delivery is off," Nate said.

Frye nodded as best he could. He hugged himself and struggled for breath.

"Have they responded to you?"

"You can see they haven't," Frye said in a wheeze.

"I'm going to give you back your phone and you're going to text them and tell them you made a mistake. Tell them the delivery is back on."

"I think you broke my ribs," Frye moaned.

"Your nose is next," Nate said. "I'm just getting started."

When Frye looked up Nate handed him the flip-phone.

"Don't screw it up."

"What if they don't believe me?"

"Then you'll have both of us to worry about," Nate said. "It's your job to make them believe you."

Frye reached up gingerly and took the phone. Nate watched as he tapped out the message.

"Let me see it."

Frye held up the phone. He'd written: *False Alarm. I was being causous. It's still a go at the usual time.*

Nate said, "Send it." He figured if he corrected Frye's spelling it might appear suspicious.

Frye sent the message. "Can I get up now? I done what you said."

"There's more. Show up to work tonight like normal," Nate said. "Play your role and don't do anything clever like trying to contact them again. You don't seem like a very clever guy."

"I don't want no part in this anymore," Frye whined.

"Too late," Nate said. "You took the money and betrayed your employer. The only way clear is to do your job. Right, Jeb?"

Pryor reluctantly agreed. He asked Frye, "Who are these guys you've let into my mill?"

Frye shot a panicked look toward Nate when the grip tightened on his ear. "I don't know their names—I really don't. Part of the arrangement is I walk away from the burner when they show up and don't come back until they're gone. I've heard their voices but I've never seen them face-to-face."

"You've been letting them use my burner as a crematorium," Pryor said. "What's wrong with you?"

"They pay in cash."

Pryor's face reddened and he narrowed his eyes. "You've earned whatever's coming to you, Wylie." As he said it, he glanced toward Nate.

"Don't even think about running," Nate said to Frye. "Just show up for work like you always do."

"What then?" Frye asked.

Nate shrugged. "We'll figure that out."

Nate and Pryor left Frye on the floor. Pryor kept the handgun.

PRYOR WALKED STIFF-LEGGED toward his truck. He said to Nate, "I'm not real comfortable with what's going on around here and what went on in there."

"It could have been a lot worse," Nate said. "I let him keep his ears." He tossed the trout club into the back of his vehicle.

"Personnel is the hardest part of running a business," Pryor said. "I could use a guy like you at the mill."

"Thanks—but I've got a business of my own." Then:

"Keep your cell phone on tonight. We might need you."

JOE CALLED BACK just as Nate was turning the ignition on in his SUV.

"You actually called me on my phone?" Joe said.

"Yes. You need to get the hell back over here as fast as you can," Nate said. "It'll happen tonight."

"What will happen?"

"I already told you," Nate said, and punched off.

30

SHERIDAN PULLED THE SNOWMOBILE TRAILER IN HER TRUCK UP THE old two-track road into the mountains as the frozen trees closed in on her from both sides. She'd remembered to check in with Mark Gordon on the satellite phone after the first hour.

"Did you find him?" he'd asked.

"I'm not there yet," she'd replied.

She was concerned that the sky hadn't lightened up much and that the forest was still muted in shadow. It looked and felt like more snow was on the way and she wanted to get to Lance's cabin and back out before a new storm hit.

She wondered how many times her dad had been in the same situation before: high in the mountains alone as a storm moved in.

She thought: *a lot.*

It was obvious that the road she was on had been tracked within the last few days and she presumed it was from Lance's truck. Very few recreational snowmobilers favored that area of the Snowy Range because there were scores of better trails and more spectacular rides above Encampment in the Sierra Madres and on Highway 230 farther south.

Sheridan rounded a corner with lodgepole pines tight to both sides and came upon a cow moose standing in the middle of the road. The moose was wedge-shaped and jet-black and long-legged for moving easily through deep snow. But instead of moving on, she just stood there staring. Finally, Sheridan tapped her brakes and honked her horn.

The cow ambled into the timber and vanished so quickly it was as if she were never there. A shiny brown pile of moose pellets steamed in the snow to prove she had been.

Now you're gonna find out why we call him Lance Romance.

What did that mean? Were they just messing with her head?

LANCE'S OLD RED Ford F-150 pickup was parked where it should have been in a wide alcove in the trees. His snowmobile trailer was attached to the rear bumper and his machine was gone.

Sheridan parked next to Lance's Ford and climbed out and checked the cab of his truck. It was unlocked, as always. He'd left his keys under the driver's-side floor mat next to his cowboy boots. No doubt he'd exchanged his everyday boots for a pair of snowmobile pacs before he left for his cabin.

There was nothing else inside the cab that was unusual or suggested that anything strange had happened.

The only thing in the bed of his pickup was a light dusting of snow from the night before and a few old empty beer bottles that always rattled around when he drove it.

She backed the Titan off the trailer and secured the pack she'd assembled into the tub with bungee cords.

Sheridan pulled on a snowmobile suit that was too large and a helmet that was a size too big. She wished she had spent a few more seconds in the Activity Center garage making sure she got the right fit.

Before she took the narrow trail that would lead to his cabin, she lashed the .30-30 in its scabbard to the side of her snow machine.

SHE WAS SOMEWHAT assured that he'd be at the end of her journey in one way or another because the trail was packed down into the light powder snow by a previous machine. In the summer, it was a twenty-minute ride through thick timber to Lance's cabin on an ATV. Snowmobiles traveled at approximately the same rate of speed.

She took it slower than that because she'd never driven there by herself in the winter. That, and the oversize helmet kept twisting to the side and she had to adjust it to see out the clear plastic shield.

It was through that slightly foggy face shield that she saw the curl of smoke from the chimney of Lance's cabin and his snowmobile parked out front. The snow around the structure had been trampled down by boots.

She breathed a sigh of relief.

The cabin was small and made of logs with a green metal roof. She'd heard Lance complain that he wished the roof had been pitched steeper because sometimes two or three feet of snow gathered on top and threatened to collapse the trusses.

Like most people who owned high-mountain cabins, Lance spent his free days in the summer re-chinking the logs and getting it in shape to last the coming winter. Two cords of fresh-cut and -split pine were lined up in a kind of wall against the southern tree line. She could see a well-worn path from the door of the cabin to the stack of fuel, and another to an outhouse half-buried in snow.

But what was he still doing inside? Had he lost track of the days of the week?

SHERIDAN LOOPED AROUND the small clearing in front of the cabin so the tub was close to the front door before turning the engine off. That would make it easier for her to load him if he was hurt or sick.

She stood up on the sideboards of the snowmobile and slid her visor back. It was suddenly still without the high whine and vibration of the motor. The sky had darkened even further and there was the anticipatory stillness in the trees that usually signaled coming snow.

"Lance?"

Nothing.

"Lance?"

Flickering yellow light from his kerosene lantern played on the frosted glass of the window next to the door.

Her boots squeaked in the packed snow as she approached the cabin.

"Lance?"

As she reached for the rusted iron door handle, the door swung out and she had to step back so it wouldn't hit her.

"Oh, thank God you're here," Kate Shelford-Longden said in her clipped British accent. She was without makeup and wearing jeans, ankle-high slippers, and an oversized fuzzy sweater. "Lance is in bad shape and he needs to get to hospital. I tried to take him there myself but I couldn't get his snowmobile started."

Sheridan closed her eyes for a moment, then reopened them.

Kate was still there.

"Come inside quickly," Kate said. "You're letting the cold in."

Sheridan rocked back, then shoved Kate with both hands so hard that Kate fell over backward and struck her face on the tabletop on the way down.

Sheridan stormed into the cabin and slammed the door behind her.

Lance was on the iron-framed bed naked from the waist down except for his underwear. A white shard of thighbone poked out from the discolored flesh of his upper leg. His body gleamed with sweat from a fever. He was unconscious and his mouth gaped open.

"What happened to him?" Sheridan asked Kate, who was scuttling backward across the floor using her feet to propel her. She raised both of her hands to her face and blood trickled out from between her fingers from her broken nose.

"He was scooping the snow off the roof when he slipped and fell early this morning," Kate said. Her voice was muffled from behind her hands. "I went outside and found him like that."

Sheridan looked around the inside of Lance's cabin. She recognized it, of course, but what struck her was the woman's touch that wasn't there the last time. Instead of the sets of antlers and old fur traps on the walls, there were nice curtains, a clean floor, plastic flowers in a vase on the table. An actual tablecloth.

Kate had been there awhile.

Sheridan said, "We need to get him out of here so he can recover. So I can *kill him myself*."

Kate's eyes widened even farther. She said, "I'm staying here, if you don't mind. But please get him to hospital."

"We say *the* hospital, lady," Sheridan said. "And you're coming with me."

To back up her words, Sheridan took a quick step toward Kate, and Kate recoiled.

Point taken.

ALTHOUGH SHERIDAN HAD a dozen rage-fueled questions to ask of Kate they couldn't talk. The whine of the snowmobile was too loud.

After binding a thick compress from the first-aid kit to Lance's leg to prevent further bleeding—he moaned while Sheridan wrapped it tight—Kate helped her half-carry and half-drag him toward the door. While Sheridan lashed him tight into the tub, she looked around for a sign of the silver 2017 Jeep Cherokee with Colorado rental plates hidden in the trees behind Lance's cabin.

It wasn't there.

KATE SAT BEHIND Sheridan on the machine and grasped her around her waist to hold on. As she drove back through the trees, Sheridan frequently looked down at the pair of British arms locked on her beneath her breasts and grimaced as if they were radioactive. She also shot glances back at Lance wrapped in blankets and lashed in the tub. He'd moaned and stirred while they did it, but he hadn't woken up even though Sheridan had jostled him around more than necessary.

She considered taking a turn extra-wide and letting the tub thump against the trunks of trees, but she didn't.

. . .

WITH LANCE STILL unconscious in the backseat of the pickup, Sheridan retraced her route down the two-track back to the state highway. She'd left the snowmobile and trailer at the trailhead to retrieve later.

Sheridan drove as recklessly as she dared to get out of the mountains, while Kate was obviously scared for her life. She hung on to the safety handle above the passenger window with one hand and braced herself against the dashboard with the other. Her broken nose was red and swollen, although the bleeding had largely stopped.

Sheridan didn't speak until they turned onto the blacktop of the highway.

After taking the truck out of four-wheel-drive she said, "Do you know how many people have been looking for you? Do you even care?"

"I haven't been following the news," Kate said.

"You created an international incident."

"That wasn't my intention," Kate said defensively.

"What the hell *was* your intention?"

Kate relaxed a little and let go of the handle above her head. She placed both of her hands on her lap and stared at them.

She said, "Until I got on the ranch, I'd forgotten what it was like to simply unplug from the modern world—to go through the days not looking at my phone, not answering constant emails and texts, not looking at Facebook or Twitter. It was like I was feeling myself slow down in real time. A weight was lifted. I had no idea what kind of pressure I was under until it started to melt away."

Sheridan looked over but didn't respond.

"You have no idea what it's like to be in a job like mine," Kate said. "The stress is incredible and there are hundreds of people—even people who you think are your friends—who are just waiting for you to say the wrong thing or make the wrong move. Especially in the age of social media, when you're in the public eye. Everyone wants you to fail in the most spectacular way possible so they can feel superior to you and comment on it. Anonymously, of course.

"I realized I craved a simpler life," Kate said. "For the first time in my life since I was a little girl, I could see things for what they were and not just out of the corner of my eye as I was dashing from one place to the other. I could watch the sun come up in the morning and see it set at night. Then I could see a whole universe of stars so bright in the sky they almost hurt my eyes. I could smell things—flowers, sagebrush, pine trees, water. I could hear again without the background white noise of traffic and people.

"I read real books again instead of watching video clips on my phone," she said. "I started a journal, writing in longhand. With a pen! I do want to go back and get my journal. I left it in the cabin."

"We're not going back for it," Sheridan said.

"But I need it. I've kept it for me. I wanted to chart my own course on the voyage of self-discovery."

"Self-discovery! You worried a lot of people. You're the most selfish human being I've ever met."

"That's not fair," Kate said with a sniff that was no doubt painful. "I don't owe anyone my presence in their lives and I didn't ask anyone to search for me."

"But that's what people do," Sheridan said. "They help each other. Someone disappears, and of course they're going to look for her. You're such a pathetic narcissist, you can't even get that through your head. Why, even your sister came all the way here looking for you."

Clearly stung, Kate said, "Sophie is a resentful and vindictive cow. She'll do anything to get attention—including playing the role of the grieving sister. I'm sure every little tearful speech she gave was covered by the press."

"I don't know," Sheridan said.

"You can count on it," Kate said. "What you don't realize is Sophie broke up my marriage and has moved in with Richard. The two of them are colluding to push me out of my own company. Now they can have it. She didn't come here to rescue me. She came here to confirm I was dead."

Sheridan had no response. But she now knew one reason for Kate's troubled expression when she thought about going back.

SHERIDAN TOOK THE EXIT to I-80. The highway was clear and dry and she accelerated to ninety-five miles per hour. It was a straight shot to Rawlins and the hospital.

"You're speeding," Kate said.

"Let the Highway Patrol pull me over," Sheridan replied. "Once they find out who's sitting beside me, they'll give me a police escort into town."

Kate shook her head ruefully.

Sheridan asked, "How did you get Lance to let you stay in his cabin, anyway?"

"He pointed his cabin out to me when we were on a trail ride. He said he never locked it, which I found charming. So when I left the ranch after that week I drove straight there without telling him. I was there for two weeks before he even found me, and when he did I made him promise not to tell anyone. I'm sure he regrets that promise now, but he kept it. He's a very honorable man. He probably thought I'd stay at his cabin for a few days and then leave and go home. I might have thought about it then as well. But every week I found the prospect of returning more and more daunting.

"I don't think he even knew what he did for me," Kate continued. "When he helped me up in the saddle or tipped his hat and called me 'ma'am.' He just didn't know . . .

"Why would I ever trade long lazy walks in the forest to going back to traffic, bad air, and insipid 'men without chests,' to quote from a C. S. Lewis phrase I read recently."

Then she recited a line.

"'We make men without chests and expect of them virtue and enterprise. We laugh at honour and are shocked to find traitors in our midst.'

"In fact," Kate said, her voice wistful, "I did try to leave once. I drove all the way to Fort Collins in Colorado, toward the Denver airport, when I nearly had a mental breakdown. I just couldn't return to England. I just couldn't. I'd left everything behind that I'd come to care about. So I called Lance and he drove down to pick me up. I left the car with the keys in it and we both thought someone would report its discovery and I'd be forced to come clean. But apparently someone just stole it and drove it away! I'm sure Lance wishes he hadn't driven down to pick me up, but he's a rare gentleman."

"He's an idiot," Sheridan said. "*He* knew what an uproar you'd caused, and he still said nothing."

"Yes, well," Kate said, "it's not his fault. I was . . . a little naughty.

When he told me I had to leave, I said I'd tell the authorities he'd held me there against my will—that it would be his word against mine." For once, Kate had the good grace to blush. "I wouldn't have done it, of course, but Lance didn't know that."

Which explained his growing anxiety and his reaction when he met her dad, Sheridan thought. *What a bitch!*

Kate continued. "He didn't know what to do, and the longer I stayed, the more difficult it was for him. I could see it on his face when he showed up hoping I was no longer there. And I was there so long there was no way he could tell anyone about it!"

She slid her eyes to Sheridan. "He loves you, you know."

"Bullshit."

"Oh, he does. It became a problem. We were never lovers. I know that's what you're worrying about. Sadly, it never worked out that way."

"*Sadly*," Sheridan echoed bitterly under her breath. "If he truly loved me, he would have told me he had a missing woman stashed away."

"Really?" Kate asked. "Tell me, what would have been your reaction if Lance had told you a woman had been living in his cabin—with his knowledge—for months?"

Sheridan didn't answer because Kate had a point.

Kate chuckled at that and then turned serious again. "I don't think I can ever go back. Can you imagine the insurmountable wall of questions, the hateful comments on social media about where I've been and why? I just couldn't face it."

"You have no idea how much trouble you've caused," Sheridan said. "Now please quit talking so I can call my dad."

"Lance really likes him, you know," Kate said.

"Shut up, Kate. I'm not as fascinated with all things Kate as you are."

As she fished her phone out of her snowmobile suit, she heard Lance moan in the backseat and saw in her mirror that he'd pushed himself painfully into a seated position.

When he saw who was in the front, he said, "Oh no. I think I'm in big trouble."

31

"I'M GOING TO THE HOSPITAL TO CONFIRM IT'S HER," JOE SAID TO Marybeth as he neared Rawlins. The massive steel hulk of the Sinclair Oil Refinery dominated the southern view out his passenger window. In the frigid dusk, clouds of steam from the refinery hung above it in the shape of a mushroom cloud. The heater in his pickup couldn't keep up with the icy wind whistling into the cab from his damaged passenger door.

"Joe, don't hurt that boy."

"I can't promise that."

After talking with Sheridan and hearing the flat sadness in her tone, all he could think about was clubbing Lance Ramsey, whether he had a broken leg or not. Joe could endure humiliation of his own—the fact that he was still working the case was evidence of that—but his vision turned red when it came to the betrayal of one of his daughters.

"I'm worried about our girl," Marybeth said. "She hasn't had many serious boyfriends . . . and now this."

"She'll be okay," Joe said, having no idea at all if Sheridan would be okay. "She's tough like you. And she solved the big mystery."

"Does the governor know?"

"I haven't called him," Joe said. "I wanted to make a positive identification first and send him a photo of Kate to back it up. We can't afford to make another mistake."

"I'd like to see his face when he sees it. I wonder how he's going to spin it so he can take credit for finding her alive."

"That's what Hanlon is for," Joe said.

HE ENTERED THE HOSPITAL for the second time in two days and the receptionist directed him to the surgical suite on the second floor. Joe took the stairs and found Sheridan, Mark Gordon, and Kate Shelford-Longden sitting in a spartan lobby. Sheridan and Gordon sat on one side of the room and Kate sat on the other.

Sheridan looked up and their eyes met for a moment before she turned away. She clamped her lips together to keep them from quivering.

Kate acknowledged him with a curt nod.

He said to Kate, "You've created a lot of problems around here for a lot of people, but I'm glad you're safe and alive."

"I was always safe and alive, why can't people understand that?"

Sheridan shot a bitter look at Kate, and Gordon sighed audibly. Joe could feel the tension in the room. It was Silver Creek Ranch versus Kate Shelford-Longden. For her part, Kate seemed preternaturally disconnected from the situation, as if she were there by mistake. That rubbed Joe the wrong way.

He held up his phone and said, "Smile for the camera."

He got two clear shots before Kate looked away, annoyed.

He attached both photos to a message and sent them to Governor Allen and Connor Hanlon with the tagline *We found her and she's in good shape.*

"Lance is in surgery," Gordon said to Joe. "We talked to the surgeon and his prognosis is good. They're worried about infection, but they said the cold temperatures probably worked in his favor."

Gordon reached over and put his hand on Sheridan's shoulder. "Your daughter probably saved his life."

"Yeah—so that's on me," Sheridan said.

"You did the right thing," Joe told her.

"Then why do I feel so crappy?"

"I did my best before she got there," Kate said defensively. "I don't have any formal training in treating injuries."

Joe ignored her as he approached Sheridan. His daughter stood up and he hugged her. She felt small again in his arms.

"Mark, I did my best," Kate said to the general manager. "I was trying to figure out how to get some help for Lance when she showed up. I would have gotten something sorted."

Gordon turned to Kate and there was a long pause. He said, "I suppose I shouldn't expect gratitude from you after all this time, but a lot of people risked their lives and their careers trying to find you. My property will forever be linked to a visitor's disappearance in the minds of potential guests. So you could at least shut up for a while."

"Oh, please—" Kate started to speak and then obviously thought better of it and closed her mouth.

Joe took Sheridan aside and told her that he was meeting Nate at the Encampment lumber mill and he'd be happy to give her a ride back.

"I'll stay," she said. "I guess I want to make sure he makes it through surgery."

Joe nodded.

"So I can kill him," she added.

Joe hugged her again.

Before he left the room, he said to Kate, "You need to stay right here. I'm calling Sheriff Neal. He'll probably have his own ideas about what to do with you. You wasted a lot of state and federal resources, you know. I wouldn't be surprised if someone decided to slap you with a whopping bill. And legal charges."

She put on a defiant look, but she looked a little shaken.

"She doesn't care about anything or anyone but herself," Sheridan said to Joe. "She doesn't care how many people she's hurt on her 'voyage of self-discovery.'"

Joe wasn't entirely sure what his daughter meant, but he trusted her judgment.

"There's another reason I'm staying," Sheridan said to Joe softly as she turned her back to Kate and showed him the screen of her phone. She'd surreptitiously taken several photos of Kate at the cabin, in the cab of her pickup, and at the hospital.

"These are going up on Twitter, Facebook, and Instagram," Sheridan whispered. "They'll go viral within hours. Kate told me one of the things she dreaded most was the social media reaction. Well, now Kate's chickens will come home to roost."

Joe gulped.

"I want to be here to see it happen," Sheridan said with narrowed eyes.

. . .

SHERIDAN *WAS* TOUGH, he thought as his boots echoed in the long hallway away from the surgical suite. But she was hurt and there was very little he or Marybeth could do about it other than to be there for her.

When the girls were young, he knew better how to deal with their problems and minor tragedies. He could distract them, or make pancakes for them, or offer to drive them into town for ice cream. He had little experience dealing with the problems of adult children. He wished Marybeth were there, but perhaps Sheridan didn't.

He raised his chin when a woman shouted from one of the hospital rooms ahead of him. She sounded angry.

"Nurse!" the woman called out. "I need to make a statement. *Nurse*."

A nurse brushed by Joe and walked quickly up the hallway toward the room with the disturbance. She said to Joe, "She just gained consciousness. I've told her to use her call button, but she'd rather yell."

Joe followed and glanced over at the open doorway where the nurse had entered. The whiteboard next to the doorframe read *Carol Schmidt*.

He paused.

Schmidt was sitting up in bed. She peered around the nurse who was hovering over her and she saw Joe in the hallway.

"Are you a game warden?" she asked him.

"Yes, ma'am."

"Good. You'll do."

You'll do?

Then: "I need to talk to somebody in law enforcement. I need to make a statement."

"You really need to calm down and get some rest," the nurse told Schmidt as she gently pushed her back toward her pillow. "It isn't good for you to get so worked up. I'll talk to the doctor about prescribing a sedative."

Joe recognized the name as the same woman he'd heard about the other day at breakfast. He removed his hat and entered the room.

"A statement?" he said.

The nurse gave up trying to get her to lie flat and she stood helplessly to the side of Schmidt's bed.

"Gaylan Kessel ran me off the road," Carol Schmidt said. "I'll testify in court it was him. At first I couldn't remember his name when I saw him, but it came to me just this afternoon."

"Gaylan Kessel," Joe repeated.

"He's that windmill guy."

"I'm aware of him. Why would he do that?"

"I made some legitimate complaints about that burner at the mill in Encampment and I identified his truck being there. I even got the license plate number and he knew it."

To the nurse, Joe said, "Keep her healthy. We'll need her on the stand."

SHERIFF NEAL DIDN'T pick up when Joe called him directly on his cell phone. Joe didn't want to call the sheriff's office itself with the news of either Kate's appearance or Schmidt's allegation, since Michael Williams thought Kessel had a mole or two within the agency.

When it went to voicemail, Joe said, "Everything has broken open. Call me back."

Then he sent the photos of Kate as well, thinking they would prompt Neal to drop everything he was doing and return the call.

JOE ROARED DOWN I-80 toward Walcott Junction and the road to Saratoga. It was dark enough now that the sea of red blinking lights from the Buckbrush Project pierced through the southern sky and cast the horizon in an unnatural neon hue.

A thousand wind turbines, he thought. A five-billion-dollar facility.

Whether operating on his own or under orders, somebody was out to protect that investment at all costs until it could go completely operational.

That somebody, Joe believed, was Gaylan Kessel.

And Nate was sure Kessel himself was making a delivery to the burner in Encampment that very night.

WHEN JOE'S PHONE lit up while he was making the exit off the interstate, he expected Neal to be on the other end. But it wasn't the sheriff.

"*What the fuck are you doing?*" Hanlon shouted. Joe had to move the phone away from his ear.

"We found Kate," Joe said.

"I saw the fucking photos," Hanlon screeched. "Are you sure it's even her this time?"

"Yup."

"Why are you even there? Why are you still working the case?"

Joe said, “I thought you’d be happy to know she’s okay.”

“I’m happy! I’m happy!” Hanlon screeched. “But that has nothing to do with the fact that you’ve gone rogue over there. Don’t you even know what ‘you’re fired’ means?”

“I guess not.” Joe smiled.

“It doesn’t change a thing,” Hanlon said. “If you thought this would buy your job back, you’re even dumber than I thought you were.”

“Maybe I am,” Joe said.

“I’m going to send the Highway Patrol after you. I’m going to order them to pull you over and arrest you for impersonating a law enforcement officer.”

“Tell them to hurry,” Joe said.

Hanlon went silent for a moment. “Why?”

Joe disconnected the call.

Then he said to himself out loud: “Because after tonight the governor’s two biggest contributors are going to be real mad at him.”

Hanlon called back immediately and Joe let it ring.

32

NATE WAS WITH JEB PRYOR AND A SULLEN OVERWEIGHT MAN WHO slumped in a hard-backed chair in Pryor's mill office. Joe had walked through the darkened and silent mill to get there. He stomped snow and sawdust from his boots as he entered the room.

"Don't worry about making a mess," Pryor said. "Where did you park?"

"Out front," Joe said. "I didn't see your vehicles."

"We hid them behind the building," Pryor said. "Except for Wylie's pickup. That's the truck you saw down by the burner on your way in."

Joe nodded and assessed Wylie, who was apparently the sullen man. Wylie hugged himself in a way that suggested his ribs hurt.

He had both ears, though. Joe shot Nate a look.

"He's a no-account worm," Nate said. "His only purpose on earth right now is to receive a call from Gaylan Kessel."

"That name again," Joe said.

The room smelled of sawdust and pizza. The pizza box was on Pryor's desktop, along with a half-full bottle of Yukon Jack whiskey. They'd already eaten the pizza and all that was left was grease-stained cardboard and a few discarded crusts.

"We found her," Joe said. "We found Kate."

"Alive?" Nate asked.

"Very much so. She was hiding out at Lance Ramsey's cabin and she'd been there the whole time. Actually, Sheridan found her and brought her in."

"Sheridan?"

"Yup."

"I'm not all that surprised about the Brit," Nate said. "Too many people around here seemed to think she just stayed. I think if you really look into it, you'll find that the Teubners sold her a little meth and the Youngbergs probably spied on her."

Joe nodded. "I really don't care about that woman anymore. She's someone else's problem. I'm more worried about my daughter."

"You've got something else to be worried about," Nate said as he held out his balled fist toward Joe. "We found this in the burner."

Joe opened his palm up and Nate dropped a light metal object into it. It was an elongated ring nearly half an inch wide.

"Recognize that?" Nate asked.

Joe held it up to the light and turned it in his fingers. The soot had been largely rubbed off of it and he could make out some kind of insignia and a series of numbers.

"It's a leg band," Joe said. "The kind the U.S. Fish and Wildlife Service use for research."

"Research on golden and bald eagles in particular," Nate said.

They exchanged looks.

Nate said, "Maybe next time you'll listen when falconers start complaining."

"They're always complaining," Joe said. "They're like farmers or outfitters."

"But this time we had a point," Nate said. "There was a reason why the feds wouldn't let us get eagles to hunt with. Too many of them were ending up in that burner down there."

"What?" Pryor boomed.

Even Wylie Frye looked up. He was confused.

"We've only got a couple of hours," Nate said. "We need to make our plan."

"Damn," Pryor mused. "All along I thought that Kate woman ran off with the game warden."

"That was your theory?" Joe asked.

"It was until now."

"Some conspiracy theories are better than others," Nate said with a smirk.

TED PANOS SLOWLY unthawed in the passenger seat of Gaylan Kessel's pickup as they drove south toward Encampment. He was glad he'd popped Percocet before they went out that night to help numb him against the cold. But it was wearing off and Kessel kept looking over at him with suspicion.

"Open your window," Kessel said.

"What? Why? It's fifteen below zero out there," Panos complained.

"You've got fucking feathers stuck to your sleeve, moron."

Panos held his arms out in front of him and placed his fingertips on the dashboard. Kessel was right. There were a number of small pinfeathers stuck to the fabric of his coveralls, as well as smears of blood.

"Oh."

"Clean yourself off," Kessel said. "Get those feathers off your arms and out of my cab."

As he said it, Kessel worked the master control on his side of the truck and Panos's window rolled down. Panos winced against the cold while he frantically brushed at his sleeves to remove the feathers, which floated away behind them on the two-lane highway.

When he was done, Panos shoved his frozen hands between his thighs and waited for Kessel to roll up the window.

When he finally did, Kessel said, "You smothered the wrong old lady last night."

Panos looked over, unsure of what he'd just heard.

"You killed some old broad named Alvarez who was in there with pneumonia. Do you not know the difference between a sixty-nine-year-old white lady and an eighty-five-year-old Mexican?"

"That's im-possible," Panos stammered, although she had looked older and smaller than he'd guessed. "I saw her name outside the room. Carol Schmidt."

"Carol Schmidt is alive and kicking," Kessel said. "My sources in the hospital confirmed it. But this Alvarez woman died last night. It's not considered a suspicious death because of her age, which is the only good thing to come out of this."

"I can't believe it," Panos said.

"When we get done tonight, we're going back," Kessel said. "This time, you're going to get it right."

Panos started to object when Kessel backhanded him hard across his mouth. Then his boss leaned over toward him with bulging eyes.

"You're fucking this up for me," Kessel hissed. "You're threatening my livelihood and my freedom. *No one does that and lives.*"

Panos shot a glance out the front windshield. The truck was wandering over the center line because Kessel was glaring at him.

"Do you understand what I'm saying?" Kessel shouted.

"Yes, boss."

Kessel swung at him again and Panos was ready for it and partially deflected the blow.

"No more fuckups," Kessel said. "And stop taking whatever drugs you're on. From now on, you operate clean. I saw you out there picking up those carcasses in my headlights. You were stumbling around."

You could have helped me, Panos thought but didn't say.

"No more fuckups," Panos echoed. "Please watch the road."

Kessel jerked on the wheel just in time to avoid clipping off his driver's-side mirror on a delineator post on the wrong side of the highway.

After he'd recovered and was once again in the correct lane, Kessel raised his phone to his mouth.

When Wylie Frye answered, Kessel said: "Are we clear?"

Then a moment later: "Hit the bricks."

ENCAMPMENT OFFICER JALEN SPANKS was parked on a side road a hundred yards inside the town limits when he saw a set of oncoming headlights veer wildly on the highway. He'd been watching pornography on his phone and had nearly missed the display of careless driving.

He quickly zipped up and returned to his home screen. He looked at the time on his dashboard clock.

Two-fifteen in the morning. No doubt the oncoming truck was being driven by a drunk who'd closed down the bars in Saratoga and was returning home.

JOE WAS SLOWLY freezing in the cab of his pickup because of the damaged passenger door. He'd jammed a few dozen balled-up citation forms into the gaps, but he could still feel the cold coming in.

He was parked hard against a wedge of plowed snow on a residential street that gave him a good view of the glowing burner and the mill yard. His Remington Wingmaster 12-gauge shotgun was propped muzzle-down on the floorboard. His phone was on his lap so he could instantly see a text from Nate.

Joe noticed that Hanlon had called him seven times that night, and he smiled to himself.

A text appeared from Nate.

It read: *Get ready.*

At that moment, a call came in from Sheriff Neal. His voice sounded groggy. "Jesus, I just saw what you sent me," he croaked. "I was out with the missus and had a few cocktails and I forgot to look at my phone. Is Kate still at the hospital?"

"I don't know," Joe said quickly. "But forget about her for now and get to the Encampment lumber mill. Bring guys you know you can trust."

"What the hell is going on?"

"I don't have time to explain," Joe said. He could see a wash of headlights on the road out in front of him from an approaching vehicle. "Believe me and get here fast."

He disconnected as the light-colored pickup with the camper shell he'd seen parked outside Pollock's house passed under a streetlight and turned toward the mill yard. Joe now recognized the Buckbrush logo on the driver's-side door.

He also noted the license plate and saw that the last three digits were *six-zero-zero*, just as Carol Schmidt had reported.

What Joe didn't expect was the sudden blinding red and blue light bar of the Encampment Police Department SUV in hot pursuit of Gaylan Kessel's truck.

"WHAT THE *HELL*?" Kessel said as his rearview mirror reflected a blast of light and a siren whooped right behind him.

"Oh no," Panos moaned. He pressed his hands to his face.

Kessel slowed to a stop. The burner glowed fifty yards ahead of them. Panos could see that idiot Frye walking away from the burner to the mill building.

"Get out and see what that stupid cop wants," Kessel ordered.

"Why me?" Panos asked. "What if he wants to look in the back?"

"Let him," Kessel said. "Now go."

Panos was confused but he opened his door and jumped out.

"Remain in your vehicle," the cop shouted. He was stepping out of his SUV as he did so.

"What's the problem, Officer?" Panos asked while he forced a smile.

"I said, *remain in your vehicle*." The cop was adamant, and as he gave the command he reached back and gripped his weapon on his hip.

Panos noticed that another set of headlights had flashed on across the road and a third vehicle was coming fast.

"We don't want no trouble," Panos said to the cop.

"Hey," the cop said as he approached the truck, "are you guys with Buckbrush?"

Before Panos could respond, there was a heavy *BOOM* and a flash from the other side of the truck. The cop dropped without even stumbling and his arms flung out to the side.

"Get in or I'm leaving you here!" Kessel shouted at Panos. Kessel lowered the Bushmaster XM-15 rifle he kept behind the seat for finishing off wounded birds.

Then he suddenly raised it again and squeezed off five rounds at the pickup that was roaring at them from the dark.

"No!" Panos shouted, but the gunfire drowned out his plea.

JOE SAW IT ALL: the guy coming out of the passenger side of the company pickup, the officer ordering him to get back in, the driver hurtling out and firing from behind his open door, the cop going down.

Then Kessel raising the muzzle toward *him*.

There wasn't time to stop or veer away, so Joe threw himself on the passenger seat as rounds snapped through his windshield and out the back window. Slivers of glass coated him.

And he was thrown to the floor when his truck crashed into the back of the stationary patrol SUV.

. . .

PANOS BROKE INTO A RUN just as the green Ford pickup slammed into the Encampment cop's car. The collision was hard enough that the cop car lurched forward and nearly crushed the downed man.

He didn't know where he was running, only that it was away from the mill and away from Kessel. His heavy coveralls didn't help and he gasped for air. It was so cold that his lungs burned.

Then he heard footfalls behind him.

Kessel?

No.

A game warden in a cowboy hat.

JOE ALMOST THREW the shotgun aside, but decided against it as he chased the man who'd run from the scene. When he'd rolled out of the cab, the man was running away right in front of him, the glow from the burner on the back of his coveralls.

It was only after fifty feet that Joe realized he wasn't chasing the shooter, but the passenger of the truck.

He glanced over his shoulder as he ran, hoping Kessel wasn't drawing a bead on *him*.

Kessel was moving as well, loping toward the burner with the rifle swinging in his hand. He didn't know that Nate was in the burner shack.

"*Stop,*" Joe wheezed at Panos. But it wasn't really necessary. Panos had run across the packed snow of the mill yard and was now foundering knee-deep in powder.

It slowed him down like a fly lighting on flypaper.

Joe launched into him and both men went down. Joe flailed and managed to get on top and he covered the tip of Panos's nose with the muzzle of his shotgun.

"Roll over and put your hands on top of your head," Joe said. He was out of breath from running and his knees ached from banging them on the floorboards in the crash. He didn't realize until that moment that he had a head wound as well. Blood ran from his chin into the snow and speckled it bright red.

"I might smother in the snow," Panos wheezed back.

"You might," Joe said.

Panos grunted as he rolled to his belly. Joe straddled him and located the cuffs on his belt. They were so cold the steel stung his fingers.

Joe cuffed the man and found a .45 derringer in his boot top. He pocketed the gun, then snapped the cuffs more tightly on Panos's wrists.

KESSEL WAS REACHING for the door handle of the burner shack when Nate stepped around the side of the structure and thumbed back the hammer of his .454. He stood with his back to the open door of the burner so his form was silhouetted against the flames. The sharp metallic click cut through the roar of the fire in the burner.

The sound made Kessel hesitate and look over. When he did, Nate pointed the weapon at the man's left eye. The reflection of the flames danced in that eye.

"Toss your rifle away," Nate said just loudly enough to be heard over the fire.

Kessel froze in place.

"Or you can go for it," Nate said. "I really hope you do."

Kessel straightened up and let the rifle drop to the snow.

He said, "I think we can try and work this out. My employers have unlimited funds."

"Of course they do," Nate said. He pointed to Kessel's vehicle. "What's in the back?"

"That's not important. You're obviously not a cop. What will it take to let me drive out of here?"

"No, I'm not a cop," Nate said. "I'm a master falconer."

The realization of what Nate said dawned on Kessel's face.

"So this is about those damned birds," Kessel said.

"I'd trade one of them for ten of you."

Nate stepped back and gestured for Kessel to return to the site of the crash. He said, "I have a friend named Joe who would like to meet you."

Kessel rolled his eyes and said, "If this is just about birds, we can work this out."

The man passed between Nate and the open doorway of the burner as he said it. Nate waited for midstride when Kessel was off balance before reaching out and shoving him inside.

It was quick. Kessel screamed and thrashed for a few seconds, but he couldn't regain his footing. Then his body went still.

One of Kessel's boots remained outside the doorway and Nate kicked it into the flames as well.

There was the strong odor of roast pork in the air.

JOE MARCHED PANOS toward the vehicles and confirmed that Officer Spanks was deceased from a bullet through his heart. He'd likely died before he hit the ground.

"It was Kessel," Panos said through chattering teeth.

"I saw it all," Joe said. Then: "Were you there when Steve Pollock's files were taken?"

"Sort of," Panos confessed.

"WHAT HAPPENED to the shooter?" Joe asked Nate after he'd guided Panos toward the burner shack. Nate had met them halfway.

"He fell into the burner."

"He fell?"

"Tripped on his own feet."

Joe took a deep breath and chose not to ask more.

Indicating Panos, Joe said, "I'm going to put this guy in the burner shack until the sheriff gets here."

Nate nodded. "I'll wait out here. But we need to check out the cargo."

NATE REACHED UP and grasped the handle of the camper shell on Kessel's pickup. He turned it and the hatch rose slowly in the cold air.

Joe flipped on his MagLite and shone the beam inside. The back was full to the top of the bed walls with dead eagles and eagle parts. The carcasses had been piled on a thick sheet of plastic that would also, he guessed, have been thrown into the burner.

"Damn them," Nate said.

"Yup."

"I wonder how many overall?"

"Maybe Ted Panos can help us with that," Joe said.

. . .

IT TOOK NEARLY an hour for the small convoy of Carbon County sheriff's vehicles to arrive. Sheriff Neal and his team started securing the mill yard and taping off access with yellow crime scene tape, despite Jeb Pryor's protests that he had a business to run.

PANOS WAS TRANSFERRED to a sheriff's department vehicle and Spanks's body was transported to the Carbon County hospital.

Joe leaned inside the patrol SUV.

"Please close the door," Panos pleaded. "I'm freezing here."

"Tell me what you know about Kate Shelford-Longden."

"I don't know much. Gaylan thought she was out there somewhere screwing a young cowboy."

"Did he tell you this?"

"Yes. I don't know how he knew that, though. We even spent some time trying to find her, but we couldn't."

"Why?" Joe asked, puzzled.

"Because Gaylan didn't like the attention her case brought to the valley. He said it attracted too many cops and reporters."

Joe nodded. It made sense.

"Did he tell you about her a couple of months ago in the Rustic Bar?"

Panos shrugged. "Yeah, that's probably when it was."

Joe leaned back and closed the door. Panos stared straight ahead as if viewing the coming attractions of the rest of his life, starting with a long stint in the Wyoming State Penitentiary in nearby Rawlins.

. . .

JOE WAITED IN Pryor's office to give his statement to Neal. Now that the adrenaline of the events had ebbed, he felt immensely tired and sad. Sad for the Encampment cop, sad for Sheridan, sad for the eagles, sad for himself.

Nate had slipped away. He was good at that.

Outside the room in the mill itself, he heard Sheriff Neal say, "Where do you think you're going?" when the door opened.

A Wyoming state trooper filled it. He was beefy and his cheeks were flushed from the cold.

"Are you Joe Pickett?" the trooper asked.

"Yup."

"I've been instructed to bring you in."

Sheriff Neal shouldered his way into the room and turned on the trooper. "This man stays," he said. "I need a statement out of him. In case you haven't heard, a cop was shot here last night."

"I heard," the trooper said. "But the command came from the governor himself."

JOE WATCHED out the side backseat window of the Highway Patrol cruiser as Encampment, then Saratoga passed by.

He was numb.

"I need to give my wife a call to let her know I'm all right," he said to the trooper.

"When we get to where we're going," the trooper answered.

"Am I under arrest?"

The highway patrolman grunted. "I don't know what you are."

Joe drifted away and watched as dawn began to paint the east side of Elk Mountain in the distance.

He paid no attention when the trooper took a call on his phone in the front seat.

"It's for you," the trooper said as he passed his phone through the slider to Joe.

"For me?"

"Yes, sir."

Joe raised the phone to his ear.

"I talked with Marybeth," former governor Spencer Rulon said. "I hear you might need a lawyer."

Joe smiled. "I think I do."

ACKNOWLEDGMENTS

The author would like to thank the people who provided help, expertise, and information for this novel, starting with Corinne White, Michael Williams, Nora Asbury, Maria Peschges, and Ron Hawkins of the spectacular Lodge & Spa at Brush Creek Ranch outside Saratoga, Wyoming.

Thanks as well to Doug and Kathy Campbell of the Hotel Wolf in Saratoga. Readers can stay in Room 9, "The Joe Pickett Room," if they choose.

I'm grateful for the extensive research and information provided by master falconers Mike and Jocelyn Barker, which proved to be the linchpin of the novel. And thanks to David Paddock for the tour of the Saratoga National Fish Hatchery and Mark Nelson for game warden assurance.

Thank you, Nic Cheetham of Head of Zeus for serving as my Brit consultant.

Special kudos to my first readers: Laurie Box, Molly Box, Becky Reif, and Roxanne Woods.

ACKNOWLEDGMENTS

A tip of the hat to Molly Box and Prairie Sage Creative for cjbox.net and social media assistance.

It's a sincere pleasure to work with professionals at Putnam, including the legendary Neil Nyren, Ivan Held, Alexis Welby, Christine Ball, Alexis Sattler, Mark Tavani, and Katie Grinch.

And thanks once again to my agent and friend, Ann Rittenberg.